WHEN THE TIDES SHIFT

GARNET SHORES

MEGAN MONTE

To Mrs. Dyl,

For nurturing my dream of becoming an author, even when I was no longer your student.

Maybe one day I'll revisit that first high school manuscript— I still have the original printout with your hand-written feedback.

CONTENT WARNINGS

For content warnings, please visit
www.AuthorMeganMonte.com

1

———

ELIZA

I'VE NEVER BEEN one to believe in signs.

Rainbows? Just pretty colors painted across the sky. Ladybugs? They only land on you because they're exhausted from flapping their wings a gazillion beats per second. Finding a face-up penny means you're one cent richer and zero-point-zero-two percent closer to buying a latte at an overpriced downtown café.

Good fortune doesn't come from exhausted beetles or wallets with holes in them. It comes from hard work and strategic decisions.

So the fact that the downpour obscuring my car windows and flooding the gravel lot seems like a promising sign shows just how low I've stooped. I'm so desperate for something good that my brain actually thinks the rain could be signaling a new beginning, washing away all the bullshit from the last two weeks that landed me in the nowhere-nothing coastal town of Garnet Shores.

Alright, maybe that isn't a fair description. Garnet Shores, Rhode Island, *is* on maps. But the weather-beaten institution in front of my windshield is one of the only reasons it's there.

Compared to Boston, it's as exciting as a desert—the kind without stunning canyons and fun cacti that look like they're waving hello. Maybe *that's* unfair, too, but I grew up in a town as confining as it was uninspiring, and this one is even smaller.

It's not that this town is ugly. Garnet Shores is actually rather cute, with its quiet rural homes, sliver of coastline, farm stands, and stretches of trees. It's quintessential coastal New England, without the preppy flair, lively atmosphere, or tourist energy I've experienced out on Cape Cod. This is a place where you come to read a book on a quiet porch, migrate to the beach to continue reading said book, and—when you simply cannot digest another page—grab a drink at the sole bar that caters to all five square miles of this town.

It isn't a place to make six figures, get promoted to Marketing VP, or network with entrepreneurs at happy hour.

Yeah, because all those things worked out so well for you.

Just like that, my chest tightens all over again.

I jerk my door open and shove myself into the rain. Promising-sign-from-the-universe or not, the downpour is relentless and distracting enough to stop my ribs from collapsing.

I'm tempted to dash across the gravel lot, but for some reason, running feels less professional than calmly allowing the rain to swallow me whole. So I keep my walk even as the smell of my new workplace cements itself in my head.

It kind of...*stinks*. Salty and briny with a hint of fish.

No surprise, given this gig is at an oyster farm, not a sterile office on the fortieth floor of a high-rise.

I'll get used to the smell. I mean, I'll *have* to. My contract is for twelve weeks, ending mid-August, and "adaptable" is on my resume. And while I might have exaggerated my skills a bit—because that's what you *do* on resumes—I *am* good at making things work.

The closer I get to the office door, the more the building transforms from weather-beaten to charmingly rustic. Wood-shingled, two stories high, and sprawling, it's surprisingly well-kempt. The shingles look freshly stained, pots of colorful flowers line the front porch, and I even see a few bird feeders. A post pinned with multicolored wooden arrows—the kind you see in the Caribbean—offers helpful directions.

Order pickups are somewhere to the right, tours start by a little dock in the distance, and farm operations all point to the back of the building, which transitions from giant wood-shingled home to warehouse. None of the arrows indicate the main office, but my welcome email told me it's the yellow door under the porch. "Gold's Oysters" is spelled out above it in carefully arranged oyster shells, which should be tacky, but is actually kind of endearing.

The whole place looks like it was designed by a grandmother—not the moth-balls-and-prunes kind, but the crafty-crocheted-blankets-and-gardening kind. It's surprising, because, if my research is correct, the whole Gold's enterprise is managed by men.

Maybe men who crochet blankets and garden?

That would be a blessing. I'm at my wit's end with the unfeeling, inconsiderate assholes I seem to attract like flies in the city.

Under the cover of the porch, I pull down my hood, check my hair for fly-aways, and peer through the office door's window. I don't see anyone, so I tentatively turn the knob, and come face-to-face with the tiniest office I have ever seen. Like, tinier than my city studio apartment.

There's one big desk with a computer monitor, a cup of pens, and an empty chair behind it. On the wall hangs a giant map of what might be the oyster farm, next to a closed door in one corner. Two cushioned chairs line the windows beside me, and...that's basically it.

Gold's Oysters is in the midst of becoming one of the region's top-tier oyster farms, distributing to Boston's best seafood restaurants, and *this* is their front office setup.

There's no one here to greet me. Not that I'm expecting a grand welcome party, but it's my first day and I'm on time.

Eying the closed door beside the desk, I call out, "Hello?"

The only answer is the heavy patter of rain.

Taking another step forward, I try again, louder. "Anyone here?"

A muffled honk slices through the still air.

I jolt. "W-what?"

"*Quack.*"

This time, I jump, stumbling back against the door-frame. Palming my heart before it jumps out of my throat, I wonder if I just hallucinated. Because that sound was *way* too loud to come from behind the mysterious closed door, which means it came from inside the office. But there's no way, because it sounded like—

A duck waddles out from behind the desk, dark bill, brown feathers, and all. It stops when it turns the corner and stares at me with beady eyes.

"*Quack.*"

This quack sounds...impatient. Like it's waiting for a reaction. But I can't give one, because I'm still trying to process if I'm actually staring at a duck in the office. A real, live, *enormous* duck.

Five seconds later, it hasn't disappeared, so I know this is real. And then I realize, *oh my gosh, there's a duck in the office.* A wild animal.

Does it have rabies? It *has* to have rabies. Rabies makes animals do all kinds of abnormal behaviors, and a duck being in an office is definitely abnormal.

"Quack."

I inch forward, one hand on the door handle in case it decides to charge me. There's no drool coming from its mouth, which is maybe a good sign. With slow, careful movements, I extract my phone from my pocket and quickly search: *How to tell if a duck has rabies.*

The results have my hand dropping from the knob. *Ducks cannot contract rabies. Rabies affects mammals.*

I'm too relieved to be embarrassed I didn't know this.

"Quack."

This one's disgruntled. Accusatory, like it knows I assumed it had a mind-addling virus.

I replace my phone and set my shoulders. The little guy doesn't have rabies, but he definitely shouldn't be here. There are wires and seat cushions for him to chew up and destroy. Leaving him here while I find help will make me look like some incapable girl, and if corporate Boston taught me anything, it's that first impressions are fast and final.

"Come here, ducky," I croon in a high-pitched voice.

It blinks.

I crouch to its level. "Mr. Duck, let's go please."

Again, it doesn't move.

Time to get resourceful.

I reach into my bag for the sandwich I packed for lunch. Peeling open the foil, I wave one end toward the duck. I'm aware this is a bird and not a dog, but given its size, it probably isn't one to turn down food.

I'm right, because it happily waddles toward me.

I slowly open the door and inch outside, taking the sandwich with me. But the bird stops just before the threshold with another disgruntled, "*Quack.*"

"*C'mon*," I groan, waving the sandwich.

It thinks about it, reaching forward cautiously with its head.

Come on. Come on. Come on.

I'm so zeroed in on whether its splayed webbed feet will take a step that I don't notice how close the duck's beak has gotten to the sandwich.

It lunges, and in the matter of a second, the entire turkey sandwich is out of my hand and in its mouth.

This is war.

"No, you did not!" I shout, lunging after the duck who's a flurry of feathers as it escapes back into the office.

I've given high-stakes presentations in front of CEOs. Negotiated pay with a stick-up-her-ass HR executive. Navigated the subway alone at midnight. I'm not letting a cocky bird with *way* too much audacity litter this office with my sandwich bits and make me look like a fool on my first day of work.

There's no time for an internet search on how to pick up a duck.

Two big steps get me right on top of it, where I reach down and scoop it up. It squawks, a wing bashing me in the face as I stumble toward the door. Something sharp scrapes down my stomach and I drop the bird, frantically palming my shirt for blood. But the only evidence is a trail of loose threads in my sky-blue blouse.

This top was one of my favorite sale rack finds.

I turn, murder in my eyes. "You fluffy little piece of—"

"What in the hell are you doing?" The sharp exclamation comes from the open door behind me.

I pivot, wild eyes landing on the owner of the deep, angry voice.

His are just as infuriated as mine, two golden orbs glaring from a rugged, scruffy face that can't be much older than mine. It's all framed by messy dark hair, just long enough to curl against his forehead and ears.

I quickly scan his dark blue rain jacket and brown pants stained with black grease. When I zip back to his face, I spot a smear of that grease near the corner of his mouth, which is turned down in a scowl.

A scowl directed at me.

Seriously?

"Oh, I don't know. Maybe I'm just trying to *save this office* from a wild bird," I snark, because does this guy not have *eyes?*

"Save the office? Wild bird?" he echoes, shaking his head in disbelief. He takes one heavy step inside, and the office suddenly feels smaller. It's clear this isn't a crochet-blankets-and-garden type of man. The exact opposite, I'd guess.

"You're *assaulting* Dave."

My jaw drops. This has to be a joke. But the structured lines of his jaw are set, humorless beneath all that thick scruff.

His broad hands settle on his hips, shoulders straining against his jacket in what's probably an intimidation tactic. I straighten.

"I'm not assaulting him," I say evenly. "I came into this office, saw an animal that belongs outdoors, and decided to take care of the problem and remove him."

Soft grunts fill the air behind me. I twist to find the bird feasting on my sandwich, pieces of spinach and bread dribbling from his beak onto the floor.

You're kidding me.

This is *not* how my first day on the job is going to go. I'm too prepared, I've worked too hard, and I've proven myself too many times for my first impression to be this terrible.

My hands find my own hips. "This mess? The one he's making right now while you stand there all high and mighty and angry-looking?" The man's lips thin. "That's *your* fault, because you're too busy scowling instead of helping, or getting out of the way."

He runs his tongue over teeth, looking like he's trembling with the effort of keeping his body right where it is. It's a solid body too—one clearly built from muscle, standing a few inches taller than my five-foot-nine. It could probably pick me up and toss me out, and the duck would definitely cheer him on.

But the fact that he stays in place suggests he's not that kind of man.

No. He's the kind that attacks with his words, because he slowly articulates, "I'm standing here all angry-looking because this is my fucking office, on *my* fucking farm."

It's like I'm a balloon, and he just jabbed a hole in me. I stare at him, gob-smacked, as his words barrel on.

"*That,*" he points angrily at the duck, who's still gobbling my sandwich, "is *Dave*. My duck." That pissed-off finger points to the floor. "And this office is *closed* to visitors."

Oh, he misunderstands. "But I'm not a visi—"

He continues over my explanation. "Tours are by-reservation *only*, and as the sign out front clearly indicates, those begin by the dock. Oyster pickups need to be made ahead of time and are fulfilled on the side of the building. None of those arrows point you to this door, so there's no reason for you to be here, in this room, *especially* when no one invited you inside."

His voice is even louder now than when he started, and a vein strains against his corded neck.

He has no idea who I am. And now, I'm wondering if he just lied about who he is. If he's actually in charge, he'd know I'm starting today.

There's absolutely nothing about him that suggests he's running this business. The water and grime coating his clothing do suggest he *works* here, but there's no way a person this unkempt is the owner of the award-winning farm that's been featured in culinary magazines.

He swings the door open wide. "Get out."

Oh no, you didn't.

I've never punched anyone before, but the urge snakes down my arms, gathering in my hands, now fisted by my sides.

I am a *damn* good professional with a *damn* good (slightly inflated) resume who confirmed my start date *and time* with my new employer when I signed a contract for this job three days ago. I subletted my apartment and moved into a ramshackle sailboat in a ramshackle marina because that was the only accommodation available on such late notice. I dumped my cheater-of-a-boyfriend and told my boss he was going to miss me when my job was deemed unnecessary and cut.

I'm not about to balk at some jerk who needs a shower.

I take two steps back and perch against the desk instead.

"I *would* get out, if I was a visitor."

His jaw works over more words, but I cut him off before they make it out. "I'm the new Social Media Director for

Gold's Oysters. Anson Gold signed my contract. His secretary confirmed my start time and directed me to this office in an email yesterday morning. I have all the papers to prove it if you want your eyes to do something other than glare at me like a toddler whose mom won't buy them a new Lego set."

His head jerks back in shock as he processes this information. Pasting a pleasant smile on my face, I tap my fingers on the desk and wait for an apology.

When he opens his mouth, however, the words *I'm* and *sorry* are not on tap.

"Lady," he bites out, and the disrespect in it makes me bristle with loathing. "My brother would have told me if he went over my head to hire someone for *my* fucking farm. But he didn't. And I sure as shit didn't hire you. It's been a hell of a day and it's only nine in the fucking morning. I don't have the time or patience to drive some sense into you, so like I said: Get. Out."

That's the last straw.

A burn slides into my throat, crawling up my face and into my eyes, which are on the verge of watering.

I know this feeling. It's the same one that made me bawl my eyes out in the elevator after HR eliminated my position two weeks ago. It's frustration, and anger, and the fact that no matter how hard I work, I cannot seem to catch a break.

And *this*, which was supposed to *be my break*, is just another mess.

The only thing that would make this worse right now is actually releasing tears in front of this jackwagon, so I'm drawing the line. I force a shaky exhale and push to my feet. Beside me, Dave is nesting in his wonderful mess of mayonnaise, turkey bits, and crumbs.

Forcing the wobble from my voice, I say, "You might want to clean that up. Mayonnaise stains."

Then I hitch my bag over my shoulder, settle my hood on my head like I have all the time in the world, and calmly bypass him. I want him to reek of dead fish, but I only catch a whiff of something salty and warm, and that pisses me off even more.

I trudge across the parking lot, already drafting an email to Anson's secretary in my mind as the rain welcomes me right back to where I started.

A sign of a new, fresh beginning, *my ass*.

"COME ON, BABY," I say, coaxing the little engine that could-not.

I send up a prayer as I turn the ignition for the twentieth time. The skiff's motor sputters, hitching twice. Then a miracle happens.

It catches, rattling to life before settling into a loud, steady buzz.

I'd cheer, but I'm too pissed off to feel anything but annoyed relief. Thanks to its tantrum, we're running two hours behind on our first tour day of the season, when we're already down a boat. This morning's downpour soaked my pants through before I had time to put on my waterproof gear, and I'm already chafing.

No fucking hip-hip-hoorays over here.

"About time," Mark grumbles from beside the open motor at the back of the skiff.

Like me, he's smeared in black grease.

Unlike me, I'm almost certain he loves it.

Mark's an old dog whose blood is half saltwater and half beer. He's a damn good oyster farmer and even better with mechanical shit, and while he'll never admit it, he likes being the go-to fixer.

"Magic hands, Mark," I say, releasing the lines from the floating dock.

"Not magic." He slams the motor cap in place, and I lower the prop into the water. "Now stop sitting on your ass and get us out there."

No one else on my crew would speak to me like that, but laws don't apply to Mark. At seventy-one, he's earned the right to be ornery, and he's reliable as hell. Not to mention, he has plenty of money to retire, but insists on sticking around and working his ass off for a thirty-year-old oyster farm owner who almost screwed the business last year. He's covered me more times than I can count.

So, yeah, Mark can say whatever he wants.

I breathe in the cool, briny air as we putz to the floating oyster cages, and some of the tension from the morning eases out of my shoulders. Being out on the water always has this effect. Something about fresh air, no paperwork, and the salt pond's pretty mix of vivid greenery and calm water always puts me at ease. Ironic, given how grueling this work can be.

Oyster farming isn't a cakewalk. The labor is tough and the days are long. We're out here during frigid December mornings, pelting spring rains, and brutal summer after-noons. Maintenance never ends, my back is constantly sore, and the trade is dirty by nature. Between weather, water, and business, problems are always arising.

But even during freezing shifts or vicious storms, there's no better workplace.

Pretty sure I'd shrivel into a brain-dead zombie at a computer in a four-walled institution.

Above, the sky is clearing, sunlight peeking through the

dispersing rain clouds. With it comes the tentative brush of heat that late May usually brings in Rhode Island.

I'm thinking it might turn out to be a nice day when fate throws another punch.

My pocket vibrates, and I slide out my beat-up phone to see Anson's name on the screen. Behind it is a picture of us flipping off Old Plum Bridge. The photo is ancient, back from when a stick wasn't lodged up my brother's ass.

Angling the boat left, I accept the call.

"Gray," I bark.

"How's your morning?"

I already know he's edging around something. It's Monday, and we're both working. Anson might be the only person I know who gives more to his job than I do. He isn't calling right now to shoot the shit.

"Fine," I say.

"Glad to hear that. Mine was, too, until you decided to create a problem for me to handle," he says dryly.

Big brother's unhappy.

The cages pop into view, and I turn the skiff toward them. "You going to make me guess?"

"Shouldn't be that hard, Gray. Unless you've suddenly decided to be an asshole to everyone and all the instances are blurring together."

I frown, adjusting the speed of the skiff.

Then it clicks.

"You want me to be nicer to random, privileged vacationers who break into a closed office and attack my duck?"

I try not to picture her, but she comes anyway. Glossy brown hair with these caramel bits in it tied into a knot. Trench coat, little heeled boots, expensive-looking clothes. Cute nose and wide, hazel eyes that regarded me with pretentious judgement.

This can't actually be about her. She's a city girl, through and through. Probably vacationing in a beach house for the summer. Maybe one of the mini-mansions over on Orchard Row.

"I have no problem with you being a dick to random vacationers who break into your place." Anson's voice takes on a gritty note. "But she isn't a random vacationer. And you already know this, because she fucking explained it to you."

I roll my eyes. "Like I'm just going to take her word for—"

"And before she explained it to you, you were informed about her. *Three. Separate. Times.*" He's starting to overpronounce his syllables, and I'd bet he's pinching his nose.

The possibility that City Girl wasn't lying slowly filters in, but I still can't believe it.

"*How* was I informed? Because I sure as hell don't remember agreeing to let some random girl waltz around my farm during our busiest season."

"Your email." He says it expectantly, like I'm the clueless one here.

"Who the fuck *emails* their brother, Anson? Text me. Call me."

"Business correspondence stays in business channels," he robotically explains.

And there he is. Mr. Anson Gold, CEO of the Gold's family businesses, in all his stiff, sanctimonious glory.

"What about practicality?" I throw the skiff into neutral, because we're almost at the cages and I can't do my job with a phone in my hand and a shitstorm on the horizon.

Just *another* delay.

"You run the oyster ops, Gray. Email comes with that. Need me to hire you a secretary?"

I ignore the question. "You're right. *I* run the oyster ops. So why are *you* hiring someone to interfere with those ops?"

Mark eyes me warily from the back of the skiff, no doubt eavesdropping on every word. I don't mind. This is about to be his problem, too.

"Because I'm in charge of marketing for Gold's, and because you've never cared about industry trends, and you're too stubborn to take advice." Anson doesn't pull any punches. Not that I expect him to. "You do oysters. I do business. That's the way you've always wanted it."

My brother's a damn good businessman. As CEO of the entire enterprise, he's head of everything—the small vineyard, my oyster farm, our distribution channels. He took what our dad had only started and exploded it into the award-winning name it is now.

He's ruthless. Cutthroat. Genius in strategy, numbers, and marketing.

But Christ, his people skills need work.

Now isn't the time to remind him of this. I have bigger fish to fry. Like the fact that Anson did, in fact, hire me a girl who's a professional at phone usage and emojis.

How is that even a degree?

"Of all the people you could've hired, why a social media girl?"

"It's a marketing channel we haven't tapped, and it's taken over the world. We're behind."

I run my hand through my hair, wondering if I'm stuck in a nightmare.

City Girl. Broken engine. This phone call. It all adds up to a bad dream. But the familiar breeze that ripples across the water and tickles my face keeps me grounded in reality.

"What makes you so convinced *she* can help us?"

"She's incredibly overqualified. I sent her resume along

in those emails." He sighs on the other end of the line. "Gray, she isn't like Mackenzie."

Every muscle locks at those three syllables.

It's going to haunt me forever—the shiny hair, fruity perfume, too-clean outfits, and baby blue eyes that lodge in my brain like hooks whenever I hear her name. And that's just the precursor to the goddamn *feelings*. The hurt. The anger and embarrassment. The soul-sucking shame caused by the person who nearly wrecked us.

Who I nearly *let* wreck us.

And City Girl this morning looked like a carbon-fuck-ing-copy. Their faces are different, and City Girl's voice is a pitch lower, but the better-than-you air is all there.

"There have to be locals who can do this job. People who respect us and what we've built," I try.

"Not with her resume or availability, Gray." Anson's voice is more understanding now.

He's talking to me like I'm a wounded dog, and I hate it. Yeah, what happened with Mackenzie messed with my head and my pride, but if anything, it was a necessary wake-up call.

Gold's isn't some casual, local oyster farm. Through a mix of luck and straight-up hard work, the farm and winery have grown into a respected regional name. We're winning awards. Just last month, I took two journalists on a tour, one of whom writes for a *national* magazine.

But everything we're building could be ripped away at a moment's notice, and every decision—from hiring, to gear orders, to the people we allow close—impacts our success. Mackenzie had been a stark warning to drop the easygoing approach and act like a fucking business owner. No distrac-tions. No thinking with my dick. Just grinding it out with the detail and diligence our goals demand.

Women and relationships can wait until things are stable and I have time to suss out any hidden hints of crazy.

"Eliza's going to drive our growth. Her references were excellent. And it's only until mid-August. Three months."

I clench my jaw, surveying the farm. The place our father started when Mom first got sick, where he'd found solace as she'd declined. It hardly made any money then, too small for anything more than local pickups and seafood shops, but it's my lifeblood now.

No matter what Anson says, this is a terrible idea. She—*Eliza*—is going to slip off a dock, hit her head, drown because she's too busy scrolling through social media, and posthumously slap us with a lawsuit. She's going to ruin our reputation with idiotic trends. She's going to be mortifying to explain when wealthy out-of-towners come for tours and spot a person wearing heels and dress pants on an oyster farm.

But there's nothing I can do. I own the farm, but he owns the enterprise, which owns it all.

"I'm not responsible for monitoring her, on the internet or on the farm," I tell him, not bothering to hide the angry edge in my tone. "Whatever bad comes out of this isn't falling on me."

Mark recognizes the surrender for what it is, and shakes his head in disgruntled disappointment.

"She's an adult woman who doesn't need babysitting."

"Well, at least there's that."

"But she's also an adult woman who deserves a damn good apology, or I'm going to have a PR headache."

I scoff. "She threaten you?"

"No," he says, and I unclench my fingers from the phone. "If I were her, though, I'd be thinking about some way to get back at us."

My chest heaves a heavy breath. I'm the stereotypical middle brother, known for my patience and good nature. Of the three of us, I'm rarely the asshole, but I was a certifiable one to her this morning. I'm not arguing that.

It'd been a shit morning, between a time-consuming motor fix, needing to backtrack for the shed key, and the skies opening up on me mid-walk. When I'd entered my office to find a random girl ready to punt Dave out the door, I'd already been pissed.

Then I'd gotten a look at her, and my mood tanked irreparably.

Would I have reacted like that before last year's dumpster fire? Maybe. Maybe not.

Doesn't matter, though, because now I have to stomp all over my pride and deliver this stranger a grand fucking apology.

"Gray?" Anson prompts at my silence.

I scratch the back of my head, grimacing. "Yeah." *Shit.* "I got it. I'll buy her apology flowers, a cake, the whole thing."

"You do that, Gray."

Anson hangs up, and I shove my phone back into my pocket before jerking the skiff into drive. I'm too aggressive on the throttle, and the eighteen-footer jumps.

"She tries anything, I'll end 'er," Mark says a little too casually from behind me.

I glance over my shoulder to see his tanned, heavily wrinkled face set. Mark has no wife or kids, and I've never heard him speak of family, but I've worked with him long enough to know he isn't a serial killer. He'd put his neck on the line in an instant for those he cares about. He'll give you shit the entire time, but he doesn't mean it.

Still, I don't want to encourage any murderous behavior. At his age, folks get inclined to try all sorts of activities. Life in prison isn't a very long time.

"Appreciate the offer, but I got it," I tell him.

"You change your mind, let me know."

———

MARK'S OFFER is still percolating in my head when this grueling day comes to an end. By some rare stroke of luck, it finishes better than it started. Tours go smoothly, the motor fix holds, and we get through every cage we planned to tumble, sort, and harvest.

I've just pulled up to my secluded home, bone-tired and ready for a beer and a burger, when my pocket vibrates again. Dave pokes the pocket with his beak from the passenger seat.

"Yeah, I got it." He retreats, giving his feathered butt a wiggle as he stares at me.

If it's Anson, I'm ignoring it—at least until I've taken ten minutes to decompress. But when I pull it out, JJ's name lights up the screen.

I answer the call and swing my door open. "Hey, man."

"What's up?"

Even without the caller ID, I'd recognize JJ's good-spirited tone anywhere. My best friend is a walking, talking, pocket-full-of-sunshine. Always has been. One interaction is enough to make anyone think his childhood was all rainbows and butterflies, but that couldn't be further from the truth.

"Take it you're back from Alaska?" I pull Dave out with me and set him on the ground.

"Yessir. Just got back this morning." A yawn fades out over the line, like he's pulling the receiver away. When he returns, it's to say, "We have to do a boy's trip up there. It's nature's playground. Would love to enjoy it instead of letting it kick my ass in training exercises."

JJ's on the fire department's dive team, and he's been in Alaska for the last few weeks for some new certification. I'd ask if he got it, but I already know he did. He's like my younger brother Dawson—born with the type of athletic genes that probably could've gotten him into the Olympics. Unlike Dawson, though, he's developed the grit and ethics to go with it.

I heave my bag out of the back seat and head to the door, Dave trailing me. Something stinks of sweat and engine fuel, and when the scent follows, I'm not surprised to learn I'm the source.

Good thing our tours are all outdoors.

No one comes out clean from a good day's work. Dad's words echo in my ears. I'd heard it as a mantra for hard work in my early twenties, but in hindsight, it was an excuse for him to let his hygiene slide.

He let a lot of things slide, toward the end.

"It's got to be a summer trip, though, right?" I ask.

I'd be geared up for a boy's trip with JJ in a heartbeat, but I can't leave the farm in peak season. It's winter travel for me, only, and even that requires thorough planning and contingencies.

"Yeah," he says. "So we only got to wait forty years or something 'til you retire."

"That's the cost of free oysters."

He chuckles. "Trust me, I'm willing to pay it. How're things at the farm?"

I wedge the phone between my shoulder and ear as I unlock the door. "The usual." The door opens, and I set my bags down with a labored sigh. Dave waddles past before I close us inside.

"What happened?"

"What do you mean, what happened?"

"Gray, that was a dramatic sigh if I've ever heard one."

I beeline it to the fridge for an ice-cold brew, because he's right. That was a dramatic sigh. I need to unwind. "Just a little problem I need to work out." The cap comes off the bottle with a satisfying pop, and I take a long draw.

"If it'd help to blow off some steam, I've been wanting to get the boys together to play some ball." He pauses. "Though me kicking your ass might just piss you off more."

"Alaska made you delusional," I say, pulling a leftover burger from the fridge.

"Pick a day, and I'll take great joy in proving you wrong."

I laugh at his challenge. JJ and Dawson aren't the only ones with some athlete in them. We all grew up playing sports, and working on the farm has kept my endurance high and body tough.

"Until then, though, tell me what's going on."

The patty goes into the microwave, and I'm digging through the cupboard for a bun as I tell him about the encounter with Eliza this morning. I don't omit our conversation. JJ knows as well as my brothers that the sainthood everyone knows me for has its limits.

"I'm not surprised Anson went around me, hiring her without consulting me first, but can't say I'm not angry about it." The three emails I'd missed didn't even *ask* if I wanted her—just told me to expect my new Social Media Director today.

My fingers find the corner of a plastic bag, and it slips weightlessly into my hands, reminding me a little too late that I'd eaten the last bun yesterday and was supposed to pick up more today. *Great.*

"That was shitty of him, but expected," JJ agrees, having been around my brother almost as long as I have. His folks were absent more often than not, so he essentially became my parents' fourth child. "Your shittiness is a little less expected, but I get it."

Thank you.

But JJ keeps going. "But you're still being a dick now, even knowing she *didn't* show up out of the blue. Your brother posted the job, and she took it."

The microwave beeps, and I pull the burger out, tossing the plate on the counter. The patty stares back at me, pathetically bare, as I mull over JJ's words.

"You're right," I decide.

A long exhale rattles over the connection. "I don't like that, man."

"What?"

"That two-word answer resigned bullshit. Means you're digging your heels in."

It's scary sometimes how well he reads me.

He continues to do so when he says, "This girl might remind you of Mackenzie, but *she* was a special kind of crazy you don't see much around here. I doubt this one's like her. I wouldn't hate her right off the bat."

"I don't hate her."

It's a half-truth. I *know* I shouldn't hold Mackenzie's likeness against her, but it's a natural defense mechanism to be wary of the newcomer who gives the same first impression as the woman who screwed me over because she thought I was cheating on her. The impression that'd somehow drawn me in last time, like a lamb walking itself right to the slaughter.

I set down my beer and lean against the counter. "It's mistrust. Wariness. A desire for her to not be here, because social media is going to make us into a gimmick."

JJ's quiet for a beat. "Well, there's nothing you can do about it. A contract is signed. It's legally binding."

"I'm legally bound to allow her to do her job at her workplace," I correct. A grin snakes up my cheek that I'm glad no one is around to see, because this town respects me, and I'm stooping lower than I typically do. Lower than I should.

But if City Girl's resume is as impressive as Anson says, there are endless opportunities she can seize—opportunities that lead to promotions, higher pay, and far more success than she could ever get at a contract gig on an oyster farm in Garnet Shores.

This wouldn't hurt her in the least. If anything, leaving would be doing herself a favor.

"There's a second part to that sentence," JJ says cautiously.

There is. "She works at the farm," I repeat, taking a swig of beer. The cold, bitter sweetness feels like a refreshing shower as it goes down. "Doesn't mean I'm obligated to make sure she likes it."

3

———

ELIZA

Mom: Suzanne find anything yet?

THE TIME-STAMP on the text is 4:30 am. One hour ago. Which means the first thing my mother thought of when she woke to her Mozart-blaring alarm was whether Suzanne, her recruiter friend, had procured any promising job opportunities that could restore my reputation in corporate society.

Not how my drastic, temporary move had gone, or how my brain was doing with all the big sudden changes. I don't think she's even once asked, since I was laid off, *How are you?*

It's not that I'm surprised. This is mom's standard. I'm just particularly crabby about it because I'm awake two hours before my alarm, pajamas soaked through and sheets sticking to my skin. The air is thick with humidity, and early morning sunlight streams through the sailboat's narrow port windows. Apparently, the owner of this boat doesn't believe in window shades.

I throw my phone aside, slap my hands over my face,

and collapse back on my pillow. Only I misjudge my position and knock my head against the side of the berth instead.

"Mothertrucking, piece of crap boat!" I curl on my side, pressing my hand against the bump that's beating pain against my skull.

And now I want to cry at five-thirty in the morning.

I shove the tears back. I've felt sorry for myself a lot over the last two weeks, and it's getting pathetic.

I'm healthy, employed, and safe. Really, I owe the world gratitude.

But as shameful as it may be, it's a little hard to feel thankful when I open my eyes to the tiny, crusty cabin of the eighties sailboat that's my temporary home. The full-sized berth I'm sleeping in takes up most of the space, the rest consisting of little cubbies and stowaway shelves I've stuffed with my belongings. The space is just tall enough for me to stand upright in, and there's no kitchen. My refrigerator is a cooler sitting out on deck, and my counter is a shelf on the wall I've stocked with a cutting board, one measly chopping knife, and a few nonperishable provisions. Tap water comes from a hose off the back of the boat, and my toilet and shower are up in the marina's ramshackle office.

I'm essentially camping for the next three months of my life.

Not that I hate camping. It used to be the highlight of my college summers—taking a week away from whatever soul-draining internship I had to stay in a state park with Kitty, my childhood best friend, staring at the stars and talking about our futures.

But back then, my future didn't involve getting laid off from the premier marketing firm I'd sacrificed *years* of my life to, all because my manager took credit for my ideas and rendered me "non-essential." My ideal future also didn't involve my boyfriend of two years cheating on me, casting my social circle into awkward disarray, and me being so overwhelmed by it all that I escaped to rural Rhode Island on such little notice that the only lodging available was an ancient sailboat.

I don't even know anything about boats.

A "reset," I'd called it in my head. A chance to slow down, breathe pollution-free air, and make a little money while Suzanne works her magic with my resume and gets me right back to where I was. But as I lay here, sheets sticking to my skin, staring at the rickety wood cabin door across from me, I wonder if this reset is more of a regression.

Eliza Attleburn, summa cum laude, spawn of two first-generation doctors, the one who "thrives" under the lifelong pressure to succeed is...here.

At least I *do* have this contract job. Anson Gold confirmed it yesterday, when he personally replied to my email and apologized for his brother's—*Grayson* Gold's—behavior. He assured me his brother was misinformed, expressed his excitement for having me on board, and clarified that *he*, not Grayson, is my boss.

Grayson might be in charge of the farm, but Anson runs the Gold's larger name, marketing operations included.

I won't lie and say I didn't briefly consider leaving yesterday. I didn't come here for more problems. An oyster farm gig in a quiet town should, in theory, be the easiest, lowest-stress job ever. A chocolatey, sugary, extra-sweet cakewalk. I'm used to Saturday fire drills, Sunday evenings in the office, and "I needed that a week ago" from pretentious, disrespectful men who think lip gloss makes me inferior. While this might not be a high-paced environment, Grayson has the *disrespectful men* part down to a science.

But my boat rental is locked in. And even if it wasn't, I'm not a quitter. Never have been. If anything, asshats like him make me want to work harder so I can stick it to them at a later date.

Granted, that ideal just failed gloriously at my last job, but this is a new opportunity.

I stoke the thought, letting it spark a little fire in me, because I need to crawl out of this pit of despair. Before I can reconsider, I throw the covers aside, toss on my faded college sweatshirt, and head up on deck.

Everything is slick with dew, but the air is sweet and fresh. I pull a water from the cooler and survey my new home while I drink.

The sky is beautiful in a sleepy way, hazy clouds parting enough to let the oranges and pinks of the sunrise slip through. Around me, the docks are quiet, save for the gentle lapping of water against hulls. This marina is nothing like the yacht club I'd glimpsed on the other side of town. Its six tiny wooden docks host a collection of modest boats, many of which are too small to have sleep-in cabins. The twenty-foot sailboat I'm on is one of the biggest here, situated all the way at the end of dock three. When I face away from the marina, it's like I'm on an island, nothing but calm, blue water and the greenery of the salt pond stretching around me.

The oyster farm is visible to my right, a few homes line the shore, and the channel connecting the pond to the ocean is somewhere across from me, but compared to the city, it feels like I'm at the edge of the world.

With plenty of time to waste before work, I sit down on a damp cushion and open my socials. That pit of despair I'd just tried to seal opens right back up when I spot a photo of my two closest city friends, Sami and Jane, looking cute at this new West End coffee shop. No doubt this is the tenth time they'd posed for this, their half-laughing smiles too perfect, but the pang of FOMO grips my chest and squeezes tight.

I should be with them.

But being with them wouldn't make me feel any better.

In fact, being with my city friends recently has only made me feel worse. That's what happens when your friend group is built around your ex. I knew it, too, the second I realized Kyle wasn't the marriage material I'd always dreamed about. That'd been about eight months ago, but I never acted on it, telling myself I was seeking a standard too good to be true.

Now, two weeks removed from him and not nearly as heartbroken as I should be, I'm certain I was just operating under fear of change. With work draining me dry, I'd clung to the small, daily comfort of a stable, predictable personal life.

I really thought I was better and smarter than that. *Stronger* than that.

Truly a bold thought to have while curled up on a worn boat cushion, lamenting over missing a café selfie before the sun is even up.

Screw this.

Whatever I've been doing *clearly* isn't working. I need to get out of my head. Before I can overthink it, I dart into the cabin, ditch my phone, and pull on my most secure bikini. Grabbing the goggles I haven't used since college, I march back out on deck. Without my sweatshirt, the morning air is chilly, but it feels good to have something other than *myself* to occupy my thoughts.

At the back platform, my blurred reflection stares up at me from the water as I braid my hair. Suddenly, I don't feel like a twenty-six-year-old career woman, but the sixteen-year-old girl about to start high school swim practice at the lake. I was good back then, ranking in the top twenty for the state, before ending my short career for an un-turn-down-able academic scholarship.

I'm completely unprepared for how the frigid water steals my breath when I jump in.

It's *icy*. A Siberian pond. Colder than the little lake in southern Massachusetts ever was. I'm in dire risk of turning into one of those Florida iguanas that freeze so hard and fast, they fall out of trees.

Survival instincts send me scrambling to the platform, ready to heave myself out. But when my fingers grasp the wood platform, I pause.

Take a shaky, tight breath.

Because the cold is starting to feel a little less painful and a little more invigorating. And it's blessedly impossible to think about anything past the sensations on my skin and the challenge the water presents.

I ease my fingers off the wood. It's probably inadvisable to do this without a wetsuit or a swim buoy, but the salt pond is warmer than the ocean, May's been above-average, and twenty minutes of discomfort won't kill me. If anything, it might *fix* me.

And I need this—need *something*.

So I force my body into a slow and steady stroke away from the dock.

WITHOUT A DOWNPOUR TO OBSCURE IT, the exterior of Gold's Oysters looks even cuter than it did yesterday. And now that I've met Grayson, it makes even *less* sense.

The flowers on the office's porch are springy and vivid, and small birds flit at the bird-feeder. Several wind chimes I didn't notice before hang from the covered porch, off-key melodies singing in the soft breeze, their stained glass designs reflecting the gentle sunlight.

An older woman bustles out the office door and stops short at the top of the stairs, big, green eyes smeared with shimmery blue eyeshadow scanning me from loosely curled hair to white leather sneakers without a hint of subtlety. She wears a colorful cardigan stitched with crocheted flowers, and I instantly know I've found the source of the butterflies and bird-feeders.

A delighted smile warms her grandmotherly face when I reach the top step. "You must be the new phone girl," she says, like she's just found a pot of gold.

Phone girl? Is that what Grayson's calling me?

I'm pretty sure *she* means nothing by it, so I smile back and offer my hand. "I'm the new Social Media Director. The phone's only half the job."

Her fingers are frigid—like every grandmother's fingers, ever—when she shakes my hand.

"My, my. He *certainly* didn't say how pretty you are," she says with a pleased chuckle.

I hold my smile, because how does one respond to *that?*

She prattles on. "My name is Joy. I'm the bookkeeper here, and let me tell you—" She pulls me in with a surprisingly strong grip, and like she's sharing a secret, loudly whispers, "These Gold boys are quite the catch."

It's getting harder to hold the smile, because I think she's trying to sweeten up my boss and the jerk of a farm owner, and her grip won't allow me to escape.

"Of course, it's obvious how handsome they are. But they're *good* boys, you know? The kind that make for great husbands and—"

"*Quack.*"

Dave cuts her off, appearing from the office door that's now held open by Grayson. The interruption makes Joy whirl, and I'm able to gently extricate myself.

Grayson's amber eyes settle on me like a heavy weight. The kind that wants to grind me into fine dust until I disappear. He peruses me with the same unabashed openness as Joy, so I scan him right back. He's wearing the same brown work pants as yesterday. But with the sun out, he's sans rain jacket, and I find myself wishing for a downpour, because he's wearing a worn, light blue *Gold's Oysters* tee with the sleeves cut off, revealing arms I can't help but notice. Tanned skin, muscled shoulders, thick forearms, veins visible beneath a smattering of dark hair. It only gets worse when I trace one of those veins to his bicep, which flexes as he holds the door open.

I drag my eyes back to his face to find a knowing smirk, and I want to tumble down the stairs. Instead, I set my shoulders and lift an unimpressed brow.

Grayson Gold has hot-guy arms. So what? They're a dime a dozen in Boston.

Oblivious to the tension, Joy claps her fingertips together in glee. "Well, I'll let you two get to know each other. Lovely to meet you—" She waits for my name.

"Eliza."

"Ah! Pretty name for a pretty girl." She sends a not-very-sly look at Grayson before waddling down the stairs.

He shakes his head and steps out onto the porch, letting the door swing shut. "So, you've met Joy." He sets his hands on his hips in a way that puts those annoying arms on full display.

"She seems nice."

His scruffy face is missing the streak of grease from yesterday, though his dark, textured hair already looks stiff with salt. He reminds me of a bear, or maybe he's just so much more rugged than the clean-swept finance men I'm used to that my brain defaults to animal comparisons. In the sunlight, his irises seem to glow, almost...gold.

Comes with the last name, I suppose.

Those orbs settle on me again, raking a path from my face to my hair, and down across my body. Self-consciousness pricks my skin at his *second* evaluation, and I remind myself I look presentable. The curls are cooperating today, my black, wide-strapped tank-top is lint-free, and my dark wash jeans hug my hips perfectly.

It's more casual than I'd normally wear, but I'd gotten the vibe yesterday that dress pants and heels don't quite belong.

Grayson must find it lacking, because he shakes his head and sighs. "Welcome to Gold's Oysters."

I stare at him for a moment, wondering how Joy could know this man and call him a "good boy." His words are fine, but his unashamed assessment of me and the dislike in his tone are so boldly rude, it's staggering.

Any efforts at civility I'd planned go right out the window. Anson said to inform him of any issues I face on the farm, but I'm not about to whine to my boss. If Grayson wants this dynamic, so be it. I can play, too.

And as far as I'm concerned, Anson already thinks his brother's the problem, which gives me *plenty* of room to play.

"How much did that hurt to say?" I ask.

Grayson blinks twice, maybe because he was expecting sweet gratitude from someone who would swallow his bullshit.

He ignores my question and says, "Apologies for yesterday. I wasn't expecting you. That's not how we run things here." God, it's like he's being held at gunpoint, the words are that disingenuous.

"Everyone makes mistakes, Mr. Farm Owner. Don't worry about it."

"Gray," he says flatly. "That's what everyone calls me."

I cock my head, squinting up at the overhang. "You're right. Mr. Farm Owner is kind of a mouthful. But you seemed so intent yesterday on making it known that you run this place."

I take a little joy in the way his jaw grinds. He's about to reply when Dave gives a mighty *quack.*

"He seems to like it," I comment, and Grayson scrapes his hand across his mouth, as if he's trying to physically block his next words from coming out.

Finally, he loses all pretense. "Look, I have concerns about you being here, but the contract has been signed. So all I'm asking is that you stay out of the way and don't cause us any problems."

I actually don't mind the directness. It's easier to work with than passive aggression.

"Despite what you might think, my goal here is to help, not hurt. Think of me as icing on the cake." He squints in confusion. "You're the cake. Your flavor and consistency aren't going to change because I'm added to the equation. You're just going to look more enticing."

For an on-the-spot metaphor, it's pretty damn good.

But all he says is, "Not the biggest fan of cake."

Of course. "You hate puppies, too?"

"Just because I don't like cake doesn't mean I'm some unfeeling asshole." My eyes widen at the golden opportunity he just served up, but he catches it before I can take advantage. "Cake is fine, but I prefer other desserts. It's not that I hate sugar or something."

No. You just hate me.

He shakes his head and gestures at the office. "Use this front office space if you want, unless Joy's in there, which is rare. Do what you need to do to fulfill your contract, but don't touch anything on the farm." He glances at Dave, who's poking a flower pot with his beak. "That includes Dave."

With that, he brushes right by me and jogs down the stairs.

Wait a second. "Hey!" I call out.

He pauses, momentum carrying him forward before he turns. His brow hikes in question, as if he doesn't know why on earth I'm interrupting his dramatic exit.

"Are you going to give me a tour?"

He twists his lips and glances around at the empty lot. "Don't have time, and no one's available. Anson said you're real smart, so I'm sure you'll figure it out."

Frustration bubbles up in my chest. Verbal sparring is one thing. Deliberately interfering with my work is another.

There's no way in hell I'm begging him for a tour, so I turn to the second problem at hand. "I can't fulfill my contract without touching things."

"Why?" He rummages around in his pocket to produce a beat-up phone. "All you need is this thing, right?"

I don't bother justifying that with a response. Even Dave can tell this conversation is going nowhere. Grayson gives a little nod—like I've just agreed to his ridiculous request—replaces his phone, and gives me his broad back as he strides away.

A back set with cocky, self-assured swagger.

Too bad I'm about to burst his big ego-inflated bubble.

After dumping my belongings in the office, I head around the other side of the building. If Grayson doesn't want to give me a tour, I'll find someone who will.

A girl comes into view almost immediately, carrying a stack of empty bins out of an open door in the side of the building. She looks about my age, clothed in bright orange bibs and a stained white tee shirt, dirty blonde hair swaying in a messy ponytail.

She doesn't seem to notice me, so I jog to catch up to her.

"Hey!"

She glances over her shoulder, and her expression shifts from curious to crestfallen. "Shit," she mutters as I close the distance.

Probably because she thinks I'm a visitor, like Grayson yesterday.

"I'm Eliza, the new Social Media Director. Anson hired me," I say with a friendly smile.

My introduction only worsens the dread on her makeup-free face, and now some of her dread transfers to me. I haven't done anything but offer my name and evidence that I work here, but she's looking at me like I'm a giant raincloud.

"Grayson was a little too busy to give me a tour, and I was hoping to run into someone who could," I try.

She sighs, takes me in, then answers, "Look, you seem nice, so I'm going to save you the trouble of going up to every person here. We've got a lot to do here, and we can't take any time to do social media stuff. Even if I wanted to, Gray told us no."

Fucking Grayson.

"And Gray is almost always in a good mood, so on the rare occasion he gets testy like this, you listen." The buckets in her hands tilt on a shrug. "I don't know what you did to get on his bad side, because it takes a lot, but just know he's not your biggest fan."

I bark out a short laugh. "Yeah. Got that memo."

Problem is, I did nothing but *show up to my job on time,* and somehow, that landed me on Grayson's allegedly elusive shitlist.

She purses her lips. "Good luck."

She's already starting to walk away when I say, "Can I at least have your name?"

I'll admit it sounds a little desperate, but I need at least one ally here, and she was kind enough to throw me a bone.

She throws me another one. "Amanda."

I commit that to memory before allowing myself to internally crash out.

Grayson's game is easy to read.

He's made it startlingly clear he doesn't want me here, but he can't fire me, so he wants to make my job impossible.

Well, if he thinks I'm going to throw in the towel and leave, he has another thing coming. I've played victim enough recently, and I'm *done.*

I'm going to kick ass at my job, blow Anson away, and make Grayson Gold drop to his ungrateful knees and thank me by the time August rolls around.

That, and touch every single thing on this farm.

4

GRAYSON

I HATE early mornings on the farm about as much as I love them.

The four-thirty alarm kills me, but watching the sunrise from the pond is one of my favorite things in life. There's something about the quiet early hours of dawn, when the water's still, those pretty colors painting the sky, just me and nature coexisting as the engine hums along, that feels transcendent.

Most of the town is asleep, and I've earned this moment of peace, because I was willing to get up at the ass-crack of dawn.

Granted, I'm only starting this early because I'm helping Anson out with Lala, our little sister, this afternoon. But still, I've earned it.

I sip my black coffee, which steams in the crisp air, as I adjust the wheel.

"You ready?"

Kenny's slouched against the side of the skiff, looking like he'd give anything to miss this sunrise. I needed someone to man the boat while I dive to fix some gear in the deeper side of the farm, and the kid pulled the short stick yesterday. He just turned twenty-one, and I know for a fact he's been spending some late nights at Dyl's Den, taking advantage of that freshly legal ID.

From the misery on his face, I'd bet last night was one of them.

But Kenny's a hard-working kid, so he showed up on time, and now he's lurching to his feet, grabbing a line to anchor us to our floating cages.

The same way I used to assist Dad, back when he was starting things up here and I was juggling college with work on the farm.

Should still be that way—me helping my father. But after cancer took Mom, he just fell apart. I can't blame him for it. Losing our mother was brutal, but losing the love of your life...I don't know how someone could handle that well. First went the state of the farm, then his health. The heart attack was inevitable.

Six years later, and it all still feels like the end of the fucking world when I think about it.

Skiff secured, I'm laying out my dive gear when my peripheral catches something splashing in the distance, toward the local marina. Straightening, I squint. Oysters and small fish are usually the only sea life we get in these shallow waters, but the pond does open to the ocean. A whale got caught up in here a few years ago.

"See that?"

The dark circles under Kenny's eyes shift as he tries to make out the shape. It's moving quickly. "Something's feeding?" he guesses.

I pull a pair of old binoculars out of the compartment beneath the wheel. It takes a second to find the shape, but when I do, I'm surprised. "Someone's swimming."

Shallow as the pond is, we don't get a ton of action in here. It's mostly kayaks, our skiffs, and the occasional small craft from Joe's docks making its way to the ocean. Swimmers prefer the open waters at the town beach. And the water's still fucking freezing.

The figure pauses and goes vertical, their head popping out of the water, and I'm no longer confused. The person swimming in the pond is too new here to know this isn't the best spot for it.

Eliza Attleburn looks a little alien with reflective goggles on her face, but it's easy to recognize her. And I hate how easy it is, because that means I've spent too much time studying her face, despite my attempts to ignore her for the last week-and-a-half.

Hard not to when it looks like *that*. All glowy skin, elegant angles, and eyes as big as a doe's—especially when they're glaring at me.

I receive about five of those glares per day, whenever we silently cross paths in the yard. Though from what I can tell, she's mostly been keeping to the office. Hopefully it stays that way.

"You know the swimmer?"

I grunt and put the binoculars away. "That's the Social Media Director."

Of all people, I wouldn't expect her to be swimming in open water three hours before she's due at work. She's toned down her look since the first day we met, but even with the jeans, she's the furthest thing from ocean-hardy.

"The one you keep telling us to ignore?"

"Not telling you to ignore her. Just do your job and don't get distracted by any antics."

Kenny's nose wrinkles. "Pretty sure you told us to ignore her, or we'd be cleaning cages for a week straight."

"You misunderstood."

Because telling my team to ignore her would be a dick move, even though I don't want her here. Impressing the importance of working hard on these busy days and not getting sidetracked, however, is perfectly respectable.

"Sure, Boss," Kenny says without an ounce of conviction. When I reach for my gear, he asks, "Think she's alright out there? She's pretty far from the shore, and the water's cold."

The same concern already crossed my mind, because no matter how much I want her off this farm, I don't want anyone to drown. But she's already kicked back into her freestyle stroke, now moving back toward the docks, and the way she cuts through the water radiates confidence and strength.

"Looks like a good swimmer. And she isn't too far from Joe's Marina."

But even good swimmers can misjudge distances and get tired, especially in frigid water.

Shit.

Now I'm pulling the binoculars out again and resting them on the console in front of me. She hasn't even stepped on the property for the day, and she's already adding to the mile-high list of things I need to worry about.

Of course.

"Keep an eye on her, just in case," I tell Kenny.

Some of the worry eases from his forehead. "She seems nice," he remarks, palming the binoculars. "Smiles and says hi to people when she walks around."

I grunt as I strip off my sweatshirt and start pulling on my wetsuit.

Eliza sure as hell doesn't smile and say hi to me. And

maybe it should bother me that I'm the only exception to her kindness, but it doesn't. At all.

Makes it easier to keep *encouraging* her to leave.

———

THE IMAGE of Eliza smoothly gliding through the water invades my thoughts more than it should for the rest of the morning. It was an unexpected deviation from the picture I'd painted of her. That picture being an echo of Mackenzie—squeaking at seaweed and avoiding sea water like the plague so her hair doesn't dry out. Not the type to get down in an unfiltered body of water that's still cold enough to freeze your balls off.

I'll admit it impressed me. Just a little.

Couple that with the fact that she hasn't caused any issues yet, and the possibility that I'm being too tough on her is starting to emerge.

That whisper of doubt is tracking through my mind when I open the door to our oyster pick-up room and see her inside one of the massive refrigerators, tip toes on the bottom shelf, hand reaching toward the temperature gauge.

Panic and anger crash into me, and I can't think straight. Can't see anything except her fingers aiming for that metal knob. The same fucking metal knob that nearly got us shut down last year, when Mackenzie cranked it to illegal storage temperatures, took a photo, and sent it to her father—who passed it, along with other false allegations, on to a local regulator—all because she'd mistaken texts to Amanda for me cheating on her.

This fucking lady.

"What do you think you're doing?" I bark, barreling toward her.

She jumps and shrieks at the same time. Her head twists, and I catch a flash of wide, startled eyes before her hand slips from the shelf that was holding her in. She tumbles back, tripping down from the shelf.

I'm already there. Quick reflexes have me catching her under the arms before she hits the floor. I set her upright and yank my hands away like her skin is hot coals.

The second she turns, though, I get right up in her space, the tension in my muscles so explosive I feel like the fucking Hulk.

The bewildered fear in her eyes pierces me for a second before slipping into outrage.

"What the *hell* is your problem?" she shrieks, red spiraling across her cheeks. "You could've killed me, coming up behind me like that!"

Her playing the victim only winds me tighter. "Why are you messing with the temperatures?"

"Messing with the—" she repeats in disbelief. The red from her cheeks is flooding her neck, which is craned back so she can meet my eyes. Eliza's not short, but I still have a few inches on her. "I'm grabbing a bag of *oysters* to take *photos* to show people what pickups look like, because that is my *job*." Her voice is breathing fire, a vein pulsing on her forehead, like a little pissed off dragon.

"There are plenty of pickups on the bottom shelves," I fire back.

"Believe it or not, *Grayson*, I have eyeballs." Her pitch rises with her volume, each word working her up more and more. "And these eyeballs are trying to find the best-looking pickup, because this is going out as a *paid ad*. But you wouldn't understand the importance of that or what it even means, because you only think and speak in shellfish!"

Her chest heaves on rapid breaths, drawing my attention right down to where it shouldn't be. To the smooth olive skin dotted with freckles above small, perky breasts that I absolutely will *not* look at.

The mere temptation only pisses me off more. "I told you not to touch anything."

"And unless you're down to two working brain cells—" she shoves a finger into my chest— "you'd know that's impossible when I've been hired to work here."

Trying to rein in my temper, I look down at the finger digging into my sternum. Technically, I was the one to make contact first, when I saved her from knocking herself unconscious, but Little Miss Professional just broke a boundary.

I'm getting to her.

The realization sinks in at the same time as her words.

She wasn't altering our refrigeration, but looking for a pretty bag of oysters. And I just turned into a goddamn gorilla.

I'm too worked up to sort it out now, so I dig my heels right in. "Did it ever occur to you that I told you that for your own safety? Last thing I need is you hurting yourself and taking it out on us."

She crosses her arms and snorts in my face. "Yeah, you definitely have two brain cells." Her finger's gone, but the imprint of her manicured nail is seared into my skin. "If you gave a damn about my safety, you would've given me a tour and explained what's dangerous and why. Not left me here to figure it out on my own."

Her logic is indisputable, and the haughty look on her face says she knows it. I stare her down—the fierce set of her shoulders, the ready-to-fight spirit blazing silver in her hazel eyes.

It stirs something in my abdomen, something that counters my dislike. Probably more of that respect from earlier.

Not sure why *respect* has me suddenly noticing the soft floral scent coming from her hair or neck or wherever it is women put perfume. Which has me noticing the trail of goosebumps along her collarbone.

I reach around her, slam the refrigerator door shut, then take a step back, because I don't need to be crowding her like this. Trying to intimidate her with my size.

Christ, when did I turn into one of *those* guys?

"I still need to find my bag of oysters," she points out, rubbing the chill from her arms.

"Not from the top shelf. Clearly, you're unstable up there."

Her brows crash together. "I wasn't *unstable* until you attacked me from behind."

I hide a wince behind a blank stare. She's waiting for an apology. One I owe her.

When I don't give it, she tacks on, "If you're done throwing your tantrum, I should be fine on my own."

Not a fucking tantrum, City Girl. I'm protecting my farm.

Self-control stops the response from coming out. Or maybe it's the fact that those flowers are tickling my nose, and I'm noticing a few freckles scattered across her cheeks that are just like the ones sprinkled across the smooth skin of her neckline, above her—

Cut it the fuck out.

I'm standing there like an imbecile, not speaking, not moving, long enough for Eliza to release a long exhale and ask, "Why do you hate me so much?"

Because social media, in that pretty little city-girl package, doesn't belong on this farm.

Because you can't possibly understand what we've built here, and treat it with the respect it deserves.

Because you remind me of my mistake, and how easily my dick can override my common sense for a nice smile and pretty face.

"I don't hate you," I say instead.

She barks a dry laugh. "Yeah, you do." Losing her anger, her hands drop to her sides. "I'm not here to ruin your life. I'm here because your brother posted an open position, and I took it."

There's resignation in her tone now, and it twists unpleasantly in my gut. I want the fire, the insults back. Maybe because it makes me feel like less of a dickhead. Makes my insolence more acceptable.

"I'm aware," I reply lamely.

She turns away, reaching again for the refrigerator door. "I have work to do."

Right.

The image of her falling down replays in my mind, and I realize that my concern for her safety is genuine. I don't want this woman smashing herself on the floor. God knows I've been beating her up enough with my words.

Fuck.

I back away and turn toward the door, but not before saying, "Just use a bag from the lower shelves. They're all the same."

I'm not expecting a thank you, and it doesn't come as I walk out the door.

5

———

ELIZA

GRAYSON GOLD IS OFFICIALLY at the top of my shitlist.

An incredible feat, given the stiff competition.

For a long time, my manager held the number-one spot. It'd been a long time coming, but he'd cemented his place there the *first* time he took credit for a strategy I developed that landed a client millions in sales.

My ex, Kyle, only recently usurped him. Cheating was that powerful. In fact, I thought cheating was such an egregious offense that it couldn't possibly be outdone by anything else—except for, like, murder.

But Grayson Gold has proven me wrong.

He'd scared the ever-living shit out of me when he'd stormed into the pickup room, barking the way he did. When he'd caught me, I thought that maybe there was a chance he wasn't a total dick. But he set me on my feet only to make false accusations, and left without a hint of apology.

I've gotten used to facing men who don't like me in corporate Boston, but those challenges were always more subtle. Political games, fake pleasantries, compliments threaded with condescension. Even Kyle, when he hooked up with his coworker, had done so quietly, behind my back, out of sight.

But Grayson is like a bull, loud and unashamed in his assholery that's seemingly based on nothing other than my existence.

I understand I'm an outcast on the farm. Respect is something earned, and to do that, you have to prove yourself worthy.

The thing is, I'm not being given the chance to prove it.

Then again, there is nothing I need to prove to Grayson. Anson Gold is my boss. Grayson is just an obstacle I have to figure out how to deal with—with*out* physically assaulting him and getting myself arrested.

Fortunately for us both, we don't cross paths for the remainder of the day.

Fire still lances under my skin as I make the short drive back to the boat. I'm not looking forward to my destination, but I try to let the journey soothe me.

Lush trees frame this stretch of the road, driveways disappearing to houses buried within them. A few home farmstands pop up along the side of the street before it opens up into a waterside route. The air breezing through the windows turns salty and familiar, and there are more cars here—though it really isn't as busy as it should be.

It might have something to do with the lack of commercialization. Garnet Shores is mostly residential. There are no state beaches; just a single stretch of sand that's part-private and part-public, and the giant salt pond's grassy waterfront. The two towns sandwiching this one are more popular spots, with restaurants, hotels, shopping, groceries, and that idyllic-summer-vacation vibe that pull in tourists like a magnet. But Garnet Shores seems determined to stay small and discreet, except for the private vacation homes scattered around.

As I take in the serene wetlands on my left and the stretch of salt pond to my right, I don't blame them. With all its quiet, this might be one of the best commutes within two hours of Boston.

In the city, it's all car horns, over-aggressive drivers, and people buzzing around like swarming flies. Some people love that energy. I used to be one of them. But lately, it's just compounded my stress after a day of headaches in the office.

This, here? It's like a demand to breathe and relax. Like if your mind is racing toward your next destination, you're disrupting the peaceful vibe. The thought has my hands relaxing on the wheel just as my phone rings.

When I see Kitty's name plastered across the screen, my entire day flips around. I pull over, parking against the barrier that separates the road from a little swamp.

Kitty calls demand full attention.

I answer and exclaim, "You're alive!"

Through a crackle of white noise, Kitty's voice comes through, all smiling sarcasm. "Yes, Mom. I told you not to worry about me."

"You're backpacking solo through the wilderness with limited phone service. If I didn't worry a little, I'd be a shitty friend."

"I'm safer out here than I am in society. No potential car accidents. No bar creeps hanging around. No flu germs to—" her voice cuts out for a second and returns with— "rather die by grizzly bear."

My nose wrinkles. "Death by grizzly bear is easily one of the worst ways to go."

"Disagree. It's natural. The circle of life."

"Please tell me you have bear spray on you. Like, you aren't inviting a grizzly to come hug you, right?"

"Still have to go bungee jumping and skydiving. So no bear hug invitations at the moment. Except from you. I miss my best friend."

"I miss you too, Kitty."

I need you here.

I don't let those words come out, because Kitty's out West living her earthy-crunchy outdoorsy dreams. She's always been an adventurous soul, and I love watching her seize it, now that she's finally free to do so after getting out of her shitstorm of a marriage.

But she's been my best friend since third grade, so she hears the desperation in my voice anyway. "You doing okay?"

Her service on the trail is extremely limited, so we only catch up when she reaches a rest stop that offers one measly bar of cell data. The last time we chatted was just days after I lost my job and found out Kyle cheated on me.

I scratch my head. "Figuring it out. Long story short, I... um, needed to get out of the city, so I got a contract job for the summer with an oyster farm. I'm currently living on a sailboat, my parents are up my ass about finding a new job, and the oyster farm owner is the biggest douchebag I've ever met in my life."

There's a beat of silence. "That's...a change," she says slowly.

I laugh a little. "Yeah. Not as put together as I'd like to be."

She doesn't hesitate this time. "Doesn't sound like that to me. Sounds like you're on a coastal retreat for the summer, challenging yourself with a new industry, and learning how to live on the water, with plans to return to your super-successful-boss-lady life soon."

"You're giving me too much credit."

"You're not giving yourself enough, per usual," she shoots back. "And what's this about the oyster farmer?"

Grayson's face pops right back into view. "If you come across any bears, ask them if I can hire them for a hit."

"That dickish?"

"Yep."

"Is he hot?"

I'm still seeing his scowling face in my head, which makes it unfortunately easy to answer her question. "Aren't all assholes hot?" When she laughs, I add, "Not my type. Someone else's, probably."

Someone who likes rugged-looking men who fill out their clothes well, have golden eyes and tanned skin, and swagger around with easy strength. It wasn't lost on me that earlier, he'd caught and plopped me on my feet like I weighed nothing.

It truly was a shame all the ovary-stimulating men chose to open their mouths and share their thoughts.

"You'll put—" her voice disappears again— "his place. Just like you did...Jack when he tried...beat you as class president."

Her one bar of service seems to be disappearing, as it usually does after a minute or two.

"How much longer will you be out there?" I ask her.

"What?" Her voice is garbled.

I repeat myself, and it must go through, because she says, "Three weeks."

Only three-quarters of a month, then, until I can get her on a video call. I'll be counting down the days.

"Call me at your next stop?"

"Of..." there's a long stretch of static, "...or ten days."

Maybe I'll have murdered Grayson by then, and I'll be asking for tips on how to hide the body. The thought makes me smile as I say, "Love you."

Her service holds on long enough for her "love you" to come through, and then the call drops.

I pull my phone from my ear to see three new texts. When I read the *Boston Bitches* group name, it's like a sack of rocks lands in my stomach. All the Kitty-induced happiness vanishes, and just like that, my day returns to its downward trajectory.

> Jane: Margs tn? New taco place in Southie.

Jane immediately notices her mistake, because she quickly follows with:

> Jane: Oh shit! Wrong chat lolol

> Jane: Love and miss you ellie bear!!

I should return the words. Heart her message at the very least. But I can't bring myself to do that when Kyle's initials are in a little circle near the group chat name. It's the chat our friend group has used for years, until a few weeks ago when it went radio silent.

Apparently they've formed a new one.

Without me.

I don't know why that makes the bag of rocks in my belly heavier. I *know* they're all still hanging out. I met Jane and Sami through Kyle, and while they're my closest friends in the city, they were close with *him* first, starting in college. Sami's boyfriend is his roommate. I'm living two hours away.

Of course they'd have a chat without me.

But talking that through in my head doesn't make me feel better.

The rest of my drive to the boat consists of me trying to shove that text thread from my mind and running through the work tasks I'll do tonight. The first posts I've made are exceeding expectations, and Suzanne doesn't need me to write any cover letters today, but there's nothing better for me to do than bury myself in work.

That plan hits a snag when I step on the rickety boat, head to the cooler to grab a snack, and meet a puddle of water and a few remaining scraps of food. The freezing morning swims have turned me into a horse, and I'm going through food faster than usual. There isn't enough here for a satisfying meal, and I can't handle another major disappointment today.

I'm trying to limit them, if that's even possible.

A quick restaurant search shows just one open nearby—a spot called Dyl's Den. It comes with a picture of a stacked burger, and my decision's made. The boat has relegated me to sandwiches, salads, and whatever I can put in the marina office's microwave, and my taste buds are now salivating at the thought of a fresh, hot, greasy meal.

I grab my laptop, and ten minutes later, I'm pulling into a busy parking lot tucked into the woods.

Dyl's Den looks exactly how I thought it would. It's a modest, older building with wood shingles, the kind of small-town spot that's well-loved but not dingy. A hum of voices emanates as I approach the entrance, the low notes of a blues tune emerging when I hit the landing.

Crossing the threshold is like stepping into a warm hug.

Inside, it's all tavern-style wood, sturdy round tables, and nineties-coastal décor. An oak bar dominates the right wall, most of its stools taken by people who look like they came straight from work. My gaze roams over the back corner, where a pool table and dart boards are being used by groups.

This isn't a place where wealthy tourists make reservations for their summer vacation. It's a local's spot.

That thought is the only warning I have before a figure by the pool table shifts and I'm graced with Grayson Gold's obnoxiously strong profile.

Fuck. My. Life.

I just wanted a burger.

I picture the half-eaten tub of hummus and single tortilla wrap left in my cooler, trying to convince myself it'll hit the spot, and then mentally slap myself. When did I become the person who lets a man run my life?

I came here to eat a hot meal while I work. I'm not going to turn tail and run because of one infuriating person, no matter how uncomfortable he makes me.

Especially because my presence here might just ruin his night, too.

And he seems to be having a good one so far. The scowl I've gotten to know so well is replaced by happy smile lines as he sips a beer and chats with a younger man beside him. I recognize the kid's shaggy blonde hair from the oyster farm. When that recognition locks into place, I realize I know some of the others from the farm.

Know being an exaggeration, unless you count self-consciously smiling and mumbling "hi" as they skirt away as a sign of acquaintanceship.

My discomfort grows.

"Welcome to Dyl's! Take any open table," a woman chirps. I jump, spinning to find a middle-aged waitress, hands filled with trays. "Menus are already out. I'll be with you in two." Even in her rush, she spares me a kind smile.

See? You're welcome here.

"Thank you," I say, but she's already rushing across the room.

I beeline it to a corner table that's as far from Grayson as possible and plop my laptop down. Then I pause.

Do I give Grayson my back so he doesn't notice me? Face him so it seems like I don't care if he sees me? One says I'm hiding. The other says I'm goading him.

Or I'm just way overthinking this, and Grayson isn't going to think anything beyond "I hate you" when he recognizes me all the way over here—*if* he even notices me.

I've been standing here so long it's starting to look weird, so I compromise and scoot one of the chairs so I'm only half-facing Grayson. It isn't lost on me that I'm allowing him way too much real estate in my mind, and now my pleasant, grease-filled evening is in terrible danger of becoming yet another tribulation when he probably hasn't even noticed me.

No.

We're not letting Grayson do that.

Easier said than done.

When the waitress stops by two seconds later and asks if I want a drink, the answer is an overly enthusiastic yes.

6

GRAYSON

ELIZA ATTLEBURN IS SITTING in the corner, typing away on her laptop like she's in a working café in downtown Manhattan and not Garnet Shores' local joint.

I'm not the only one who's noticed.

The only big shiny electronic screen that's ever been in Dyl's Den is the one on the wall showing local lottery numbers. Eliza sticks out like a sore thumb.

Doesn't help that she'd catch eyes without the giant computer. Her hair, which was down earlier, is thrown into a ponytail that shows off her pert cheekbones and the straight line of her stubborn nose. Lips that I know are slightly pouty twist as her face wrinkles, her entire focus on that screen.

Like the laptop, that level of focus doesn't belong here either. Not when Dyl's is the type of place you go for a casual drink and comforting meal to unwind after a work day.

Then again, it's that level of focus that's responsible for the neatly typed words I'd read just before coming here.

After hanging with Lala for the afternoon, I'd finally opened up Eliza's resume.

I might not be as versed in marketing-speak as Anson, but it's clear Eliza Attleburn has one hell of a track record. Graduated top of her class. Worked in Boston, generating strategies that earned millions for clients in the technology sector. Got promoted twice within one year at her first job, before making a vertical move to a new fancier-sounding company. She still doesn't belong on the farm, but Anson's hiring decision makes more sense now. And our earlier conversation in the oyster pickup room seems a little more egregious now, too.

Sure "conversation" is the right word for it?

I turn back to Kenny and take a long pull of beer to hide my grimace. Unfortunately, he saw exactly where my eyes just went.

He grins. "Checking out the video girl?"

"Social Media Director. And I'm not checking her out." The cheery glint in his eyes tells me he's just about at his alcohol limit. The kid's young and still learning where it is, which seems to be at a whopping two beers.

"What then? Trying to scare her away with your eyes?"

Eliza Attleburn doesn't scare.

Except when I barged in on her and she nearly split her head open earlier. Even then, she recovered like a feral cat and came back at me, claws extended.

Fuck, I owe her an apology. I knew it the moment she'd set me straight about what she was doing in the pickup room. The guilt that'd been planted then has been growing ever since, and Lala piled on the fertilizer when she'd stared at me with her big green eyes and declared I was her "favorite big brother."

Granted, she said it when we were pulling into Missy

D's Dairy Freeze, but dessert-motivated or not, it was a bucket of ice water to the face. I'm supposed to be her role model, and today I raised my voice at someone who didn't deserve it. Even worse, that someone was a woman.

I'm better than that.

"Is it 'cause she looks like...what's her name?" Kenny snaps his fingers, attempting to jog his alcohol-impaired memory. "You know, that chick who fucked us over last—"

I pull the beer right out of his hands.

"Hey, man! Come on."

I slap it on the high-top behind me and block his access with my body. I'd bought the beer for him as a thank you for helping so early this morning, but now, it's fueling his stupidity. Kenny sure as hell wouldn't be prodding his boss about last year's fuck-up if he was sober.

Everyone on the farm knows what happened. I'd had no choice but to sit them down and warn them that they'd potentially be out of a job on short notice. A one-off accusation of unsafe storage temperatures might get you a simple inspection, but Mackenzie's father—one of the waterfront mansion-owners who wants us off his front lawn—is buddies with a local official. He piled on enough false allegations to make the situation into a solid clusterfuck, and it was only Anson's connections that saved us from a suspension and investigation that would have destroyed our reputation. We'd moved past it, but the whole thing was nearly disastrous, and everyone had the sense to know it was a sore subject they should stay the hell away from.

"There are different kinds of drunks in this world," I tell Kenny. "Some get funny, some get quiet, some get sad. And some, like you, unfortunately get a little stupid. You're going to want to get that under control." Or he'll end up getting smacked in the face by someone he offends at a bar.

He opens his mouth to protest, but Amanda saves him by butting in. "Someone's mouth getting them into trouble?"

Kenny shakes his head and waves us off. "I'm gonna go kick Steve's ass at pool, then I'm coming back for my beer." He jams his thumb into his chest as he skirts away, and declares, "That's *my* beer, Boss!"

Over his head, I catch an eye roll from Steve, my farm manager. Everyone knows Kenny sucks ass at pool.

Wednesday nights are when the team typically hits Dyl's after work. It isn't some exclusive, planned occasion. Just something locals tend to do around here, to break up the workweek and take advantage of the weekday dinner specials. Some of the construction guys are throwing darts, and I recognize most of the residents scattered around.

"The kid needs a chaperone," Amanda grumbles, taking a sip of her water.

I chuckle. "He just turned twenty-one. He'll learn."

"I'd pay to be there to watch that lesson." Her eyes dart to the corner for a second. "Eliza's here."

"She is." I'm way too aware of it.

"She looks lonely."

"She looks *busy*."

"Maybe she's making herself busy because she doesn't want to look like a sad, lonely puppy in a place where everyone has someone to talk to."

"Or maybe she's a workaholic who doesn't know how to slow down and enjoy a quiet town like this."

Amanda raises her brows. There's something she wants to say, but all she gives is a lackluster, "Maybe."

I steal another glance at Eliza. She has a glass of wine in hand now, the other furiously scrolling across her keyboard.

She's either incredibly busy, or doing a damn good job pretending to be.

I've made no introductions. I've warned my team against being distracted by her. I've officially outcast her. Another week or two, and she might finally leave.

Mission accomplished.

Except seeing the results of my actions—this pathetic picture of her sitting alone while everyone else is chatting together—has me feeling like even *more* of an ass.

Goddammit.

"You're the keeper of Kenny's beer," I tell Amanda. She opens her mouth to protest, but I make my way across the room before a sound gets out.

My presence must shift the air, because Eliza's head tilts up like she senses me coming. When her eyes lock onto me, her entire face falls into a scowl. Except that scowl is framed by a few pieces of hair that fell out of her ponytail, making it less mean and more like a disgruntled kitten.

I have a feeling she'd shank me if I shared that comparison out loud.

"That seat is taken," she says as I pull out the empty chair across from her.

"By me," I finish, plopping down and settling in.

"By my sanity, actually," she fires back. When I don't move, she blinks at me expectantly. "I'm afraid you're squashing it right now."

"Not squashing it. Replacing it."

"With what—your giant propensity for assholery?"

I deserve that. "With an apology."

She crosses her arms, and her lips tip up in a rueful smile. The bottom one is a little fuller than the top, and like the pieces of hair, the feminine detail softens the edge she's trying to have.

Kara arrives with a tray of food. "Oh, perfect!" she exclaims, cheeks red from the dinner rush. "I have both your plates here. Was going to bring yours over after, Gray, but here it is."

Before Eliza can say something, Kara drops a burger beside her laptop, steak tips in front of me, and breezes away like a tornado.

"You're not eating here."

I glance down at the steak. "Appears I am."

"Then get your vision corrected."

"I could move, but that would just dirty another table, and Kara's already slammed tonight."

That approach seems to work, because while Eliza's jaw works over more words, nothing comes out. Instead, she closes her laptop, picks up her burger, and takes an enormous bite. She doesn't even finish chewing before she takes another one, like she can't wait to finish eating so she can leave.

I don't mind, because I only need about thirty seconds. Cutting a piece of steak, I get right to it.

"What I did today was out of line." Her jaw stops mid-chew, but I'm focused on her eyes, more brown than hazel in the tavern's warm light. "I'm sorry for raising my voice at you like that. It was unacceptable. That isn't something I normally do."

I wasn't planning on tacking on that last part, but I don't want her to think I'm one of those men who gets off on power trips and bullying. And while I'm far past the point of trying to impress other people—especially this woman I want gone—my gut twists at the possibility of being viewed as antagonistic scum.

Though from my recent behavior, I fit the fucking image.

Her face gives nothing away as she finishes chewing and takes another bite, bacon and ranch oozing out from the bun. I dig into my own meal as I wait, marinating in the awkward silence.

I have a feeling it's intentional. A tactic to make me suffer a little. We both know I want her to accept the apology so we can be done, but she isn't the type to let me off easy.

It's both frustrating and respectable.

Another man would prompt her. Prattle on about how sorry he is. Desperately find a way to repair his ego.

I wait.

It's at least two minutes before she breaks for some fries and finally responds. When she does, it's not at all what I'm expecting.

"You don't trust me."

I didn't come here to rag on her more, but I'm not a bull-shitter. "I don't."

"I'm very good at what I do," she says between fries.

"I know. I saw your resume."

She considers this, like her mind is flipping through possibilities. She comes up empty. "You don't know me, and I don't know you. But I trust that you're good at oyster farming, because of your track record."

So why don't you trust me with my job?

The unspoken question hangs in the air.

"You don't have experience in this industry."

"I didn't have any experience in tech before I started, and that wasn't an issue." The statement isn't cocky; it's confident. Spoken by a woman who's proud of her successes and owns it. From what I read, she absolutely should be.

I could give her another small part of the truth, but something tells me she'd find some way to challenge it. Poke holes in my careful construction. So I lay it all out—sans the part about her semblance to Mackenzie.

The more I learn about Eliza, the less of a likeness she has.

"We had an incident last year. Someone who I trusted came in and almost screwed us over. You're not from here. You might not respect the business, and you're out of here in less than three months. This is my baby. It's just a few bucks and a short summer to you." I shrug. "Besides, we've been steadily growing without social media. You've seen our awards and write-ups. Your position here is entirely unnecessary. If anything, it has the potential to do more harm than good."

Part of me expects her to jump up in outrage. Maybe throw a fry at my face. But instead, she takes another calm bite of her burger as she mulls over my words.

"Not just a few bucks and a short summer," she corrects once she swallows. "It's a reference and possible introductions from a leader in a local industry, if I do my job well—which I fully intend to."

"Not buying it. Based on that resume, you don't need references or introductions from little Garnet Shores."

"I don't want to be a one-dimensional hire."

"And I don't want you to lie to me when we're having an honest conversation," I say, calling her bluff outright. A high-achieving woman like her wouldn't go from the city to rural Garnet Shores amidst a successful career, just for more fucking *dimensions*.

The burger hits the plate.

"You and I are not buddies," she says, waving her finger between us. "We don't have heart-to-hearts over dinner. You'll dislike my presence no matter what I tell you."

"You want an official tour of the farm?"

She scoffs. "Are you seriously bartering with me right now?"

It's worked for civilizations for years. "How about oysters? They're award-winning, I hear."

"I don't want your oysters."

"How can you work that social media magic if you can't even describe how our oysters taste?"

She tilts her head. "Oh, so now you care about my work?"

Something tells me she can play this game all night. So I give her a flat smile and declare, "Tour tomorrow. Going once. Going twice."

Her sarcastic mask drops, and I swear I see her cheek muscles spasming on a *yes*.

"This is a once-in-a-lifetime offer. And it's about to be sold in two seconds to no one."

Stubbornness keeps her mouth shut.

So be it. "And it's so—"

"I needed to get out of the city," she rushes out. Quietly, like it's a confession.

"You rob a convenience store? Running from the mob?"

I watch as she visibly sets her shoulders back. "My position was cut from my previous job, and I needed a break from the people I know there. This fit the bill, and I liked the challenge of learning a new industry. It's a reset."

A break from the people I know there is vague as hell, and I want to press. But her shoulders are tensed up, and pressing would go beyond the professional boundaries of this conversation.

Her personal life is no business of mine. I've gotten the information I need. Yet I still find myself shoving down a niggle of curiosity.

"There are plenty of towns around. There weren't other

jobs with better potential? Something actually worthy of your resume?"

She shakes her head slowly. Resigned, almost. "Everything happened a little unexpectedly, so I couldn't pre-plan anything. My options were limited. And now I'm locked into my summer rental here."

In other words, she isn't going anywhere until August, even if she wants to.

I nod at her closed laptop. "Working over dinner at a restaurant doesn't seem very reset-like to me."

Her eyes flick from the silver device to the people around us, and I'm reminded of Amanda's words about her being lonely.

Her tight smile makes those words louder in my head. "I have wine. It's relaxing to work at a slow pace."

That's the biggest pile of duck shit I've witnessed in a long time.

I'm acting before I can overthink it. I scoop her plate out from under her and grab mine, too.

"Hey, what are you—"

"Come on, Boston. Eat while you play."

7

ELIZA

"*BOSTON?* Did you just try to give me a nickname?"

I don't care if neighboring tables can hear me. Grayson Gold just took my burger hostage and gave me a nickname like we're good ol' pals.

"Don't forget your drink," he says over his shoulder as he gives me his broad back and saunters away.

With my *burger*.

I stare at him, trying to decipher what is actually happening. First, the apology. Then the getting-to-know-you questions. Now a label and an invitation to join his little crew for a round of pool.

Maybe this is his way of trying to make things right, or maybe he's finally accepting that no amount of terrible behavior is going to push me out of this job, because I'm planted on that boat until my contract is complete.

Or maybe he feels bad that I've been sitting over here alone like a loser when everyone else in this place is grouped in conversations or laughing together.

All these possibilities suggest Grayson isn't the completely heartless ass he's made himself out to be. But

I'm not allowing one small moment of grace to change my impression.

I down the rest of my wine before shoving my laptop in my bag and following my food. He sets it on a high-top and slides right back into conversation, and I can't help the self-consciousness that floods me as I make my way across the room.

It doesn't matter that I'm an adult. There are few things more intimidating than inserting yourself into a group you've been outcast from. And I'm not sure Grayson's kindness will extend as far as an introduction to his locals clique.

Get the burger and leave.

But Amanda's familiar face appears in the crowd, and Grayson turns to track me with those golden eyes and a smile I know isn't attributed to me. It's the energy of this space and his friends. The kid I recognized from the farm and a few other guys turn with him.

"Social Media girl!" the kid exclaims with a goofy grin. He's cute, with shaggy blonde hair and a face holding on to its boyishness. His flushed cheeks tell me the water in his hands has recently replaced something stronger. "Hey, Boss, this mean we can talk—"

"Kenny, shut the fuck up." Amanda skirts a few people to join them, telling Grayson, "And, yes, I kept him away from his beer, so don't blame me."

"This is Eliza," Grayson cuts in before Kenny can fire back. "Steve, Amanda, Kenny from the farm," he introduces, nodding at each of them. "And this is Darian and Bob."

The two new men tip their heads in a greeting. One of them, Bob, wears a ring, but Darian's finger is free, and his face is...*not* a sore sight.

His blue eyes are bright and curious as he asks, "You

vacationing here for the summer?" He reminds me of Grayson in his build, though he's a little shorter, his hair closely cropped like his beard.

"No. I'm working on the farm for the summer. Social media marketing."

Recognition sparks across his face. "Oh, is that, like, the little dances people do? People go viral from that stuff, right?"

I laugh. The assumption usually annoys me, because it's typically spoken by men trying to belittle me. But Darian's questions seem genuine.

"This isn't that type of social media. It's more strategic marketing via short-form content."

He looks perplexed. "So no dances?"

"For certain businesses, a trending dance or two might work, based on brands and audiences. But I've never used them."

Beer in hand, he nudges Grayson's chest. "Man, oyster dances. Think about it."

"No oyster dances," Grayson and I say at the same exact time.

Our eyes meet, and my lips tip up. "Though Grayson could probably go viral if he was willing to get down." Dark, salty hair curls around his baseball cap, while the bill shadows his face and the scruff running along his jaw.

There are women who'd go wild to see that shadowed face attached to some shaking hips on their phone screen.

His lips flatten. "Absolutely not."

"Are you self-conscious about your dancing?"

"I just have self-respect."

"Your dancing must be *really* bad." I bet he's starting to regret taking my burger captive, and I revel in it. "It's all in the loose hips, you know."

He inclines his head, something sparking in his eyes. "My hips are plenty loose. That's not the problem."

His double meaning isn't lost on me. "Then it must be a grumpiness thing. Too busy scowling to let loose and have fun."

"Grumpy?" Darian cuts in. His face scrunches in disbelief. "Nah, that's more Anson. Gray's the happy one."

So people keep saying.

"And he's the one who's about to very *happily* kick your ass at pool," Grayson says, the game behind him ending. "We're up."

My cheerful teasing disappears. I didn't think his invitation to play was serious. I expected a stand-here-and-watch, jump-in-if-you-want sort of thing. But Grayson has already claimed a cue and is extending the other toward me.

Shit.

"I need to finish my meal." It isn't a total fib. Two bites of burger and a few fries are growing cold on my plate.

Grayson shakes his head, one side of his mouth slowly hitching. "Scared I'll win?"

I snort. "I'm scared you'll throw another tantrum when you lose."

That one is a *complete* fib. I've never played pool a day in my life.

"I don't think we need to worry about that, Boston."

"That is not my name," I grind out.

"And you're not stalling as subtly as you think you are." The half-grin hitches higher, flashing a row of white, straight teeth I'm close to knocking from his mouth.

"Not stalling," I lie again. "Just giving you the chance to change your mind." Before I can overthink the ramifications, I snatch the cue out of his hands.

He nods at the neat triangle of balls arranged at one end of the table. "Ladies get to break."

I stare at the rack, feeling the weight of eyes on me. Not everyone in this corner of the tavern is watching our game, but a handful of people are paying attention, including Darian and Bob.

Which means my utter failure is about to be a show.

Bluffing my way through challenges is nothing new. My career path has practically ingrained it in me. When competition is high and impressing your superiors is tantamount to success, you never say "no" to unfamiliar tasks—you say "sure thing," then stay awake until two in the morning figuring out how to get it done.

The problem here is I have *no* time to figure it out.

But it's just hitting some balls with a stick and trying to get them in a hole. Can't be that hard, right? I've watched people play pool before—in shows and in movies. I've got this. I just need...a quick refresher.

"Now you're chivalrous?" I point out, squinting in confusion. "Not buying it. You break the rack."

One of the bystanders whistles, but Grayson just shrugs. "You can still back out, Boston." The words come out a little tight, his torso stretching as he leans over the table and sets his free hand on the edge. The narrow end of the cue is tucked under his pointer finger and braced on his thumb, like some sort of kickstand.

I watch as he pulses the tip toward the lone white ball in front of it, and my eyes trace his thick forearm up to the shirt sleeve wrapped tightly around a bulging shoulder. The entire display is a tapestry of veins, lean muscle, and tanned skin dusted with dark hair.

By the time I remember to watch his form, it's too late. The cue hits the ball with a clap, and all I've effectively done is map the impressive sinews and dips of Grayson Gold's arm. My focus rushes back to the pool table, where balls clatter against one another and bounce off the edges.

"Now, ladies first. House rules."

You can do this.

I circle the table like I have some mysterious strategy, but I already know my target. It's the solid red ball close to the white one, somewhat aligned with a hole in the corner.

Hit the white ball, so it hits the red ball and goes into the hole. Easy.

I picture Grayson's hand as I lean over the table like he did. The position feels awkward, like something is bent where it shouldn't be, another limb angled the wrong way, and I'm struck with the reality that this isn't easy at all. I'm doing this horribly wrong, and everyone can see it.

But I'm already here. I can't disappear into the wood floor beneath my sneakers. I need to follow through.

I set the end of the cue between my fingers, but it slips. I try again. Again, it slips to the side uselessly.

"Don't know how to play?" Grayson asks. It isn't mean, but it's teasing, and it sends a hot blush crawling up my cheeks.

"Just been awhile," I say lamely.

"Sure."

"Not all of us practice handling our balls as often as you, Grayson."

There's a burst of laughter. It's Darian, whose brows are raised so high they might launch into the ceiling. Bob and Amanda cough beside him.

I expect to find Grayson scowling, but he's simply watching me like I'm an object of fascination.

Then his lips twitch. "Not about handling balls, Boston.

More about small holes and working them with good technique."

"Amen, brother." Darian raises his beer, filling the silence, *thank god,* because I'm stunned.

His employees are within *earshot.*

He's just trying to fluster you.

Recovering, I offer an unbothered smile. "Well, that's not my forte."

"Here," Darian cuts in, handing his beer off to Bob. "Let me give you a quick refresher." He extends a hand for the cue, and I hand it over.

He quickly shows me how to set up for my shot, then returns the cue and coaches me into position. "Not quite. Move this back." He nudges my back foot with his toe. "Yeah, like that. And then your hands—here." He applies gentle pressure to my bracing hand and helps me form my kickstand correctly. It'd be a sleazy come-on if not for the fact that his fingers stay politely at my hand. "Yeah, there."

When I try again, the cue rests comfortably on my fingers.

"Appreciate it," I say as he backs away. Before my attention returns to the white ball, it snags on Grayson.

The levity on his face has vanished.

Probably because Darian just set me up with a chance to actually win.

———

I DIDN'T WIN. But I didn't embarrass myself, either.

At some point, a beer made its way back into Kenny's hands, and he ended up racing to the bathroom to throw up when we were only a few turns into our game. Grayson bailed to check on him, and left to drive him home soon after.

In some way, I owe Kenny a *thank you*, because in just three turns, Grayson demonstrated just how capable he was at whooping my ass into next Sunday. Had he finished, it would have been much more difficult to show my face at work today.

I'm not so naïve as to think last night's social invitation has changed the dynamic on the farm. Grayson might have realized he needs to deal with my presence, but he still doesn't like that I'm here, or trust me to treat his brand with respect and care. So I'm surprised when Amanda intersects me before I enter the office, wearing a Gold's sweatshirt in the chilly morning air.

"You're coming with me today," she calls out as she approaches.

I stop mid-step. "What?"

She grins. "I'm showing you what's what here on land, and then you're joining a farm tour I'm leading. Gray's orders."

So Grayson *is* carrying through on yesterday's barter. I wasn't sure he would.

"Part two of Gray's orders is that you don't wave your phone in our guests' faces," she tacks on. "They might not want to be on video."

"Part two of Gray's orders clearly doesn't think I have a brain."

Her wry exhale hints at agreement. "You know what? I can't tell him that, but you can."

A high-pitched giggle cuts across the parking lot, and we twist to see a Grayson Gold-shaped figure walking to the back of the building from a dock, a small human skipping beside him.

Oh my go—

"You could do it right now. Lala will probably back you up." Amanda turns back to face me, like seeing Grayson with a child is an ordinary occurrence. "She's a girl's girl."

Grayson Gold is a...a *father?*

Oh my gosh, is he a *husband?*

I think back to his fingers last night on the pool table. There was no ring. But he also does physical labor all day, most of it in the water. He might leave a ring at home so he doesn't lose it.

It's like the parking lot has dropped from beneath my feet as I watch the young girl, no older than seven or eight, bounce alongside him, giggling like a maniac. He smiles back at her with adoration, then lunges and scoops her into his arms. There's an eruption of squeals, and then she's upside-down, dangling by her legs as Grayson swings her back and forth. All the while, Dave the duck waddles behind them like he's the second child in the family.

Biology is the only reason my ovaries tickle. A natural response to seeing a grown man being heart-wrenchingly adorable with a little kid.

But I don't have an explanation for why I feel so entirely bewildered that Grayson has a child and wife. His personal life doesn't concern me. I just...never considered it.

I force my attention away to see Amanda awaiting a response, one brow cocked high. *What was she saying?*

Talking to Grayson. Phone in guests' faces. Right.

"Maybe, um, not right now," I stutter out.

She nods slowly. Awkwardly. Then she informs me, "That's his sister."

I blink.

Sister?

The math struggles to compute, because according to

Gold's most recent write-up, Grayson is thirty. Besides, his parents passed away. When was that—five years ago? Ten?

This must all be written across my face, because Amanda continues. "She's like one of those miracle children. His mom had her right before she passed. Anson's her legal guardian, but Gray helps out a ton."

The parking lot solidifies beneath me, but I'm still struggling to find words, because Grayson's put her—*Lala*—back on her feet, and he's half-heartedly running away as she tries to launch herself on his back.

"Um, you ready?"

I clear my throat, because wow, maybe I actually *don't* have a brain. It's a man and a child. Not a kangaroo in the middle of rural Rhode Island.

"Yeah," I chirp, a little too brightly. "Let's go."

Amanda's lips twitch as she leads the way to the dock. Gravel crunches underfoot as Lala's giggles fade and the two disappear into the warehouse. A warm, salty breeze washes through the lot, and I welcome it, hoping it'll wash the image of Grayson out of my memory.

"He's single, by the way."

My head jerks to Amanda. She says it so casually, like she's discussing the weather. Like Grayson's relationship status is as trivial as today's humidity levels.

Because it is.

But if that's true, why did a little jolt of energy zip through my chest?

8

GRAYSON

IT'S BEEN two whole weeks since I found Boston trying to punt Dave from my office, and she's already published nine social media posts.

This isn't information I necessarily want, nor is it my responsibility. I'd explicitly told Anson I wasn't going to manage her. But despite all my talk, I care too much about this farm to ignore the content she's putting our name on. And while I think social media is the most useless invention of this era, and thus don't have any, Kenny was all too happy to inform me about the posts yesterday as he worked the Sunday tours with me.

I expected to hate every single one.

There were already a few old posts on the page, back when the company was smaller and Anson made some basic content to have something available if people searched us through socials.

Eliza's additions knocked them out of the park.

First up was a shot of the Gold's Oysters shell sign above the office door, then two short videos of the premises, a photo of the pick-up bag, and a montage of clips from the area, with infographics sprinkled in between. The quality was exceptional, the captions were simple and to the point, and all the information was correct. There were a few shell emojis among the nine posts, but nothing egregious. And people liked them enough to comment on them.

I *wanted* to hate them, just to justify my assumptions.

But, much to my displeasure, I didn't.

This doesn't mean they're bringing any real value to us. Anson could still be wasting the business's money. But at least she hasn't made a mockery of us yet. A good thing, considering she isn't going anywhere for the next two-and-change months.

My phone buzzes, and I curse at the alarm.

Fucking tours.

They bring in a solid boost of income and help us educate visitors about sustainable practices and encourage them to support local producers. But man, they can be a nuisance. Especially on days like today when Amanda's out and Steve's sick, so I'm the only one here qualified to give a solo tour.

I could grab two other team members to do it, but if I go, it's only one body pulled from work during our busiest season instead of two.

Shoving the tracking paperwork I've been working on in a folder, I head out of the warehouse. The tour doesn't start for fifteen minutes, but the excited ones tend to arrive early, and customer experience is everything on these visits. People don't necessarily come to see the farm through our eyes, but for the exclusive, on-the-water, sea-to-table Gold's experience—high price-tag included.

My annoyance cools when I catch Boston's figure by the touring boat. She's in a Gold's sweatshirt—a new one, because that green is too vibrant to have met much sun and salt—and her dark jeans stretch around toned thighs as she crouches for an angled shot of the skiff.

The same way they stretched when she set up each pool shot last Wednesday. Something I only noticed because Darian's eyes couldn't help but fucking wander all over her.

Only natural my gaze should track his.

The floating dock shifts when I step on it, and Boston flies to her feet. A long, glossy braid whips around, little wisps of free hair scattered across her features. For a second, her face is open and curious before settling with wariness.

"Enjoy your tour last week?" I say as I stroll up to her.

There's a light tan across her freckled nose, and I wonder if she pulled herself away from her laptop to spend the weekend outdoors. Hell, I hope she did. The mornings are still cool, but a sunny afternoon is finally warm enough to strip down to a tee-shirt and soak in some sun. Winter down here can be miserable, but summer beach days are one area where Garnet Shores truly shines.

"I did. Amanda's great."

"Sure is."

From anyone else, I'd expect a thank you. But we both know that tour was long overdue, not to mention I'd used it as leverage to wrangle some truths out of her. Our night at Dyl's had revealed a few things, one being that she's beyond attempting civility with me. If anything, that smart mouth of hers suggested deliberate *incivility* is her current game.

Something I don't mind.

I can't stand fakeness and pretenses. Never could, and last year with Mackenzie only decreased my tolerance.

I hop on the boat, grab a rag from the center console, and start wiping moisture from the seats. After my third seat, Eliza still hasn't moved.

"Need something?" I ask.

"No. Just waiting for you to be done."

I glance up at her. "I'm not drying these for fun. I'm about to use this boat for a tour."

Her hand hits her heart. "Thank you *so* much for clarifying that. I thought you just really enjoyed mopping up dew. Silly me."

There's that smart mouth again. "Maybe I do. It's the least stressful thing I do all day."

"If wiping off seats is your idea of unwinding, you need to reevaluate."

"Yeah?" I return to my task, which feels less tedious than usual. "And how *should* I unwind, Boston?"

"Meditation. Yoga. Bubble baths." She pauses, as if she's genuinely contemplating this. "Mm-hmm. Those are perfect for you, I think."

"My way of unwinding involves a little more activity."

"Let me guess. Kicking puppies? Dismembering flowers? Oh—" She snaps her fingers and points at me. "I've got it. Parking at the entrance to the town like a little bridge troll and harassing vacationers who dare cross your path."

I shake my head, chuckling as I make my way to the seats at the bow, right beneath her. This woman and her wit.

"Close." I pause and look up, catching the hint of a smirk creasing her cheek. I wink. "More the kind that makes me so good at pool."

She rolls her eyes. "I so deeply pity the women in this town."

"That's a waste of pity."

It's mostly all talk. My early twenties were a montage of pretty faces, late nights, and questionable decisions. But after both of my parents passed, casual one-nighters lost their appeal, and I turned into a long-term kind of guy.

Case in point: falling head over ass last year after two decent dates.

But Eliza doesn't know that. And I'd be lying if I said I wasn't curious what creative insult she'd sling back at me.

She doesn't disappoint.

"I'll save my pity for you, then, because it must be exhausting carrying around so much ego." Eliza crosses her arms impatiently. "Why are you still standing there? Seats are dry."

"Well, now I've got to wait for my guests. What's *your* excuse for being here?"

"I was in the middle of shooting content when you came down." She wiggles the phone in her hand. The case is clear and utilitarian. "I just need two more seconds to finish up. No one's here for the tour yet, so I was hoping you could step out for a second so I can get what I need."

The skiff is clean and cushioned for guests, but it isn't anything special. "Why are you filming this thing?"

"To promote tours. No one else was taking photos or videos on Amanda's tour, so I kept my phone away, too." She gives a tight smile. "Lost my only chance to film the actual experience itself, so I'm making do."

Multiple car doors slam in succession, tourists in bright, preppy colors blurring in the distance. Eliza mutters a curse, her shoulders deflating. "Nevermind." Her tone is resigned as she starts turning away.

Shit.

"Join this tour," I blurt.

She freezes mid-twist, blinking like she's trying to decide if I really just threw her a bone.

The surprise is warranted. Hell, even *I'm* surprised. But if there's nothing I can do about Eliza working on this farm for the summer, I might as well make it easier for her to present us in a respectable light. Boat's going out regardless.

And I'll admit that watching her shoulders shrink just now, after seeing her so confident, pinches the part of my gut that finds her sharpness entertaining.

"If they're into taking pictures or videos, you can wave your phone around, too. Get some content," I add lamely, because she still hasn't responded. Maybe she's waiting for a punchline, or another barter for information.

When nothing comes, she lets out a soft, "Okay."

Then she bites her lip in a piss-poor attempt to stem a smile. Like allowing herself to smile at something I've offered is a grievous crime.

I'm tempted to tease her for it, but I know the almost-smile would vanish in an instant.

And, *fuck me*, I don't want it to go away.

Before I can dig into the meaning of that, I'm back on the dock and heading to greet our guests. Eliza still hasn't boarded the skiff when I return with the three older couples who arrived together.

She greets them with a shy smile that is clearly well-manufactured, because this woman's anything but timid. "Hi! Hope you don't mind me crashing your tour. I'm here visiting on my own, so I got joined together with you all."

Relief sinks in that she's pretending to be a guest. The last thing I want is to field concerns about blasting their faces across the internet, or complaints about their paid experience being used for work.

That relief, however, is short-lived, because one of the men replies, "I thought six would be a full boat."

I know their type. Just retired, mid-range wealthy, like spending their money on name brands and vintage wines. Vacationers from one of the ritzy neighboring towns, if I had to guess. Doesn't automatically make a person an asshole, but on occasion, these types of guests are snobs.

Lucky me, this is one of those occasions.

"Eight is capacity," I tell him, bringing his condescension away from Eliza and to me. "Unless you select the private tour when you book."

"I thought you *did* select the private tour," the woman beside him fusses. His wife, most likely, from their matching paisley windbreakers.

"It was an extra charge. I figured six of us would automatically be a private tour," he grumbles, deep grooves cutting down from his mouth.

What a miserable fucking life you've got to lead to have frown lines like that.

"Not the case here," I say plainly. "Anyone need to use the restroo—"

"Can we reschedule?" the wife asks.

"We have a twenty-four-hour cancellation policy."

"But this isn't what we were expecting."

Eliza nudges my arm. "Maybe I can just join the next tour," she cuts in hesitantly.

My brows furrow. There's no way she's balking at these people.

But if intimidation isn't behind her offer, that means she's trying to help me. Trying to save me from this misery by putting herself out.

"Next one's full," I lie, dragging my gaze away from her and back to the guests. "Are we continuing with your tour?" I ask point-blank.

"Cindy, Tom, it's okay," one of the other women says. "It's just one extra person."

From the frowns on Cindy and Tom's faces, you'd think

they're being forced into a surprise root canal. But they begrudgingly nod and shuffle toward the boat.

I step into the skiff and help them in with a hand.

"I'm all set," Tom waves me off.

"Farm rules," I tell him. "Safety is our priority."

He obliges, and everyone is settled on a seat when Eliza steps up to the side. She eyes my hand like it's a cockroach.

I smile. "Rules apply to all guests."

"Of course." I swear I hear an eye-roll in her voice.

She slips her hand into mine, and I'm struck by how delicate it is. Then I'm wondering why I'm even struck by that.

Maybe because her verbal sparring makes her seem so much tougher than she is.

But that sharp tongue is nowhere to be found as she mutters a "thank you," nor as we stop at the upweller to peek at the millions of juvenile oysters that'll slowly make their way out to the farm as they get big enough. In fact, as we head further into the salt pond, she dives full-tilt into her role, asking, "What's your favorite part of the job?"

I've just finished answering Cindy about what a day of work is like here when Eliza poses the question. I wonder if it's for some social media caption, but she's leaning in, face tilted up inquisitively, like she genuinely wants to know.

"Can't choose one favorite," I tell her. "I love oysters. I enjoy the sustainability aspect, too. Oysters filter the water they live in, and they grow here naturally. No fertilizer or chemicals needed. And there's no better workplace than this."

I glance away from the farm ahead to look at her. The breeze has loosened more hairs from her braid, and they're whizzing around her head as she nods thoughtfully.

"Definitely a beautiful workplace," Cindy remarks.

"Makes up for the dress code, I suppose." The comment, tainted with derision, comes from Tom.

I keep my expression unbothered as his buddies chortle. Years ago, I would have chirped back. But experience has taught me that no matter how successful your business is, if it involves manual labor or servicing others, there are folks who'll put you beneath their boot.

If only they knew how ass-backwards that was. He wouldn't survive a morning doing my team's work. But I'm man enough to not get defensive over something so trivial. Plus, putting him in his place would only get us a bad review and make him more self-righteous.

It's better to find entertainment in that kind of ignorance.

But Eliza doesn't. Leaning forward to get a clear view of him, she says, with utter innocence, "Better that than the ugly, bright golf polos everyone wears at my office. Those were invented for the green, and they should stay there. Am I right?"

Above the neon salmon collar peeking out of his windbreaker, Tom's smug grin fades.

She catches my eyes as she leans back in her seat, and I can't stop my lips from tilting. The corner of her mouth twitches, and for a moment, it's like we're on the same team.

And I realize I don't hate that. At all.

9

ELIZA

"NOT A FAN OF GOLF POLOS, HUH?"

It's the first thing Grayson says as we stand in the skiff, watching the tour from hell pile into their expensive cars. I'm shocked they stooped so low as to sit in a small, helicopter-less boat.

"I don't care what people choose to wear," I tell him. "Just not a fan of the attitudes."

I've come across plenty like them. Growing up, my parents' social circle didn't exactly consist of the kindest souls. Just successful and wealthy ones—the sort that bridge you to better opportunities and promotions.

It's a minor miracle my parents never adopted that disposition. Maybe it's because they come from the types of families many of their "friends" would look down on, or maybe, despite their high expectations and detachment toward me, there's some gentleness hiding in their hearts.

If so, it's in some mysterious, elusive place I can no longer find.

Grayson nods toward the idling vehicles. "That kind of attitude doesn't come from a happy life. I'd bet our friends there are miserable. You've got to be, if someone's forcing you to wear a paisley-print windbreaker."

"Doesn't mean they need to share that misery with you."

Grayson quirks his head at me. "You worried about my feelings?"

"I'm worried they'll make you more insufferable than you already are."

He chuckles, the sound rumbly and resonant. "Careful. Keep saying stuff like that, and you'll make me blush."

Yeah, right. Oysters will grow fins before the man's self-assurance crumbles enough for him to blush.

The guests' cars bumble out of the lot, and Grayson wordlessly begins loosening the lines from the dock.

"What are you doing?"

He shoves the boat away from the cleats and takes his post behind the wheel, starting up the engine. "Got to go check on something," he says over his shoulder.

I blink. "You know I'm still here, right?"

"Boston, you talk too much for anyone to forget your presence."

I hope he can feel my glare through the back of his head. "Where are you taking me?"

"Over to the new intertidal system," he answers, as if that terminology is common knowledge.

"How long will we be there for?"

"Not long."

Boat time might be a precious commodity to me, but his deliberately obtuse approach is quickly getting old. "You realize this is basically kidnapping."

He glances over his shoulder, his expression dry as a desert. "No way in hell I'd kidnap you. I'm not a masochist."

He turns back, pressing the throttle forward. Shouting over the engine, he asks, "Can't you just go with things?"

No.

Especially with someone who probably wants to strand me on a remote island.

My silence must give away my answer, because Grayson offers a real explanation. "We'll be back at the dock in thirty minutes. It's a new farming system I'm testing out, and I made a repair two days ago that I need to check in on. Think of it as a tour extension."

The warm breeze coasts across my face as I silently digest that, despite his nonchalant wording, Grayson is helping me for the second time in a single afternoon. Completely unprovoked. He isn't exactly going out of his way, but he's not leaving me out, either.

He's being...thoughtful.

Though he seems determined not to make a big deal out of it. So I shouldn't, either. After all, it's just an *inkling* of decency.

He slows the skiff to a crawl as we approach a shallow sand bank tucked close to shore. Sitting on it are three long rows made of short posts, with oyster baskets suspended between them. The bottoms of the baskets are barely submerged.

Grayson cuts the engine, and the machine whirs as he lifts the propeller from the water. Momentum carries the skiff forward, until the water's so shallow I can make out the white shells scattered on the dark, muddy bottom. The hull gently scrapes the sand, and Grayson hops out, drawing us to a stop. The water only reaches halfway up his rubber boots as he walks to the hull, pulls out an anchor, and tosses it several yards away.

"The boat doesn't get stuck here?" I ask as he situates the anchor's line around a cleat.

"Tide's coming up," he explains. "And I can shove us off easily enough." With that, he makes his way over to a post halfway down one of the lines.

He seems completely intent on leaving me in the skiff, like a child in a shopping cart at a grocery store, allowed to look at all the yummy snacks but not touch.

Okay, buddy.

I take off my sandals, roll my jeans to my knees, secure my phone in my back pocket, and gingerly scoot over the boat's side.

Grayson must hear the tiny splash of my landing, because he pivots. The disgruntled groove between his brows is so deep I can see it from here.

"Get back on the skiff."

In lieu of a response, I wade toward him. Soft mud oozes between my toes, cool water lapping around my calves, little shell fragments pressing into my feet, just shy of painful.

"There are crabs hiding in the mud," he threatens.

The statement almost makes me pause. *Almost.* But I wouldn't put it past Grayson to scare me with a white lie, just to get his way. *His way* being me out of his hair, stranded on a little boat while he does his rough-tough manly work.

When I continue my advance, he puts his hands on his hips. "You're gonna cut your feet on a shell, and I'll have to carry your ass back to the boat."

"As if I'd let you."

"It's either that, or listen to your dramatics."

"You're the one being dramatic."

He glances away, a tendon thrumming in his jaw. He

rubs his forehead, like I'm the active cause of a migraine, then mutters, "Suit yourself."

Grinning triumphantly, I trudge onward, stopping a few feet from where he fiddles with a post to observe the network of suspended baskets, thousands of oysters contained within.

The system doesn't look like a hack-job, but it's rugged. Utilitarian, like everything else on the farm. "Did you build this yourself?"

His attention on a post beside him, Grayson answers, "With my team." He grunts as he jerks something into place. "My buddy Jay who owns a farm up in the bay helped out."

"They don't make ready-made systems?"

"Some parts are proprietary, but we modify and custom-build a lot. Needs to suit our conditions and production goals."

I'm reluctant to give Grayson any veneration, but it's admittedly impressive—the breadth of knowledge and skill he has. Every day makes it clearer that Grayson does more than pluck oysters from the water and zip around the pond like a grungy James Bond. He's part-mechanic, part-engineer, part-maintenance-man, and a billion other occupations. Anson may be the business lead of the operation, but Grayson's a respectable force of his own.

Though I'll shake hands with a crab before I ever share that compliment.

"Your floating system's obviously doing well." I step over a basket and move closer to see what he's doing. "Why try this one out? Expansion?"

"Not looking to expand." He straightens, examining the attachment point he was tinkering with. "Just seeing if we can improve our product. Offer a little variety."

"You don't want to expand? Go big?"

"Absolutely not."

This surprises me. Anson brought me on board to help grow the Gold's name, value, and awareness. But I figured he and Grayson also want to increase production. Distribute nationally.

"Why?" I ask, genuinely curious.

"Quality over quantity," he says simply.

I think he might stop there. Make me beg for more information, just to be difficult.

But he keeps going, his tone earnest. "And even if we could maintain quality with higher production, getting bigger, relying on automations, expanding the team—it takes the personal touch out of it. Feels wrong. Unnatural." He shakes his head. "I'd end up stuck in an office all day, drowning in paperwork, separated from the actual work out here. And I didn't get into this business to sit in front of a computer under fluorescent lights while machines and people I don't know put our oysters into the world."

I consider him, this man who continues to draw outside the neat little box I first drew him into. He's like an onion you'd leave at the grocery store. Stinky and rotting at first glance, but each layer proving more redeemable and edible the further you peel it.

Wait, am I calling Grayson edible?

No, you're calling him an onion.

A rotting onion.

"There are many bosses who enjoy that separation," I say, shaking myself loose from that doomed train of thought. "Not doing the actual work, but reaping all the benefits."

"I'll sell this farm before I do that."

I snort. "I wish you could have a conversation with my old manager."

"He the reason you lost your job?" His eyes regard me with honest curiosity.

Swallowing my self-loathing, I smile bitterly. "No. *I'm* the reason I lost my job."

Regret hits me the second that honesty slithers out. It's a harsh, shameful truth I haven't shared with *anyone*. Kitty's phone calls are too short to get into that kind of therapy, my parents are too judgmental, and my Boston friends are, well...yeah. But here I am, blabbering it to a man who hates me, in a moment of temporary insanity.

I expect him to smile in glee. Store away this stupid, vulnerable nugget to wield against me later like a flaming sword.

So I'm taken aback when he drawls a slow, "Yeah, no. Not buying that."

I shouldn't argue with him, but his knowing smirk grates on me.

"My manager sat back, let me and my team do all the work, and took credit for our final outcomes. I thought this was normal. That this was the standard dynamic at this company, and his bosses saw through his posturing and understood who really was driving our success. So I did nothing, and I let him screw me when the company made budget cuts." I was so oblivious that I thought I was getting a *promotion* when HR called me in.

"Was that supposed to convince me I'm wrong?" His tone suggests there's some serious malfunction in my brain. "Because all you did was tell me you lost your job because your boss is an asshole."

My brows slam together. "Well, duh, he's an asshole. But I enabled him—"

"No."

I stare at him. *No?*

"No, what?"

"No, you're wrong. And no, I'm not gonna let you argue it with me."

"I—"

He cuts me right off. "Boston, this conversation is just as ridiculous as the whole self-blame game you're playing."

"It isn't a game. It's reality. And playing victim won't do me any favors moving forward, when I inevitably encounter more of his type."

"So acknowledge the lessons you learned and bring them forward. But don't absolve that piece of shit for what he did. And don't let it beat you up. That kind of absurd thinking is shocking for someone with your GPA." With that, he bends over to unlock the opening to the oyster basket between us.

I sputter on a come-back that won't form. Grayson is being infuriatingly black-and-white. But he's not the platitudes type, which means he's also being honest, and that honesty feels a lot like the comfort I've been needing. Reassurance that I didn't epically fail.

A *thank you* wants to tumble out, but I'm unsure if it should.

I never have to decide, either, because that is the exact moment a seagull swoops above and takes a giant shit on Grayson's head.

His body freezes, hunched over the basket. My jaw pops open as the white blob dribbles from the crown of his baseball cap.

There's...so *much* of it. I don't think an ounce of the bird's droppings *missed*.

Grayson's giant, belabored sigh tells me he's aware of what just happened.

And just in case he isn't, the laughter that bursts from my chest makes it very, very clear.

I can't help it. Completely uncontrollable giggles shake my body. The irony is Shakespearean. All the *shitting* he's done on me, and now...

My fit only worsens when Grayson stiffly removes the hat from his head and observes the generous glob with utter disappointment.

"You think this is funny?" he asks slowly.

Trying to stifle my next string of laughter—and failing miserably—I shake my head.

He levels me with an annoyed look, sighs, and shakes the hat around in the water. It does nothing but make the fabric wet and encourage the droppings to spread further.

Another sigh. "Hilarious," he mutters, sloshing it around again. The bill flicks when he forcibly pulls it out, sending a little splash of water toward me.

I jolt back a second too late. Grayson glances up at my jeans, splattered with water.

It was probably an innocent accident—a byproduct of his frustration and me standing a little too close.

But Grayson's mouth hitches into a subtle smirk, and he says, without an ounce of apology, "Whoops."

Whoops.

Whoops.

I take the only reasonable course of action.

Bending down, I scoop my hands into the water and send a wave cascading toward his face.

I couldn't have aimed better if I tried. Water smacks his nose, sluicing over his hair.

Grayson doesn't react right away. Just like when the bird imparted its gift, he freezes for a moment, eyes closed, like he's processing whether this is reality. Whether I really just splashed his face like a five-year-old.

I guess...I did?

"You don't know what you just started," he states, straightening, amber eyes snapping up to mine. *Danger,* they scream. *Get away.*

"You're the one who started it," I defend weakly, taking a nervous step back.

"That was an accident."

"No, it wasn't."

"Yes, it was."

"No, it *wasn't*. And besides, you're wearing waterproo—"

I'm interrupted by a swoop of his arms. A wall of water slams into me, covering me from knee to chest.

For a moment, I stand there, shell-shocked. Then my chin tips down, and I take in the carnage.

He's wearing waterproof waders up to his chest. I only got his face. But *he* just...he just *soaked* me.

And from the satisfied, humored grin spreading his cheeks, he's freaking *elated.*

I drop all pretense, shove my hands in the water, and send him the best tsunami I can muster. It splatters unceremoniously against his waders, reminding me how sorry of a disadvantage I'm at without any gear.

Not that Grayson cares.

He lifts a brow. And that's the last time the water between us stands still.

Like someone's fired a starting pistol, we engage in an all-out splashing war. He soaks me with his stupid, giant hands as I fling water back at him. *Rude.* Splash. *Overbearing.* Splash. *Jerk.* Splash.

Salt stings my eyes, my arms aching as I try to wipe the

shit-eating grin from his face. Except at some point, I start wearing a grin too.

I start *laughing*.

Because, I mean, this is *ridiculous*.

His next splash goes straight up my nose, and I sputter like an asthmatic pig. His assault pauses, and the rumble of his chuckle filters in above my gasping. Blinking water from eyes, I scoop low, come up with a pile of muddy sand, and chuck it at his face.

This one, he dodges. He comes back with a rigid finger pointed at me. "Now *that* was a dirty move." His words are scolding, but his smile is amused, softening all the hard, rugged edges I'm used to.

His smile grows when he sees my eyes latch onto the giant mud-ball in his hand.

I falter.

These are my favorite jeans, and this Gold's sweatshirt is new.

Water darkens his hair and spikes his eyelashes, making his irises glow brighter. Or maybe that's the pure, vengeful glee lighting them up, because I am completely at his mercy, and we both know it.

"Apologize," he demands.

"For what? You're the one who started it."

"Like I said, it was an *accident*." When I remain silent, he cocks his hand back. Mud oozes between his fingers. "Admit I'm right and apologize, Boston."

It doesn't matter whether he's right, because I'd rather spend hours scrubbing a stain out of my clothes than apologize to the guy who spent the last two weeks erecting a giant hill for me to climb.

Accepting my fate, I close my eyes and wait.

One second ticks by. Two, then three. Water laps gently and a soft breeze hums through the air.

Tentatively, I pop one eye open to find Grayson's hand by his side, head shaking in exasperated wonder. Little droplets of water fling from his hair with each movement. "Jesus, you're more stubborn than Anson."

In this context, it sort of feels like a compliment.

"Are you going to do it?"

The Grayson I met two weeks ago would have already slung the muck at my face and taken a photo to hang like a trophy, then thrown darts at it all day.

But *this* Grayson just keeps shaking his head. "It'll stain that sweatshirt, which means you'll end up needing another one. And they're supposed to be for *paying* customers, not freeloading employees."

The sweatshirts are inexpensive to produce, and there are literally *hundreds* piled in the stockroom. Grayson's too aware of the farm's operations to *not* know this.

But he sticks to the weak excuse. Shaking the mud from his hand, he turns toward the boat, wet shirt glued to the muscles of his upper back and shoulders. "Come on. Before you get cold, Boston."

I trudge behind him, tugging my useless, sopping sweatshirt over my head. The sun's out, and the fabric was thick enough to save my black tee underneath from most of the water. Still, I can't help but shiver a little in the sea breeze as I board the skiff.

"The bow," Grayson says, as he shoves the boat off and jumps in with practiced ease. When I look over in question, he glances at my shirt, then my plastered-on jeans, a frown marring his scruffy mouth. "Sit on the floor at the bow. It'll protect you from the wind."

"The sun's out. It isn't bad."

"Just sit at the bow." His nostrils flare on an exhale. "*Please.*"

The sky must be falling, or I'm already hypothermic and hallucinating. Because there's no way that six-letter word just came out of him.

But it did.

Just like his invitation to join today's tour, despite the headache it caused. Just like his poorly worded conviction that I'm not at fault for my layoff.

So, for once, I don't fight him, dutifully heading to the bow and hunkering down.

And he's right. It does protect me.

10

ELIZA

THE STAINED, off-white backboard and rickety hoop stare back at me blankly, like they're wondering why in the world I'm standing in front of them with a basketball.

Or maybe I'm projecting.

I'm not a middle-schooler. Nor am I a washed-up D1 athlete. I haven't actually touched a basketball since sophomore year of high school, before swim and school took over every ounce of my free time. I have zero business being here.

But it's one of those ugly early summer weekends, where it's cloudy and cool, and even the sand and picnic warriors aren't interested in the beach. After a full week of work and a morning spent writing cover letters for two positions Suzanne found, I needed a break from the screens and the house. Or, boat.

I could've gone to one of the vacation towns sandwiching Garnet Shores, but they remind me of the neighborhoods I used to visit with my friends. The ones with cute cafes, shopping, and pretty sidewalks. The thought of doing that without them only reminded me of my current predicament, and all *that* did was twist my gut.

It didn't help that Sami had texted this morning, asking how I was. She didn't respond to my reply, probably because she's at brunch with Kyle and the others—something we've always done on Saturdays.

So I grabbed the lone basketball hiding in the boat cabin's storage bin and walked here, trying to pretend this is completely voluntary and not as pathetic as it feels.

Fresh air. Exercise. Some good old-fashioned fun.

Kids beg their parents to let them do this stuff, right?

I shoot from the free-throw line. The ball hits the rim but bounces awkwardly, flying out to the side. I watch as it lands and rolls all the way to the tree line surrounding the court.

Fresh air. Exercise. Some good old-fashioned fun. I mentally recite the words as I make the long jog to retrieve the ball.

My next free-throw is an air-ball, bouncing twice and coming to a stop on the grass behind the hoop. An improvement from flying all the way to Timbuktu, maybe, but *come on.* I used to be a starter. I should be better than this.

I snag the ball and march back to the free throw line, and that's when my motivational mantra dies like a plant that's caught fire. Because two cars roll into the dirt lot, and the worn forest-green pickup looks a lot like the one I see parked daily in the oyster farm's lot. The other is black and shiny, and the driver looks awfully familiar from my internet searches.

Anson Gold. Grayson Gold. Both here. With me.

Karma, what have I done to you? Was it throwing mud at Grayson's face?

My worst fears are confirmed when they pile out of

their cars with another man I don't know, all dressed in athletic clothes and sneakers.

"Shit. Shit. *Shit.*" Is it too late to dart into the trees and pretend I was never here? As if in answer, all three heads turn in my direction before I can move.

Wave, you idiot.

I force my hand up, because Grayson is here *with my boss* and I need to act normal and respectable, not like a panicked, anxious mess. Anson returns the gesture as the men make their way over, basketball in hand.

The ball of anxiety in my chest stretches bigger with every step they take. Between my tours and Grayson's mercy with the mud, we seem to have entered a fragile truce, as if he's finally accepted my presence on his farm.

But every interaction still requires me to be on top of my game, and if my last two shooting attempts are any indication, I am, in fact, at the very *bottom* of my game. Like, below sea-level. I refuse to make a fool of myself in front of him, never mind my employer—who may as well be auditioning for a cologne commercial right now.

Anson Gold is like the Boston, Gucci-model version of his brother. Where Grayson is shaggy and rugged, Anson is clean-cut and controlled. His dark hair is cropped short in a buzz cut, and neat stubble covers his jaw. His face is a little more square, but with the same tawny eyes, straight nose, and confident stride I'm coming to know, he's very obviously Grayson's sibling.

He's also the type of man I'd normally give a quadruple-take if we crossed paths on Boylston Street. But I find my attention settling on Grayson instead, who's traded his perpetually-stained work gear for a clean tee with a charity's 5K plastered on the front. His ball-cap is backwards, which means there's no shadow to hide the way his gaze rakes over me as I approach.

"Boston," Grayson greets. "Play ball as much as you play pool?"

Anson raises a brow at his brother before extending a large hand my way. "Eliza, pleasure to meet you in-person."

"You too." I return his handshake firmly, as if that professional firmness will make up for the fact that I'm wearing skimpy running shorts in front of *my boss*.

Anson has built an impressive miniature empire in an incredibly short amount of time. Despite looking casual in athletic gear, this man is something of a shark. His reputation is one of ruthless business—which is why I trust a reference from him will be valuable.

"How have you been enjoying the job?"

It's laughable how loaded that question is. Ignoring Grayson in my periphery, I smile. "It's been a wonderful experience. Thank you again for the opportunity."

"That's great to hear." His tone suggests he sees right through my bullshit. "Not sure if he's swung by the farm yet, but this is our friend, JJ." Anson gestures toward the third man with them. He's handsome. Short blonde hair, cut military-style. Kind blue eyes. Clean-shaven, strong jaw.

Very Captain America-esque. If Captain America had a sleeve of tattoos.

He gives me a good-natured grin and offers his hand. "Heard a lot of great things about you from Gray, here."

My eyes skate to Grayson as I shake his hand. "Great things, huh?"

I can't tell if it's annoyance or amusement painted across Grayson's face. "What can I say? Farm wasn't complete without you."

"You're too kind."

"No, really. I thought we could use a new skiff, or maybe upgrade our sieve. But you and that phone is what we really needed."

"So glad that you recognize that already."

Beside him, JJ's smile has grown, while Anson's evaluating gaze moves between us. *Right.*

"Well, the court's warmed up for you. It was wonderful to meet you both," I say a little too brightly as I skirt around them.

"Hold up." JJ's voice cuts my escape short.

My eyes close in disappointment before I school my face and turn around.

"You don't have to leave," he says. "Happy to share the court. We're not kicking you out."

"I don't feel kicked out. It's just—" An excuse about having plans runs across my mind, but Grayson and Anson know I have no friends or family here. "I have work to do."

Grayson's brows crash together. "It's Saturday."

My chest tightens again, because he's right. It's *Saturday*—a day for seeing people you love and laughing and smiling. "Exactly. A great opportunity to get ahead," I push out.

He crosses his arms. "No. A great opportunity to give yourself a break, because Anson was just giving me the stats from your first three weeks, and they're pretty damn good. "

"*Extremely* good," Anson clarifies, though he's frowning. "And I don't want you working beyond your contracted forty hours per week. That's why it's in the contract."

"Okay," I say, because being the reason for a frown on my boss's face is never a good thing. I flounder for a new excuse to leave. "I don't want to crash your game. And I have, um, grocery shopping to do."

I don't.

I did it last night, when I had zero Friday plans. I'd technically had a video call date with Jane, but she cancelled on me.

Oblivious to my plight, JJ waves me off. "You won't be crashing our game. If anything, you can make it happen. Our friend dropped out on us, and we can't play with just three people. Wanna step in?"

The word *no* is dying to burst from my chest, but I'm out of flimsy excuses, and Anson's involved.

The anxiety filling my chest drops into my stomach, tying it in knots. If my two shooting attempts are any indication, I've lost every ounce of basketball ability I ever had. And there's no intoxicated Kenny around to save me in the middle of another game.

I go with some honesty. "I'm a little rusty."

"So are we. You'll fit right in," JJ says.

I *certainly* don't fit in with these three chiseled bodies. Grayson isn't the only one with arms that belong on a protein powder label.

"I really don't want to intrude," I try.

"Well, there's no game without a fourth person." When I hesitate, JJ has the wherewithal to look a little sheepish. If a sturdy, six-foot-something man with a tattoo sleeve can look sheepish. "Sorry, I don't mean to pressure you. It's just an invitation."

Grayson jerks his chin. "What is it? You nervous?"

I stare at him, wishing it was appropriate to throw the ball straight at his face. He should be cheering at my attempted departure, not daring me to join them. Yet here he is, poking at my pride like an annoying five-year-old.

It works, like I'm sure he knows it will.

"Not nervous," I say, committing to my demise. I'm not pretending to be any good, so I can handle losing, but I won't balk in front of him and Anson. "Just managing your expectations. I'm a liability, not an asset." I glance at Anson who seems intrigued at this turn of events. "I also want to note that my basketball abilities are not in any way correlated to my professional abilities."

God, I sound like such a loser.

The smirk that ghosts over Anson's lips is either appreciative or amused. "Noted."

JJ points at me. "You're with me, Eliza. We're gonna kick their asses so bad, they'll have to change their last name from *Gold* to *Participation Trophy*."

Leaves rustle in the wind. A bird squawks overhead.

Then Anson says, "Was that supposed to embarrass us, or you?"

"Hey, trying to keep things polite for the lady. It limits me."

"Trust me, the *lady* can handle it," Grayson snarks. "You might even inspire her."

"I have all the inspiration I need with you," I say sweetly.

"Must be why your work has been so exceptional," Anson comments with mild amusement. "All that *inspiration*."

JJ rolls his eyes. "Man, you can't help but slip work into every conversation, huh? It's like a fucking reflex."

Anson raises a brow. "Know what else is a reflex? Mopping this court with your chatty ass."

"Hope you brought some of your fancy wine to wash down those words when you choke on 'em." JJ taunts, jogging onto the court. "Two-minute warmup."

I follow him, tossing my ball when he opens his hands for a pass. "When I said I was a little rusty, I mean I haven't touched a basketball since high school."

He shoots, and the ball swishes in. "Don't worry. Grayson's always sore from work, which slows him down. And Anson will be too busy thinking over his next business deal to do much damage." He retrieves the ball and passes it to me. "If anything, you're leveling the playing field."

"I'm fine with leveling it. I just don't want to sink our end." I line up, shoot, and completely miss.

My face floods with heat, but JJ isn't put off by my failure. "Your follow-through," he says, returning the ball to me. "You're cutting it short. You want your hand to point all the way through the shot."

I nod, remembering I used to be good at that. I line up and shoot again, this time focusing on making a swan with my arm and hand.

The ball swishes in.

JJ tosses it to me again, and again, I shoot. The ball sinks right in.

"Rusty, who?" he calls out, as he grabs the ball and sinks an easy layup.

A cautious grin crawls up my cheek, and I catch sight of Grayson taking a shot—that ends as an air-ball.

Well, then.

11

ELIZA

JJ TAKES THE BALL FIRST, dribbling with easy swagger as we get into position.

"You ready, Boston?" Grayson sidles over, placing his bulky body between me and JJ.

Apparently, we're matched up, but this isn't a surprise. It'd be weird to get physical with my boss, and two-person teams don't leave many options.

"Ready to make you regret inviting me to play? Yes."

"Careful about underestimating us."

"It's impossible to underestimate you."

A chuckle erupts from his chest, one that's immediately cut off when JJ suddenly drives to the basket.

Anson's on him like glue, so I dart to the side, hands open for a pass that JJ throws. Either Grayson is taking it incredibly easy on me, or he just wasn't ready for the game to start, because I have a wide-open shot that I *drain*.

JJ howls. "You boys are fucked."

Jogging backwards, I open my arms wide at Grayson, whose jaw is parted in surprise. "That regret sinking in yet?"

"You have two points. Cool it," he chirps, starting a slow, controlled dribble down the court.

It's smart to give him a little space and conserve energy until he gets inside the three-point line. But it's a short game, and that point I just scored lit a fire within me that'll carry me through to the end.

Even if it doesn't, my desire to pummel Grayson into the ground will.

The whole *I can deal with losing in basketball?* Yeah. Not happening anymore.

I get right up in his face, stance wide, jabbing at his dribbling hand.

"So that's how you want to play." The soft words are barely out when he crosses the ball behind his back and darts left. I sprint to catch up, but he fades back before I can stop. The ball hits the backboard and goes in.

I snag the ball before I have to hear whatever bullshit Grayson's two points just inspired, and send it to JJ, who's already halfway down the court. Anson and Grayson aren't expecting the fast turnaround. A second later, JJ reaches high for an easy layup. "Gotta be quicker, boys!"

"JJ, you talk too fucking much." Anson's face is set in stern lines as he comes down the pavement.

"Check your panties." JJ winks, closing in on him. "Pretty sure they're twisted."

Anson fades right, then passes left. I'm in line to intercept when Grayson flies in front of me with way more speed than JJ described. He yanks the ball from the air and drives to the basket.

In it goes. Four-Four.

Apparently he's learning, because he doesn't stick around to gloat, joining Anson to hustle down the court.

This is the pace for several points. I shoot and pass

quickly, because my dribbling is abysmal. Grayson doesn't try poking at my hands like I do to him. In fact, he's careful not to make contact with me at all. He just edges to my right, forcing me to move to my weak side or give up the ball. Luckily, JJ is an evasion artist, getting open for a pass again and again.

Until he doesn't.

With Grayson all over my right side, I hold the ball and prepare to pass. But Anson's figured out JJ's game, and he can't get free.

"What trick you gonna pull now?" Grayson taunts, bringing his broad chest right up in my space. He's like a goddamn brick wall.

"I don't know," I lie. Planting one foot, I duck and drive my elbow into his rock-hard gut. I hear his expulsion of air as I pivot back, using the space I created to get a shot off.

In it goes.

I wink. "Maybe a little something like that."

"That was a foul," Grayson accuses.

"Can't handle a little roughness, Grayson?"

His mouth curves, all rogue. "It's all about the setting, Boston. Just don't want to set a bad precedent on the court."

There's no chance for a retort because Grayson turns for the sideline, calling a timeout. His arms flex as he pulls his shirt off and tosses it aside, and all my wit withers away.

Grayson Gold doesn't just have hot guy arms. He has hot guy...*everything*. My eyes shamelessly rivet to the tapestry of tanned skin and thick muscle, not overtly chiseled like a bodybuilder, but honed for function. Perfectly proportional, all male, with a light dusting of hair across his chest and a happy trail that disappears beneath his waistband.

And, *yeah*, there's a hint of a *vee* that also disappears into his shorts.

Why, universe. Why?!

JJ, guardian angel that he is, also whips off his shirt, and his equally incredible physique dulls the shock of Grayson's —but not before Grayson catches me watching him and develops a smug smirk that makes me want to dive face-first into the pavement.

I remind my eyes that they're *not* to look below his neckline as he jogs over.

"See something you like?"

"What makes you think that?"

JJ's still making his way back on the court, and Anson's thankfully out of earshot.

"Just looking a little focused there, that's all."

"I *was* focused—on the idea I just had."

Grayson steps closer, bringing a wash of body heat with him. It brushes against my skin, as taunting as his tone. "No, you can't take a photo of me and frame it on your wall."

I roll my eyes, too aware that he doesn't smell as rancid as a sweaty man should. "When we win, you're taking me with you for a full day of work on the farm." When he blinks, I add, "For content."

Knowing him, he'd twist my request and force me into physical labor all day.

"Fine."

It only took him a second to consider my offer. "Really? That easy?"

He glances around guilelessly. "It appears so."

"You're going to take me out with you for a full day of work," I state, just to make sure he *truly* understands me.

"No, I'm not." When my face scrunches in confusion, he says, "You're not going to win."

And that's when I know I will do *anything* to beat him and Anson to twenty points.

The next few points come fast, each of our teams matching the other. By the time we're tied at eighteen, my forehead is slicked with sweat. JJ calls me over to the end of the court, where he's dribbling the ball.

"You want to win this thing?"

"Yes." I'm trying not to wheeze, while JJ sounds like he's out for an evening stroll.

"Know how to set a pick?"

When I nod, he quickly relays the plan, and we lope down the court to where the brothers wait.

Anson comes up to guard JJ, while Grayson slides over to me. JJ dribbles hard toward me, and I run just past him, forcing Grayson and Anson to swap their defense. Anson's slow on the uptake, leaving me free to get right in Grayson's way as JJ drives across the court.

The pick works *perfectly*.

Too perfectly.

Grayson's too focused on keeping up with JJ to notice my placement and barrels directly into me with the force of an eighteen-wheeler.

I'm flung off my feet. Grayson comes with me, throwing his hands out just in time to catch himself.

Unlike me.

I slam into the pavement, and there's the whoosh of a basket finding home. But I can't celebrate the fact that we just won because I can't breathe, my lungs frozen in my chest as a primal panic sets in.

"Woah, Boston." It's Grayson, crouching right at my side, face etched in concern. "Breathe."

Breathe. How do I make myself breathe? I never have.

It's an automatic process that I've never had to do manually and *oh my god I'm going to suffo—*

"Hey." Two pools of whiskey dip right into my vision, calm and grounding. "You just got the breath knocked out of you. You've got this."

I've got this.

A sliver of oxygen slides down my throat. It disappears, and my ribs stutter on another inhale that draws a sip of air. I shove it out, and my next breath is a little more full.

Pull it together.

As my body remembers how to breathe, the panic ebbs away, making room for a storm of sensations. My smarting ass. The burn on my palms. The heat of Grayson's body that is nearly touching mine, all that bulk crouched beside me and head angled low toward mine. There's no air between us to pull away the salt and warm musk that radiate off his skin.

For a fleeting moment, I'm glad. It's the same moment that I meet his gaze again and find it steady and sure, void of the mocking light and irritation I've come to know.

"Eliza, you good?" JJ's voice shatters the fragile peace.

Grayson pulls away to glance at his friend, though he stays crouched by my side.

"I'm—" big breath, "fine."

I am.

My body feels like it was hit by a freight train, but nothing is broken. My ass will bruise, and my hands have a little road rash, but there are no real injuries.

JJ crouches on my opposite side, concerned eyes running over me. "Shit, that was not supposed to happen."

"What the hell were you thinking?" Grayson's tone, which isn't directed at me, but his friend, has me sitting up straighter. He sounds angry, so vastly different from the calm he just exuded.

JJ runs a frustrated hand across his jaw. "You've never gone that hard into a pick. Thought you'd see her."

"I could've seriously hurt her."

"Yeah, I realize that now. It was a bad idea—"

"You think?" Grayson interrupts sharply. "You don't normally have those, but that—"

"*Hey.*" I glance between Grayson's stormy expression and JJ's sorry one, settling on Grayson—this man who was just my lifeline, who's still crouching above me like he *cares*. For the second time in a matter of days, the neatly defined image of him in my mind doesn't seem so bounded, the edges blurring as that picture tries to morph. All my thoughts start to jumble, but this isn't the time. I don't even know if they *should* be jumbling.

Shoving them back into their organized boxes, I say, "I'm fine."

Both of them look at me, still in a pathetic heap on the pavement.

Handle yourself.

"I lost my breath and needed a second to get it back." I start to stand, and they move back, making space for me. Grayson's hand is the first drop down. I trace it to that chiseled arm and up to his face, then jump to Anson's face high above it.

Handle. Yourself.

Ignoring his offer, I push to my feet, forcing a smile through the aches. "You shouldn't be upset with him. I would've suggested the plan if he hadn't."

This doesn't appease him. His mouth parts to argue back, but I beat him to it.

"Besides," my smile turns genuine, "it got us the win."

The stern lines of Grayson's face slowly morph into incredulity, and I twist the knife.

"What time do we start on Monday?"

12

GRAYSON

THE SUNRISE PAINTS the clouds with bright reds and fiery oranges. It's the Garnet Shores Special. A stunner. The kind that stamps itself in your memory and resurfaces whenever you reminisce on home.

But the only image my memory currently cares about is Boston's long, toned legs in those little black running shorts. It doesn't stand alone. There's also the unfiltered triumph every time she scored a point. The poorly veiled interest in those expressive eyes when I stripped away my shirt. The challenge set in her small jaw when she agreed to play with us—the same kind that usually accompanies her insults. That wide vulnerability when I ran her over and she lost her breath.

Over the past two days, I've revisited it all more times than I'm proud to admit, and every time, JJ's words ghosted along with it.

She's not Mackenzie.

He'd said it when we got back to Anson's estate, while Lala ran off to retrieve her soccer ball. Anson was hogging the kitchen, giving us a minute alone.

"*No,*" I'd agreed.

"*I invited her to play ball, but you goaded her into it.*"

"*We were kicking her off the court, and she's alone in Garnet Shores. I felt bad.*"

"*Sure.*"

Lala appeared in the distance, little legs pumping as she ran back to us.

"*I get it,*" JJ had continued. "*That situation fucked with your head. Made you take the business even more seriously. No distractions, all that.*" Lala gave him just enough time to deliver the blow. "*But I think it made you scared, too.*"

He'd timed it perfectly, the fucker. Lala started our game, and there was no telling him off.

But he's wrong.

This isn't about fear. It's about being thirty years old, and being focused on building a business alongside my brother. A wife and kids will happen someday, but now isn't the time to test the waters—to fuck around *again*. I don't have the attention to spare, and the risk isn't worth the reward.

My phone buzzes in my pocket, jolting me back to the sunrise I'm watching from the dock. I pull out my phone as I head toward the warehouse.

> Anson: Positive Vibrio case. Not sure whose oysters, but one of yours was apparently on the plate.

Just like that, my Monday morning flips from serene to exceptionally shitty. I'm not one to panic—never have been. But raw edges are bursting into frame, and I can't completely hold them back.

We're incredibly strict about our oyster-to-ice timing and proper storage, and nothing's happened recently that would cause a water bacteria spike. The chances this gets traced back to us are slim. But having last year's accusations on record somewhere, even though it was dismissed, could be a mark against us and lead to a deeper investigation. The kind that tarnishes reputations.

People won't consume raw seafood from a farm they think could make them sick. And Vibrio's the type of sick that can kill a person.

The fragility of what we've built here shoots to the surface as I ditch my early morning plans to double-check our records are sorted correctly. I'd intended to work out. A few pushups, pullups, and squats in the back corner of the warehouse. My bare-minimum maintenance routine to try to stave away the aches and injuries that take farmers out of the game.

So when it's nine o'clock and I'm heading to a skiff with Kenny, I haven't done anything to take the edge off. That edge only grows more jagged when I step onboard and Boston's little sedan still isn't in the lot.

I'd be lying to say part of me wasn't looking forward to our day together all weekend. To say I wasn't curious about what witty remarks she'll string together, or what she'll find interesting enough to film, or what her face will look like when her sharp mind learns something new.

But now it's two minutes past nine, and I'm standing on the skiff, staring at the lot, when there's a metric fuck-ton of work to do and more records to check, and I don't have a minute to spare.

I *want* Eliza to show, but she hasn't.

For all her snark, she's responsible. She respects this business. Success and excellence are her priorities. That's what I was coming to believe about her, but now she's late, and whether it's this morning's shitstorm or common fucking sense, I'm realizing maybe those beliefs could be wrong because I've only known her for three weeks.

I've been horribly wrong before, and everyone knows where that got me.

On top of all that, I wouldn't wait around like this for any other team member coming along for a joyride.

Which means *this* waiting elevates her from colleague to distraction.

One I can't afford.

"We waiting for someone?" Kenny asks from the stern.

I glance at the parking lot one last time, finding the gravel empty.

"No," I say, and shove us off the dock.

13

ELIZA

THERE'S an inferno in the sky, brushed with neon reds and oranges, and it blinds me every time I lift my head from the water for a breath. It's just beginning to fade as I emerge from the water and step into the cool morning air.

All my As, studying, and successful internships, and I didn't know the sky could look like this. Maybe the sun has always put on this show in the city, and it's the high-rises and office lights that dim its blazing hues. Or maybe I've always spent my early mornings taking in the bluish glow of my laptop screen.

Or maybe I've just never had the bandwidth to pause, breathe, and look up.

At this hour, the marina is at its prettiest. The gentle morning glow softens all the chips and stains and ugly lines, while water gently laps against hulls. It's serene.

Until my phone buzzes on the seat beside the cabin.

Water pools on the deck as I wrap myself in a towel, toss my new swim buoy aside, and retrieve my phone. *Mother* stares back at me.

I consider leaving it, because my morning has been going well. My swim was strong, Michelangelo just painted the sky, and I get to tag along with Grayson today. But my mom will just call every hour until I pick up. It's more efficient to handle her now.

I sit down and put it on speaker.

"Eliza." From the way she says it, you'd think I just entered a boardroom for a meeting.

"Hi, Mom."

"How are you?"

I recognize the question for the formality it is. "Great."

"That's good."

There's no gladness behind her reaction, and I'm not expecting any. She doesn't blame me for my lay-off, but she's made it clear how much she disapproves of my decision to leave the city. In her mind, I should be chasing down every door with the slightest crack in it, or at least attending networking events. It doesn't matter that Kyle upended my personal life.

For all her frigidity, she's asked enough questions over the last year to figure out Kyle and I were no longer in love. To her, him cheating was almost a favor to me. Not a betrayal, an embarrassment, or a giant elephant in what was supposed to be my close friend group.

"How is the job?" she asks.

"Fantastic," I recite, though the jury's still out on that statement's accuracy. "I'm certain I'll receive strong references from the CEO when the contract is over, and I'm glad to add some diversity to my resume."

"I trust Suzanne has been sourcing opportunities for you?"

"Yes. We've submitted several applications."

I don't know why she's asking. Suzanne updates her regularly, as if I'm not an independent twenty-six-year-old, but some prodigal child.

"You'll be back at it in no time, then."

I don't know if she's trying to comfort herself, or me.

Finally, she gets to the point of her call. "Your brother's commencement ceremony is in two weeks. I know you'll be there, but I need to know if you're joining us on Friday night. I'm making reservations."

I'd almost forgotten about the event. Or maybe that was me trying to preserve my sanity. James, the family prodigy, my parents' most prized child, is graduating from law school. He already took his final exams and landed at the top of his class.

"I'll be there Saturday."

"Why not Friday night?"

"I'm attending a virtual conference," I lie. The last thing I want is to have my face rubbed in my brother's success while my parents have unfettered access to me—their current disappointment—for two nights in a row.

"Well, we look forward to seeing you on the Saturday. We'll circle back that week to determine your arrival time."

I watch water drop from my hair onto the phone screen, distorting the letters of her name. "Sounds good."

"Talk soon."

She hangs up before I can tap the red button. Slouching back with a sigh, I gaze at the water that's still calm enough to reflect the cloud-speckled sky like glass. As Grayson said on Saturday—and seemed to genuinely appreciate—my early metrics are looking promising. In two weeks, I might be able to report major milestones to my parents, when they inevitably ask for specifics over dinner.

My ride-along today should help with that.

If someone told me two weeks ago I'd be stuck on a small boat with Grayson for an entire morning, I would have thought I'd been arrested and this was my prison sentence. But I've actually been looking forward to the ride-along all weekend. And no matter what I tell myself, it isn't just because it's a content goldmine, but because the thought of Grayson is no longer accompanied by loathing.

Now it comes with something lighter and more energizing than hatred, and the memory of his steady reassurance as I gasped for breath.

Hero worship, maybe?

I get ready quickly, not wanting to be late. Grayson might owe me this, but anyone can see how long and hard he works every day. The last thing I want is to get in the way of his productivity, which is why I leave extra early, giving myself plenty of time to stop at a coffee shop I discovered my first week here. They serve nothing but the basics, but everything feels like a warm hug, and the staff are always smiling.

The bell jingles as I step into the homey space—right in front of an elderly woman who's too busy looking at the tray of drinks in her shaky hands to notice me.

I try to step back, but it's too late. Moth balls assault my nostrils as the woman trips into me. I catch her but miss the drinks, and they hit the floor, ice clattering on the wood as dark liquid runs everywhere.

The shop freezes, then everyone jolts into action.

"Eliza! Nancy! Are you alright?" It's Joy, Grayson's bookkeeper, bustling toward us with two other customers and a barista.

"I'm okay. Are you?" I ask the woman, Nancy.

Her arms are fragile in my hands as I set her back on her feet. "I am so sorry. *So* sorry. Oh, what a mess."

Her face is completely distraught, like she's just run over a deer, rather than spilled a few drinks.

"There's nothing to be sorry for," I reassure her. "Everyone is fine. It's just coffee."

"But look at this mess!" A wavering hand motions to the coffee that's currently being mopped up. "And your shoes!"

"It's almost cleaned up already. And my shoes are brown. You can't even notice the drops."

"Nancy, dear, just calm down." Joy thankfully steps in, because Nancy seems on the verge of losing it, and I'm not entirely sure what to do. "Here, let's take a seat while they make you some new drinks."

As Joy guides her to a table, I grab more paper towels and help on the floor. Two minutes later, it's like the accident never happened. Nancy's given two new coffees, and the weathered wood floors are dry.

"Let's walk you to your car," Joy tells her.

Nancy's hands are visibly trembling as she apologizes *again*.

"I'll help," I offer.

Joy carries her drinks to her car, parked in the handicapped space, as I give her my arm and walk her to the driver's door.

Joy bustles over. "I've got it from here. Thank you, dear," she says with a grateful smile.

As I step away, I hear Nancy say, "Now that is a lovely girl."

"She works on the farm—with *Grayson*."

"What a wonderful young man! So handsome, too."

"Wouldn't they be..."

I remove myself from the vicinity and pull out my phone to check the time—and realize I'm about to be late to my ride-along.

Swearing under my breath, I forget about coffee and hop in my car, pushing the pace to the farm and wishing I had Grayson's number so I could give him a heads up. It's buried somewhere in my hiring paperwork, and I never thought to add it to my phone.

Two minutes past nine, I whip into the lot. I shove the car in park and hurry to the docks, where Amanda's carrying two buckets off a boat. Grayson's nowhere to be seen.

"Hey!" I call out to her. "Is Grayson still here?"

"He just left," she says, glancing over her shoulder at the water, where a skiff retreats into the distance.

I stare at the Grayson-shaped figure behind the wheel, all my hope and happy anticipation collapsing like a house of cards.

I'm two minutes late. *Two minutes.*

And he...left.

That *asshole.*

"Was he...not supposed to leave?" Amanda asks cautiously.

I lick my lips, head wobbling in stunned disappointment. "He was supposed to take me with him. We had a deal." And I thought he was starting to respect me.

Maybe...maybe there was an emergency? Something that required his immediate attention?

When I ask, Amanda purses her lips. "Not that I know of."

My disappointment expands into a ball in my throat, and the sensation triggers a swell of anger.

Because that sensation feels a lot like when I learned that Kyle cheated on me, that Jane and Sami still spoke to him, that I'd been laid off.

I'd come to Garnet Shores to get *away* from all that.

And Grayson had done *just* enough over the last week to make me think he *wasn't* such an asshole—setting me up perfectly for this pathetic fall, right here.

"What the hell is she doing down here?"

Apparently my day is on the greatest upward trajectory of all time because Mark, the farm's oldest team member, marches toward us with a scowl plastered on his grizzly face. Everyone else on the farm has acknowledged my existence at least once, even offered a "hello" or an introduction. But Mark treats me like I'm trying to infect them all with chicken pox.

"Just doing my job," I reply plainly.

He grunts. "Do it somewhere else. Far away." He grumbles under his breath as he brushes past us.

"Don't take it personally," Amanda advises.

"I won't." With Mark, anyway.

With Grayson? I'm taking this so personally it'll be written into my obituary.

Never mind that we had a deal, or that I thought we were edging away from enemies and toward, I don't know, whatever it was he'd been stirring in my gut. The reality is, the content I'm no longer getting today is going to impact my entire workweek.

Grayson just *screwed* me.

"You look like a very dangerous person right now," Amanda observes, studying my face.

Good.

I am.

Because Grayson Gold doesn't know the ins and outs of my mind. He doesn't know that I've been toying with a content idea from the first day I saw him, in all of his rugged, grouchy glory. An idea I'd shoved away because I knew how much he'd despise it, though the results would undoubtedly please Anson.

An idea that's now slithering to the front of my mind.

I smile at Amanda, who's growing more wary by the second, and head back to my car.

I have some planning to do.

14

GRAYSON

"CAN BARBIE TAKE ME FISHING? Please please *puh-lease.*" Lala lays it on thick, green eyes batting and hands clasped together in a plea.

I thought puppy-dog eyes ended at age five, but at eight, Lala's got it down to a science. While Anson might be immune to her sad little petitions, she knows *this* big brother is the world's biggest sucker.

Gave up trying to fight it a few years ago and accepted my place, which is wrapped around her little finger.

I search the farm's evening cookout for *Barbie,* and spot him chatting with some of the boys by the fire. There's a water in his hands.

"Let's ask. Can you go grab him for me?"

"Yay!"

"That's not a yes," I call after her, as her little body weaves through the campfire-lit crowd until she reaches Kenny. She tugs on his hand, and his head cranes to hear her. Then he makes the fatal mistake of looking into the heart-yanking hope that's inevitably all over her face, and a second later, he's following her.

Lala's got her small hand wrapped around his big one, tugging him until he's standing right in front of me. Some eight-year-olds are shy, or quiet, or hampered by the beginnings of self-consciousness. But my baby sister doesn't know what any of those words mean.

"Barbie said he'd take me!" she declares.

"Barbie said this?" I ask, looking at Kenny.

He shrugs. "Barbie said he'd check with you, but sure."

Him using her ridiculous nickname makes her smile even bigger.

It came around two years ago, when Kenny started working with us and Lala was still in her doll phase. I shortened his name to "Ken" one day, and Lala latched right on, connecting him to her favorite blonde-haired, blue-eyed, plastic surfer boy. Kenny instantly went with it, and that put him in my good graces faster than any amount of work on the farm could.

"You had any drinks?" I ask. Like all our monthly cookouts, this one's BYOB, and it's a Friday night, so there's plenty of alcohol floating around. As good as Kenny is with Lala, he's not about to take her near the water if he isn't one-hundred-percent sober.

He waves the plastic bottle in his hands. "Just water so far. Promise I'm in excellent babysitting condition."

"Babysitting?" Lala's nose scrunches in disgust. "I'm eight. I'm not a *baby*."

"No, you are not." Kenny bops her head with his bottle. "You're the best fisherman in Garnet Shores, and we're gonna go see what big catch you can drum up tonight." He glances at me, asking for permission.

It's easy to give. "I'm expecting a tuna. Maybe a shark."

Lala's eyes widen. "What do I get if I bring you a shark?" *That* question is all Anson's influence. He keeps her away from work conversations, but his business mind is part of everything he does. No doubt he's equipping her to successfully wheel and deal her way through life.

People are going to need to watch out, myself included.

Thankfully, sharks don't like to hang out in the pond, so I can safely promise, "Unlimited ice cream."

That sends her bounding off, hand clutching Ken's again, dragging him over to the warehouse where the fishing gear lives.

I owe him for this. He's happy to hang with her, but it's only so much fun entertaining an eight-year-old when your buddies are gathered around a fire, passing a bottle of Mark's moonshine as they trade stories and strum a guitar. And Lala being Lala, she'll leach Kenny of every minute he's willing to give, especially because she's been stuck by my side for a full Friday of work.

I do my best to make the hours entertaining when she's around, and she's at the age where doing an "adult" job feels special, but work's still work at the end of the day.

Events like this, though, inject a little fun back into it.

There's maybe thirty people here, some from my team, some farming buddies from a few towns over, some regulars from town. Laughter and conversation buzz through the air, and fresh oysters are laid on a table beside a platter of Italian grinders and Anson's stuffed Quahogs, which are almost gone. No surprise, considering anything my brother whips up is Michelin-star worthy.

It also isn't surprising that he prepped them for us, despite his inability to attend because of a business event. As much of a hard-ass as he is, he's never once skipped a food delivery for the farm's summer cookouts. He values our little community here just as much as I do.

The smell of campfire fills my lungs as I use Lala's absence to take a deep breath and sit in the moment for what feels like the first time all week. That breath gets stuck on its way out when my gaze snags on the figure near the food table.

A gentle smile rounds Boston's cheeks, her feminine face cast in a soft glow from the fire as she speaks to Amanda. Her hands are swallowed by the sleeves of the same Gold's sweatshirt I spared last week, light jeans loose around her thighs, two cute braids dangling to her chest. Everything about her is casual. Sweet and soft and very unlike the snarky hellion she usually is.

Or maybe she just seems that way because I haven't been on the receiving end of her snark since our basketball game last Saturday.

I haven't been on the receiving end of...anything.

She didn't rip into me for leaving without her on Monday. Hasn't demanded an explanation or another ride-along. Hasn't seared me with glares or even passive-aggressively avoided eye-contact.

No. Any time we've passed on the farm, it's been a subtle chin dip of acknowledgement. A polite *I see you there.*

It's been the worst kind of punishment, slowly peeling the wrapper away from the ball of guilt I'm doing my best not to acknowledge.

She was *late.*

I left on time. Like I had every right to do to any colleague who didn't take the work schedule seriously.

It shouldn't make me feel like the world's biggest dickhead, but it's threatened to with every civil, silent pass-by. And that constant undercurrent of shame has somehow—despite all my efforts—made her an even bigger distraction than she would have been had I just waited for her to show before leaving the dock.

Which is why I'm done giving her headspace.

Now.

Mark's moonshine suddenly looks far less deadly and exponentially more medicinal. I'm stepping toward the fire when Joy intercepts me.

"Grayson, dear. How's that little angel of yours?"

We chat for a minute about Lala, whom Joy babysits whenever we're in a tight spot, and then she tells me about her new garden.

"Nothing like your brother's operation, of course," she laughs, batting my chest. "But it's lovely. Gives me an excuse to get away from my husband when he starts to annoy me."

I doubt her husband minds that one bit.

In fact, I find myself wishing for a garden to materialize when she glances around and pauses at the very direction I'd just stared too long at. "Ah! There she is. That wonderful phone girl."

"Social Media Director." The correction slides out automatically.

Why do I care what Joy calls her?

"Sure. That's what I said," she agrees amicably, gaze still aimed at Boston. "I owe her a thank you for Monday morning. Excuse me."

She pats my chest in dismissal, but the day of the week registers and I blurt, "Thank her for what?"

"Oh, you didn't hear?"

No, I didn't. Unlike Joy, not everyone mainlines town gossip. I arch a brow in question.

"There was an incident at the coffee shop. Nancy tripped into Ms. Director there and spilled coffee everywhere. It was a total disaster. Poor thing, that Nancy." She tsks in sympathy. "That girl helped us clean up and walked Nancy out to her car. Then she ran off in this big rush before I could thank her, or she could even get her own coffee."

I'm no longer smelling the campfire, or thinking about Mark's moonshine, or hearing the genial buzz of conversation.

"Joy, what time was this at?"

She takes too long to think about it. "Just before work. Nine or so, I'd say."

The wrapper flies off my guilt in one clean pull, and the sense that I'm a total asshole is no longer just a niggling thought.

It's front and fucking center.

Eliza was late because she was helping an elderly woman with an unfortunate accident.

Not because she didn't prioritize the farm schedule or respect the time we set.

Because she was busy being a good fucking person.

Goddamnit.

My eyes zero right back in on her. She's alone now, inspecting a closed oyster at the unmanned table. She's chewing on her lip, glancing from the oyster in her bare hand, to the shucking knife on the table, and back again.

She picks up the blade, and it sets my feet in motion, carving through the clusters of people with an urgency that has no place at this cookout. Because this stubborn woman is about to do exactly what I think she is.

And she does.

She jams the blade into the shell, using the same technique I demonstrated during the guided tour last week.

But then something makes her jump, and the blade slips, spearing right into her gloveless palm.

AMANDA MIGHT BE my first friend in Garnet Shores.

We've chatted all week—small talk that flows into conversations about our favorite seasons, what brought her to the farm, whether oysters are better grilled or raw. They're surface-level topics, and we haven't exchanged phone numbers or followed each other on social media, so *friend* might be a slightly desperate stretch. But she invited me to the farm's cookout tonight.

She also caught me filming Grayson from afar several times this week and said nothing, just giving a conspiratorial twist of her lips that suggests she's onto my game and is, at the very least, entertained. And everyone knows there is no bond stronger than the one forged between a vengeful woman declaring war on a man, and her confidant.

The farm's parking lot is humming with chatter and the easy thrum of guitar strings when I pull in. The sunset is lost behind dense clouds, a large bonfire casting a soft light over the gathering that's more crowded than I expected. A table is set up near the warehouse's entrance, filled with platters of food.

Some of my nervousness eases. If Amanda isn't here yet and I fail at inserting myself into conversations, I can at least look occupied by stuffing my face before calling it an early night.

Still, my fingers play anxiously in the oversized sleeves of my sweatshirt as I head over, the smell of burnt wood swirling in my nose and dredging up memories from high school and my camping trips with Kitty.

It's funny. Campfires should smell bad, but all that chemical combustion brings a wash of nostalgia instead. I've sat by my fair share of evening fires in the city, but those propane patio firepits never get the scent right.

Amanda pops out of the gathering with a drink in her hand, giving me a friendly wave. My relief is immediate, and I have to hold myself back from breaking the rules of early-almost-friendship and giving her a giant hug.

"Glad you could make it." She's wearing an army green trucker jacket, and her hair is thrown into a haphazard knot, streaks of pale yellow and brownish-gold reflecting in the firelight.

"Thanks for the invite."

"'Course. These cookouts are a summer tradition around here." She glances over shoulder and sighs. "Besides, the ratio of dicks to women is always way off. It's nice having some more of us here to stop this from turning into a frat party."

I laugh a little, realizing that the ratio *is* quite off. I spot Joy bumbling among the crowd, a few ponytails scattered around, but it's mostly men—and Dave, who's plucking food scraps off the ground.

I set my gaze back on Amanda before my survey can confirm Grayson's presence. Though, who am I kidding? Of course he's here.

It's his farm.

Amanda gestures toward a cooler. "You want a drink?"

"Amanda!" The shout has us both spinning toward the fire. "You bring that electric sander?"

"Yeah! I'll go get it." She turns back, wincing. "Sorry. I'll be five minutes, max. Just got to grab this thing from my car and give him a tutorial. He shouldn't need one, but he already fucked up Steve's." She points her beer toward the food table as she backs away. "You should get something to eat! The sandwiches are good, but the stuffed Quahogs could give you an orgasm."

Then she's gone, and I'm standing on my own, contemplating the groups around me like a lost puppy.

To the food it is.

I plop a stuffed clam on a plastic plate and wander to a platter of ice filled with whole oysters. A blunt blade sits next to a basket of discards.

I pause.

Have I ever shucked an oyster in my life? No.

But Amanda's over at her car, and I'll jump fully clothed into the salt pond before I seek Grayson's help. Some team members mill around, but we aren't exactly friends, and the last thing I want is to look like some damsel, afraid to crack open a shell when it's probably in Garnet Shores' kindergarten curriculum. Besides, the two demonstrations I watched on-tour were simple enough.

I pick up the shucking knife and an oyster and initiate step one: the lollipop. The tip of the blade slides between the two shells, lodging there like it's supposed to.

Easy. I've *so* got this.

Firming my grip, I go for the twist. A mighty *quack* assaults me mid-movement. "*What the—*"

The blade slips—

And slices right into my hand.

I see the cut before the sensation registers. In that second, masked by the low light, it doesn't look bad.

Then the sharp bite of pain flashes as blood floods the wound—and keeps coming. I gasp.

The oyster and knife clatter to the table as I slap my other hand over the injury, cursing Dave as the pain tightens my breathing and blood drips out of my grip.

Crap, this is bad.

Like, might need *stitches,* bad.

Dave, the traitor, casually waddles away.

I survey the table in a panic, searching for a towel, napkins, anything to stem the bleeding. My eyes land on a roll of paper towels just as a large hand swipes it up. I follow that hand to a too-familiar body rushing around the table to my side, and this stroke of bad luck transforms into a full-fledged *heaven-hates-me* curse.

"Here." There's no greeting, no mocking comment. Just quiet urgency as Grayson tears a few sheets free and grabs the wrist of my injured hand. "Lift your hand."

The pain must be overriding my frontal lobe because I instantly comply. Grayson replaces my grip with his own, pressing the paper towel to the wound hard enough to make me hiss.

"Sorry. It needs pressure."

"Mm-hmm," I manage, shifting on my feet to try to distract myself from the tears beating against my eyes.

He lifts the paper towel for a beat and curses low, his breath ghosting across my forehead. "Can't see how bad it is. We need light."

He tugs on my wrist, hanging between his, leading me into the warehouse. My brain must be short-circuiting because I follow him voluntarily, unable, for the life of me, to think of a better course of action.

I don't even have a first-aid kit on the boat.

Voices from the gathering fade to a muted buzz as we enter the cavernous space and he leads me to a card table I've seen the team eat at. Three vases of flowers sit in the center. They must be from Joy, because otherwise they'd be from Grayson, which simply does not compute.

An image of him frolicking in a field and picking flowers pops into my mind, and I hiccup on a giggle.

Grayson eyes me in concern. "Going delirious on me, Boston?" He kicks out a chair and guides me down, keeping pressure on the wound as he crouches before me.

"I was just picturing you picking flowers."

The groove between his brows deepens. "Picturing me picking flowers?" he repeats to himself.

My head tilts down to find my hand swallowed in his. His nails are clean and trimmed, but little white scars and scabs speckle those long, calloused fingers.

These are hands hewn by hard work. Definitely not flower-picking hands.

I snort a small laugh again.

"Hey, seriously—you lightheaded?" His free hand moves, landing softly on my chin. Gentle pressure lifts it until I'm snared by two amber orbs that should feel too pretty for a man like him.

But it isn't the color holding me captive. It's the steadiness. The earnest concern. The same calm intensity that helped me get my breath on that basketball court.

It shoves the pain down enough for other things to register. The back of his knuckle, rough and hot as it softly braces my chin. His tight pressure on my wound, his free fingers resting quietly on my palm, callouses tickling my skin.

The heat from his hold on me seeps into my skin, warming my face as he finishes his perusal and meets my gaze. "Your color looks good." His murmur settles deep within me. "How's the pain?"

I stare at him crouching before me, the messy scruff along his jaw, the faint lines starting to show beside his eyes. Lines born from smiles.

Smiles he never gives me, unless they're sarcastic, or smug, or paired with some double-edged remark.

All that invested concern, and he still left without me Monday.

I jerk away. My hand stays in his grip, but I lean back into the seat, the voodoo spell broken.

Misreading my reaction for pain, his concern deepens. "That bad?"

"Not sure why you care, Grayson." Logic is quickly regaining function, and with it, all the reasons I should not accept this man's help roar back. "I can handle this myself."

I tug on my hand, but he doesn't let it move.

"Of course, I care."

"Because you're worried I'll file a safety complaint or something?"

He frowns. "Because you just stabbed yourself in the hand and you might not be okay."

"I'd think you'd be cheering. Just another strike to *Boston.*" I smile bitterly. "Another thing that might make her dislike this place enough to leave."

"I'm well aware you're not leaving."

"So why are you still *so* determined to screw me over?" My voice echoes through the warehouse, exasperated chords suspended in the air.

All week, I've refused to show him how much Monday bothered me. Small nods. Polite smiles. That's all he's gotten. But whether it's my throbbing hand or exhaustion from the week or just a damn tipping point, I can't hold onto that apathetic mask anymore. Which is why words keep tumbling out.

"You left without me on Monday. We had a deal at the basketball game. I spent all of Sunday planning content around that ride-along, and then you left. So either you still hate my guts and want to ruin my life this summer, or you're a sore fucking loser, or you're one heck of an actor because everyone in this town thinks you're a good man and they're dead wrong."

I expect him to fire back—to tell me I don't belong, that it's my fault for showing up and staying when I'm not wanted here. But all he does is stare over my shoulder at the wall, like it holds all the answers to life.

When he meets my eyes again, he isn't frowning anymore. Or confused. Or concerned. I don't know what he is, because his expression is carefully blank.

"I left because you were late," he says quietly.

Leaning in, I inform him, "I was late because I was helping to clean up an accident."

"I know."

Okay, yep, he's *definitely* a Grade A dickhe—

"Joy just told me. Tonight."

My mental insult pauses.

He gives a belabored sigh and briefly glances at the wall again. His throat bobs.

"Eliza, I owe you an apology." His tone is stone-sober, just as sincere as the concern in his eyes a minute ago. "I assumed you were late because you didn't respect my time."

"You realize how that sounds, right?"

"I know exactly how it sounds," he answers with a level of seriousness that stops me from interjecting. "This farm is everything to me, and it's a hell of a lot to my brother. It's our business, yes, but it's also our father's legacy. Nothing is guaranteed, and if we want it to succeed, if we don't want to get eaten by all the sharks out to get us or shut down by careless mistakes, we need to treat it with the care and discipline it requires. You're smart as hell. You're excellent at your job. But I've only known you for a few weeks."

"Yet all you do is assume the worst of me," I state.

The way his eyes soften is the only admission I need.

"Do you do this to every new person you meet? Or is this only reserved for me?"

He readjusts his grip on my hand, reminding me he's still stemming the bleeding. This entire time, he hasn't let go. I swore at him, insulted him, and he didn't drop my hand or even tighten his fingers in frustration.

"I mentioned at Dyl's that there was an incident last year," he says in that low timbre. The knob in his throat rolls again, like he's choking on whatever he's about to share. "There was a woman, an out-of-towner here on vacation, who I...got involved with. Her father owns one of the waterfront homes on the pond. He's one of those summer residents who wants us out of here because he thinks we're ruining his front yard."

"You sure know how to pick 'em," I joke, unclear where this is headed. "Didn't know you have a thing for playing with fire."

"Why else do you think I talk to you?" he teases. Then he clears his throat. "She thought I was cheating on her, and decided to fuck us over. She had access to the farm, and she lowered our storage temps, took a photo as evidence, and sent it to her father, who's friends with a regulator. He made some other false allegations and could've gotten us shut down."

The shame emanating from him is nearly suffocating.

"That's a little extreme," I say. "On her end and the regulator's."

"Oyster regulations are strict. The accusations had some serious health implications, and the regulator didn't question his friend. Even if they didn't suspend us while they investigated, that type of attention destroys a farm's name."

"So how'd you get out of it?"

A flash of a smile. "Anson might be the only person in this town who has more power and connections than the ritzy folks who want us gone."

"Then they'll never win." Now I'm the one staring at the wall, though I'm not searching for answers.

I already have them.

It doesn't take a senior analyst to connect the dots between last year's events and...us. Another woman might throw his story in his face and remind him there's never a good reason to treat others poorly. Maybe that woman is stronger than me.

But I'm not her.

And Grayson Gold is literally *kneeling* before me, swallowing all his pride in a confession that most other men would talk themselves out of. Even if they didn't, their egos would swallow it whole before it ever came out.

Heck, in my two years of dating Kyle, the words "I'm sorry" never left his mouth—not even after I'd caught him cheating.

Meeting Grayson's eyes, I say, "I've worked my ass off to get to where I am. Sacrificed weekends, nights, a lot of my own sanity. Woken up in a cold sweat because I thought I forgot to put a certain statistic in my presentation. Stayed in a dying relationship until he cheated because I was too invested in work to deal with the fallout of a breakup."

I don't mean to include that last confession. It just slips out. And maybe it's because of all Grayson just shared that it doesn't feel as vulnerable as it should. Or maybe it's the way he's watching me in simple, quiet observance, not passing judgment on all the things Kyle used to berate me for: trying too hard, thinking too much, caring too much about my goals instead of football and the high score he got gaming.

Still, I cut to the chase before any other confessions slither out.

"I understand the sacrifices, discipline, and attitude necessary to build your own success. And while I've only been here for a few weeks, it's clear to anyone that you put everything into the farm. I don't ever want to interfere with that. Not just because I'm a professional, but because I *get* it." My lips curve up softly. "I respect it."

Regardless of how he's treated me, Grayson is one of the hardest working people I've encountered. Working before I arrive, staying late, laboring beside his team day in and day out. He loves this work. He lives it, breathes It. I wouldn't be surprised if little baby oysters are running through his veins.

There's a thoughtful silence before he says, "Your successes, your work ethic. I respect that, too. Admire it."

"Just not on the farm."

His cheek hitches and he admits, "You've done good work on the farm."

"I'm sorry, can you say that again?" I reach for my phone in my back pocket. "Just want to record that."

"I would, but you're bleeding out, and we shouldn't waste any more time."

Before I can point out that we just sat here talking for the last five minutes, and therefore I'm obviously not on my death bed, he removes the paper towel and lifts my hand out of the shadow of our bodies.

He whistles low as he tilts my palm in the light. "This is going to need stitches. Maybe glue, if you're lucky."

"You don't think that's a little extreme?" I argue weakly. He simply lifts a brow as he covers the wound again, and I sigh. "I'll drive myself to the ER."

I must have mispronounced my words, because Grayson regards me like I've just suggested a dive off the dock.

"No," he says. Simple. Firm. Like it's an established fact.

It makes my muscles stiffen against the hard plastic seat. "You don't make my decisions."

"I don't," he agrees. "I do, however, need to make sure you're okay. And while you're the smartest, most impressive woman I've ever met, you don't need to do everything your-self. So I'm going to give you two very reasonable options, and you can decide which one you'll take."

16

GRAYSON

HER FACE IS PINCHED in exasperation as she looks down at me.

I much prefer it to the pain-fogged acquiescence of when I'd first brought her in here. Or the angry hurt when all her carefully constructed apathy from this week vanished.

Knowing I caused it made me feel like the smallest fucking man in the world. When I left Monday, I wasn't thinking of her. I was thinking about *me*. But anyone with a single functioning brain cell would've known it'd be another insult, another blow to her.

I did it anyway, not even considering that she might be busy helping a grandmother cross a street, or saving a lost puppy, or being the kind of good person she's shown me she is. The kind I usually am.

The kind who's as lost as fucking Waldo wherever she's concerned.

I'm not ignorant enough to think confessing last year's situation, no matter how painful it was to wrench out, will magically make up for everything I've done.

"I don't need help," she says. Sweet notes of her flowery perfume mingle with the campfire smoke sticking to my sweatshirt.

"You don't *need* it, no. But I want you to have it."

"It's a little cut. There's nothing wrong with me driving myself to the hospital."

"Some rational people would disagree."

"*I* am a rational person."

I glance at her hand, braced in mine. It feels as delicate as it did when I helped her into that boat, except this time, it's leaking blood. A hand as nice as this one shouldn't have a gash like that.

Eliza's a smart fucking woman. But what she did? That was putting-diesel-in-a-gas-engine stupid.

"Need I remind you that you just tried shucking an oyster *for the first time* without a glove or towel, which is the first, most basic step to the process?"

I'm not an idiot. It isn't good practice to insult a person after apologizing to them. But what the hell was she thinking?

Her tongue swipes across her lips. "You said on the tour that the blade's supposed to have dull edges. I didn't think it was a big deal."

"I also said to always use a glove or a towel, then proceeded to use a glove for the demo." Which she's too bright to forget.

"There wasn't one handy."

"Should've been." Steve must've taken the towel with him when he left the table. "Why didn't you ask someone?"

"Amanda was off getting something from her car."

"There are plenty of other team members out there."

"I don't know them well enough to interrupt their conversations."

Because I made sure she didn't know them at *all,* back when she started.

More guilt piles on to the Everest-sized mountain in my gut. It comes out as frustration. "Then why didn't you ask me?"

Her mouth forms a rueful smile. "Sure, Grayson. Let me give you another thing to rag on me for, because you can't find enough on your own." Her voice lowers into a piss-poor imitation of a man as she says, "Don't know how to shuck oysters, Boston? They didn't teach you how to find a towel yourself up in the city?"

I'd laugh at how terrible her impression is, except I'm caught up in the sting behind it. Her exhale stutters out and her expression flattens.

"It's okay to not know how to do something." I say it gently, because right now, it seems like the wrong combination of words could make her crack.

"It is, when you're not fighting daily to gain the respect you deserve."

The pool game at Dyl's, playing basketball last weekend —it all rushes back. Both times, I'd *dared* her to play. Not to embarrass her, but because she seemed lonely and it rubbed me the wrong way. I wanted to give her something to do. Something that could replace that loneliness with a triumphant smile or that ball-busting attitude.

And I guess teasing is more in my nature than saying something like that straight.

She's always so confident. I never once thought she was saying yes because of some absurd pressure to *prove* herself.

"I do res—"

"Hey, Eliza! Been looking for you!"

Amanda's voice booms through the warehouse, cutting me off. Eliza's hand flinches, like there's some instinct to pull away. Like she's been caught revealing parts of herself she's not supposed to.

I don't release her.

Looking over my shoulder at Amanda's shadow, I call out, "Can you go get Martha? Eliza cut her hand open. Might need stitches."

"Oh, crap! Sure—be right back."

I turn back and level Eliza with my gaze. "Here are your two options. Either I'm driving you to the ER, or you'll let Martha, who's an ER nurse, fix you up."

Her forehead knits. "Or, option three, I can drive myself to the ER."

I'm not one of those men who gets off on controlling women. People can make their own decisions. But I'll slice my own hand open before I let Eliza get into a driver's seat right now.

"You need two hands to drive, and one of them is out of commission." She hasn't gotten woozy yet, but fainting from the sight of blood isn't a non-possibility. "You're not driving yourself," I state, not caring one bit that I sound domineering. "I'll take you. Or, you can get someone else to drive you. That's your option three."

Her sigh breathes fire. "I really do not like you right now, Grayson."

"That implies you *have* liked me, and will like me again."

Her tongue darts out over her lips. They're supple and smooth with a little shine, like she's wearing lip balm.

Kissable.

I'm too aware of how easy it'd be to test that theory. Kneeling before her, I'm situated between her knees, my fingers wrapped around her hand. She's leaning toward me again, her braids dangling, close enough to see every detail of the long lashes swooping away from her eyes and the streaks of gold slicing through her olive irises.

"Were you put here to annoy me?" she murmurs, but it lacks her usual bite.

"Are you really that annoyed?"

Something flickers in her hazel eyes—until a commotion at the warehouse's entrance interrupts us.

She straightens as Amanda bustles over with Martha, an older woman I've practically known since birth. I recognize the small purple kit in her hand, all too familiar with it myself. The thing must be twenty years old at this point.

She's stitched me up four times now. Anson, maybe twice. Dawson, probably ten. Consequences of her living next door to three wild brothers, and having a damn soft touch to boot. Even as adults, we've always preferred going to her than waiting hours at the ER for a tired doctor to jab you with a needle and the front desk to slap you with a two-thousand-dollar bill.

Plus, visits to Martha always come with cookies.

She tuts when she's close enough to see the blood-stained paper towel. "What have we got here?"

Amanda peeks over my shoulder. "What the hell did you cut yourself with?"

Eliza's chest heaves a tired breath.

"Some idiot dropped the shucking knife into the sand-wich platter," I say, answering for her. "There wasn't enough light over there for her to see it. Sliced her hand right open."

Eliza's eyes clash with mine, flaring in surprise. The corner of her mouth twitches, and I know covering for her was the right call.

"I think the word *idiot* is too kind for whoever did that," Amanda says matter-of-factly.

Martha's kit clatters against the table, and she nods at Eliza's hand. "Put it here on the table. Let me see what we've got."

For the first time in—hell, I don't know—ten minutes, my fingers peel away from her palm. The feel of her skin lingers on mine, like holding her for so long has imprinted it there.

Martha puts on her glasses and hunches over, inspecting the wound as I stand, hovering over them. "I think you can get away with glue. It's fairly deep, but not terrible." She straightens, all five-foot-two of her. "I can do it here, right now."

"I don't want to ruin your night," Eliza defers.

"It takes ten seconds. It wouldn't ruin my night. But it'd probably ruin your night, and the night of whoever drives you, if you go to the hospital."

That's the other part of Martha—the unapologetic straight-shooter. I've started to think she makes those cookies just to soften her hard edges.

Eliza nods slowly. "Do it here." Her tone is threaded with nerves, and it doesn't take a genius to know why. She's the furthest thing from a wimp, but getting a medical-grade treatment outside of a medical facility, no matter how minor, is daunting.

"It wouldn't ruin my night to drive you," I find myself saying. "But if you'd prefer to do it here, it'll hurt way less than you think. I've given Martha plenty of practice over the years."

"Dawson even more so," Martha grumbles. "That's the most reckless boy I've ever met."

"Dawson?" Eliza asks.

"My little brother," I explain.

"Does he live around here, too?"

"God, no. He ran off as soon as he could—couldn't stand Garnet Shores. He's in Ohio now, playing professional soccer." *As long as he can keep his dick in his pants and his image clean.*

Eliza hums thoughtfully. "Seems I'm not the only one who can't stand to be in your presence."

I bark a laugh. Leave it to her to let loose something like that. She's more invested than anyone I know in having a polished, respectable reputation, but I'm not included in that equation.

I wouldn't want to be.

"That's because I set the bar too high for him."

"Think you have your directions mixed up there, Grayson." She turns to Amanda. "Are you sure he's qualified to steer boats?"

Amanda bursts into a laugh that she quickly tries to rein in. "Sorry, Boss." She raises a hand and turns away. "Not laughing."

There's a lightness in Eliza's face when she faces me again. "I'm good. Let's do it here."

Amanda slowly backs toward the entrance. "Not that I don't support you or anything, but I might pass out if I watch. I'll have a drink waiting for you when you're done."

As Martha sets up her tools, I debate whether I should stay or take off like Amanda. Eliza's gone mute, latching onto the tube of glue as Martha snaps gloves on her hands and palms a saline solution.

On her list of people to comfort her, I'm not at the top. I'm not even on the list. If there *is* a list I'm on, it's for people she'd keep out of the room or run over with a car.

But she hasn't dismissed me, and I'm certain she would have if that's what she wanted. She isn't afraid to tell me to fuck off.

She might, however, be too proud to ask me to stay.

Martha tears open a sterile syringe, and Eliza's free hand slaps onto the edge of her seat, squeezing in anticipation.

Decision made.

Braced for rejection, I offer my hand. It's enough to make her unglue her eyes from the syringe being filled with saline. Questions swirl in her startled gaze, but none of them seem to scream *what the fuck are you doing?*

"This is your chance to break the bones in my hand," I say lightly. "Might just turn your night around."

She peeks at Martha, who's preparing to clean the wound. Eliza's free hand shoots into mine.

And I know I made the right call.

Words of comfort might feel patronizing, so I shove them down and say nothing as Martha works. Just let Eliza squeeze the ever-living shit out of my hand.

She's got one hell of a grip, too. Must be all the typing and phone-holding.

Her face twists, a hiss escaping as Martha flushes the wound, then another when she pinches the cut closed, but she takes it all like a champ. By the time Martha's covering it with a bandage, her death grip has eased.

But Eliza's hand doesn't drop. Her fingers stay tangled with mine as Martha cleans up and rattles off after-care instructions.

Either she forgot, or she still needs the comfort.

Whatever it is, my nerve endings don't care. They're too busy absorbing the feel of her silky skin against mine, which suddenly feels criminally rough.

Maybe I should use some lotion. Do I even own lotion?

Why the fuck am I thinking about lotion?

"Let me give you my number in case you have any problems," Martha says.

Eliza's hand slips away to her phone, and I shove my empty hand in my pocket so it won't try to find an excuse to touch her again. She types in her number, and Martha heads back to the cookout, leaving us alone again.

I jerk my chin toward Eliza's phone, which she's putting away. "Put mine in, too."

She pauses.

"In case Martha doesn't answer," I explain. It feels like crossing a line, the invisible marker that keeps us on opposing sides, so I add, "Or in case you come up with a creative insult and can't wait until you see me to share."

"It's just glue. I'll be fine." But she opens a new contact anyway. When I'm done rattling off my number, her eyes spark. "What makes you think I'm even thinking about you in my off-time, Grayson?"

"You're a planner, Boston. Wouldn't surprise me if you map out all your witty little comebacks on Sundays," I say.

But it's a cover-up for my gut response.

Because I find myself thinking about you.

More than I should.

17

———

ELIZA

SOME BILLIONAIRE MUST BE PAYING off the sky in Garnet Shores, because another pristine sunrise is putting on a show above the salt pond.

It's so magnificently vibrant, every single garnet hue shows through the screen of my phone as I film it from the farm's dock. The dew-damp wood soaks through my jeans as I sit, cross-legged, but it's an easy sacrifice.

This isn't a sunrise to snap a picture of and walk away. It's one to savor.

And savoring is slowly becoming my new favorite hobby.

The long, relaxed morning swims. The sound of water softly splashing against the boats and docks when I wake. The salt-tinged air that comes with skies like this. Little details that have gradually woven themselves into my life and feel like a warm, weighted blanket over my constantly buzzing brain.

It feels indulgent to savor them. Like it's distracting me from...*me.* My success. My forward progress. The next thing I should be doing.

But in about two months, I'll be hustling my butt off again. Sunrises will be replaced by early morning getting-ahead emails, quiet drives will become busy subway commutes, and those long, open swims will be a solid hour-drive away. So maybe a little savoring is okay for now. Besides, it's not like I'm being lazy. I drove here before dawn to film the sunrise for part of this week's content.

The farm is still quiet by the time the colors of dawn fade and I push to my feet. It's Monday, so the warehouse and docks will be whirring with activity within an hour or two. For now, though, it's completely peaceful.

Soaking in the blissful quiet, I head to the warehouse to film while no one's there. But as I approach the massive sliding door at the back, it isn't quiet anymore. There's—is that...

Grunting?

The scrape of metal comes a few beats later, and then another low rumble of noise.

I only hear it because the door, which should be locked, is cracked open—just enough for a body to slip through.

All that peaceful savoring flips on its head, and my heart gallops into a fast drum. *Oh, crap. Has someone broken in?*

I peer through the cracked door, but a pile of red crates blocks my view of the far corner, where the noise seems to be coming from. Fingers tightening around my phone, I silently slip inside. My goal isn't to be a hero, but to confirm the crime, slip out, and make the necessary phone calls.

But when I creep to the stacked crates and my vision wraps around the side, the only crime occurring is Grayson slapping my eyeballs with the sight of him doing shirtless pushups on the concrete floor.

And then *I'm* the criminal, because I don't jerk away or close my eyes.

I *stare.*

I stare at the sinews rolling in his corded arms as he brings his chest to the floor and pushes up. I stare at the thick muscles of his abdomen as he stands, bulging with every breath. I stare at the backwards baseball cap holding his short, sweat-licked waves as he starts squatting, oblivious to my presence.

My body has been possessed by a horny, muscle-starved spirit, and for the life of me, I cannot look away.

"Quack."

I jump, ramming the side of my body into the crates.

No no no no no.

I lunge behind them, spinning to see Dave. He quacks again for good measure, then ruffles his wings smugly as he waddles around the crates, toward the man I just visually assaulted.

The man whose footsteps are heading my way, judging by the rapid thud of his sneakers.

My phone almost slips from my hand as I whip it up, hit record, and start panning the camera around the wall of the warehouse. The blank, boring wall.

Dave, I'm going to kill you.

The footsteps stop just behind me. "You could just ask me to do pushups when you need a look." I don't need to turn to know he's smirking. "Don't need to take a video to save for later."

The amusement in his deep voice rankles me. Or maybe it's the fact that I just openly gawked at him. Either way, I let that rankling into my voice as I say, "Believe it or not, you're not the most interesting thing in this warehouse."

"You're telling me that blank fucking wall in front of you is interesting?"

Calmly, I finish panning the camera to the door that I

never should have entered. When I turn around, my focus is strictly on Grayson's face, which glistens with sweat. Sweat I should find repulsive, but don't, for some certifiable reason.

"It's a behind-the-scenes thing. People like taking a peek behind the curtain."

"Just like you." He glances at the stack of crates. "Though I guess it's more of a wall than a curtain."

His expression is as smug as Dave's stupid little waddle, and I berate myself for wearing a scoop-necked shirt, because a blush is crawling up my collarbone and neck.

I want to pretend I'm blushing from frustration, or anger at his audacity to think he's so mesmerizing. But I can't, because even now, as I'm fighting for my ego's survival, I'm thinking about how Kyle couldn't hold a candle to him. We'd worked out together from time to time, and while he was in shape, it was always so...curated. Stiff. His muscles were shaped for looks, not function. Looks he cared so much about, he'd never wear a backwards hat because it would mess up his coiffed hair.

Grayson Gold is anything but coiffed and curated.

And while I've known this since the moment I met him, right now, it's laid bare right in front of my face, and it's pricking at unbidden biological things low in my belly.

Knowing I have no good defense, I turn to insults. "You're awfully full of yourself."

"Now, that's a mean thing to say, Boston."

"Didn't realize your feelings are so delicate."

"If they were delicate, you'd have run me off by now." He angles his head, planting his hands on his hips.

My eyes ache to track those hands, but I don't let them, because I know what lines and dips they'd find, and they'll want to cling there like the little traitors they are.

Grayson innocently continues, "It's just that I'm going to do something very nice for you today, and you might feel bad about being mean when you find out what it is."

My eyes narrow. "You, doing something nice, for me?"

The corner of his mouth hikes up. "Yes. Though you'll be devastated to know it involves me fully clothed."

"Thank god," I blurt.

He chuckles and backs away. "Be ready at seven-thirty, sharp."

"For..."

"You're coming out with me."

I blink. "A ride-along?"

"Yep." At the corner of the crates, he winks. "Thought you might want to appreciate my presence up-close for the day."

Then he disappears around the crates that are the same shade as my cheeks before I can come up with a desperately needed retort.

I turn all my annoyance to Dave, who wandered back and is happily sitting on the floor, wings tucked in tight.

"You know, people eat duck," I tell him.

"*Quack.*"

———

AS PROMISED, Grayson is fully clothed when I meet him at the dock. He has a new ball cap on, one with a sports team logo, spun forward to shade his face from the early morning sun. His hair is wet, strands heavy against his forehead like he's just come from a shower. Loose waders that were once a bright orange but are now stained with dark splotches match the bundle in his hands, which he holds out to me.

"Suit up," he orders.

I glance down at my outfit. Old sweatshirt, five-year-old-jeans, sandals already stained from last week's coffee incident. It's grungier than my usual work outfit, but at four-thirty in the morning, all I wanted was comfy, well-worn clothes.

"It's fine if these get a little dirty."

He shakes the bibs persistently. "It's brisk this morning. Your clothes won't dry quickly if they get wet, and we're not coming back here until I've done what I need to."

Giving in, I take the pile of rubber, find the straps, and shake it out. "Didn't realize this was going to be a waterpark ride."

The bibs don't have boots attached like his, but they're still heavy. Careful not to disturb the cut in my hand, I try to figure out which side is the front.

The weight is suddenly removed from my hands as Grayson takes the bibs back. He flips them around. "You say it like you don't like waterparks."

"I don't like the idea of paying a hundred dollars to have my stomach flung into my throat," I say as he squats in front of me, the bibs' legs pooling on the dock.

"Well lucky for you, this ride's free. Technically, you're getting paid." He jerks his chin toward his hands. "Now hop in."

"I can dress myself." Says the woman who couldn't tell the difference between the front and the back.

Instead of pointing this out, Grayson says, "You're injured. Can't have you tripping and falling onto that hand." He inclines his head and adds, "Liability and all that."

"My hand is fine," I argue, but lift my right foot anyway,

aiming for the hole. My foot lands on a pile of fabric, the bib leg bunched beneath it.

"Lift your foot a little. Yeah, there." He drops the straps and gathers the fabric trapped beneath my foot. My standing ankle wobbles. "Hold onto my shoulder."

My eyes roll, and I'm about to tell him I'm fine when my ankle shakes again. Yoga's never really been for me—too slow, too zen—but I'm quickly reevaluating its relevance, because my balance is apparently *dismal.*

His sweatshirt is a soft, thin cushion against his rock-hard shoulder as I give him my weight. He steers the bib over one foot, then the other, moving deftly like he's done this before. Like he's practiced with soft touches and attentive care, despite having such rough hands.

It must be from helping raise Lala.

The image of him swinging her around on the farm comes to mind, and just like that, my inner cavewoman activates.

"You're good." Grayson's voice is low and soft. He's looking at me again, face just inches from mine as I lean on his shoulder. If I shifted my weight, my lips would meet his, which I'm now paying attention to for the first time. They're surprisingly smooth amid all that coarse facial hair.

It's a dangerous combination—his blend of rough masculinity and composure.

Overhead, a seagull squawks, pulling me back to the feel of my feet on the dock, the bibs bunched around my calves, the fact that I'm *staring at his mouth* like it holds the answers to life.

I jerk upright, and he smoothly stands with me, pulling the bibs up as he goes. His toes come to mine as he slips the straps over my shoulders, and his head lowers as he focuses on tightening the first strap. The scents of soap and a warm, salty musk mingle in my nostrils. A musk my brain has categorized as "Grayson" at some point, because as I stand here with my nose practically in his ear, it smells...familiar.

Fitting.

Nice.

Really nice.

Grayson shifts to my other side, fingertips tickling my shoulder as he toys with the clip. This close, I realize his eyelashes are darker than his hair. Maybe that dark contrast is why his eyes appear so gold.

He backs away and studies his handiwork. "They're a little big on you, but you should be okay."

I feel like that white, puffy tire mascot with rubber billowing around my waist and thighs. Except I'm neon orange.

"Wasn't expecting to be walking in a fashion show this morning," I joke.

Mom would have a heart attack if she saw this. Maybe even send me to a psychiatrist to figure out what could be so wrong with me that I've chosen this over pantsuits in a nice, clean office.

"You make us all look bad, Boston. We've got to tone you down sometimes." The skiff gently rocks beneath him as he steps on and extends a hand. His gaze roves over my face as he murmurs, "Though I don't think that's even possible."

Words stall in my throat, because this isn't a dig. It's a sliver of soft honesty that sounds a lot like a compliment, like Grayson thinks I'm—I don't know—

I slap my hand into his so abruptly, his brows raise. But I desperately need to stop this overthinking before it jumps to conclusions—especially when those conclusions are the type to make my chest flutter.

He helps me in, and I busy my brain with filming as we set out on the water.

The docks are far behind us when Grayson's voice floats over the soft hum of the engine. "Haven't seen you here this early before."

"Wanted to capture the sunrise from the farm," I explain, cutting my video and cradling my phone against my thighs. "Plus, no morning swims for the next week, thanks to this." I hold up my bandaged hand.

Day three into my water ban, and I already miss it.

Funny, considering I hadn't thought about swimming once in the last few years before coming to Garnet Shores. Swimming had been bucketed with water balloon fights, real campfires, and nights spent video calling friends until two in the morning. Childhood. The good ol' times. The pieces of you that a successful adulthood requires leaving behind.

Yet here I am, now, arms aching to power through the water.

It must be something to do with routine. A few weeks of starting my days with a swim, and my body's come to expect it.

"You ever try swimming at the town beach?" Grayson throws the question over his shoulder. When I cock my head curiously, he continues. "I see you swimming out here some mornings. But there's a local group that swims at the town beach every day."

Here I was, thinking my swims were private. I rarely saw a soul, save for the occasional small boat beelining it for the channel. "Are you stalking me, Grayson?"

I catch a flash of white teeth before he turns back to his post. "No. I was just mighty curious when I saw a giant, awkward-looking fish flopping around in the distance a few weeks ago. Got my binoculars out and discovered it was you."

"Yet you still let this giant, awkward-looking fish catch your attention in the mornings."

"You're out there swimming solo. Someone's got to make sure you don't drown." His tone is cast in humor, but the words themselves aren't.

"Have you been worrying about me?" The question doesn't contain the snark it should.

"If you drowned, Anson would think it was me."

"That's your own fault."

"Which is why I'm trying to prevent the scenario altogether," he counters, before the engine's hum settles over us again.

A few minutes later, the cages appear in the distance, a field of dark, boxy shapes bobbing on the water's surface.

Grayson speaks again. "Your form is solid."

"Thought you said I was flopping around."

I get another flash of his strong profile, enough for me to see the lines crinkling by his eyes. "Your form is solid for an awkward fish," he clarifies.

We both know that's not true. "I was on the swim team in high school," I find myself saying. "Competed at States and everything. Used to be a lot faster than I am now."

"What happened?"

I shrug. "I just stopped."

"Why?"

Isn't it obvious? "I grew up. More responsibilities. Other priorities."

He scoffs. "Boston, there are fifty-year-olds in that swim group at the beach. They're a lot more grown up than you, they've got kids to worry about, mortgages to pay, and they're still showing up every morning. They just make swimming into one of their priorities because it feels good."

Whether he means to or not, his point prods at me. It's the ignorance in it. The obtuse disregard for what I really mean.

Or is it the fact that it's true?

"How long did Martha put you out for?" he asks.

"Ten days." Which means I'm in for some boring early morning runs. At least it'll increase my basketball stamina, if I'm ever bored and desperate enough to stare down a net again.

"There's these special waterproof patches you could use," he informs me, gently turning the boat. "They don't let anything through."

I nod, because I'm sure there are. Special order, probably.

Our conversation ends there as Grayson pulls up to the shallower side of the farm, cuts the engine, and secures the boat.

As he hops in, the water just below his chest, I can't help but toy with the idea of spending a Saturday driving somewhere for an open-water swim when I'm back in the city. It would probably be the highlight of my week.

Then swimming becomes the last thing on my mind, because for the next two hours, I watch Grayson work his farm—harvesting oysters, hauling gear around, analyzing his product. And he doesn't slow. Doesn't take breaks. Just works with capable hands and muscles I know are flexing beneath his baggy sweatshirt and waterproof gear. There's an occasional grunt when he jerks something into place, or heaves a heavy cage up into the skiff, which rocks with the weight.

All I can do is try to ignore everything stirring at the sight of this man doing his physical job, and doing it well.

Kyle was a spreadsheet wiz. Capable with a laptop, knew algorithms like the back of his hand. But seeing him at his laptop did nothing for me. It was as stimulating as seeing a squirrel.

This is different. It's inciting that strangely sweet tightening in my belly, the same sensation I felt when I saw him earlier in the warehouse.

This is...this is *hot*.

I tell myself it's biology. A reaction to witnessing physical capability. The animal wiring that attracts you to your best chance of survival.

But the thing is, I don't think it would be nearly as hot if it was anyone other than Grayson.

18

GRAYSON

JOY JUST DELIVERED a platter of her homemade cinnamon buns. Anson informed me this morning that we're clear of the vibrio case. And Dawson has officially kept his name out of the news—and therefore his dick in his pants—for three weeks in a row.

In short, it's a hell of a good day.

Doesn't matter that the first heat wave of summer has hit and I'm sweating my ass off. A new problem will inevitably arise tomorrow, so I'm taking the opportunity to fully bask in today's good fortune. Which is why I'm whistling under my breath like I'm JJ when I make my way to the warehouse for lunch and catch Eliza coming out of the front office.

A flowy, denim dress flounces against her thighs as she strides across the lot. Her hair's in a pile on top of her head, the kind that's supposed to look lazy but shows off the long, elegant lines of her neck. The straps at her shoulders are thin. Dainty. Way too dainty for a workplace like this, yet she doesn't look one bit out of place.

Her forehead's pinched, lips pressed together as I

approach. It's her focus face. The summa-cum-laude expression that suggests some kind of genius is turning over in her mind. I watch it melt into soft curiosity when I get close enough for her to notice.

Not long ago, it would've been wariness. Displeasure. An expression armed for war.

I don't miss that.

"Got something for you in my truck," I call over to her, gesturing for her to follow me. My truck's parked alone in the lot's far corner, under the shade of a giant oak.

She eyes it suspiciously, even as she follows me. "You planning to kidnap me?"

I give her a once-over, noticing a plain, thin gold chain around her neck. She's a sight in a baggy sweatshirt and worn jeans. In a simple dress like this, delicate chain links resting on her collarbone, she's point-blank pretty.

Pretty in a way that makes a schoolboy crush on a girl, or makes you halt mid-conversation on the street because it takes your breath away. The same way that makes it near impossible to look at anything but her right now.

"I already told you my stance on kidnapping you. That cute dress isn't fooling anyone, Boston. You'd rip a kidnapper apart."

From the smug tilt to her lips, this pleases her. "Scared of little old me?"

"Not scared," I correct, though her scathing mouth might make other men run—like idiots at a bar looking for an easy one-nighter, or who think late-night drinks make a respectable second date. "Just picking my battles."

"That implies you think you can win some."

"It does."

There's a spark in her eyes as she replies, "Well, I won't be offering any tissues when you don't."

"That's why I have Dave," I supply. "He's my emotional support duck when mean out-of-towners like you come in and beat me down."

She snorts. "Yeah, well, your emotional support duck is incredibly violent. I wouldn't have cut myself if it weren't for him."

"Now hang on a second. You didn't tell me Dave stole the towel you were going to use."

She pins me with a droll look. "He *quacked*."

I blink. "He's a duck."

"He's a duck who snuck up on me, waited until I was prying the shell open, and released the loudest quack I've ever heard." She rubs her bandaged hand, like she's reliving the experience, and grumbles, "It was entirely pre-meditated."

I can't help but laugh. "Boston, you jumped him on your first day. Not a great way to start a relationship." Her mouth opens to protest, probably something about how sorely I started *our* relationship. But I'm already swinging my truck door open and reaching inside. "Besides, he brought you a peace offering."

I swipe the small box from the passenger seat and hold it out. She regards it like mystery meat, so I explain, "They're the waterproof patches I was telling you about. Had a few extra at home that I don't need right now."

She doesn't say anything as she takes the box and turns it over, so my words keep on coming. "I always put a little piece of gauze along the wound, then seal it on with the patch. Never had a problem. Dawson's used them for years to cover new tattoos when he's doing cold-plunges or hot soaks for recovery."

I stop there, because anything more would be rambling, and I'm not a rambler.

But Eliza's silence is starting to make me question if I've just crossed a line. If I was wrong in telling myself this is a no-big-deal act of decency.

Yesterday's ride-along didn't raise any of these doubts. I'd wanted to do it, but even if I hadn't, I would have eventually *needed* to for her work.

This little favor can't hide behind the same excuse.

But Eliza doesn't call it out. "Your duck went into your bathroom, opened a cabinet, and grabbed these for me?"

My lips wobble. "Yes."

"You have an indoor duck?"

"He sleeps inside so he doesn't get eaten by anything, but he's got free reign of the farm and my yard during the day."

Her head slowly shakes. "How did you even *get* a pet duck? Who does that?"

"I didn't *get* him." Consciously deciding to purchase a pet duck would be strange. "I found him on the farm a few years ago as a duckling with a broken leg. I nursed him back to health, and he's never left my side since."

I'm not an idiot who thinks he can domesticate any wild animal that stumbles into his yard. I tried multiple times to set Dave free, but he kept on coming back, and when winter came, I didn't have the heart to stick him outside in single-digit temperatures. I'm not a duck murderer. So now I'm a duck...landlord?

Anson thinks the little guy sees me as his mother.

"Well," Eliza says, soft smile playing on her lips, "I don't think Dave has the hands needed to open a bathroom cabinet. So thank *you*."

I dip my chin in acknowledgement and close the door. She's quiet as she falls into step beside me, and I find myself speaking again.

"Not sure if you heard, but Joy dropped off some of her cinnamon rolls this morning," I tell her. "The team's probably digging in right now. We should grab some before they're gone."

That pulls her attention from the box, lips parting like I just told her Martha Stewart's our own personal chef today. Again, she makes me wonder if I'm doing too much.

Nothing I wouldn't do for anyone else on the team.

Joy's cinnamon rolls are so damn good, they can send a sinner to heaven. Plus, from what I can tell, Eliza always eats by herself in the main office. Maybe that's her preference, or maybe it's a circumstance I forced her into.

"What would your team think if this mean out-of-towner came and stole their cinnamon rolls?"

"Not stealing if you have permission."

"*Permission,*" she repeats derisively. "See, having your *permission* actually makes those cinnamon rolls less enticing."

My head wobbles in a slow shake. "No way you're a rule-breaker, Boston."

Her head's on straighter than a ruler. I'm no rebel like Dawson, but I was known to toe the line growing up. Trespassing into the old power plant two towns over, sneaking into the middle school gym at night to make out with a crush, ignoring homework and using a polite smile to get away with it. Fun, harmless adolescent stuff.

"I'm not a rule-breaker," she admits easily, then points at me with the box. "But you don't make my rules, Grayson. Your big brother does." She halts, stopping me in my tracks. With the coyness of a Cheshire cat, she finishes, "And he said nothing about taking the rest of the cinnamon rolls from you."

One second, she's standing beside me. The next, she's

all billowing skirts and maniacal laughter as she races toward the warehouse.

For a second, I let her go, watching in disbelief because there's no way she just pulled a Lala on me. Then my ass kicks into gear, and I race after her.

The owner of this farm, racing across his parking lot like a kid at recess who wants his stolen cookie back. Except I'm not running to beat her to the pastries in that warehouse. Cinnamon buns aren't on my mind at all. Just this woman, who I'm hearing laugh with pure joy for the first time ever, and who is running way faster than she should be able to in those cute sandals.

Eliza might be a little speed demon, but my legs are longer than hers. Twenty feet from the warehouse, I catch up with her.

"Hope you weren't looking forward to those," she pants.

"Oh, no you don't, city girl."

I don't even think as I lunge and sling my arms around her waist. With a heave, I swing her up and around, plopping her on her feet behind me. Her mouth pops open in an astonished "O," and it's only then that I realize what I just did.

And it doesn't feel remotely wrong.

If it did, I'd be dropping her like hot coals. Instead, I keep my hands planted on the curve of her waist, a captivating combination of soft and athletic beneath my palms. Feminine and strong. Her hands find my forearms as she steadies herself.

I wait for her to shove me away, but she doesn't. Her mouth just opens wider, and another laugh sings out. A laugh I'm responsible for.

"That is *so* not fair, you cheater!"

"How am I a cheater?"

"*Because*," she jabs a finger at my chest. "You can't just use your muscles to win a race!"

Like they've been summoned, the muscles in my hands flex, gripping her waist tighter. "Now, *that's* not fair," I admonish. "You're a hell of an adversary, Boston. Can't strip me of all of my weapons."

Her hand finds my arm again, all the confirmation I need that I'm not doing something wrong. I inhale the warm, flowery notes of her perfume, my voice dropping an octave as I say, "And if yesterday morning was any indication, I know how much you appreciate these weapons in particular."

Her attempt to play it off had been as skillful as Lala feeding Dave her vegetables and pretending she's eaten them. And the hint of sunburn on her cheekbones isn't doing anything to hide the blush creeping over her face.

"Well—"

"Hey!" Mark's gravelly voice cuts the moment like a knife. Eliza and I drop each other, jerking apart like two teens caught kissing under the bleachers.

Jesus.

I twist to see Mark stalking past, wearing a scowl despite the cinnamon bun in his hand. Pretty much everyone here has warmed up to Eliza, except for him. He hasn't offered to plot her murder since that first day, but his glowering avoidance whenever she's around makes it damn obvious how he feels.

"You took too long. There's only one left," he hollers. It's accusatory, like I've been picking flowers all morning instead of working.

Kenny exits the warehouse then, demonstrating exactly how thirty-five cinnamon rolls have managed to already get eaten down by twelve people. He's stuffing one in his mouth and carrying two in his hands when he spots us, eyes flaring in urgency.

"Hey Boss!" His voice is muffled by cinnamon bun as he jogs over. "Amanda wanted me to tell you—the tour schedule just got crazy. Got a waitlist of, like, twenty groups." He breaks for another bite of cinnamon roll. "She's gonna need help coordinating."

My brows slam together. "We never have a waitlist."

He shrugs. "We do now."

Our farm tours do well, but we price them high so they're actually worth our time, which means we usually have a few unfilled slots each week. Anson's been wanting to fill them in—not just for the money, which is a decent supplement to our usual operations, but for the publicity, too. If what Kenny says is true, this is the kind of news that can produce one of Anson's rare smiles.

It also makes no sense. Our last magazine piece came out months ago. We haven't had any recent big breaks that should cause a spike like this.

When I say that out loud, Kenny draws out a long "Ohhh" that flashes way too much of the soggy mush in his mouth. "Here, Boss." He reaches into his back pocket and pulls out his phone. "Forgot you don't have socials."

Socials? I glance at Eliza, who's studying something in the distance, then lean in to see his screen.

The first thing I see is a pan over the Gold's Oysters sign—a professional cut I've seen leading one of Eliza's videos before. Except this time, it doesn't fade into a bag of oysters or a panorama of the farm.

It cuts to a shot of *me*.

A close-up of my hands showing off a few mature oysters during a farm tour.

A distance shot of me hauling a bin of ice and oysters off a skiff.

A side angle of me pulling off my hat to wipe the sweat from my forehead.

Another closeup of my hands working to open an oyster, my sweatshirt sleeves shoved up to bare my forearms.

The whole time, clean, little white letters are splayed across the top of each frame: *Reason no. 23 you should book that tour of Gold's Oysters.*

"Oh, shit, forgot the music," Kenny mumbles. He presses the side of his phone, and the slow, easy melody of a James Taylor tune floats over the images. The song is way too fucking casual and innocent for what Eliza Attleburn has done.

It only gets worse when Kenny's dirty thumb taps over the comments. "The women have gone wild for you, man. Amanda said she's getting calls from bachelorette parties."

Drooling emojis. Heart eyes. Some woman named Linda wants to *take a tour of the oyster FARMER.*

I tear myself away from the screen before I read whatever the fuck *Rachel* said that got her one-thousand-nineteen likes, and set my sights on the woman at the center of this all.

Her jaw is twitching like she's trying to hold in laughter. She doesn't look nearly as sheepish as she should, never mind apologetic.

No. Eliza Attleburn's hazel eyes dance with conspiratorial light as she crosses her arms and stands there like she didn't just turn me into a schedule-flooding *thirst trap.*

"Ken, I need a word with our Social Media Director."

I don't wait for a response. Stiff steps start taking me to the front office, because if I stand by that phone any longer,

I don't know what I'll do. For once, Eliza's silent as she tracks behind me, showing just how smart she is.

Or maybe that's survival instinct.

The hum of the office's air conditioning greets me when I swing the door open. I hold it for her before closing it with a softness I don't feel.

"Let me explain," she says calmly, hands up like she's talking to a rabid dog.

I settle my hands on my hips and glare at her, molars grinding.

"Anson told me one of his goals was to fill our tours. Your visitors are mostly men, so we needed a way to attract a female demographic, too."

My jaw is locked, letting her marinate in my pissed-off silence.

"This strategy *clearly* worked," she tries.

When I remain quiet, she shifts on her feet and sighs. "They can't even see your face. No one knows it's you, and it's just a few clips of you doing your job. The music was tame, and so was the caption. The fact that the women went feral has nothing to do with me."

"You're way too fucking smart to actually think that." The words burst out of me, though I keep them low. The outrage in my tone does more than any volume would.

What it's supposed to do, though, I'm not sure. Because Eliza doesn't balk or start apologizing. I swear, her spine straightens instead as she leans back against the desk and crosses her arms. "I passed it by Anson, who loved it. And before you tell me it turned your farm into a gimmick, it hasn't. It was tasteful, fun, and showed a little personality that consumers appreciate. And, as I said, it *worked.*"

I can't fucking argue that last point, and that just strings me tighter. "You knew I wasn't going to like this."

"I did."

She doesn't even *try* to deny it. And she doesn't sound the least bit sorry.

My body thrums, and I take two big steps toward her. Crowding her. Close enough for that damn perfume to tickle my nose as she cranes to look at me.

"You knew I wasn't going to like this," I repeat, annunciating slowly, "and you did it anyway."

"Just like you knew I wasn't going to like you leaving without me last Monday."

My frustration sputters for a moment. "I thought we were past that."

Friday's cookout had felt like a turning point. An end to the war. And yesterday's ride-along had been easy. Fun, even. Hell, I've been looking forward to our next one, more than I should.

"We are *now*," she clarifies. "But I published this post last week."

After I'd ditched her.

No fucking way.

"This was, what? Revenge?"

"Revenge? Now that'd be unprofessional," she croons innocently.

The bullshit is so obvious, there's no need to call it out.

Eliza Attleburn, straight-and-narrow professional that she is, used her job to get *revenge* on me. That should piss me off even more, just like her playing coy.

But all my hot ire twists into something else that has me stepping in *again*, closer to that perfume, closer to that face tilted up at me in challenge. Closer to this smart, ballsy woman who meets me at every step.

"You're real pleased with yourself, aren't you?" The question rumbles out of my chest.

A dare.

When those smooth, pink lips curve into a smirk, I move in. My hands hit the oak desk on either side of her thighs, my face coming inches from hers.

Her smirk wobbles, nostrils flaring on a quick intake of breath. But she doesn't lean away. She sets those shoulders tighter and leans *in*.

Fuck.

"I'm incredibly pleased with the results." Her breath brushes across my skin as her eyes flick between mine, long pretty lashes deceptively innocent around the hot challenge in her gaze. Then, Eliza being Eliza, she takes it fucking one step further.

Her tongue slips out, licking her top lip and dragging my attention with it. "You should be pleased, too. Tours are good."

It's a visceral effort not to close the distance and stop that smart mouth with my own. Then all that desire shoots straight to my cock, which is eager to help with that effort.

The smooth skin of her thighs taunt my fingertips, splayed inches away at the edge of the desk. A desk that's old and sturdy enough to fuck someone over, hard and good.

Fuck.

My brain is two fragile seconds away from thinking about flipping this pretty little dress up and seeing exactly what smart words her mouth is capable of with my fingers playing on her pussy and my cock driving into her.

Would she be into that? Her face is still an inch from mine, thrumming with enough heat to suggest she—

A car door slams outside, and those thoughts shatter like a sheet of ice. All at once, I'm aware of the wide-open windows. My team working out back. The giant parking lot right next to us.

I shove back from the desk and take an extra step to where it's professionally acceptable to stand.

But the distance does nothing to cool the fire wisping through my veins. My voice is gravelly when I say, "You're right. Tours are good for the farm." I force myself to retreat to the door. "But they're good for your content, too. So you'll be coming with me, because I'm not suffering through a goddamn bachelorette party on my own."

I shove myself out into the muggy, hot air, waiting for shame or regret to sink in. Because now it's plain as day that no matter what I told myself when I grabbed those waterproof patches, I'm not treating Eliza like another team member.

I don't *want* to.

But the regret never comes.

19

ELIZA

"SO, tell me. What's it like driving to your own funeral?"

Kitty is on one. She's gone delirious from dehydration, ate too much candy on the trail, or tangoed with a bear and now, in her second chance at life, has decided to throw away her filter. Because there's no other reason she'd be making a joke like this when I am, in fact, delivering myself to my own demise.

Or maybe I'm being too sensitive and overblowing her attempt to make light of my predicament, because I'm stressed out of my mind.

Yep. That's probably it.

"I just hope you're planning a good eulogy for me," I reply, trying to lean into her humor.

I'm currently on my way to my little brother's commencement ceremony. James Attleburn is about to be a fancy Manhattan lawyer. I'll stand beside him, sun-tanned from the small-town oyster farm I've relegated myself to, and Mom and Dad will have ample opportunities to remind me of my layoff and criticize my decision to escape the city for the summer.

It's going to be oh-so-amusing.

Not.

At least I'm meeting up with Jane tomorrow. A bright spot in my weekend away.

"Who do you want invited to the after-party?" Kitty's voice isn't jumbled by poor service, for once.

"Jane, Sami, some of the other girls from college. Maybe some old high school friends," I throw out. It isn't a long list, but as long as Kitty's there, it's complete.

"Anyone from Garnet Shores?"

I huff out a laugh. "Well, Grayson might be pretty sad if he missed the best day of his life."

"I'm assuming Grayson's the dickhead oyster farmer."

My mouth opens to confirm, and that's as far as I get. Because it doesn't feel fair to make "dickhead" a permanent addendum to his name any more.

In fact, it feels dead wrong.

So I gently correct, "He's the oyster farmer."

"Either this backwoods California service is warping your voice, or you just said his name like you *like* him."

"I didn't say his name. I said he's the *oyster farmer.*"

"Don't use semantics to get out of this." There's a quick intake of breath on the line. "*And* you didn't deny it. Oh my god. How the tables have *turned.*"

"Okay. Slow down." I thought her ex-husband drained the hopeless romantic out of her, but apparently it's back. At my expense. "All I did was remove the 'dickhead.'"

"*Mm-hmmm.*"

I want to be annoyed, but I feel my cheeks pulling up instead. "Kit, you're jumping to conclusions."

"I hear a smile in your tone," she sing-songs, like she can see me through this phone screen. "You guys hook up?"

My hands slip on the wheel, and the car jerks in the

middle lane. *Oh my god.* Righting the sedan, I calmly say, "No."

But he looked at me like he wanted to.

And I wanted him to keep looking at me like that.

I've revisited that moment in the office more times than I'm proud to admit in the last three days. Analyzing it inside and out, inspecting it like an FBI detective, searching for indications that my brain and hormones blew it out of proportions. But then I think about his cocky little smirk and that backwards hat and those muscles when he caught me watching him in the warehouse. And the way he worked with his hands on our ride-along. And him taking care of me when I sliced my palm.

And how thinking of a downtown finance man no longer does anything for my libido.

That's when I land on my libido as the cause. Sex with Kyle had been rare and dissatisfying in the last few months of our dying relationship. Heck, it'd *never* been satisfying. I'm probably just starved for an orgasm.

Case closed.

"You haven't hooked up with him, but you *want* to," Kitty concludes. Or she's taking a shot in the dark and hoping I slip and confirm it.

"I do not want to hook up with Grayson Gold," I state, like it's a journal entry that I'm trying to manifest. "He's too—"

Dirty. Unrefined.

Those are the adjectives I should say, but I don't, because like the word "dickhead," they aren't entirely honest.

"Hot? Sexy? Scrumptious?" Kitty supplies oh-so-helpfully.

"Kit, you don't even know what the man looks like."

"Well, I'm about to when I have reliable internet and can look him up." *Of course.* Maybe it's a blessing she's decided to extend her hike another six weeks. "And in the meantime, you now have the perfect distraction for the weekend."

"What's that?"

Kitty sounds way too delighted as she answers, "Figuring out Grayson Gold's new adjectives."

———

THE BLEACHERS ARE a sea of styled hair, proud smiles, sundresses, and ties, everything cast in the dead, grayish hue that indoor stadium lights have down to a science. Or maybe it only appears that way because I've gotten too accustomed to the warm tones of sunshine.

It's easier than it should be to spot my parents in the bleachers. They're the only couple wearing formal black, mom's white-blonde hair an abrupt contrast with her tailored dress.

I used to want hair just like hers—a short bob, always curled, bleached to such an unnatural shade it demands attention. Thank goodness Kitty told me about color theory. I scoot my way down the row, and Mom's perfectly done-up face tracks my progress.

"Eliza." She stands up for a stiff side-hug when I arrive.

Dad glances up from his phone. "Good to see you." You'd never think that from how he goes right back to analyzing his stocks.

"It *is* good to see you," Mom says, giving me a once-over as she sits. "What happened to your hand?"

"Cooking accident. It's fine."

She harrumphs. "You look...tan."

"It's summer." I lower into the seat they left open between them.

"It is summer, but you're also working hard in your free time to find another job, yes?"

And so it begins.

"I am. I finished two more applications for Suzanne last night." One of them had involved a test assignment that took me three hours to complete—which should honestly be illegal. It's free work from people that company will never have to pay.

"Only two?"

"I would do more this weekend, but James is graduating and I'm here with you."

She's not impressed with that retort, but before she can respond, an announcement is made and the ceremony begins.

Speeches, names, and awards go on for the next three hours, and I might be the only person here who wishes it was even longer. Fortunately, it takes another thirty minutes to find James after the event, and even longer for him to take photos with all his freshly minted lawyer friends.

He's a chatterbox in the car as we head to dinner, buzzing with excitement, and I'm reminded this weekend isn't about me; it's about celebrating my nerdy little brother, who's worked his butt off since elementary school and just fulfilled his dream at an incredibly competitive program.

I'm proud of him.

It doesn't matter that our parents have always held our successes over the other's head, or that he and I aren't as close as I'd like. This is a *huge* deal.

I elbow him as my parents take a corner. "You realize I'm calling you for any and all legal trouble."

He's the spitting image of my father, all dark hair,

Roman nose, and intelligent brown eyes. "Don't know if you can afford me, sis."

"The sibling discount's one-hundred-percent off."

"It's subject to change." He's only half-kidding, which doesn't surprise me. We've never been the type to trade heart-to-hearts or take pictures with each other.

Besides, a bit of snobbishness is probably necessary for the environment he's about to be in.

The dinner conversation is mostly about James. How much he's already prepared for the Bar Exam. If he's excited to move into his new apartment. Which of his friends are working for equally prestigious practices in the city.

I think I might be getting off scot-free when the bill comes and the conversation unfortunately turns to me.

"Mom said you're working at a clam place?" James asks, leaning into the table.

Clam place? "It's an oyster farm," I correct. "And I'm the Social Media Director. It's a contract job."

He waves me off. "Clams. Oysters. Same thing."

"Aren't details supposed to matter in your profession?"

A cocky grin he never used to have in high school pops up. "The important ones."

Mom swirls the remainder of her wine. "Well, the good thing about contract gigs is that they're easy to get out of when a better opportunity comes along."

"They're legally binding, Mom. The word *contract* is in the name." I look to James for support.

My brother simply shrugs. "But who's really going to sue if you leave a few weeks early?"

So much for support.

"If there's someone capable of suing in Garnet Shores,

it's my employer." Anson Gold's wrath is the last thing I ever wish to encounter.

"Well, as soon as James passes the Bar, we'll have a lawyer who'll put him in his place," Mom replies, unbothered.

I glance between the two of them, struck silent.

They really expect me to up and leave the farm the second an opportunity from Suzanne comes through. Never mind all the other reasons I left the city, or the commitment I've made to the Gold brothers, or my rental contract for that boat.

Then again, why am I surprised?

"I'm not leaving until my contract is up," I state.

"Now that would be foolish." Mom sets down her wine glass. "An employer might need you to start within days of your hiring, two weeks at most."

"I'll inform them I can't start until late August."

Dad watches me from their side as Mom scoffs. "Honey, I understand why you might think you can do that, but that's silly. Impressions matter, and that sets a bad one."

"Commitment matters, too."

She drops all pretense then, voice turning stern as she says, "What you're doing? Right now? That is not the real world, Eliza. You need to get back there as soon as you can, or you'll be left behind."

As if I haven't already thought that. That blame, the feelings that I'm not doing enough, that I'm falling behind, have been a constant undercurrent since I fled the city.

It only *just* started to fade. Probably because I've finally accepted my current circumstances, and my social strategy is driving genuine growth at Gold's. Or maybe it's that, for the first time in my career, I'm...enjoying my days.

There's the sunrises and swims. The pride of achieving

results all on my own. The fact that I can wear an old sweat-shirt to work and don't have to be so stiffly professional all the time. The man who spars with me like no colleague ever would and trapped me against a desk in the most unprofessional way.

Unprofessional. There's one of Grayson's new adjectives.

Mom's criticism is still unanswered, and she takes that as an invitation to drive her point home. "All the time and energy you've invested in yourself, all the hard work you put in at school—it deserves more than *this*." The hard edge in her tone buffs out, and it sounds like loving concern when she says, "You're experiencing a hiccup. Don't let it derail everything you've worked toward."

She's being overdramatic.

That's what I want to think.

But instead, the truth in her words slithers into my eager doubts. I might be in Garnet Shores for the summer, but I'm still Eliza Attleburn.

"It won't," I say confidently, and she settles back in her chair. "It's only temporary."

The affirmation should make me feel better.

But all it does is weave a knot in my stomach.

And when I get a text message from Jane an hour later, canceling our lunch date because of a family event she forgot about, that knot tightens.

20

———

ELIZA

SUZANNE and my mother have a lot in common.

Both are career professionals. Both like to work weekends. And both like to wake before the sun rises and send messages that ruin my day.

> Suzanne: First batch were all rejected. We need to adjust your strategy. Be advised, I'm reviewing your resume and suggesting changes. Return the revised document to me by EOD.

It doesn't matter that rejections are standard and competition is fierce. When I see the message through bleary eyes, the news stings, casting a dark cloud over my morning that's barely even started.

And that's only the beginning.

Because my eyes rove over the time to see that it's seven-thirty-five.

I explode out of bed, stumbling to my makeshift sink—a big plastic bowl—to splash water on my face and brush my teeth. Missing my alarm wouldn't normally be a big deal, but Amanda offered to do a sorting tutorial if I leave the dock with her at eight, and I *need* this content. I teased it on Friday, dammit.

Throwing my hair into a bun, I burst back into the main cabin, searching for something to wear—only to realize my clean clothes are still in my car from last night's laundromat run.

Not caring that I look like a maniac, I run barefoot down the dock, wincing as I gingerly shuffle across the parking lot's gravel to the car. Then I'm lugging the laundry basket back with me, brainstorming the outfit I should have laid out last night. This morning is especially chilly, so definitely a sweatshirt, and my old—

My foot catches on a cleat as I step back on the boat, and I stumble. On instinct, my hands release the basket, flailing for the railing to stop myself from going in. But the basket doesn't catch.

On anything.

In slow motion, I watch the basket drop between the side of the boat and dock. It splashes unceremoniously into the water, landing perfectly upright.

For a second, I think I'm the luckiest woman on the planet. That fate has decided to cut me some slack.

Then I watch, helpless, as the basket tips and all my clean clothes spill into the water.

Fuck me.

Lunging across the deck, I scoop up the giant fishing net stuffed in a rod holder and shove it into the water. Three sweeps retrieve every piece of clothing I can see before I flip the net around and use the rod to scoop up the useless basket by one of its holes.

A sopping wet pile of clothing stares back at me from the teak deck. Water from the basket drips onto my feet, reminding me that I not only have a full load to re-wash, but a basket I need to hose down.

It's a later problem. Just like Suzanne's edits, which I'll have to magically work in between a laundromat visit and the grocery run I need to do if I want dinner.

A thick ball lodges in my throat as I rush back into the cabin, searching for any clean items to wear. Workout gear and a new Gold's sweatshirt are the only options, so I yank them on, telling myself a tank top and leggings aren't as sloppy as I think. Then, for the second time this morning, I'm running down the dock like a madwoman. A rush of air follows me into the car, and my phone buzzes.

It's from Sara, one of Kyle's fringe friends I've only ever met once.

Weird.

Curiosity riding me hard, I spare a second to open the message.

The seat beneath my thighs completely falls away.

I'm staring at a photo of Jane and Kyle.

Not in a group. Not standing by each other. But full-on making out in the middle of the fucking day at some kind of backyard party.

And the photo's timestamp is yesterday—when Jane and I were supposed to be having lunch, until she cancelled on me.

> Sara Last Name??: Sorry, you're so nice. Thought you should know.

My heart stalls, betrayal flushing my body cold. I feel like throwing up. Like the car is too small and too big all at once. Like this is some weird anxiety dream, because Jane is one of my closest friends, and she—I mean, she couldn't have *actually* done that.

But the photo isn't grainy, or fuzzy, or altered in any way that allows room for doubt.

It's Jane, with her wavy chestnut hair and a new mini purse around her shoulder, and Kyle, blonde hair slicked to the side, swallowing each other's faces.

With robotic movements, I turn the car on and stiffly drive to the farm. I can't find calmness in the draping trees, or the salt marsh, or the soft morning sky. I don't even *see* any of it, too busy trying to prevent whatever's mounting in my chest from escaping, because I'm about to be at work.

Through a haze, I park in front of the farm's office and jog down to the dock, hoping I'm not late.

But Amanda isn't there to meet me.

Instead, I'm greeted by Grayson—and Dave.

"Did I miss her?" I pant out.

Grayson's in his orange waders as he loads empty baskets and crates into the back of a boat, Dave's head following every movement. "Nope."

I don't understand. "We had a ride-along planned for this morning."

"We also have a divorcee tour this morning." The final crate hits the deck, and he straightens, planting his hands on his hips. "And one of them emailed last night to ask if 'the hot farm owner' would be leading that tour, so I asked Amanda to take it."

His displeasure should be entertaining. At the very least, cause a little chuckle to bubble in my chest. But my chest just feels like collapsing. Like it's been stuffed with too many things in too short a time, and can't adjust to the weight of it all.

"Are you taking me with you?" I ask tiredly.

Grayson doesn't answer right away, like he, too, is waiting for me to find delight in his demise. When I don't, he nods toward a bench seat with a pile of orange on it. "Got your bibs all set. Hop on."

Dave waddles by my side as I shake out the rubber, recognizing the same pair of bibs I wore last week. Maybe Grayson's assigned them to me.

"Finally figured out which side's the front?" he asks over the engine's hum as he releases the lines.

"No." The front and back look too similar.

We pull away from the dock, and he sets us on a straight course out to the farm before coming over. "You can get straight As, but you can't figure out how to get dressed, huh," he says lightly, pulling the bibs from my hands and twisting them around.

I also can't figure out how to choose good friends.

Or land an interview.

Or make my parents proud.

Grayson observes me beneath the brim of his hat as I grab the straps from his hand and say, "I've got it from here."

The plastic bench is cool and damp through my thin leggings as I sit to pull the legs on. In my periphery, Grayson lingers for another beat, probably making sure I'm actually capable of pulling on pant legs before stepping back to the wheel.

Seagulls fly overhead, squawking as they battle the unusually cool breeze rippling the water. Most mornings are calmer and warmer than this, but I don't mind the cold air whipping my face or the hair whizzing around my head. If anything, I want more of it—more sensations to keep the memory of that photo at bay, to remind me there's a big world that exists outside my exceptionally shitty morning and that everything is *fine.*

The second Grayson stops by the cages, I throw myself

into filming every tiny, little detail, even though I only need about two minutes of footage for the week.

"Amanda said you wanted to film a sorting tutorial?" Grayson asks, as I crouch and take a close-up shot of the oysters he's pulled in.

"Yes, but I'll reschedule with her."

"No need," he says, peeling off his gloves. "We're stopping at the new system next, then the sorting float. I'll do your video."

He's not even going to make me ask? I glance up to see his face matching the sincerity in his tone. "Thanks."

A tiny splash of water pulls my attention to the side of the skiff. Through the rippling blue surface, a school of baitfish jerk around in tight formation, like they can't decide where to go. Beneath them lurks a long, dark gray shape.

National Geographic: Oyster Farm Edition. The content takes shape in my head, and I lean over the side of the skiff, stretching to get a clear video. My shadow must spook them, because the fish shift, moving closer to the float that's just beyond my hand.

"Careful there."

Grayson's unnecessary warning comes as I stretch further, bracing my free hand on the float so I don't fall in. The bigger fish stills, and I wonder if I'm about to witness a baitfish murder. Maybe someone can do a David Attenborough impression for the voice-over.

There's a flurry of sound, like flapping wings, then a storm of movement careens into my back. I startle, my hand slipping from the float.

I try to pull back into the skiff, but my entire body-weight is forward, over the water, and then it's—*crap.*

I flop face-first, cool water rushing into the bibs within a millisecond. Desperation throws my injured hand up in the air, *barely* saving my phone from the fate of the rest of me.

My feet catch on the bottom, and I pop up, every loose hair on my head plastered to my face as I sputter. The wind hits first, a wall of ice against my skin. Then I register Dave beside me, bobbing his head in the chest-deep water.

Then the deep, rich sound of Grayson's laugh.

"Shit, I should've warned you. Dave will do anything for bait." My eyes blink open to find Grayson grinning ear-to-ear, like this is the best reality TV show he's ever seen. "As unlucky as that was, you're *real* lucky we're not in a deeper section." He kneels at the side of the boat, extending a hand.

The speeding steam train in my chest charges right off the end of the track.

And I do the most humiliating, unrecoverable thing I have ever done.

I burst into tears.

For a desperate second, I think I can play it off, the first few tracks blending with the salt water clinging to my skin.

But when Grayson says, "Fuck," I lose every last bit of control I have.

I cover my face with my hands, wanting to die as my breaths saw in and out and the tears pour free. Grayson curses again, and the water around me shifts as he hops in and wades toward me.

No. No. No.

I want a whale to swallow me whole. For an underwater sinkhole to pull me down. For a waterspout to whisk me away. I cannot believe I'm doing this, but I can't stop it, the stress and disappointment and—

"Hey. *Hey*. Are you hurt?" There's no more amusement in his tone. Two big hands land on my shoulders and carefully pat down my arms, which I'm holding awkwardly above the water to keep my phone and bandage dry. When he doesn't find anything, he moves to my face, his hands folding over mine and gently tugging. "Eliza? You swallow some water?"

Sniffling, I shake my head, giving him the answer he needs so he won't remove my hands. My face is a giant, blotchy mess, and if he sees it, I won't have a shred of dignity left.

He releases my hands, but his touch stays, fingers smoothing back over my hair, pulling the soaked strands away from my forehead. "Let's head back to the dock."

My body wants to melt into that low, soothing timbre. But I shake my head. "It's f-fine. Y-you can finish up here. It's just water."

It's not at all fine. I'm a pathetic disaster. But I can handle it, once my lungs stop spasming and my eyes stop leaking.

No one's dead. No one's threatening me. It's just my fucking brain.

One of his hands settles softly on the side of my face, while his other skates down to my shoulder. "You're out of your mind if you think we're going to keep going."

"Y-you told me l-last week that if I get wet—" a sniffle— "we're not turning back until y-you're done."

"I meant splashed with water. Not you falling in on a cold morning."

"You d-didn't specify."

His soft exhale mingles with the breeze. "Well, I am now." He lets go of me, only to place a hand between my shoulders and nudge me forward. I go, dragging my hands across my cheeks as the tears begin to slow.

He leads me to the skiff and hovers behind me as I drag

myself up. The chill starts immediately, the breeze freezing every piece of wet fabric sticking to my skin, despite it basically being July. I huddle in on myself, slinking to the bench seat and twisting away from him, out toward the water. With any luck, the wind will ice out my tears.

"Take off the sweatshirt," Grayson says, rounding on me.

My face is a swollen, puffy balloon as I shake my head. "It's not bad. I'm used to swimming in this."

Rustling fabric has me spinning around to see Grayson lifting his sweatshirt. Even in this state, I can't help but notice how his biceps flex under his short-sleeve shirt as he peels the layer off.

Guess my hormones don't feel as defeated as the rest of me.

He looks at me expectantly, the fabric bunched in his hands. "Put my sweatshirt on, Eliza."

Eliza. Not *Boston.*

The three syllables rumble out of his chest in a way that makes me want to grab his sweatshirt—and shove it in my face and inhale.

Because you haven't embarrassed yourself enough.

"Really, I'm fine," I insist, grateful the tears have stopped.

Grayson doesn't budge. "My ship, my rules."

"Ship? This is a toy boat."

His lips compress. "Eliza."

That's the third time he's said it. I think I want a fourth. Just as much as I want to put on his warm sweatshirt.

My own sweatshirt feels like it weighs ten pounds as I lower the straps of my bibs and pull it off. I reach for his, but Grayson's already lowering it over my head. Salt, detergent, and the warm notes of *him* surround me as my face pokes out of the soft fabric. His hands linger as I thread my arms through, then he tugs the material down.

I don't fight any of it, never mind that I look like a toddler who needs help putting on her PJs.

Or maybe you just look like a woman being cared for.

And Grayson...he's good at the *caring* thing.

Good at knowing what I need before I do, and delivering it with confident hands and steady eyes. Almost as good as he is at raising my hackles and egging me on.

But he hasn't done much of that lately.

Besides, does it count as "raising my hackles" if I enjoy it?

Grayson doesn't say another word as he takes us back to the dock, pushing the pace. We wave to his team when we pass the sorting float and zoom by Amanda's tour in the distance—a vision of styled bobs and lipstick.

All the while, shame sinks in, adding its name to the pile of this morning's emotions.

When he ties off the skiff and cuts the engine, I say, "I wasn't upset because of the water."

That's probably what it looked like. The prissy city girl fell in, got her hair wet, and threw a tantrum. But I need him to understand that isn't me.

"Figured that, considering how much you swim." Grayson leans casually against the steering console. "Do you want to talk about it?"

There's no pressure in the question, and the last thing I want to do is linger on what just happened. But words tumble out anyway. "I had a bad weekend, followed by a bad morning. The fall just...put me over the edge."

"Okay," he says with simple acceptance. His eyes rove over my face, and I can only imagine the red marshmallow-y mess he's seeing. "Why don't you head home and get changed."

A reasonable suggestion, except, "I don't have any dry clothes." When his forehead wrinkles in question, I explain, "I dropped all my clean laundry in the water this morning trying to bring it back to the boat."

His lips twitch. "That does sound like an unfortunate morning."

"I don't cry over spilled laundry, Grayson," I inform him, because that would be just as ridiculous as crying from an impromptu swim. "It was just one of several unfortunate events."

"I know you don't cry over spilled laundry." He shrugs. "I didn't even think you were crying at all. Thought some salt water flooded your retinas when you fell in."

It doesn't sound mocking. More earnest with a side of amusement, the way a friend tries to lighten the mood when your sky is falling down.

"Does that ever happen to you?"

"Nah. I know enough to close my eyes whenever I go face-first into the water."

I'm surprised to feel my lips curl up, even if only a little. Another breeze washes in, slithering down my bibs and reminding me how sopping wet my leggings are.

As if he's reminded, too, Grayson says, "Keep my sweat-shirt for now, and take the rest of the day to do laundry and get sorted."

I shake my head. "I'm not sick, and there's stuff to do here. I'm working today."

"Anything due tomorrow that you haven't already done?"

"No, but I have some reports I need to send your

brother for Wednesday, and content I need to shoot for the rest of the week."

And if it isn't early, it's late. One of my parents' mottos that has actually served me well over the years.

Grayson pivots easily. "Alright, then take an early lunch. Do your laundry, then come back this afternoon, and we can go out on the water then."

"I don't want to put you off-schedule."

"You aren't," he argues. "That's my new schedule."

We both know that's bullshit. He'd be going out of his way and moving his schedule to fit me in. But from his uncompromising expression, he's not willing to budge.

And it makes things so much easier for me if he doesn't —which he knows.

Finally, something *other* than disappointment, shame, or misery swells in my chest. It's appreciation. Gratitude for this man who owes me nothing, who I've insulted more times than I can count, but who always seems to pick me up whenever I've face-planted.

Figuratively *and* literally.

Not once have I even had to ask. And not once has he shoved it back in my face, even when we're dealing blows.

So I nod and accept, to which he smiles and says, "Now let me demonstrate how to step off a boat without falling in."

21

GRAYSON

> Anson: Lala wants you both here for the
> Fourth on Saturday. 2:00 pm.

IT'S the first message in our brothers' group chat since April that involves something other than wishing Dawson good luck at a game. Setting my paperwork down, I reply right away.

> Me: I'll be there

> Anson: Daw, you need to answer this one.

Even with that message, it'll be a miracle if we hear from Dawson without two reminders and a phone call.

The fact that this doesn't disappoint me shows just how bad it's gotten. We've had this group chat since we got phones in high school. Used to text in it every day without fail. Through breakups, graduations, girlfriends. Mom's funeral, then Dad's.

Then two years ago, Dawson slowly fell off, at about the same time as his all-star career blew up—along with his reputation for partying, women, and other stupid shit people do when they're famous and rich.

I used to blame Anson for it. He would send screenshots of Dawson's bad press into the chat and question him on it when he'd ignore our calls. But Anson didn't do it to shit on him. He did it because he was concerned, and he's painfully direct.

And now it's like there's a giant fucking canyon between us and our little brother.

We've been to a few games, seen him at holidays, but it's nothing like it used to be. Our visits are like hanging out with a long-distance friend—you know each other from a bond forged back in the day, and now that old bond is the only thing still linking you together. Anson treats him like a black sheep, mostly because he hasn't given Lala the attention a big brother should. Meanwhile, I spend the whole time hoping this is temporary—hoping he gets his shit figured out, while knowing any attempts to give him advice will shove him further away.

A gaggle of high-pitched laughter sounds outside the warehouse, loud enough to be heard over the oyster packing in front of me. My watch tells me Amanda's tour just finished up.

I scoot my chair back a touch so I'm fully concealed from the entrance by a stack of crates. Call me a coward, but the last thing I want to deal with is that swarm of feral forty-year-olds. I'm not a tiger, and this isn't a fucking petting zoo.

Alarm punches through me when someone appears around the crates, but it's replaced by warmth when I register who it is.

"You owe me a thank you," Eliza says, sidling up to the card table where I'm working.

From her pressed khaki shorts to the glossy hair brushing her chest, you'd think I dreamt up this morning's events.

Relief sinks in. I don't know what I'd do with more tears. Hers had churned my stomach.

"What do I owe you a thank you for?" I ask.

My folded sweatshirt in her hands, she drapes her forearms on a chair back and leans on it. I wonder if she realizes the neckline of her fitted white tee dips a little, teasing me with the smooth curves of her chest. "Those women out there *really* wanted to say hello to you, but I told them you were gone for the day."

Folding my arms, I lean back in my chair, working to keep my eyes on her face. "Now, why would you spare me like that?"

"You gave me your sweatshirt this morning." She hands me the folded fabric, then straightens, hugging her own arms across her chest. The posture is protective. Like she's trying to defend her earlier vulnerability.

I don't think she even realizes she's doing it. And I don't like it one bit.

Not on a woman who's such a constant force.

So I don't tease her, instead closing my binder and shoving to my feet. "You ready to go?"

Her eyes float down to my work. "I don't want to interrupt."

There it is again. That professional consideration I never gave her credit for in the beginning. Turns out she has it to a fault, and right now, it's rubbing me the wrong way.

"In case some water got in your ears earlier," I start, coming around the table, "taking you out is part of my new schedule for the day. You aren't interrupting anything."

For once, she doesn't argue back.

"Meet me down at the dock. I've got to grab a few things before we head out. And before I do *that*, I need to make sure the coast is clear."

The side of her mouth lifts. "They're just women, you know."

"Exactly," I say. "Terrifying. And you're here every day to remind me of it."

Her grin widens, and the warmth in my chest spreads even more.

———

"ISN'T THE FARM THAT WAY?" Eliza's hair whips around her face as she raises her voice over the engine.

"Sure is," I yell back.

"Then where are we going?"

I eye the sandy cove in the distance. "You'll see."

Planner that she is, Eliza doesn't accept that level of mystery. A second later, she's standing beside me, one hand braced on the console as we speed along. "We have that sorting demo to do."

"I had Amanda and Kenny film it this afternoon." I peek over, watching her lips part in surprise. "Figured they were already out there doing the work. Just took them a few minutes to add a phone to the equation."

Her mouth closes, then opens again. "Why would you do that?" Her shoulder nudges into mine as we skim across the textured pond.

It's the same question that popped into my head when I made my plan for this afternoon and asked Amanda and Kenny for a hand. That was four hours ago, which means I've had plenty of time to figure out my answer.

I did it for her because she reached a breaking point

today. She isn't the drama queen type. She's a hard-working, driven woman who'd finally been pushed to the edge, and then my dumbass comment shoved her over it. Just like my dumb ass undoubtedly played a role in pushing her to that brink.

All I want to do is fix it. Get her back to being the woman who drives me mad.

Because I fucking *like* that woman.

It only took me five minutes to reach that conclusion, which means the next three hours and fifty-five minutes were spent thinking about all the reasons I *shouldn't* like her.

Like my inability to do casual. My propensity to get tangled up and mesmerized, like a fucking lovey-eyed tween. How last year's royal fuck-up proved just how unreliable my feelings are.

I thought that experience had permanently turned off my dick. Shut down my feelings for the opposite sex. But Eliza's turned both back on. And when she leaves in six weeks, they're both going to be sorely disappointed.

It's inevitable. And I don't need that clouding over the things that matter, like this farm, this business, and raising Lolo.

That conclusion should've stopped me right in my tracks. Hell, maybe I should've left the dock without Eliza again, just to shove a self-preserving wall between us.

But I didn't.

I decided to do what I'm doing right now, telling myself I'm merely helping a friend. And as she waits for my answer with wide-eyed gratitude, I don't feel the slightest bit of regret.

Of course, I don't tell her any of this. "All you've gotten is content from the farm," I go with. "If you want to really convey the atmosphere of this place, you need a different perspective on the area."

She looks like she wants to ask another question, but just nods in acceptance and wanders back to the bench, watching the cove draw closer.

The tiny half-moon beach greets me the same way it has since I was a kid. Backdropped by leafy trees and brush, speckled with shells and driftwood, it's completely empty. Once we're as shallow as we can get, I lift the engine, throw out the anchor, and grab the supplies. Then we wade to the beach.

"What is this place?" Eliza asks, head swiveling as she takes it all in.

"Secret Spot."

She turns around to face me, brow cocked in question. "It faces the open pond."

"That it does." The cooler and bag make a soft thud as I drop them in the sand. "But we've always called it the Secret Spot, so that's its name."

"And how does a not-at-all-secret spot get called the Secret Spot?"

I plop down on the sand, sore muscles sighing in relief as I rest my arms on my knees. "Goes back to my dad." The air shifts as she sits beside me, criss-cross like the prim little student I'm sure she once was.

"There are about five beaches within twenty minutes from here, and our own town beach is all built up with nice facilities. But my dad refused to 'spend hard-earned money to be with a crowd,' so he and my mom would always take us here." I can picture his face now, wrinkled and scattered with gray scruff, griping about the public beaches back when paid parking and someone shaking their beach blanket out in your face was our biggest concern.

"Being kids, we wanted to go to the beaches our friends went to. Not this free scrap of sand in the middle of nowhere. So my dad started calling it the Secret Spot to make it feel special."

"Smart," she says.

"Yeah, it was." My next breath is weighted with memory. Like all parents, mine had their faults, but they gave us a damn good childhood.

"I've been to the town beach, and it's nice, but I have to agree with your dad. This place is special."

She drops her hands onto the sand, leaning back like she's settling in. Maybe feeling some of the calm and contentment this place brings me. Her gaze finds mine, irises appearing green in the sunlight. "I know it's been years, but I'm sorry about your parents."

The years don't matter. I still miss them. Still feel like we were robbed, still remember the suffocating grief that closed in when Mom got sick, and didn't end until after Dad met her in the grave. Sometimes, on birthdays or holidays or Lala's milestones, remnants of that grief try to burst out and drag me under again.

Guess that's just part of living life and loving people.

"Appreciate that," I say, meaning it. Because it turns out, after a year or two, most people just assume you've moved right on.

I don't think anyone does.

She nods quietly. "Wish my parents ever thought to take us somewhere like this. Somewhere away from all the noise and standards and people."

"Childhood me would've disagreed."

She snorts. "Not if 'childhood you' had to sit under a beach cabana, pretending adult conversations were more fun than building sand castles, just because your parents saw every outing at their beach club as a networking opportunity. God forbid we didn't look like the picture-perfect suburban unit."

I frown. "Don't tell me you've never been buried in the sand."

"My mother would have had a heart attack."

"Climbed a tree?"

She shakes her head. "They're doctors. Seen too many pediatric injuries."

My brow furrows. "Had a snowball fight?"

Her eyes finally roll. "I've done that."

"Makes sense. You're so combative." This earns me a laugh, and she playfully shoves my arm. Then she eyes our surroundings again, and her expression sobers.

"I know how this all sounds, but my parents—they're not, you know, *bad*. At all. They love me, even if they don't say it much anymore, and they've given me so many opportunities. I'm so lucky. They've just...they've worked so hard to get where they are, that it's the only way they know how to live. Naturally, they expect my brother and I to do the same."

It's clear her parents were strict as hell. Suffocating. Anyone raised in that environment would be a high-achiever, like her. But I can't think of many people who'd be as empathetic.

The way she defends them, trying to understand their motivations, when it'd be so easy to rag on them, spears right into my chest.

Eliza's wholly *good*. She can sling digs, tease, and roll her pretty eyes as much as she wants, but deep down, at the foundation of it all, is a sweetheart.

"They must be proud of you," I say.

She scoffs. "Not exactly."

"Now, you didn't say anything about your parents lacking common sense."

"They see me being here as a failure. A waste of time. Not that their opinions should even matter when I'm my own adult." She scoffs again, then abruptly stops. "Sorry. This place is so beautiful and peaceful, and I'm being a total buzzkill."

The chemicals gleefully buzzing through my bloodstream would disagree.

"It isn't too quiet for you here?" I ask, genuinely curious. It's nothing but sand, trees, and water. No music, no noise, no people. Nothing to do but sit and just *be*.

"Not at all. It's..." Another deep breath, like she's trying to absorb it all. "It's like a little paradise. Like...we're not part of the world right now."

A salt-tinged breeze wraps around us, and I stay silent. Not on purpose, but because I'm too busy absorbing the soft, calm bliss painted over her face.

She mistakes my silence for disinterest, maybe, because she suddenly shakes her head. "And now I'm getting philosophical."

"No, I think you got it right."

It's like that simple agreement opens the tap to her thoughts.

"This whole place is sort of like that, actually," she says, fingertip drawing random shapes in the sand between us. "I know I'm working, but it doesn't feel like it usually does."

"Which is?"

"Like you can never really relax," she answers, finger stilling in the sand. She hugs her knees. "Like you're fighting a constant uphill battle against people who think they're better than you. And then you leave, and there's people and traffic and noise everywhere. And then you go home and keep working, because that's the culture, and you're tired but you say yes to every social outing, because that's just what you do, and you give all of this time and energy to people who you *think* care about you, but actually don't give a shit, because they cheat on you, or hook up with your ex behind your back—"

She cuts herself off, closing her eyes for a moment. When they open again, they're flat. "That's, um, actually just me. Not a city thing." Her mouth twists in self-deprecation as she glances over at me. "I'm *really* great company right now, huh?"

"You are," I state. Sincerely. Intentionally, so she knows that opening up won't chase me away like she thinks it will.

I want to dig, to find out what kind of corporate idiots would ever think they're above this woman, what kind of shithead would cheat on her, what kind of fake friends would betray her like that. Then I want to go have a private word with all of them. Get them all to see how stupid they are, how fucking *wrong* they are, to cast her aside like that.

It isn't lost on me that I was no better than them just a few weeks ago. But now I want nothing more than to remove that slump from her shoulders that looks dangerously close to defeat.

"It's no wonder you're so damn talented at dealing with dickheads like me." I'm trying for humor, but grooves appear in her forehead.

"You aren't a dickhead, Grayson."

No, I'm usually not. But, "I was."

Finally, a hint of a smile. "Good to keep me on my game. Don't want to lose all my dickhead-handling abilities. I'll be needing them again soon."

"I can turn it up, if you want. Just let me know."

"So generous of you."

"I'm a generous guy." I drag the cooler and bag in front of me and start unloading the supplies, keeping the oysters on the ice.

"You brought oysters?" she asks, her delight feeding my ego.

"Like I said, you need a different perspective on the atmosphere of this place." I unscrew the cap on the hot sauce. "That includes oyster consumption."

She shifts, folding her knees around and twisting to face me. I make a point of wrapping a towel around my hand before shucking, to which she huffs in amused annoyance, and present her with an open shell.

"Ladies first."

Slurping oysters—slurping *anything*—shouldn't be attractive. Hell, I've witnessed enough of it to know. But I find myself riveted to the way Eliza tilts her head back, exposing the long column of her neck, as she downs the oyster in the most ladylike way possible. Her throat rolls as she swallows, and then her tongue darts out to lick some of the briny liquid off her lips.

The sight heats my own throat. There's a gravelly note to my voice as I grunt out, "Good?"

Dainty fingers place the empty shell back in the cooler. "'Good' isn't a strong enough word."

I hardly taste the salty sweetness of my own oyster, and then I'm handing her another, telling myself to cool the fuck off, when she has to go and say, "I think the whole aphrodisiac thing is a myth."

My cock stirs, like she just summoned it. "What do you mean?"

"My ex loved getting these when we went out." The graceful line of her collarbone shifts as she shrugs. "Never felt a thing."

She tilts her head back, sucking the oyster down. That sound, that silly little *slurp* that has no right stirring anything besides mild disgust, has me shifting my weight closer to her.

I'm too aware we're all alone, too aware that it's just me and her in this little corner of the pond.

Removed from the real world—just like she said.

So all those real-world *rules* I remembered earlier, all the self-defensive reasons I can't afford to *like* this woman, and sure as fuck shouldn't act on it, don't apply here on this little strip of sand.

I don't want them to.

Which is why I don't stop myself from rumbling, "Well, that's just because you weren't eating them with the right man."

22

ELIZA

THE LOW OCTAVE of Grayson's voice rumbles straight to my belly, curling down and hooking itself there. I've been viscerally aware of him from the moment I sat beside him, closer than was work appropriate. Close enough to make my skin tingle with awareness.

But not close enough to satisfy the desperate, aching pull toward him.

I know that pull.

I felt it stir when I saw him in the warehouse. When he trapped me against that desk. Attraction. *Desire.* Hormones that've had enough of staying away from this man, and are begging for me to jump his bones. Chemicals I was determined to *ignore*, because...

Because they're unprofessional.

Because I had a bad morning, and I'm probably not emotionally responsible right now.

Because this is *Grayson.*

But *Grayson* just shifted that big, sturdy frame closer to me, leaning down on one arm. His gaze keeps traveling down to my lips, still salty from the oysters. And he just laid down a blatant dare, knowing full-well I never back down from them.

That's just because you weren't eating them with the right man.

"How can you be so sure?" I whisper, my chest frozen in anticipation.

"Do you really want me to answer that?" His body is as still as my lungs, eyes molten as he waits for my response.

I may not have had many partners, but I *know*.

What this is, what he's asking. What my answer will lead to.

And whether it's from being out here, so far removed from *everything*, or exhaustion from constantly needing to make the right, smart, success-driven decisions, I shut off my brain.

"Yes," I answer.

His nostrils subtly flare.

That's his only reaction before he smoothly shucks the oyster in his hand. He leans in closer so our forearms brush. "Have another one." He lifts the shell toward my mouth, but I barely look at it, too fixated on his smooth lips and the neatly trimmed scruff around them. Scruff I'd once found unkempt, too rugged, but now has me wondering what it'll feel like on my skin. Between my thighs.

The cold edge of the shell meets my lips, and I open my mouth, allowing him to press it inside enough for me to suck the flesh away.

He applies pressure, dragging the bottom of the shell down my lip as he removes it. Then he dips in, catching that same lip between his own, giving it a gentle suck that shoots straight to the ache between my legs.

He pulls away, slowly licking his lips.

"You're right." His hot breath ghosts across my mouth. "'Good' isn't a strong enough word."

I gasp when the bumpy, rounded exterior of the shell lands on my chest, just below my collarbone. He presses, gently nudging me onto my back. His body follows, so he's lying on his side next to me, eyes on that shell.

He moves it, dragging it across my upper chest, then down to trace the scooped neckline of my shirt, the shell's cool, rough texture lighting a path of little fires. My nipples harden against my bra, waiting for the shell to pass over them. *Craving* it.

He stops just above my left breast. "So what do you think, Boston?" The words vibrate along my side as his body curls closer, half-covering me. His head dips, eliciting a full-body tremble as his lips brush the edge of my ear. "Those oysters working?" he whispers.

His face roves over to mine, so close our noses brush. That shell remains still on my skin, my chest heaving beneath it.

I didn't expect this from him.

I expected what I've always gotten. Dispassionate patterns of movement, the same old routine that always ends in the guy's release. Not this torturous seduction and these rumbled words. Not for every single nerve ending to throb in frenzied anticipation of this man's next move. And all he's done is half-kiss me and caress me with a freaking seashell.

It isn't nearly enough.

Not even close.

"You're going to have to discover that for yourself, Grayson," I say, hardly recognizing the throatiness of my voice. His jaw tenses, encouraging the next sentence to fall from my lips. "Though I'm not quite sure you know where to find it."

His lips part in a cocky grin. The kind he wears so easily, that puts us back on familiar footing. "Someone's impatient."

"Not impatient. Just making sure you know your way around at age thirty."

"I've never told you my age. You asking around about me?"

My eyes want to roll, but they refuse to leave his face. "I did my research before I took the position."

For a moment, that grin flashes into a genuine smile. "'Course you did."

Then that smile disappears and the shell moves, crossing over my neckline and onto my shirt. He pauses there, flipping the shell, so that its blunt edge presses into my skin through the fabric.

Then he starts to drag it.

The gentle scrape is *wicked*, tracking down, down—*ohmygod*. The abrasive edge passes directly over my nipple, and my chest arches up before I can smother the instinct.

"You wonder if I know my way around," he drawls, looping low across my belly with the shell, and starting a track up toward my other breast. "But the thing is—" he pauses as the edge passes over my nipple, and my chest jerks again— "I farm oysters for a living."

That wicked scrape draws a track down the center of my chest, past my belly button, pausing just above the juncture of my thighs, where I'm already soaked. Helplessly *dripping* with need, and he hasn't even touched me with his hands. "Which means I'm exceptionally good at finding pearls."

The shell flips again, and he presses the rounded exterior to my throbbing core.

My entire body jolts, and yet a small laugh still manages to escape my throat. "No way you just used that line out loud."

His fingers increase their pressure, and my breath catches. "Like you once said, I only know how to speak in shellfish."

Another laugh bursts from my gasping lungs.

There's some sort of witty remark waiting in my head, I'm sure, but I'll never know, because the shell disappears, and the next sensation I feel is his rough fingers at the edge of my shorts. My laughter dies away.

The only thing that exists in my head—in the world—is his strong body engulfing me, the smell of his hot skin, and those fingertips playing at my thigh, inches from where I burn.

His eyes are molten gold when they meet mine, and he dips his head, speaking his next words against my lips. "Tell me, Eliza."

Tell me.

Permission. He's asking for permission. To touch me, to cross the line we'd etched in permanent marker when we first met.

I nod, incapable of coherent words.

Grayson doesn't delay.

Like he needs it as much as me, his fingers slip under the fabric and bury themselves beneath my panties, slipping against me.

"Fuck, you're soaked." The curse is low and strained against my lips, his fingers stroking long and slow.

My hips tilt up, needing *more*—pressure, speed, words, for the life of me *I don't know*—just whatever will get me that release that's wrapping bands around me, threatening to explode. I've never been more turned on my life and I just, I *need*—

"There it is, that pretty little pearl," he murmurs, grazing my clit with two fingers.

Ego be damned, I *moan*, eyes squeezing shut. Those fingers become knuckles, rubbing, again and again, eliciting more moans from my chest.

"And those are some pretty sounds," he grits out. His knuckles trap my clit and squeeze. Lightning shoots up my spine.

Not skipping a beat, two fingers slip into me, stretching me, while his thumb continues circling. "Should've expected it, with how fucking pretty everything else about you is." His voice is stiff, strained, the words like gasoline to waiting flames. His hips meet my thigh, a long, rigid bulge pressing into me. His fingers rub, and stroke, and flick.

Within seconds, I'm gone.

A cry shoots straight from my throat as I come all over his fingers, harder than I think I've ever come before. His fingers stay there, caressing me, until the last trembles drain from my body and awareness begins to seep in.

I pant, feeling the sand beneath my head, the breeze washing over my cheeks, as his fingers slip from my shorts. Maybe I should be embarrassed, self-conscious about how desperate I just was, but Grayson appears just as affected as me, his face pulled in tense lines, his erection grinding against my side.

He's looking at me like I'm the only thing that exists in this salt pond, like I'm some kind of wonder, and for a heart-beat, neither of us moves, caught up in some kind of spell.

Then, in one smooth motion, he threads a hand into my hair and kisses me.

His lips are confident. Firm, but completely unrushed, laced with something so much sweeter than lust. Despite what his fingers just did, this somehow feels like *more*. His scruff tickles my skin as his tongue sweeps in, dragging against mine with easy intent, and sensation explodes in my chest, a whimper flying loose. He swallows it, fingers tightening in my hair as his cock twitches against my thigh.

I reach for his pants, hand pressing against the outline of his thick, hard length. Our lips move, becoming frenzied, as he leans back and I shift onto my side, my intent as clear as his want. My fingers fumble for his button when the smooth, velvety notes of a song wash over us.

It's soft at first, enough to make me wonder if I'm so caught up in him, I'm hearing things. But then Grayson breaks away.

He catches my hand, the half-lidded desire in his eyes morphing into awareness as he sits up.

"*Fuck.*" This curse isn't gritty with desire. It's agitated.

When I follow his gaze, I understand why. A fishing kayak drifts toward our beach, an old man mouthing the words to—is that Frank Sinatra?—playing from his large speaker.

"Thought this was the Secret Spot," I mutter through swollen lips, running my hand down my sand-coated hair.

He releases a drawn-out exhale, raking his hand across his jaw. "Like you said, it faces the open pond."

I track his hand as he adjusts his bulge, which still hasn't gotten the message of the moment. We sit there, breathing, as the man casts his line, drifting closer and closer, completely oblivious to what he's interrupted.

And what, exactly, did he interrupt?

My mind is eager to overanalyze, to start drawing conclusions about what just happened, to find answers now.

But it doesn't get the chance, because Grayson faces me then, notices the sand in my hair, and begins dusting it off.

With a hitch to his cheek, he says, "Think we can safely conclude you were eating oysters in the wrong company, Boston."

My shoulders relax. "I think you just have really potent oysters."

He barks out a light laugh. "Tell yourself whatever you want."

I glance pointedly at his hard-on. "And what's your excuse?" I ask. "You only had one."

His hand pauses, resting on my head. His tongue drags across his lip. Slowly. Thoughtfully. And he gives me the last reply I expected. One that doesn't deflect, or tease, or end with a challenge.

"I don't need an aphrodisiac with you."

Oh.

His words hang in the air between us, like an epic declaration, the summit of a peak appearing through clouds I assumed would never part. Maybe he didn't mean them to be so...*big*, but that's the impact they strike me with.

His ringtone cuts through the air.

For a few moments, he ignores it, his eyes steadfast on mine.

But the electronic notes keep going. I watch as he recedes from the moment in slow-motion, his lips pressing together. Then he breaks away completely, removing his hand, sitting up, and pulling his phone from his pocket.

"Sorry," he says, brows drawn as he reads the caller ID. "I need to take this."

"All good."

He cleans up as he talks, and I help him, trying not to blush as I pick up the shell he'd touched me with. I hear

Lala's name mentioned, Grayson's tone low and serious, and wordlessly file back into the skiff with him.

We're almost at the docks when he finally hangs up. "Lala's got a fever," he informs me over the wind. "I've got to go take her to the doctor's. My aunt's watching her, but her husband has her car."

I nod in understanding and say, "I hope she's okay."

He looks at me over his shoulder, then.

I don't need an aphrodisiac with you.

His words themselves are a freaking aphrodisiac.

I wonder if he's replaying them in his head, like me.

Though if he was, he probably wouldn't have so much resignation in his eyes. Resignation that suggests he's shoving what just happened between us far, far away. Redrawing the line we'd just temporarily erased in permanent marker.

When we arrive at the dock, there's no opportunity to confirm that hunch, because Mark's there, whisking Grayson into a conversation. And three minutes later, his truck bumbles out of the lot as he rushes to pick up his little sister.

23

GRAYSON

I DRAIN the last of my beer and signal to Kara for another.

"Got it," she says, whipping past with two platters full of empty glasses and plates.

"No rush."

I mean it. It's the Fourth of July—a Saturday, no less—and Dyl's is slammed. It's one of those rare, twice-a-year nights they've had to stop letting people in and shut down their waitlist. Noise fills the space from wall-to-wall, drinks flowing, bodies everywhere, despite having half the crowd out back, staking their chairs for the fireworks that'll happen in a few hours.

"You good?" JJ asks, sitting across from me at the high-top, eying my fourth empty bottle.

I counter by nodding to his third. "Are you?"

"No work tomorrow," he says.

I'm not buying it.

JJ's never been a big drinker. Neither have I, but it's even more out of character for him to down three beers in an hour-and-a-half than it is for me to have four. My guess is it's something to do with Alex, his high school sweetheart.

The anniversary of her death isn't for another two months, but her mom always calls him on holidays, and he's never totally right afterwards.

He also doesn't like talking about it, so I choose not to pry, answering his question instead.

"Dawson didn't reply."

I'd held out hope that he'd still show up to Anson's earlier today—for Lala, at least—but he never did. And our little sister noticed.

Fortunately, JJ swung by after seeing his parents and managed to put a smile back on her face. Thank fuck.

"He have a game?" JJ asks.

"Two days from now." His schedule was easy enough to look up. "That's fine if he couldn't make it, but at least answer. Call and say hi to Lala."

My little brother was never a jackass. A reckless moron, sometimes, but he always had a good heart. Not sure where the hell it is now.

But that's not the only reason I'm welcoming the buzz in my head.

My vision drifts to the door again, like one of those annoying automatic sprinklers that keeps swiveling around.

"He'll get right. Eventually." JJ takes a long swig of beer. "He'd do the dumbest shit when we were kids, and then he'd come around and apologize."

"Weeks later."

"Sure, but he still did it, and you wouldn't even need to ask for it," he says, resting his elbows on the table. "He knew when he was wrong. I don't think you just lose that when you grow up."

I toy with the label on my bottle, trying to find comfort in that. Anson's far past the point of goodwill. Maybe JJ and

I are the fools here, but it's better than believing Dawson's changed *that* much.

The front door opens, and my chest jolts. But it's just a few locals making their way back inside.

Jesus, I need that beer.

"You gonna make me guess who you're waiting for?"

Caught red-fucking-handed.

"I'm with you. Lala and Anson are out back," I play dumb. "Not waiting for anyone."

"So why are you watching the door?"

JJ's grin grates at me. "I'm not."

His eyebrows raise. "Brother, I'm trained to spot shell casings buried in the mud in zero-visibility water conditions. I can easily see that your eyes—" he points at them— "are glued to that door." His finger moves, pointing at the dark oak slab I've spent way too long staring at.

My teeth clench. "I'm not *waiting* for anyone."

"So you're—what? *Hoping* someone walks in? *Preparing* to duck and cover if they do?"

Rarely do I ever want my best friend to shut the hell up, but right now is one of those scarce moments.

Even through my annoyance, though, I know it's not his fault.

It's mine.

I took Eliza to that secluded stretch of sand. Said to hell with self-preservation and gave in to my impulses. Jerked off to the memory of those breathy little moans and her pussy spasming around my fingers every day since Monday.

As predicted, the tendrils of attachment have latched right on.

So I've spent the week trying to pry them off. Neither of us have brought up what happened. I'm not avoiding her—

she still joins me on some tours. But I haven't gone out of my way to re-engage her, and she's done the same.

It's like we've both reverted to the mean, shooting surface-level comments at each other, pretending our time on the sand never happened. Like two teenagers embarrassed about their first kiss.

Maybe we should talk about it like responsible adults, but communication is key for *relationships*, and I'm actively *not* trying to have one here. Besides, even without a conversation, we're clearly on the same dismal page.

Though the fact that I'm stuck between hoping Eliza appears in that doorway, and desperately hoping she doesn't, shows just how much I'm struggling to *stay* on that page.

I'm still figuring out what my reply should be when JJ speaks again.

"Hope you know your answer, because I'm pretty sure that someone's walking in right now."

For probably the thirtieth time, I look up to see JJ's spot-on. Eliza's following Amanda through the door—probably how she managed to sneak in when they're turning folks away. And when her body crosses the threshold, I don't care that JJ's watching for my reaction.

I can't look away.

Eliza's not wearing much of anything. A white, lacy tank-top ends at her belly button, exposing an inch of smooth skin above dark-wash shorts that sure as *fuck* aren't work-appropriate. Doesn't matter that I've been beneath that fabric, explored more than what she's showing. How she looks is like a drug.

Goddammit, I need that beer. To give me limp dick, if nothing else.

She scans the crowd as Amanda leads her toward the

bar, and it doesn't take long for her eyes to find mine. For a beat, she just stares. Then her mouth tips into a friendly smile.

The same friendly, professional smile we've been giving each other all week.

Eliza whispers something in Amanda's ear, then leaves her there as she makes her way to us.

"Need me to flip this table so you can hide behind it?" JJ asks.

I glare at him. He drains the rest of his beer, chuckling, before standing up to greet her. "Hey, there's my long-lost teammate." He pulls her in for an easy hug. "How you doing?"

"Good." She draws back, glancing over at me. It's quick, a flicker of movement, but her eyes track down my body, stopping on my arms before coming back up. "Grayson."

Her hair's pulled back, cheeks extra rosy, from the night's warm temperatures or a drink, maybe.

I tilt my bottle toward her. "Happy Fourth."

Can't believe I actually just said that out loud. That's the meaningless formality you say to neighbors. Cashiers at the grocery store. Not people you *know*.

Not women who've moaned beneath your fingers.

She tips an imaginary hat. "Happy Fourth to you too, sir."

JJ's eyes track between us in the succeeding silence. "Beer sometimes makes Gray extra formal," he comments, trying to save me.

"Formal?" Eliza repeats. "Grayson doesn't do formal."

"And what does *Grayson* do?" I ask.

Whatever pops into her mind first makes her cheeks even rosier, and I can't help the satisfaction that slides through me. It only deepens when she tries playing it off. "Grumpy. Standoffish. Rude." She pauses. "Cocky."

Maybe she emphasizes the word. Maybe she doesn't. But she's regarding me with an unreadable expression, like she's thinking about the first four letters. Or maybe that's just me in my own fucked-up head.

Since I'm apparently a masochist, I reply.

"Cocky. Hmm." I purse my lips in mock thought. "You say it like it's a bad thing, Boston."

"I find that cockiness is usually a form of overcompensation."

"Is it, in this case?"

We both know what the answer is.

Her jaw works as she mulls over her response. This is the closest we've gotten to talking about Monday, and she has the chance right now to bring it on home. I've practically dared her to, because I can't fucking help myself.

Kara, where the fuck are you?

Finally, she sucks in a breath and says, "I'm n—"

"Hey! Grayson, JJ, my guys."

The deep, boisterous voice shatters the moment. I physically rock back in my seat, not realizing I'd leaned closer to hear her response, as Darian sidles up. His blue eyes are slightly glazed, his face ruddy. The beer in his hand isn't his first.

Those buzzed eyes land on Eliza, and they beam. "Eliza! Wasn't expecting to see you here!" He slings an arm up, giving her a side-hug.

My fingers tighten on my bottle when he lingers longer than he needs to. Just like his gaze lingered all the fuck over her when we played pool.

"Amanda invited me last-minute," she explains.

"Well, I sure am glad she did." He squeezes her

shoulder before dropping his arm and turning to us. "JJ, how was...where was it—" he snaps his fingers. "Canada?"

"Alaska," JJ amends good-naturedly. "And it was epic. Wild place up there. The training was just as wild, but I learned a lot."

"Hell yeah." Darian fist-bumps him, then nods at Eliza and me. "What about you two? How's working together on the farm?"

"Good," we reply at the same time.

Jesus, we're stiff as boards.

"Cool." Darian gives a sharp nod. "Well, I'm gonna get a refill. You boys want anything? Eliza?"

JJ and I both decline, but Eliza says, "Yes, actually. I haven't gotten anything yet."

The way Darian's face lights up, you'd think she's made his whole damn night. "Perfect. It's on me." His hand lands on her upper back, and I lock onto his palm like a targeting radar. "Come on, pretty lady."

Acid burns in my gut as he whisks her away. I'm experienced enough to recognize the smolder of jealousy. And I'm self-aware enough to know I sure as shit shouldn't be feeling it when I'm trying to put distance between us.

"Alright," JJ starts, voice low. "Either you two fucked, or you made a move and she shot you down. Or you really *want* to fuck her, but won't, for some reason."

He pulls away as Kara swoops in with my beer like a superhero. She's gone before my thank you reaches her ears, and I take a few long drags, trying to find peace in the cold brew as it slides down my throat.

"I don't want to talk about it."

JJ's a certifiable guru when it comes to advice. But admitting this whole thing out loud makes it *more* of a real problem.

"Fine by me." He raises his hands defensively. "But don't expect me to sit here and deal with your moody ass all night. This is the first Fourth of July I've gotten off in three years."

"I'm not moody."

"You just looked at Darian's hand like you wanted to cut it off," he says as I take another sip. "And now you're scowling. In the middle of a party."

I drop my beer on the table and rub my eyes. JJ's a fixer, through and through. It's part of what makes him such a damn good guy—and why I know he won't let this go.

"I like her," I blurt, ripping off the band-aid. "I like her, and we messed around a little bit, but we shouldn't have. She's leaving next month."

There. I said it. Part of me expects the weight to lift from my chest, but it doesn't. Just fucking digs its claws in.

"Don't see what her leaving has to do with anything."

That third beer must be messing with his cognition. He *knows* my tendencies. Knows I have a hard time with casual.

"She and I can't go anywhere," I say, driving it home. "I can keep on liking her, but she's going to leave, and I'm never going to see her again. Why would I sign myself up for that?"

"Gray, she lives in *Boston*. Not Wisconsin. It's only, like, two hours from here." He says it like it's so simple, which frustrates me more, enough for my thoughts to tumble out.

"Two hours of time, but it's a different world up there." *With a giant pool of successful guys who climb ladders and chase promotions, just like her.* "She might be taking a detour to this world right now, but she isn't staying." I trace the rim of my bottle, not sure when I became a fucking philosopher. "And you know how I got after Mackenzie.

Couldn't focus. Couldn't think straight. I'm not doing that again."

JJ nods, fingers tapping on his drink. "She already have a job lined up in the city?"

"Not that I know of."

"So how do you know she's going back?"

I'm pretty sure my friend just sprouted two heads. "It's her spot. Where she wants to be."

"You seem so sure of that."

"You would be, too, if you knew her like I do."

Yet as I say it, I remember how *wistful* she'd looked the other day, observing the pond from that quiet strip of sand. She's killing it with her marketing, and with every day that passes, she looks more at home on the skiffs, at the farm, despite that polish she always wears.

A cheer goes up by the bar, and my head swivels—past the commotion, to Eliza, who's laughing at something Darian's saying with animated gestures. Part of me wishes he was a shithead, so I'd have an excuse to rip him away from her. But while Darian might have appreciative eyes, he's a good guy. He won't make any moves unless she makes one first.

My next breath is tight as I reset on JJ. But his eyes have followed mine, staying on the scene behind me. And he has to go and say the last thing I need to hear.

"All I'm gonna say is if she doesn't have a job lined up, you don't know for sure that she's heading back." He takes a heavy breath. "And if Alex taught me anything, it's that when you find someone special, you hold on like hell and cherish it. 'Cause if it slips away, you'll always wonder if that, right there, was the best part of your life."

24

ELIZA

MY BRAIN LIKES to overanalyze a lot of things.

Emails. Small talk with baristas. Whether an exclamation point makes me sound too cute or too angry. But there's one thing that'll always top that list: job interviews.

This morning's phone interview with a tech startup is on replay in my mind, torturing me as I plan the next two weeks of strategy. My ROI and engagement for Gold's have been outstanding, which means I'm finally at a place where I know what works—a good thing, because I can't focus on anything but the hiring manager's unimpressed responses to everything I said.

I *know* my answers were solid, but I'm eighty-percent sure she hated my guts.

The door to the oyster farm's office swings open, and in walks the *other* item at the top of my "things to overthink the heck out of" list.

Grayson.

Wearing a cutoff tee shirt and that backwards hat he looks too good in.

"Bachelorette party is here," he informs me, with the

consternation of a general announcing an invasion. He jerks his head. "Come on."

A chorus of giggles drifts through the open doorway. "You're really that scared?" I ask as I close my laptop and follow him out.

"Not scared," he corrects flatly, jogging down the steps beside me. "Just already annoyed. And if I have to be annoyed, you have to be, too, since this is your fault."

"*Technically*, it was your fault for leaving without me that day."

He shakes his head, mouth quirking as he prepares his response. But then he swallows it down. Literally. I watch the apple in his corded neck roll as he chooses silence.

And here we are. Just another one of the awkward, stilted conversations we've been having since he brought me back to the dock last Monday. The *only* conversations we've been capable of for one week and two days. Not that I'm counting.

It's like some amateur mason built a rickety, half-finished wall between us. Sometimes, we come across a hole, falling into how we acted *before*. A suggestive remark. A playful insult. Something that pushes professional bounds. But then we revert right back to surface-level comments and small talk, or end the conversation altogether.

It bothers me, even though it shouldn't. Because that amateur stone mason is comprised of me and Grayson, united in unspoken agreement that what happened at the Secret Spot can't happen again. That we can't let *that*, whatever it was, go any further.

I don't know his reasons. But I do know mine.

Objectively, it was just a hookup. Completely non-problematic on its own. But the *feelings* around it—around *him*—

well, that's where the problem is. Because *Grayson* isn't just a hookup. He's been the bane of my existence, my calm and steady hero, and the fun in my days since I came here in May.

And in one month, I'm gone. Back to the real world, to working Saturdays, to hustling my ass off and making things happen. This little summer daydream I've been living doesn't fit there—not if I want to achieve my goals.

So despite how much it sucks, mission try-to-forget-the-hottest-orgasm-of-my-life and don't-catch-feelings-I-might-already-have is officially a go.

I thought flirting with Darian at Dyl's on Saturday would jumpstart that undertaking, but no matter how hard I tried, I couldn't get lost in his blue eyes. I spent the whole time peeking at Grayson to see if he was flirting with any women.

He didn't. Just downed beers with JJ, glared daggers at Darian, and watched the fireworks with his brother and little sister.

It pleased me *way* more than it should have.

Gathered at one end of the parking lot, the bachelorette party is a scene of sparkles, sashes, and—are those *cowboy boots?*

We're in *Rhode Island.*

One of them spots us, and like a pack of meerkats, six other faces whip our way.

"Oh my god, we got *him!* I *told* you!" One of them squeals, clapping her hands together. I squint to read the words on her sash.

Maid of Dishonor.

Oh boy.

The others are quick to join in, bouncing in their wedge sandals, lipstick-painted smiles painfully big.

"We're off to a good start, ladies," the *Wife of the Party* exclaims, glittery eyes hungrily checking out Grayson like he's a hired stripper and not their tour leader.

His cutoff isn't helping matters.

"Welcome to Gold's. I'm Grayson, owner of this farm. This is Eliza, who'll be helping me today," he announces blandly. "There's wine with your tasting, but I can't take anyone out if you've already been drinking."

His dispassionate welcome does nothing to deter their enthusiasm.

"Oh, we know. We're rule followers," the *Maid of Dishonor* assures him, stepping forward. "Though you're welcome to check for yourself if we have any drinks on us." She winks and spreads her arms out wide, preparing for a pat-down.

I choke on my saliva.

My need for revenge might be long-gone, but this is pure *gold*.

Grayson rakes a hand down his jaw. "Not necessary. If you have everything you need, we'll get started." He waves a tired hand toward the dock, signaling them to go first.

"He's chivalrous, too!" This comes from *Hot Mama*, who fans her face as she and the other women teeter down the dock.

Grayson's lips compress. "It's an extended tour, too," he mutters. "Who the fuck thought we should offer extended tours?"

"At least you're making a couple grand," I offer.

He adjusts his ball cap in agitation. "I'd pay a couple grand *not* to do this."

Helping the women into the boat is an ordeal of its own. They eagerly grasp his offered hand, beaming as they take all the help he's willing to give. One girl—the *Man Magnet* —films the process with her phone.

He keeps his hand extended for me, even though I'm not posing as a guest, and I take it automatically, trying not to think about the rough texture of his fingers and how those callouses felt when they were—

Nope. Not going there.

"What's she helping with, exactly?" someone asks.

"You never know when you need an extra set of hands on the water," I say, smiling amicably. "And I'm happy to take all the photos and videos you'd like."

Instantly, I'm their new best friend.

"Can you get photos of us with him? The Gold's sign is the *perfect* backdrop," *Wife of the Party* asks eagerly as Grayson pulls away from the dock.

"This is a working farm," he answers for me, his tone flat. "Once we're done with the tour, I'll have to get right back to work."

"Got to respect a hard-working man," she hums in response, the others murmuring in agreement. "And it shows—just how hard you work." Her eyes trace the sinews of his arms with blatant appreciation.

Can't blame you, girl.

Nope, that's *also* not a helpful thought.

Grayson wisely starts talking then, droning on about the farm and oysters, leaving no space for any more of their comments. The first stop is the floating dock where the upweller lives, millions of baby oysters incubating in flooded baskets beneath the dock's planks.

He opens one of them up, lays on his stomach, and scoops a hand low into the basket to show us what the oysters look like. He springs to his feet to move us right back onto the boat.

"Wait, don't one of us get to do it?" the *Maid of Dishonors* asks, stopping him in his tracks. "I saw on one of your tour videos that sometimes you get a volunteer to scoop some!"

Grayson plants his hands on his hips, shoulders slumping, because this is a hands-on activity he was clearly hoping to avoid. Digging into the upweller means reaching your entire arm into the water, and the tour leader usually holds the ankle of whoever does it so they don't fall in.

"I'll go!"

"No, me!"

"No, the bride should do it!" the *Maid of Dishonor* declares.

But the bride-to-be shakes her head, face wrinkling in disgust. "It's smelly."

Grayson jumps at the opportunity. "I don't want to start an argument among you ladies." His gaze finds me, a desperate gleam to them. "Eliza, thanks for volunteering. Come on over."

"Wait, we can choose between us. Whose birthday is next?"

"We're on a tight schedule," Grayson says as I come around next to him. "Don't want to cut into your tasting time."

I eye him, half amused, half in awe that he can be so blatantly rude and still have them fawning over him. Must be the hot-asshole effect.

"On your stomach," he instructs.

The easy command shoots straight past those flimsy professional boundaries into the deranged part of my mind. The part that won't forget the low words he'd rumbled on the sand.

Feeling a little shaky, I comply, waiting for his next instruction. "Roll up your sleeve."

He's crouched beside me, and I'm too aware of how his body hovers over mine.

You're scooping oysters, for heaven's sake.

But "oysters" aren't a safe, neutral item anymore, not when he used that shell the way he did.

Never in my life did I think shellfish could be sexual, but here we are, still learning things at twenty-six.

I fumble with my cap sleeve, trying to shove it up.

"Here, let me." Grayson's hands bat mine away and roll the fabric, my body *buzzing* at how his fingertips drag along my skin.

My gosh, get it together.

But when Grayson delivers his next instruction, I swear there's a gritty note to his voice. Like his mind has wandered down the same horny gutter as mine, despite us being in the middle of a tour.

In public.

Doing something he's done with volunteers before.

"Go for it. Nice and slow." His body shifts back, and I feel the warm weight of his hand on my—*thigh?*

It's supposed to be the ankle. It's *always* the ankle. But his fingers are wrapped around my thigh instead, and I think we've stumbled across another one of those holes in the stupid wall between us.

I shove my arm into the water, needing a distraction, and come up with a handful of baby oysters.

"That's deeper than expected," I comment, because I need to ground myself back in reality. Seven pairs of eager eyes are on me, and with how much they're paying, we need to give them a valuable experience on the farm.

But *Hot Mama* has to ruin my good-faith efforts by commenting, "You'll never hear me complain about that."

And I spend the rest of that tour recounting all the reasons I can't be attracted to Grayson, as if that'll condition my body and my mind into agreement.

———

Suzanne: Updates for this week - we should hear from last week's phone interview tomorrow. No rejection yet is a good sign. And a contact at one of the marketing agencies told me your resume is standing out. We're on standby.

THE MESSAGE COMES as another violent stroke of thunder roars outside the boat's cabin. The squall is moving in quickly, a fierce-looking band of red on the radar fast-tracking to Garnet Shores, a swath of dark green right behind it, ready to ruin everyone's Sunday night.

I've taken the necessary precautions. Added two extra fenders to the side of the boat. Threw on an extra line, after watching a quick tutorial of how to tie to a cleat. Pulled all the cushions, my cooler, and my shoes inside, just like the renter's manual told me to do. Still, I can't shake the worry settling into my chest, even with Suzanne's good news splayed across my phone screen.

The sky cracks again in warning, and a mighty band of wind whips against the boat. I curl tighter into my sheets, reminding myself that boats weather storms all the time, and this one's been doing it for decades. Just last week, the sky rumbled with distant thunder all night.

I'm *fine*.

Determined to make that true, I grab a bag of chips and throw my favorite guilty pleasure show on my laptop—a cheesy, soap-opera-esque teenage drama that brings back high school nostalgia. Tucking the blankets up around my chest, I settle in.

Not long after, the rain starts.

Though "rain" seems too passive a word for it.

Lightning flashes outside the tiny port windows as a deluge hits, so loud and heavy, it nearly drowns out the show. Wind lashes rain against the windows, like it's trying to break in, and angry thunder splits the air. The boat rocks beneath me, wobbling violently as the lines battle the storm.

I lean forward and turn on the show's captions, telling myself it'll be over soon. Fast-moving storms like this don't last long. Heck, people out West who deal with tornadoes would probably go out and dance in this weather.

One hour later, my hunch proves correct. Rain pummels the boat and the sky still growls, but the wild intensity has calmed. I open the radar on my phone to see that Garnet Shores is now swimming in a swath of dark green. All that red's moved on.

The worry recedes, and I pause the show, slipping out of bed. My bare feet touch down, the carpet unusually cool against my skin.

No. Not cool.

Wet.

It's just a spill. All the rattling must have shaken my water bottle off the...

Shelf. Where my water bottle rests, upright and capped.

Shit.

Trepidation sinks in. If it isn't my water, it's a bigger problem—like a leak from the cabin door. A *big* leak, because the carpet practically squelches underfoot as I approach the entrance.

I snag a towel on the way, hoping it's enough to plug the crack.

But when I inspect the small wooden door, there's nothing to plug. The area's completely dry.

Is...is there a leak in the walls? Some cracked seam?

Feeling foolish, I begin perusing the cabin's walls, looking for signs of moisture. After checking the right side, I move to the left—and find my feet submerged in a full-blown puddle. I glance down.

Right by the trim, the water is *pooling*. Which means there's enough water in here *to* pool, and the boat is listing to the—*oh my god*.

Trying to hold panic at bay, I tear the edge of the carpet from the buttons that hold it down. The waterlogged fabric is heavy as I fold it back, revealing what I feared. A hatch to a compartment deep in the boat. The bilge, I think it's called.

Liquid slips out of the frame and onto the cabin floor.

Digging for courage, I lift the hatch—and find myself staring into an overflowing pool of dirty water.

My heart catapults into my throat as I drop the hatch and lunge for the control panel. The bilge pump switch is on, but the little light beside it is red.

Ohhh shit.

I shove open the cabin door, stand on the sill, and stare with wide eyes at the inch of water flooding the deck, its surface jumping with more heavy rain.

Rain that isn't stopping any time soon, according to that radar.

I don't know how much water a boat needs to sink, but I really, *really* don't want to find out.

Stumbling back into the cabin, I lunge for my phone, flipping quickly through the renter's manual for the emergency repair guy's number. The ringtone goes on, and on, and on, bringing me to voicemail. I try again, because the point of being the *emergency* guy is being *available for emergencies*, even late at night, but I land at his voicemail again.

"This can't be happening," I mutter, phone trembling as my fingers begin to shake. A gust of wind blows rain into the cabin as I try the boat owner.

Again, voicemail.

I try two more times, fear sinking in its claws with every unanswered ring.

This boat is going to sink. Or at the very least, flood. Damage electronics. *Fuck.*

I don't know what to do. I'm not a boat person. There... there might be a bucket around but I don't know how to repair this, fix this—what to even do.

My fingers are tapping my contact list and scrolling to his name before I even realize. Tears prick my eyes, my system near full-blown panic, as the dial tone rings.

"Please pick up. Please pick up," I pray, more rain soaking the entrance of the cabin.

"Gray." His voice, tired and annoyed, hits me like a ton of bricks.

"Grayson," my voice shakes as much as my hands. "I need help."

"Eliza?" It's clear and sharp. Alert. "Where are you?"

"On the boat. The—"

"What do you mean, 'the boat'?"

"The piece of crap I'm renting out, in Joe's Marina," I rush to explain. "The bilge is flooded. The pump isn't working. No one's answering and there's so much water." My voice cracks on the last word as I fight to keep the panic from paralyzing me.

"I'm on my way." There's no hesitation. No big sigh. Just a rustle of movement as he asks, "How much water is there?"

Too much. "It's leaking up out of the bilge. There's some in the cabin."

"Okay. And where are you right now?"

"In the cabin."

"Alright. You're going to go to your car and stay there, out of the storm," he instructs calmly. My entire body latches onto that steadiness, desperate for an anchor. "I'm going to be there in ten minutes. It's going to be okay."

"'Kay," I manage, not caring how small I sound.

"What slip is the boat in?"

I give him the letter and number.

"Got it. I'm going to hang up so I can make some calls, but call me again if something happens before I get there."

"Thank you," I breathe out, hanging up before I start sobbing on the line.

Thunder roars in the distance, drawing me back to the cabin door, to the gallons of water in the boat.

Grayson is coming.

He's going to fix this.

The realization settles me, enough for me to finally *think.* I'm not about to sit in my car, useless, waiting for Grayson to come and do all the work.

I'm distressed as hell, but I'm not a damsel.

Rummaging through the cleaning supplies for a bucket, I get to work.

25

GRAYSON

MY HEART IS in my fucking throat as I leap into my truck and rip out of my driveway. Rain hammers the windshield, water spraying up from my tires. It's one of those nasty summer thunderstorms, the kind that come in with a bang and leave a mess before you even realize what hit you.

I battened things down at the farm before I left, but I always head over to check in after storms like this. It's the only reason I was awake to pick up Eliza's call, and thank god for that. If I'd known she was living out of a goddamn *boat* in the area's most rustic marina, I would've warned her about the weather. Hell, I would have added her to my check-in list, despite the space I'm trying to keep between us.

The obvious panic in her tone was a bomb straight to the chest. Still is.

Fuck.

Keeping one eye on the road, I dial Mark's number.

"The hell you want." His grumble tells me I woke him up.

I don't waste time with an apology. "I wouldn't do this if there wasn't an emergency."

Mark's been with me long enough to know what I'm asking. "Need me to check on things?" he asks right away, the edge gone from his voice.

"Yeah."

"Done."

No questions asked. He's like a goddamn guardian angel.

"I owe you."

"You need something else, you call me," is his only response before the line goes dead.

I take a turn faster than I should in this weather and dial my brother. It might be ten-thirty on a Sunday night, but he's no doubt sequestered in his office, starting his workweek.

He answers on the second ring. "Gray?"

I swerve around a downed tree branch. "Eliza's living out of a boat at Joe's place, and she just called me. It's flooded. Bilge pump doesn't seem to be working."

"You heading there now?"

"Yup." I take a breath, knowing I'm about to hit him with a big ask. "Any chance you can swing by the farm, grab the manual pump, and bring it to us?"

I could do it myself, but it'd add ten minutes to the drive, and I can't accept that kind of delay. Not with Eliza sounding the way she did, ready to crumble with panic. And not with her stubborn tendency to try to solve problems herself.

She better be inside that car.

"Done," Anson says.

I wince. "I know it's late and Lala—"

"Stop," he cuts me off. "Lala loves adventures. She's

either going to go crazy for this, or she's going to sleep through the entire thing. I'll see you soon."

I end the call, beyond thankful. He might be a tight-ass, but he'll drop anything for the people he loves.

The last two minutes of my drive are a collage of shit visibility and lightning strikes, and then I'm racing over potholes in the marina's gravel lot until I'm next to Eliza's little car. It's the only other vehicle in this lot.

It's also empty.

Fuck.

The pond is a mess of white caps and dark, churning water as I jog down the slick dock, vibrating underfoot as boats clang into it. Eliza's vessel is easy to spot, its mast bobbing at the end of the row, the only boat here big enough to hold a livable cabin.

And if I had any doubts, the person-shaped shadow scurrying around the tilted deck confirms it.

Goddamn this woman.

"What the hell are you doing?" I bark as I bear down on the boat.

She must not hear me over the wind and rain, because she keeps furiously filling buckets and dumping them over the side in a *fucking tee shirt.*

Thunder growls in warning, lighting up the sky with white-hot energy as I hop onboard. "Eliza!" I bellow.

She hears me this time, stumbling, and the full bucket in her hands drops into the open bilge hatch beneath her. Her mouth falls open, hair plastered to her face, eyes blinking through the rain.

Without another word, I move in and haul her over my shoulder. Not caring that I'm being a Neanderthal, I march to the cabin.

"Grayson!" She wriggles against me, and I clamp an uncompromising hand around her thighs.

Even infuriated, my blood heats at the feel of her bare skin and the knowledge that her perky ass is right next to my face. If she was mine, I'd swat it for this stunt.

Instead, I lower her at the threshold.

"I have to—"

"Not a word."

Jesus, where's her self-preservation?

She drops into the cabin and I come in behind her, slamming the door shut. My hands land on my hips as I stare down at her, part-infuriated, part-worried, part-relieved she's in one piece. One sopping wet piece, that is.

Her hair hangs in dark ropes, a Cape Cod tee-shirt plastered to her skin, dripping water onto the carpet at our feet. It's either a blessing or a curse that she's wearing a sports bra beneath the see-through fabric. Her eyelashes are wet spikes around big, vulnerable eyes that gaze up at me.

"I know you told me to stay in my car, but—"

"Eliza, there's *lightning* outside," I articulate, sweeping a hand to the tiny-ass windows.

Her face scrunches in distress. "I wasn't just going to sit there. I had to do *something!*"

Yeah, like *wait.*

The reply is on the tip of my tongue, but I shove it down. She isn't as panicked as she sounded on the phone, but she's upset. Shaken.

Moving on instinct, I gather her in my arms. She comes without resistance, pressing her cheek against my neck and hands on my chest as I secure my grip on her frame. Her chest moves in shallow, quick breaths against mine, belying just how upset she is.

Save for the soaked floor, the small, rickety cabin is a startling contrast to the clusterfuck outside. Plants, fluffy pillows, and lamps emitting a soft yellow glow have made the space warm. Feminine. It even smells like her perfume in here.

And I'm reminded that while she's been out of her element since she first came to Garnet Shores, she's done an incredible job adapting.

Gentling my voice, I say, "You *did* do something. You called me."

"And here you are, saving my ass. Again. Your ego must be through the roof at this point." Her head nestles further into my neck, like hugging me is an easy habit.

Hell, it feels like one to me. Her body, both strong and soft, fits against mine perfectly.

"I think there's some kind of curse in Garnet Shores," she adds, "because I've never been part of so many disasters in my life."

"Nah, I think you're just clumsy."

"The bilge pump has nothing to do with clumsiness."

"Then this one's karma for all the times you've been a pain in my ass."

She shakes against me as she laughs. My arms tighten, sealing her there.

"I swear, you've gotten the worst version of me."

"What's that supposed to mean?"

One of her fingers starts drawing little shapeless designs on my chest. "I was cheated on and laid off before coming here. One of my closest friends is hooking up with my ex. My parents are up my ass about getting my career back on track, and I'm living on a sailboat stuck in the eighties. I think it's pretty clear what I meant," she says, almost apathetically.

I hate the defeat in her tone, almost as much as I hate

her piece-of-shit ex and her so-called friend. *Who the fuck does that?* Especially to a woman like her?

I hate it all enough to peel my arms from her back and cup her cheeks, forcing her to look up at me. Rainwater's still caught in those eyelashes, her damp skin gleaming in the soft light.

"Could've fooled me." My eyes flick between hers, making sure I have her full attention. "Because the so-called worst version of you is pretty fucking impressive."

Her lips part for a beat, then pull into a barely-there smile that makes me feel like I've just crested Everest. But I'm not sure *that* view could even beat this one.

She's fucking beautiful.

I want to savor it. Want to keep holding her like a glutton, my self-imposed rules be damned. But the rain isn't stopping any time soon.

Reluctantly, I drop my hands. "You're going to grab what you need for tonight and tomorrow, then you're going to go sit in my truck while I take care of this."

She frowns. "I'm going to help you."

"By sitting in the truck," I re-emphasize, hoping she listens *for once.* "With your current track record, you'll probably get struck by lightning outside. And then I'll be stuck dealing with a new social media girl, and I've just figured out how to deal with you."

"You're ridiculous," she replies, though she gives in and starts rummaging around the cabin.

"Who rents this thing to you?" I ask as she packs.

"Some guy named Gary," she answers, opening what I'm pretty sure is a bin full of underwear. I divert my eyes before I can discover what's inside, not needing that kind of torture. "He was planning to use it this summer, but got called down to Florida or something for a few months to take care of his sister."

"You have Gary's contact information?"

She nods toward a flimsy binder splayed on the bed. "He didn't pick up."

What kind of person rents their boat to someone with zero boating knowledge, then isn't available for emergencies? A stupid, self-serving one, that's who.

She starts shutting off the lights, but I stop her, telling her I'll take care of it before ushering her out into the storm.

"Jacket?" I prompt.

She glances down at her soaked shirt, glued to her pert breasts. "Kind of pointless now, isn't it?"

The rain is unrelenting as we splash across the deck and make our way to my truck. A pair of headlights cut into the lot just as I toss her bag into the backseat and open the passenger door.

"Who is that?" she asks, slipping inside.

"Anson."

Her eyes widen in horror. "You called my *boss*?"

I level a flat look her way. "I called my *brother*, who was happy to drop off the portable pump so I could get to you sooner."

"It's almost midnight, in a storm." She runs an agitated hand through her hair. "Your brother is going to think I'm an idiot."

"Hey." I grab her hand before it can make another pass, wanting to keep all the pretty hairs on her head. "He's only going to think you're an idiot if you run out there and try to help. You have nothing to do with the scuppers being fucked and the bilge pump shitting out on you."

Her shoulders marginally relax, some of her resistance fading. Gravel kicks up nearby as Anson parks.

"Now stay in the truck."

She looks like she wants to argue, but after a moment, she sinks back into the seat. "You are so bossy," she grumbles.

"I have a feeling you might like that trait in a different setting."

Knowing I shouldn't have said that, but not giving a shit, I close the door before I can see her reaction and head over to Anson, a navy-blue shadow unloading something from the back of his truck.

"I got it," I tell him over the rain, helping him set the pump on the ground. "Can't thank you enough."

"You really think I drove all the way out here just to leave?" He straightens, hitting me with his signature scowl, which suggests he's either about to rain down hell, or is working through how stupid I am.

"You've got Lala," I reason.

"I do, and she's passed out in the back. Didn't even wake up when I carried her out," he says. "Now do you want to keep standing here in the rain, arguing about it? Or go help out the Social Media Director that you clearly don't hate as much as you want to?"

Shaking my head, I haul up the pump and head down the dock.

———

"YOU REALLY DON'T MIND me staying over?" Her question comes over a yawn that cues my own. "I can get a hotel or something."

It's three in the morning, and my entire body wants to sink into the driver's seat of my truck. My brain is buzzing, though, because Eliza's curled up in my passenger seat, looking right at home with her cheek pressed against the headrest, sleepy face turned toward me.

Her eyes were heavy with exhaustion by the time Anson and I returned to the truck, and she barely managed to stave off sleep during our drive.

"If I bring you to a hotel, you'll pass out before you even reach your room."

"M'kay." Another mighty yawn fills the cab, and she nestles in, the frizzy waves of her hair smushing against the leather. "Maybe I'll just sleep here."

No way is she sleeping outside in my truck. I'd give her my own bed and sleep on the floor before I'd allow that. "These seats are leather, Boston. I'm not letting you get your drool all over them."

I hop out, the wind rustling my wet hair. The rain stopped an hour ago and the thunder is long past, thankfully, but the evidence of the storm is everywhere, from flooded roads and the water pooling in my driveway to the mossy smell of the woods surrounding my home.

After grabbing her bag from the back seat, I circle the hood and pop her door open. She twists around, face crinkled in thought.

"You know, that bachelorette party from the other day wasn't far off."

I'm really not sure where this is going. That bachelorette party said a lot of things, many of which were objectively wrong. Morally speaking.

"You *are* pretty chivalrous," she decides.

I step aside so she can slide out. "Complimenting me? You must be awfully tired."

Proving my point, she yawns *again*. But then she says, with complete sincerity, "I mean it."

I'm not sure what to say to that, just know that it makes

me feel like I'm doing something right. Closing the truck door, I lead the way inside, where Dave greets us.

Eliza pauses at the entryway, like she's facing off with a hulking bouncer. "Can we call a truce for tonight?" she asks him wearily.

Dave stares at her for a few seconds, then turns and waddles back to his little bed by the couch.

Viscerally aware of her presence in my home, I watch as she scans the open living room in front of us, tracking the wood beams across the ceiling and the sparsely furnished space beneath it. For probably the first time in my life, I wish I had a fucking candle lit. Something to warm the space up, make it less of a bachelor pad.

At least it's not a mess.

Her scan ends on me, dark circles heavy under her eyes. She's had a hell of a night. We both have.

"It's a nice place," she says softly.

Clearing my throat, I nod toward the hall. "Let me show you the guest room." She nods and files in behind me, head swiveling as we pass the kitchen.

I kick myself for not cleaning the counters after dinner, saving the work for the morning.

Since when am I self-conscious about my home?

"This is usually Lala's room," I explain as we enter the guest room.

"Did you do this all yourself?" she asks, taking in the pale pink bedspread, soccer-ball shaped pillows and sparkle nightlight.

I nod, setting her bag down on the carpet. "Just want her to like sleeping over here." I've never felt as lost as I did walking into the home goods store, searching through all the frilly pink and stuffed unicorns for stuff she'd like.

A small smile plays on her lips. "I'm sure she'd love sleepovers with her big brother, regardless."

"Try my best." Half the time, I don't even know if I'm doing it right. How Anson stepped right in as her parent-figure is beyond me. To say it's not easy is the understatement of the year.

Eliza quietly circles back to me, her drying shirt hanging loosely off her frame, almost swallowing her. She tilts her head, considering me. "You aren't who I thought you were."

In the dead, empty silence of this room, it sounds like a confession. Her quiet honesty pulls a reply from my tongue.

"You aren't, either."

But you're leaving.

In what—four, five weeks now?

The countdown fades to the background when her tired gaze drifts to my lips. I wait for it to flick away. I *need* it to.

Instead, it lingers, something soft and warm feathering through her fatigue. It's magnetic, *imploring*, and I find myself stepping closer, to encourage whatever thoughts are behind that look.

My hand lifts to reach for her—

Until her eyes squeeze shut, her face crumpling into a giant yawn.

My legs are stiff as I force them back a step, away from her. Away from *temptation*. "You should get some rest," I say stiffly. "Sleep in, too. Anson says not to worry about work tomorrow."

Every fiber of my being wants to stay, but I find the strength to retreat. The door's nearly closed behind me when her soft voice reaches me.

"Grayson."

She's still standing in place when I crack the door open.

"The things you've done for me..."

Her delicate throat works as she shifts on her feet. I wonder if they're trying to close the distance between us.

Hell, I *want* them to.

Because then I could play the victim. Excuse myself for standing here, letting *her* come to *me*, and succumbing to whatever happens after that.

But she stays put as she says, "I appreciate you being there for me—having my back. It means more than I can express."

I want to have a hell of a lot more than your back.

I want you, in my bed.

I want you, in Garnet Shores.

I'm pretty fucking sure I want your heart, too.

I can't speak those thoughts, but unable to think of any other response, I nod my head and close the door—like the snick of the latch will make me forget Eliza's sleeping in my home, just a wall away from me.

It doesn't.

26

———

ELIZA

THERE'S something about waking up to the soft sounds of another person starting their day. The muted footsteps, the careful thud of a coffee mug, the soft wash of water from the sink.

It's comforting.

Always has been, even when that other person was Kyle, and I no longer loved him as I once did.

Maybe it's childhood nostalgia, the sounds of my parents getting ready when I was waking up for school. Maybe those noises stop my to-do list from shoving to the forefront the second I open my eyes, or maybe it's that humans aren't meant to live alone.

Whatever it is, the quiet sounds of Grayson moving about the house have me waking up much calmer than I should be, considering last night's events. Events that he'd handled with that confident assurance that's quickly become the antidote to my panic.

The sunlight streaming into the room finally registers, and I check my phone to see it's nearly ten in the morning.

Why isn't he at the farm?

Sliding from bed, I throw on sweatpants and a bra beneath my tee-shirt, check my face for drool, and pad into the hallway.

The rich aroma of coffee hits me first, followed by sizzling butter. Then I'm struck by the sight of Grayson standing over the stove with his back to me, hair mussed, Dave cradled in one arm while he works a spatula with the other. He's wearing a cut-off that hangs off his broad back, every muscle curled around my feathered nemesis on full display.

If I thought the *sounds* he made were nice, this is...a visual blessing.

The floorboards creak under my next step, and he twists.

"Morning."

Dave's neck cranes, those beady little eyes spotting me. I might hate this duck, but my ovaries want to explode at the sight of him nestled in Grayson's arm like a baby.

"Didn't mean to interrupt your private time."

"Don't worry. Dave gets to hang with me all the time. He's just helping me make breakfast." He turns back around. "You gluten-free or anything like that?"

"No," I answer, a little dazed.

Grayson is making me *breakfast*. After all he did last night.

"Shouldn't you be at work?" I ask, edging into the kitchen.

"Heading in late today." He flips what looks like a pancake. There's a bottle of maple syrup and a bowl of fruit on the eat-in counter, and a carton of cream next to a pot of coffee and an empty mug. "Team's there and everything looks fine after the storm, so there's no rush." He jerks his head toward the coffee machine. "Rest is yours if you want it."

I have caffeine every morning. Of course I want it.

But I don't move.

Because the sudden realization that hits me is paralyzing.

I want this man. *Him*, who's going into work late just to make me breakfast, who's going out of his way to take care of me.

I want him beyond what he did to me on the beach. I want him beyond our stupid digs, our banter, the tension we're both trying to deny.

And no imaginary rickety stone wall is going to change my mind.

I can't pretend he doesn't make me feel both safe *and* strong—calm when I need it, and *alive* every other minute I'm with him. I can't pretend he doesn't feel *right*—make *me* feel right—despite being the rugged, boorish, provocative antithesis to my expectations.

Which means he's going to follow me back to the city and haunt my sorry ass, and I'm just going to have to make space for that misery until eventually—months later, prob-ably—I forget about him.

Because that's the only way Grayson will be with me outside of Garnet Shores. The last two weeks have made it clear that he's not interested in pursuing anything serious. And I'm not going to try to convince him otherwise, because despite this realization that he's something, *someone*, rare in this world...I just can't see how we would work. Not when I'm two hours away and he works seven-day weeks, just like me.

I owe myself *more*. Grayson deserves more, too.

Well, at least he's uncovered what your actual type is.

What a pathetic consolation prize.

"Don't have any sugar, unfortunately." Grayson's voice jolts me back to the moment.

"Cream is great," I say, composing myself as I move to pour a coffee. He flips the last two pancakes onto a plate piled with steaming, pillowy goodness. "You didn't have to do this."

"Do what? Make myself breakfast?" He gently sets Dave down and carries the plate to the eat-in counter.

I trail behind him as he rummages through a cabinet. "You're telling me you make yourself pancakes on the regular?"

"Sure do."

I'm not buying it one bit.

Taking a seat, I hug my coffee in my hands. "You shouldn't be making me pancakes after last night," I say honestly. "You've already done so much."

He sets a plate before me and grabs two forks. "I'm about to deliver some bad news. The pancakes will soften the blow."

Grayson sits next to me and drags the pancakes over, depositing two on my plate before serving himself. When he hands me the maple syrup and continues to say nothing else, I prompt, "Are you trying to build suspense?"

"No. I'm waiting for you to take a bite before I say it."

Dousing my pancakes, I take a giant forkful and stuff it in my mouth. "Ready." My voice is muffled around the pancake.

Grayson lifts a humored brow, but his voice is serious as he says, "Your boat's being hauled for repairs. Gary doesn't want you to live on it while it's out of the water. It's last in the queue, so it could be a few weeks."

The pancake turns to ash in my mouth. "How do you... did you call him?"

"I called him early this morning and explained the situation. Not because you can't handle it yourself, but because I know you'd want to wake up with solutions, which I have."

He looks like he expects me to be outraged by him going over my head, but with his explanation, I'm not.

I'm grateful.

And instantly stressed. I'm out of a *home*.

"Anson has a guest house on his property that no one's using. He's offering it to you, no charge."

"I can't take a hand-out from my boss." The reaction is immediate. "I'll get a hotel or...or a rental or something."

As if anticipating this response, he smoothly continues, "Any rentals in town have been booked for months, and one night at a hotel in the summer will cost you a couple hundred. So if you don't want to stay at Anson's, the other option is that you stay here in the guest room until your boat's back in the water."

He goes quiet, observing me as I take this in.

Surely, there has to be some other option. Something better than depending on my *very* intimidating boss for housing, or invading Grayson's space. But apart from car camping or...or *actual* camping, there's nothing I can do. I don't have the budget to stay in a hotel for weeks.

"I really don't feel comfortable mooching off my employer." As it is, the fact that he drove out in a late-night storm to help me makes me want to shrivel up inside.

Grayson shrugs. "Then you're staying here." He resumes eating his pancakes, like he didn't just nonchalantly decide I'm moving in with him. Like the butterflies in my stomach aren't throwing a house party right now.

"You have a lot going on. I don't want to impose," I argue weakly.

"You're not. Though you'll have to get along with Dave."

I glance at the feathered monster, waddling little circles around the living room, then back to Grayson. My chest is full of giddy, starry-eyed excitement that clearly hasn't gotten the memo that this is going to *suck.*

Teasing myself, playing house with a man I can't have, who just elevated himself to *superhero* status by offering me his place.

Maybe he clogs the toilet with massive dumps, or eats out of the trash, or doesn't wash his hands, and everything I feel for him will effectively be squashed.

The thought is a small comfort.

"If I can handle week-one Grayson, I can handle a bird," I tell him, digging into my pancakes.

He spares Dave a sympathetic look. "Sorry, buddy. You have no idea what you're in for."

———

HOT, lemon-scented steam blasts my face as I open the oven and remove the chicken for the fourth time in six minutes. Using two forks, I carefully open the slice I made in one of the chicken breasts to see if it's finally done.

God forbid I overcook it and Grayson eat rubbery poultry. The entire world will collapse. So here I am, being shamelessly obsessive.

The juices run clear, so I shut off the oven and start setting the table. There isn't much dishware to choose from —just a handful of mismatched plates, a random collection of utensils, and some scratched up glasses. It's on-trend with what I found in his fridge earlier: condiments, a few eggs, milk, maple syrup, and three too-soft apples.

I'd categorize it as bachelor living, but that's not entirely fair. I've seen guys' homes with speakers galore, couches stained from *way* too much NSFW activity, and a fine layer of dust on floors that have never been properly cleaned. This isn't Kyle's manicured, modern apartment, but it isn't gross, either. Just...bare.

It's the home of someone who literally comes here to sleep and eat dinner, and spends almost every other hour in his day working.

A car pulls up outside, and Grayson walks through the door just as I set the rice on the table. Dark circles cut under his eyes, telling the story of a man who was my savior until three in the morning, woke early to solve more of my problems, then busted his ass at work before returning home at— I peek at the oven clock—eight-thirty at night.

Yet somehow, his exhaustion lifts when he steps in and takes in the scene. "You made dinner?"

Dave scoots in behind him as he saunters closer, tossing his keys on the counter. He doesn't have anything else on him. No water bottle. No lunch box. He just...raw-dogged it all day.

Now that I think of it, I don't know if I've ever seen him bring lunch to the farm. The few times I've passed the warehouse during break, it's always sandwich wrappers and chip bags, or take-out on the table. What was he expecting to eat for dinner? Eggs with maple syrup and a soft apple?

Men.

"Had to top your pancakes," I say.

"My pancakes are damn good," he murmurs, wandering over to the table.

"They are. So is my chicken."

I'm no chef, but there are few things I've learned to whip up when I'm trying to impress, and this herby lemon butter chicken is *it*. Kyle loved it. His friends loved it. Jane loved it, maybe as much as she loves being a lying, weaselly, fake-as-her-tan friend.

Grayson's about to be the first *deserving* person to mouthgasm from it.

I hope. Because I don't actually know what his food preferences are, aside from sugary, floury treats and coffee.

I scrutinize his expression as he surveys the spread of green beans, rice, and chicken. It's frustratingly neutral, until his head bobs in a slow, approving nod.

"Alright, Boston. Let's see what you got." He lifts his ball cap and shakes his hand through his stiff, sweaty hair. His hand freezes. "I, uh, should probably shower first."

Sheepishness is funny on him, so poignantly out of place among all those gruff lines.

I doubt I'm the first woman he's met after a long day. Maybe they expected him to impress them with a little curated gentility, but this isn't a date. It's me putting Grayson out of his home and trying to look after *him*, for once.

Plus, I don't want some manufactured, glossed-over version of him.

I start piling his plate high. "Do you normally shower, shave, and put on a tux for dinner after work?"

"Dave appreciates it when I'm presentable."

I roll my eyes and nod toward the fridge. "Not sure if you're a cold-beer-after-work guy, but I picked up some options."

He peers at me for a moment before heading to the fridge and opening it wide. "You went grocery shopping," he states.

"I did."

It's like he's staring at an alien spaceship and not a full refrigerator. Tentatively, he rummages around, bottles clinking.

"What's this?" He produces a baby pink can.

"A seltzer water."

A groove appears between his brows as he turns it over in his hand.

"You should try it. I won't tell anyone how much you love girly drinks. It can be our secret."

He hits me with a dry look before returning it to the shelf and producing a beer. "I didn't leave much here for you to work with."

Why does that almost sound like an apology?

"You're a single guy, Grayson. I was expecting moldy cheese and three-week-old leftovers." I spoon more of the buttery, lemony liquid over his chicken and rice and set his plate down. "Come eat."

"You cook one meal in this kitchen, and now you're giving orders like you own it," he grumbles, opening his beer and sitting across from me.

"Is Chef Grayson feeling threatened?"

The thick sinews of his stubbled neck shift as he takes a long, tired drink from the bottle. "Boston, you've been threatening me since day one."

"I can safely say you started it."

His amber gaze is warmly assessing as he murmurs, "And here you are, still at it."

It seems like there are multiple meanings lying beneath it, meanings I want to peel apart and latch onto.

"I think you'll forgive me when you try this chicken."

"Talking a big game, per usual." He takes a long sniff of

his steaming plate before cutting off a giant bite and stuffing it in his mouth.

His eyes close as he chews, and I can't tell if it's because he's savoring the flavors or trying to hide disgust. Finally, he swallows, and there's a pleased tilt to his eyes when they pop back open. "Your home should flood more often."

He might as well have told me I just got a promotion. I try not to grin like a dork as I dig in. "I'm glad you like it."

If I thought his flood comment was flattering, it's nothing compared to when he says, "Tastes like my mom's cooking." He shovels another heaping forkful. "She'd always have a nice hot meal waiting for me and my dad when we got back from the farm...until she couldn't anymore."

For a moment, I fear the memory might come with sadness, but he's practically humming with contentment across the table. The satisfied "mmm" sounds he makes every few bites fill me with an insane, silly pleasure.

"How old were you when your dad started the farm?"

"Twenty. Middle of college," he says after a massive swallow. Half his plate is already gone.

"Did you always know you wanted to work there?"

He chuckles. "I was determined *not* to work there. That was *his* adventure. I just helped out around classes and during breaks."

"What did you want to do?"

"Finance."

I choke on my food.

His fork pauses. "That surprise you?"

He says it like it *should* surprise me. And, well, *of course* it does. Sticking the man across from me in a fluorescently lit cubicle wearing an endless rotation of suits would be like putting a lion with rabies in a cat carrier.

Clearing my throat, I say, "Did twenty-year-old you

know that career path involves hair gel, regular beard trims, and cologne?"

He grunts. "I trim my beard. It's neat."

"Not Wall Street neat."

"You got a problem with my facial hair?"

Yes. I want you to rub it all over my skin.

"No. It lends itself nicely to the whole disgruntled bear image."

He shakes his head, muttering something that sounds like, "*you* make me disgruntled."

Then he says, "To answer your question, no, I didn't know what I was getting myself into. I did well in school, and wanted a way out of Garnet Shores. To go have an adventure in a big city. Make lots of money."

"Do you ever wish you ended up doing that?"

"Hell no," he chokes out. His next bite pauses midway to his mouth. "When my mom started declining, Dad wasn't able to spend as much time at work, so I took the semester off to help him full-time. It was...good for me, being out on the water, doing labor all day. Kept my mind off of her. After she died, Dad started letting everything go, buyers started making offers, and I just..." He shrugs. "I couldn't let it go. Couldn't see myself doing something else."

And what he's done with it has been incredible.

I always knew Gold's was his father's legacy. That's what my research told me, what he says when guiding farm tours. But those are just nice-sounding words without...all *this* behind it.

For most business owners, their business is their baby. But to Grayson, the farm is *more* than that, and I'm embarrassed to realize the true depth of it never dawned on me until now.

What happened last year, the farm being threatened—it wasn't just business at stake. It was memory. Love.

I, too, would have morphed into Big Foot if a new girl showed up one day with unlimited access to the business's public face and a very limited understanding of my craft.

"I didn't know your parents," I start cautiously, wanting to get this right, "but I can't imagine they'd be anything but proud of what you've done. What you're doing now."

"I appreciate that," he says, lips curving as he chews. "What about you? Did you always dream of corporate life?"

"If a child ever said they wanted to grow up and sit in a cubicle worrying about spreadsheets, I'd be concerned."

Humor dances in his golden gaze. "If any kid did say it, I bet it'd be you. Your kind of drive has got to come pre-installed."

I huff a dry laugh. "Pretty sure my parents had me speaking complete sentences by two months old. Their daughter had to excel, just like them."

"So why'd you choose to do that in marketing?"

"Plenty of job opportunities. A clear path to leadership positions. You get to occasionally be creative. And I don't ever want to hold someone's life in my hands like my parents," I list. "They hated that I chose something outside of medicine, law, or finance. They didn't really respect it until they realized how relevant it is in today's business world."

This might be *one* area where I've actually been thankful for Suzanne's close relationship with my parents. She showed them the possible salaries and career trajectories, and suddenly, their daughter no longer needed a career intervention.

"And do you like it?" Grayson asks.

"I mean, the money's good, it's—"

"No," he cuts me off, pulling my eyes up from my plate. He leans in on the table, his utensils still. "Do you *like* it? Are you happy doing it?"

Am I happy?

I'm...satisfied with my paychecks. Proud of my progress. Content when a week actually goes smoothly. But *happy?*

That'll come when I've *made it.* When I've earned enough money and power to enjoy time off, write the rules, and take my pick of who I work for.

"I'm busting my ass right now so I *can* be happy. In five, ten years, maybe."

His forehead wrinkles. "Why do you have to wait to be happy?"

I wait for a punchline that never comes. "You have to *earn* it. Do your time," I say, spelling out the obvious. "Success doesn't come right away."

His befuddlement doesn't budge. "You're implying that happiness hinges on success."

"It does," I confirm. "I know that doesn't sound very romantic or fun, but I think it's true for a lot of us. We want to hit milestones, achieve goals, see our work pay off."

"I understand that."

Nodding, I return to my plate, only for Grayson to stop me in my tracks. "But why does your 'success' need to be so far away?"

Is he just...challenging me for the sake of argument? Trying to say I'm behind, or something? Promotions take time. Career trajectories follow a tried-and-true ladder.

Trying to cool my bubbling frustration, I say, "I highly doubt an established company will just promote a twenty-six-year-old to VP."

He blinks. "Success doesn't *need* to be a title. A corner

office in a big high-rise that's a decade away. That can be part of it, sure, but success isn't intrinsically tied to *work*. It's tied to *life*." I open my mouth to argue, but he barrels on. "Making good friends. Waking up excited to start the week. Smiling three times per day. Reducing stress. Swimming every day for a month straight. These are milestones, too. Just like making strides at a lower-stakes company that doesn't drain you dry. Or starting your own business, where you're in control and don't have to suffer under a shitty manager."

None of his statements are objectively offensive, but each one prods at all the wrong places. Places that have always reassured me that what I'm doing is worth it, even when I'm stressed out of my mind or dreading a week. Ones that comforted me when I skipped school dances to study, or when my parents prohibited sleepovers because they'd ruin my swim performance.

Struggling to keep my tone calm, I say, "I've been working toward my goals for *years*, Grayson. There might be many ways to define success, but there's nothing wrong with *my* definition."

"But is it actually yours?" he asks gently. "Or is it what you've been told—by your parents, schools, society?"

"It's mine," I state, jamming my fork into my chicken, my ire bubbling far past its legal bounds. It's like he's *trying* to plant doubts I shouldn't be having, make me question everything I've been doing. I snap, "You know that having a little bit of a beard doesn't make you wise."

His mouth twitches. "Never claimed I was."

The calm, easy way he says it—I *hate* it. Hate that he doesn't match my irritation, or give credence to my mean-spirited words, because it makes regret sweep right in.

"I'm sorry. That was mean."

"I'm insulted that you're apologizing." His eyes meet mine. "I can handle you."

I exhale heavily, grateful he's brushing right past it. "It's late. You've had a long day. Figured you might be a little sensitive."

"Sensitive? Now *that* deserves an apolog—" A mighty yawn cuts him off. It's almost comical, the timing, but it's a sobering reminder of his exhaustion.

Standing, I begin gathering the dishes. His chair scrapes on tile as he starts to help me.

"I've got it," I tell him.

Of course, he ignores me.

I plop the plates down and stop him with a hand around his thick wrist. This gets his attention.

It also gives me a healthy whiff and, yeah, this doesn't smell like the Grayson who laid me down on that beach and enlightened my vagina. This smells like a Grayson who sweat in the sun for ten hours.

"I've got it," I repeat. "You're tired. Go take a shower. Get some rest."

His mouth compresses, but after a stubborn beat, he murmurs, "Thank you."

"You're welcome." I release him, and he trudges from the table.

I'm by the sink when I hear, "You don't have to do this, you know."

I spin to see him paused before the hallway. He must read the question in my eyes from all the way over there, because he explains, "You staying here—it isn't an exchange. That was really fucking good, but I'm not expecting you to cook and clean and do stuff like that."

Never once did I think he *was* expecting some kind of payment.

Many others would. When I'd stayed with Kyle for a week between leases, he'd joked about letting me pamper him for seven days straight. Only it wasn't a joke. And I did it, because I was still half in love with him and pathetically wanted to ensure he felt the same about me.

Facing this man in the hallway, I can't for the life of me remember what I ever saw in Kyle.

"I feel indebted to you. Anyone would," I say honestly. "But that's not why I cooked you dinner."

Yes, it was part *thank you*. But I *wanted* to do it. Treat him. Make him feel good.

Take care of him—this man who's always taking care of everyone and everything else.

Which is why, after he goes to bed, I don't stop myself from packing him leftovers, or leaving a note by his keys telling him he better take it for lunch. Then I sit down with my laptop to review the list of interview prep questions Suzanne sent to me.

It turns out the hiring manager from last week didn't actually hate me. In fact, she liked me enough to invite me to an interview in Boston next Monday. Better yet, I'm one of only *two* candidates they moved forward with. The odds are incredible.

It's *great* news. A big, sparkling opportunity. The chance to get back on track.

Yet, as I dive into prep and start constructing my responses, I can't help but feel like this is a giant, obligatory chore.

Like...like maybe this isn't a big, exciting step toward my *success*.

It's just because of the twenty-four hours you've had, I tell myself.

Yeah.

That must be it.

27

GRAYSON

"ARE you *sure* this isn't a pity invite?"

I grunt. *Pity invite.* That's a new one.

It's genuinely impressive how many different ways Eliza can ask the same question: *Are you sure I'm welcome at your brother's?*

We're at six—no, seven—iterations now.

"I'm as sure as I was twenty minutes ago when we got in this truck. Which is as sure as I was right before we left the farm. Which is as sure as I was—"

"Okay. I get it." Her fingers play nervously in her lap as she watches Anson's street roll by.

Though street's an inadequate term. The private single-lane road is framed by lush, green trees that link together up top, like this antique bureau mirror Mom used to have. No matter how many times I've driven it, it's still stunning.

There's a little intake of breath, then, "It's just, he wouldn't be inviting me if I wasn't squatting in your house."

With her nerves, it's like I'm taking her to visit royalty.

Yeah, Anson's made a name for himself, and he's in

charge of her employment. But he's also the kid I'd noogie in middle school when my growth spurt came before his.

And he sure as hell wouldn't have specifically invited Eliza along if he didn't want her there.

"If you were squatting, I would've kicked you out by now."

She snorts. "You could've tried."

I plant her with a dry look. "You realize that stubbornness doesn't trump physical strength, right?"

She's decently tall, and more than a little toned, but I could toss her over my shoulder, walk to the salt pond, and dump her there without batting an eye.

Or go for a much shorter walk to the bed. Set her down and show her just how fucking much I want her to keep on staying at my place.

"You've come home the past two days walking like a seventy-year-old and creaking when you sit down," she points out. "Pretty sure my stubbornness would win."

"You want to test that theory?" The challenge runs out of my mouth before I can drag it back.

Who the fuck am I kidding? All my restraint is gone.

She's fucking *living* with me.

All that distance I tried so hard to shove between us was obliterated the moment she called me for help with that boat.

Eliza puts the ball right back in my court. "Do *you* want to?"

Fuck yes.

That one, I manage to keep down. "You've had a bad week. Don't want to crush your ego along with it."

She hums. Disappointed, maybe. Or just being the smarter of us two and not chasing the conversation any further.

Again, I find my focus off the road and on her. The woman who's cooked me dinner and packed me lunch two days in a row, who's suddenly got me looking forward to something other than sleep at the end of the workday.

Which is just as well, because I *can't* fucking sleep. Not with her just down the hall. In my grasp, playing house, giving my imagination too much material to run away and dig my grave with.

Offering her my place to stay was the most self-sabotaging, asinine thing I could have done. And the fact that I don't regret it yet goes to show just how thoroughly fucked I am.

Because the regret will come.

When she's gone, and my place is empty, and her fiery quips and proud little chin and intelligent eyes are just a sorry memory that I jerk off to because I can't let go.

I force my eyes back to the road, because the street's about to open up, and learning what wonder looks like on her face will dig my grave deep enough to touch hell.

As it is, her little gasp makes my chest swell with satisfaction.

"Holy crap. The photos do not do this place justice," she breathes.

I can confirm they don't.

Framed by the tall trees of Garnet Shores' signature woods, Anson's vineyard is like stepping into a little oasis straight out of the Italian countryside. Perfect lines of grapevines frame the long drive leading to a recently updated stone villa, the property's crown jewel, where tours and tastings are held and small batch wines are made. We hang a right, circling around to the house located a healthy stretch behind it, its façade similar to the main building, only smaller.

The vineyard is tiny, relatively speaking, but Anson has used the scarcity principle to turn it into a coveted, shining jewel. Separated from the main road, enclosed in trees, you can't help but feel like you're stumbling upon some little treasure.

"What's that?" Eliza asks, nodding to a ramshackle structure tucked against the trees in the distance.

"The bane of my brother's existence." Also known as the one thing he hasn't been able to mold to his will. "It's this old woman's house."

"On your brother's property?"

"Yes and no." The truck creaks as I park in Anson's driveway. His pickup is so shiny, I can see every scratch and chip on my truck's hood in its reflection. "Tell me what you know about this property's history."

We both know she researched it before she came here.

"Years before your brother purchased it, it was a working vineyard. The previous owner struggled to compete with other local vineyards and the imported stuff, so he went bankrupt. The property went on the market for a few years until your brother picked it up and turned it around."

"That's right. But before the previous owner bought this land, it was a farm. That abomination used to be part of that farm, and the old owner kept it for his sister. For whatever reason, he made that house and the little plot of land around it legally hers, so when he sold the vineyard, the house wasn't included."

"Does she still live there?"

"Nope. Nursing home."

She squints at the dilapidated house. "The house is a wreck. Why wouldn't his sister just sell it to Anson with the vineyard?"

"Don't know. But Anson's ready to throw the state's most expensive lawyer at it."

While I don't support him waging war on a grandma, the structure will probably collapse if anyone steps foot in it. Buying it might save a life.

To our left, the front door bursts open, and a maelstrom of action tumbles out—Lala, dressed in soccer gear, a ball in hand, and Runner, my brother's German Shepherd, right on her heels like the perfectly trained dog she is.

"Get out of the truck!" Her voice bounces with her feet, moving at an impressively fast clip for an eight-year-old. "Anson said I can't play after the tasting, so it needs to be—"

Lala skids to a stop, braids flying over her shoulders, when she sees my passenger through the open window.

"Who is *she?*"

Sharing a humored glance with Eliza, we exit the truck. "La, this is Eliza," I introduce as she comes around the front. "She works on the farm with me."

Lala shamelessly evaluates Eliza, her little head tilting with a full-body scan. "You don't *look* like you work on the farm."

No, she doesn't, in a pretty little sundress that shows the smallest glimpse of her thighs.

Eliza smiles kindly. "My work is different from your brother's. I do marketing."

Lala bulldozes right on to her next question. "Do you play soccer?"

"I didn't grow up playing soccer, but I can play sports."

"Can you do goalie?"

"I can probably figure it out."

"Then you're the goalie," La declares.

"Honey, she's wearing a dre—"

"It's alright," Eliza says, taking me by surprise.

Not because I doubt her athleticism, but because she came over for a tasting of Anson's newest wine—and looks the part, glossy lips, strappy sandals, and all.

Apparently, she takes Lala by surprise too, because my little sister loudly states, "The last girl Gray brought wouldn't play goalie."

Kids and the shit they say. "La, that's not—"

She barrels on. "All she did was twirl her fake hair and flutter her eyelashes—"

"Enough," I say sternly.

Lala recognizes my rare not-messing-around tone and sheepishly eyes her cleat-covered feet, kicking the ground. "Am I being ill-mannered?" she asks.

That choice of words would throw me if she wasn't being raised by Anson. *Ill-mannered.* Christ.

Pulling on my parent-role pants, I tell her, "Talking about people who aren't here in a negative way isn't nice."

"But she was mean to you, and she made you sad. How can I talk about her in a *good* way?"

My heart warms at her protectiveness, even as I say, "It just isn't a good way to welcome a new guest, who just offered to play soccer with you."

"Okay. I'm sorry." She hits Eliza with her signature green doe-eyes. "Welcome to our home. Will you still play soccer?"

Eliza fights a smile. "Thank you. And yes, soccer sounds fun."

Lala beams just as Anson leans out the front door, wearing a button-down. "Hello, Eliza," he greets with the formality of a board meeting. To our little sister, he says, "You have twenty minutes. Do not kick the ball at her face."

"Thirty minutes."

"Twenty," Anson says firmly.

The gears in her little mind turn as she thinks over her next offer. Anson knows it, which is why he says, "I'm willing to change it to ten."

Lala's eyes widen. "No, thank you!" She heads for the backyard, shouting "Hurry up! We only have twenty minutes!" over her shoulder.

Eliza meets my eyes as we follow. "So...you dated the daughter of a man who hates you, who also refused to play soccer, huh?"

Thank you, Lala, for bringing up Mackenzie. Not sure why I thought Eliza would let that one slide.

I opt for a lame, "Yep."

What am I going to say? That I'm a poor, sappy bastard who was thinking with his dick?

"Is that your type?" Eliza asks.

Ahead, Lala sets the ball down in front of the little goal Anson built her and gives it a mighty warm-up kick.

"No." My throat burns with more words. Since I'm already fucked, I just say them.

"You are."

I watch Eliza's mouth open into a little "O." Then, coward that I am, I take off, jogging over to Lala.

And Eliza goes on to prove my point for the next twenty minutes as she kicks off her sandals and posts up in the goal, letting enough of Lala's goals through to make my little sister giggle with glee—and, in true Eliza style, blocking all of mine with a shit-eating grin.

———

"THIS IS a new Cayuga and Seyval blend scheduled for launch next year," Anson explains as he pours our glasses at the antique oak dining table, the rich aroma of truffle risotto filling the air.

Sitting across from me, Lala's already downing her glass of white grape juice, cheeks flushed from running her little behind off outside. She's still at the age where my sheer size and strength trump any soccer skills she has, but soon, she'll start whooping my ass.

Eliza murmurs a polite thank you, her back ramrod straight and fingers playing in her lap as Anson sets down the bottle and sits.

"Tell me your thoughts." Anson initiates his routine, holding his glass up in the low light to inspect the white-gold liquid. A little swirl. Some sniffs. All that scientific bullshit someone somewhere once deemed necessary for enjoying wine.

Eliza picks up her glass, observing my brother's twenty-seven-step process before turning hesitantly to me.

"*I'm not a wine expert. At all,*" she'd told me when I first shared the invite earlier today.

I'd assured her it wasn't required. When Anson shares the final iteration of a product, he's already decided to produce it. This little family tasting is just tradition. Our opinions mean nothing.

With a pointed look at her, I haul the glass up to my mouth and throw back a gulp like it's cheap beer. There's a subtle, amused shake to her head before she delicately brings the glass to her mouth and takes a polite sip.

"That's delicious," she says.

She isn't kissing his ass. I'm not a wine guy, but it *is* delicious. Tastes like summer.

"This will be our first blend that trends slightly sweet," Anson informs us, no doubt dumbing it down for our unrefined ears.

"It's *very* good," Lala declares from the rim of her juice cup.

Anson's lips tip into the warm smile only Lala can pull from him. "So good that she's been asking for it every day."

Lala nods emphatically. "I've been telling everyone at school about it."

His smile slips. "Have you?"

"Mrs. Johnson said it's not appropriate to talk about in school, but I told her it's just grapes! What's wrong with grapes?"

My shoulders shake as I fight a laugh.

Anson runs his hand across his chin. "There's nothing wrong with grapes, La. But as you know, wine contains alcohol, which is an adult topic. We've talked about this many times."

Her little face wrinkles in confusion. "But *I* have wine."

She has grape juice from the grocery store. But Anson doesn't want to ruin the magic. "You have a special *kid* wine, which doesn't contain alcohol. But we only produce it for you, so no one else knows that. We can talk about these things as much as you'd like, but only at home."

"But I bet Mrs. Johnson drinks wine."

"Mrs. Johnson is just trying to do her job and make sure everyone follows the rules, which includes not discussing activities that are illegal for those under the age of twenty-one."

"You said that sometimes you have to make your own rules."

"I did, didn't I?" Anson looks to me for help, but I'm not the one giving an eight-year-old daily business lessons. "Remind me to talk to you about the importance of discernment."

"*Dis-cern-ment*," Lala repeats, frowning at all the syllables. "Is that my new word of the week?"

"Yes."

"Speaking of new words," I cut in, finally taking pity on him, "Got a name for this blend yet?"

"No." He takes a long, belabored sip and sets down his glass, sharp eyes sliding to Eliza. "Do you have any thoughts?"

Eliza takes a moment to drink before answering, like she needs to gather her courage.

"Sweeter wines obviously appeal to wine enthusiasts, but they also attract more casual drinkers. They're more approachable." She clenches her hands in her lap, like she's trying to force her nerves away. "Brand consistency is important. But if you do want to reach those more casual, summertime day drinkers, I'd go with a warm name. Something inviting, maybe with a local spin. A Garnet Shores Blend, Waterfront White, something like that."

I don't think her chest moves as she waits for Anson's response.

When it comes, it isn't what either of us expects.

"How much do you know about the wine industry?"

"Very little," she answers honestly.

"How quickly do you think you could learn it?"

"I'm a fast learner."

It's the first note of confidence in her voice all night. I want to appreciate it, but I'm too busy working out why Anson would ask that question.

There's only one plausible reason.

He confirms it when he sets his glass aside and says, "I've been outsourcing most of my marketing efforts until now, but Gold's is reaching a point where it'll be more efficient and effective to have an in-house, full-time team. I want you on it."

For a second, my mind goes blank. From shock, maybe. Then a tidal wave of hope and possibility crashes in.

Anson is offering her a full-time job in Garnet Shores. A reason to stay. A damn good one, too, as he adds, "I understand you come from the Boston corporate environment. Your salary would be competitive, and you would be my Director of Marketing, reporting directly to me."

Beside me, Eliza is a wide-eyed, unmoving doll, her jaw hinged open.

"Take time to think about it, then tell me if you want to discuss this further. I do not want an answer now."

I want an answer now. I want her to nod her head and scream yes. Say she'll give it a chance. Stay in this place that clearly makes her happier than the city does, despite her bullshit deflections last night.

But I can't demand her agreement. Can't make her decisions or choose what's right for her.

For all I know, she might already have a job offer elsewhere, or a new lease signed in the city.

"Wow. Okay," Eliza finally stammers out. "Thank you. I'll let you know."

Anson dips his chin, like he didn't just rip the fucking rug out from both of us, and heads into the kitchen. I jump to my feet, right behind him, because if I stay at that table, I'll just study her face like a scientist observing amoebas for any signs that she wants this.

And because, once again, Anson's blindsiding me with hiring decisions that affect my farm.

"Didn't think to give me a heads up?"

"It isn't a farm position," he states, not bothering to turn around as he plates the risotto.

Man, the deliberately obtuse thing comes *so* naturally to him.

"She'll be doing marketing for all of Gold's, which includes the farm."

"She will." He carefully sets the seared scallops on top of the risotto. "But marketing for all of Gold's has always fallen under me, and in this role, she'll be spending most of her time at headquarters, here. You've never even interacted with the outsourced teams when they've occasionally stopped by the farm."

"This is different."

Anson pauses, a scallop suspended in the air. "You clearly don't hate her anymore. So is this different because you want to fuck her?" The scallop descends onto its plate. "Or because working with Eliza now has you interested in our marketing operations?"

"You shouldn't be talking about your employee that way," I grit out.

"And you shouldn't be *thinking* about an employee that way." He sets the tongs down and faces me, his expression indifferent. "Though I guess it doesn't matter, because she's my employee and not yours. You're colleagues. You can do whatever you want."

Growing up, Dawson and him would go at it like bulls, taking backyard wrestling and play fights too far. Enough for one of them to sport the occasional bruised eye or bloody nose. I was always the one to break them up, but right now, I'm feeling inspired by my little brother's volatility.

The girls are right around the corner, so I settle for a humorless chuckle. "You're a real dick, you know that?"

He lifts his chin, giving me a deductive scan like the expert analyst he is. "So it's none of those two options, which means you have feelings for her." His eyes narrow.

"But if that's the case, I don't know why you're pissed. This is a happy surprise for you."

It *is*. But I've just spent the last couple of weeks resigning myself to the inevitability that she'll leave. Torturing myself with it.

When I don't say that, because it sounds too damn pathetic, Anson does what he does best and sucker punches me. "Tell me, what difference would it have made if you knew? She hasn't accepted."

This offer means nothing, dumbass.

Doesn't mean this is what she wants. Doesn't mean she's staying. Doesn't mean she'll even consider it at all.

That's what he's saying. As always, he's indisputably right.

"Just would've been nice to have a heads up." Done with this conversation, I palm two of the plates and carry them out.

Before I round the corner into the dining area, Anson, in all his apathetic glory, says, "I do hope she says yes. It'll be good for this business."

For the first time, I don't give a damn about the business.

But I go on and *hope* right alongside him as we all share dinner together. And every time Eliza answers one of Lala's silly questions, or lets her intelligence fly in a debate with my brother, or sets her delicate fingers around the wine glass, that hope morphs more and more into permission. Premature, ill-advised-as-hell permission.

It's gasoline and a spark to the giant pile of tinder inside of me that she's been stacking since the day she showed up and spat fire at me in the office.

28

ELIZA

MY HEAD SPINS as the truck rumbles through Garnet Shores' quiet, low-lit streets.

It isn't from the wine.

Anson Gold just offered me a full-time *job*.

One that comes with a promotion and a leadership position.

And instead of saying an eloquent *This sounds like an incredible opportunity, and I appreciate the consideration*, I sat there like an electrified fish before stuttering an awkward collection of syllables. I think I redeemed myself when I debated the efficacy of data-driven personalization with Anson, and he didn't rescind the offer before we left, but still, it wasn't my finest moment.

Grayson sits quietly beside me, both hands on the wheel, his posture unusually tense. He hasn't said a word since we closed ourselves in the truck ten minutes ago.

"Did you know?" I ask into the silence.

He glances over. "That he'd offer you a job?" When I nod, he responds with a grim-sounding, "No."

So he's upset. At Anson, for not telling him? Or at the possibility that I might stay?

I replay our earlier exchange.

Is that your type?

No.

You are.

His confession threw me for a giant, rollercoaster-sized loop. Unspoken tension—this quiet, torturous attraction—was one thing. But speaking it out loud made it...real. *Actionable.* Showed me that his neurons are just as lit up for me as mine are for him, and they're done trying to deny it.

Yet here he is, stiff as a board, fingers tight around the wheel like the worn leather is all that's keeping him from losing it.

"The wine was delicious," I say, wading into safer territory.

"It was."

I try for a joke. "Your brother's risotto makes my chicken look like cheap takeout."

"No, it doesn't."

Oookay, then.

The truck bounces as we enter his driveway. When I open my door, the shadowed woods around his property sing with crickets and cicadas that haven't gotten the message about strangely moody Grayson.

And I can't stand moody Grayson, so I take a page out of their book and keep talking. "I'll be up and out early tomorrow morning to go for a swim."

This one, Grayson acknowledges with a flick of his eyes, but then he leads the way to the front door without a word.

To hell with dancing on eggshells. "Did I do something wrong?"

"No." He unlocks the door, swings it open, and holds it for me to enter first.

"Did your brother?"

"This isn't about my brother."

Entirely confused, I brush past him, trying to read whatever's in his eyes and finding them too shadowed to discern.

"Then why are you upset?"

He follows me inside and closes the door, flicking the low entry light on. Every plane of his face is pulled taut as he says, "You're misreading me."

"What *should* I be reading?"

Instead of answering, his gaze leaves mine, dragging down to my lips. Pausing there, then descending my neck to the lines of my collarbone and thin straps of my dress. He's three feet away, stock-still except for his roving eyes, but every nerve ending he scans goes sharp with keen awareness.

Those honeyed eyes drag back up, slow and deliberate, before gripping mine.

Now, in the soft glow of the entry light, I can see the intent in them. The ardent, single-minded focus as he disregards my question and asks, "Are you at least considering the job?"

The gravelly edge to his voice, the stiff stillness of his body, gives his question an uncompromising weight it wouldn't otherwise have. Like the words *yes* and *no* stand at the edge of a cliff, each one with the power to tip some invisible scale.

Or break it altogether.

Which is why, as my response forms in my mind, I take a single, small step toward him. It's maybe ten inches, but with the way my pulse kickstarts, I might as well be hurdling across a ravine. Landing somewhere I can't return from.

It's there that I say, "Yes."

His nostrils flare, and his eyes roam again, following the same path they've already blazed. Except this time, they don't return to their starting point.

They stop on my lips.

With utter decisiveness, he grinds out, "*Fuck it.* That's good enough for me."

And like an animal finally released from its cage, he erupts.

His mouth crashes into mine, arms scooping around my back and hauling me against his hard body. There's no pretense. No slow seduction like the beach. It's feverish, almost jarring in its intensity, his tongue pressing against mine as he kisses me.

But *kiss* is inadequate.

It's consuming. Unapologetic. *Needy.* Like I'm oxygen, and he's held his breath for far too long, denying himself what he aches for.

His fingers tighten and the room spins, the hard wood of the door meeting my back. One hand cushions my head and stays there, bracing me as he increases the pressure, demanding more. He tastes of wine and man and heady desire, and I moan into his mouth, drowning in it all.

There's firm pressure on my ass, a broad hand, and a bolt of need shoots to my clit. He uses his grip to press himself into me, his erection grinding into my lower belly, and just like on the beach, I'm fucking *finished* in a shameful amount of time.

Doesn't matter that it's been thirty seconds. That we're dressed. Grayson is the storm, I've been dropped into the eye, and this isn't ending without him absolutely wrecking me.

I start hiking up my dress, needing more. Needing what only teased me at the Secret Spot.

"Quack."

I freeze.

My lips are wet and swollen as Grayson breaks away, searching for the source of our interruption. His hands stay where they are, his body glued to mine, but panic rides me hard. "Please, don't stop," I breathe.

The plea is unnecessary, because Grayson's already moving. His other hand lands on my ass and lifts. My legs wrap around his waist, and we move through the house, his pace steady but urgent. A man set on his intent.

It sends my already-buzzing hormones into goddamn orbit.

Never in my life have I been carried to a bedroom like this, and *oh my gosh,* it has to be the hands-down *hottest* thing in the world.

I nibble at his neck, nuzzling into his heat, the musk of his skin. *I need a car air freshener that smells like this.* We pass through a doorway, and I lift my head to take in Grayson's room bathed in a soft light. There's a plain oak bureau. A few picture frames. Cream walls.

He kicks the door closed, and the snick of the latch slices through the room, as decisive as a gavel. Some kind of decree that all pretenses are over. He wants me, I want him, and neither of us are leaving this room without giving in to it.

It must strike him the same way, because some of his urgency dissipates as he carries me to the bed and lowers me onto the neat navy comforter. I prop myself on my elbows, knees open in invitation, wanting all that urgency back. Wanting him to jump my bones and break this bed.

Instead, he slows down *even more*—to a freaking *standstill*—standing over me at the edge of the mattress.

He cocks his head, lips quirking with intrigue. "That's the first time you've said please."

Does that really matter *right now*? "Didn't realize you were keeping track."

His hands travel to my knees, leaning on them. "I pay very close attention to everything that comes out of your mouth."

Knees. What an unsexy part of the body. But the heat of his sprawling grip has my pulse thrumming impatiently.

He applies pressure to his right hand, and that knee straight-up swoons, falling open like an automatic door. That hand slowly slides up my bare thigh, pushing the hem of my dress up with it, as he drawls, "All those insults. All those clever quips. A *please* stands out."

His fingers stop mid-way up my thigh before he shoves my left knee open, his left hand now beginning its unhurried crawl up my leg.

"Since you like it so much, let me give you another." My voice trembles in time with my thighs. "*Please* stop stalling and show me you know how to fuck a woman."

All his forward momentum *stops*—the exact opposite of my request. "Did I leave any room for doubt on the beach?"

I lick my lips, drawing his attention there. "On the beach, you had the help of an aphrodisiac. Who knows if you can do it without one?"

A lazy, smoky chuckle comes from deep in his chest. "You and that smart mouth. Never stops, does it?"

"Never."

Whiskey eyes blaze brighter. "I don't think that's true."

In one smooth motion, he levers up and pulls his shirt off. Then, with the efficiency of a man who works with his hands all day, he jerks my dress to my waist, lifts my back, and slides it up over my head.

There's no shame in the way he looks his fill, pausing on my bare breasts and panties. My chest is small, my underwear a plain and utilitarian black. But when he gruffly mutters, "Yeah, I'm a fucking goner," any doubts about whether he likes what he sees begin to scatter.

And when he grips my ribs and plops me further back on the bed like I'm an empty oyster cage, those doubts completely snuff out.

Because I'm keenly aware of how he's *handling* me. The way he's used his strength to put me right where he wants me since we started this at the entryway. No hesitations. No guessing.

It might be the biggest turn-on of the century. Worthy of the history books. At least five chapters in my autobio*graphyyyy*—

He drags a knuckle up my seam through my damp panties. "Let's see how *smart* that tongue is while I fuck you." He punctuates it with another pass of his knuckle, and my entire body jolts. Rough fingertips hook inside my waistband. "That a yes?"

It's an *If you don't insert your cock into my vagina right now, I'll combust.*

I nod shakily.

"Already out of words, and I haven't even filled you yet," he teases, removing my panties with an efficient jerk. "A little disappointing, Boston."

His playfulness gets my neurons firing again. "Wouldn't want to crush your ego so early in the game, Grayson."

"Early?" he repeats, shoving out of his pants, his boxers

going with it. His cock juts out from a neat nest of dark hair, thick and long and erotic as hell. "You think this is *early* in the game?"

Yes. No. I don't even know, because my heartbeat ratchets to its highest gear as he leans toward his nightstand, retrieves a condom, and tears it open with his teeth.

Turns out I don't need an answer, because as he kneels before me and rolls the condom on, he corrects, "Baby, we've been playing this game since I found your sweet little ass in my office, and you leaned back on that desk like you own it, and effectively told me to fuck off." He lowers toward me, one hand bracing beside my body, the other gripping my hip as his blunt tip teases my opening. "But now? The game's done." All his momentum pauses, his only movement his chest brushing my breasts and his eyes, flicking between mine. "We aren't playing it anymore. Are we?"

"No, we're not," I whisper. Honestly. Easily.

His throat bobs, and he drops his head to kiss me—a short, sweet press of his lips that spears right into my chest.

Then he pulls back and thrusts. All the way in.

Oh my—

A primal groan spirals out of my chest, like his dick just punched the sound out of me. Is that even anatomically possible? I'm entirely *full,* stretched around him, aching with the abrupt invasion, reveling in the rawness of it all. My fingers dig into his solid chest, having flown there at some point.

"Thatta girl, squeezing me so damn *well.*" The words are near-pained grunts, his eyes squeezed shut, that sinewed arm braced at my side trembling with restraint.

He retreats and thrusts deeply again. Another moan escapes me, and his eyes flash open. "Yeah," he drawls, pulling out, then thrusting in again. "You've got no words."

No, I don't.

I clamp my mouth shut, holding the next cry in as he thrusts again, and again, his hand on my hip ensuring I meet every plunge.

"No, gorgeous," he pants, moving in a steady rhythm now, pleasure stacking with each deep drag of his cock. His hand leaves my hip to cup my cheek. A stern thumb shoves into the corner of my mouth, urging my mouth open and staying there. "I'm gonna hear every pretty, nonsense sound you make."

Those rough words alone yank another moan from me, and then my eyes close, my body lost to the feel of him, mouth braced open under his hand as he increases his speed. His breath pants out in a fast staccato, laced with low curses and grunts that prove he's just as undone as me.

Without warning, that hand jerks out of my mouth and targets my clit. Twists. Presses. His sweaty forehead falls into my chest, hot breaths sweeping across my skin as he locks in, and I'm enveloped in the heat of him when the orgasm sweeps through me.

Spasming around him, I cry out. He removes his hand, hips now jerking wildly as he works for his own release. A few more seconds, and he's coming, the muscles of his shoulders twitching as his tempo slows, then stops altogether.

Our heavy breaths mingle in the air, my chest heaving beneath his forehead, still pressed between my breasts. His sturdy body is a heavy, heated weight on my torso, comforting and soothing as my body finds its equilibrium.

When he finally lifts his head, pure male satisfaction colors his golden gaze.

I wait for that satisfaction to morph into regret. Pray that it doesn't, because I don't think I could recover.

But all that gaze does is shift to my breasts, which are right in front of his face. "Didn't get to enjoy these as much as I'd like," he says quietly, kissing the curve of each one before extricating himself from me.

"Maybe I'll give you another opportunity."

He glances down at me, star-fished out on the bed. With a knowing hitch in his cheek, he says, "No need to include the maybe."

I should have some witty reply, but I don't, because he's right.

He's about to have plenty more opportunities—*endless* opportunities.

Until you leave.

No—if I leave.

Because now, returning to the city, *leaving* Garnet Shores, is no longer my only realistic option.

And when a gloriously naked, half-hard Grayson returns from the bathroom with a damp washcloth and proceeds to wordlessly clean between my thighs, I let myself lean in to the possibility of staying here, even though I haven't made up my mind, haven't even *started* to unpack the pros and cons and long-term outlooks of each potential path.

Grayson closes the lights, rejoins me in bed, and tugs me back to curl around me, and my brain turns into straight-up happy mush as he kisses the back of my neck and says, "For the record, Eliza, I love every single word that comes out of that smart mouth."

29

GRAYSON

I WAKE to the revelation that Eliza is a koala.

A soft, warm, cuddly-as-hell koala who smells like flowers and sex, and snores quietly like a kitten.

I'm lying on my back, the entire left side of my body immobile. She's wrapped around me, one leg hitched high over my abs, half her chest pressed into mine as her head rests on my shoulder and nuzzles into my neck. Her arm locks her in, wrapped tight across my torso.

Warm affection settles into my chest, along with pride and wonder that I get the privilege of witnessing this side of her. Eliza Attleburn may be a strong-willed, independent woman, but she's a goddamn sweetheart with a thousand soft layers beneath that sharp-witted shell.

I've seen glimpses of those layers before, but usually when she's hurting or distressed.

This isn't one of those instances. It's freely given.

And it feels like a gift.

One I'd like to continue enjoying for the rest of the morning, but dawn is coloring the sky outside the window, and it's busy season. Part of me is tempted to say *to hell with it all* and soak in the feel, the *rightness*, of her in my arms, but I can't throw work to the wayside. I'm the fucking farm owner. Responsibilities don't take a day off. Problems don't magically disappear.

Doesn't mean you can't put them off for a few more minutes.

Eliza's thigh shifts, dropping closer to my up-and-ready dick, and I decide *that* logic's fucking flawless.

I take my free hand and drag it down her back, reveling in her toned curves and soft, bed-warmed skin. I was too fired up last night to take my time and savor it all. Then I was too spent from a grueling few days of work and the best sex of my life to start up a second round and do it justice.

Now that I've taken the edge off and slept, it's a new playing field.

I cup one round ass cheek and lightly squeeze. Her face nuzzles further into my neck. Fingers splayed wide, I caress that perfect globe, sweeping close to her pussy before making another pass. This time, her hips shift, pressing into me.

My cock hardens all the way.

I repeat the cycle, dragging my fingers close to her heat, then grabbing a palmful of ass, coaxing her awake. With every second, the sleepy rhythm of her breathing changes, growing stuttered. Aroused. Her fingers curl into my skin.

When her hips suddenly shift to bring her closer to my fingers, I'm certain she's awake. Still, I softly ask, "You with me, gorgeous?"

She nods against me.

So on my next pass, I stop teasing us both and dip my fingers right into that tight little spot to find her dripping. *That's my girl.*

A husky moan shudders out of her chest, and I can't

wait anymore. I roll her onto her side, back facing me. She goes easily, limbs still lax with sleep even as she hums with need.

The shadowed column of her spine imprints itself in my retinas as I work a condom onto my length. Then I slide in right behind her, secure her back right into my chest, and enter her with one easy thrust.

We groan at the same time.

I set a slow, lazy rhythm as I palm one of her pert breasts and squeeze. *Perfect little handful.* Then I bury my face in her soft hair, focusing on the feel of her supple body, the way she grips me like a vise, the hypnotizing sounds that float from her mouth as I fuck her.

It's indulgent. Thick with languorous pleasure.

Her body is both relaxed and trembling, welcoming every thrust, trusting me to take care of her.

I've got you, baby.

When her breath begins to quicken, and her core shakes against me, my fingers wander to her clit. One of her hands flies on top of mine that's still kneading her breast, anchoring herself to me as those trembles grow more violent.

It doesn't take long. She's silent this time, head thrown back toward mine as she comes.

Five more seconds, and my balls explode. I come hard inside her heat, hissing into her hair.

Then I'm as lax as her, floating on a little cloud of endorphins, content as hell. I should get up and go—at least remove myself from her body—but I can't bring myself to right away. Instead, I borrow a few more seconds from work to enjoy this. Enjoy *her*, here in my arms.

Because even though this might not last, even though she might leave, I've got her right now. And considering I'm in for a world of pain if she goes, I might as well make that hell worth it.

She's the first one to speak, her voice rough with sleep. "Do I sleep in my own bed tonight?"

The directness of the question puts me at ease. There's no night-after awkwardness. No attempt to reclaim some of that piss-poor distance we'd tried to shove between us the last time we got close.

Thank fuck, because I have no desire for that.

"Can't help but plan ahead, huh?" I tease.

"It's ingrained in my bones." She sighs, giving the hand she's still holding onto a little squeeze. "And I don't want to stress about it all day."

Her honesty flays me.

"You're sleeping in my bed tonight," I confirm, every part of that statement feeling right.

"Good," she says, a smile in her tone.

"Though if Joy brings us cinnamon rolls and you try to take them all from me again, we might have to reevaluate."

"Hmm." She wiggles her bum into my groin. "Challenge accepted."

———

A YEAR of celibacy and I'd forgotten what a fucking miracle drug morning sex is.

The shitty overcast weather that welcomes me at work might as well be sunshine. Defouling our gear is therapeutic. The oyster cages don't feel as back-breaking when I haul them out of the water.

And when Amanda reminds me that we have a table at an oyster festival in two days, a loaded tour schedule coming up, and that Steve—the only other person besides us who's qualified to lead tours—is taking time off, I'm not concerned.

"Think Kenny's ready to do some on his own?" she asks, pen tapping on the schedule open in front of her.

"He's got the license, but he doesn't know the script. And I don't think he's ready to talk to adults on his own." Who knows what shit would come out of his mouth? "Assign them between you and me however you want."

"There's two more bachelorette parties. You definitely don't want those, I'm guessing?"

"Whatever you want."

She blinks in surprise. "You specifically told me a few weeks ago to keep you off those tours."

Yeah, I did. But she hates them as much as I do, and those tours are an excuse to take Eliza out with me.

"Split them with me," I tell her. "Anything else?"

Puzzlement twists her features, but she doesn't press. "Nope. All good." Her eyes catch on something behind me in the warehouse.

I track them to Eliza, in khaki shorts and a Gold's tee, hair wavy as it falls down her back. Salty, probably, from her morning swim. My blood heats at the sight of her, using a phone tripod to film a wide-angle shot of my crew packing a restaurant shipment.

Never thought something so pretty would look right at home in this place.

"I heard what happened to her boat," Amanda says. She's no longer looking at Eliza, but me. Maybe it's the light, but there's a gleam to her eyes.

"Yeah. Unfortunate," I say.

"Wonder where she's staying," she muses.

I like Amanda—a lot. She's reliable. Responsible. Good

at what she does, bullshit and drama-free. But this seems suspiciously like she's nosing into my business.

Eliza and I aren't trying to hide that she's staying at my place. We drove here together early this morning. But we're also not actively announcing it to the team.

Even if we did, what would we say? That we're platonically living together? That we've entered a—what do the kids call it—*situation-ship?*

Stupid fucking term.

"You know, my buddy Jake works over at the marina," Amanda casually continues. "He told me they're down a few guys, and it's looking like her sailboat won't be repaired until after she's gone." The corner of her mouth quirks. "Guess she'll be staying wherever she's staying until her contract's up."

I smother the instinct to smile like an idiot. "Sounds like it."

Amanda's grin spreads, but I'm spared more of her innocent *musings* by my phone ringing.

It's Anson.

For a second, some naïve part of me thinks he could be calling to tell me Eliza accepted the job. Then common sense rolls in to remind me it's only been a day, and she'd probably give me that news herself. Which means Anson's calling to deliver some kind of problem.

I answer. "Hey, brother."

"Gray, where are you?" Anson's always got a serious edge on work calls, but this time, his tone's urgent. Severe.

Wariness sinks in. "In the warehouse."

"Operating anything dangerous?"

"No. What's going on?"

In true Anson fashion, he rips off the bandage right off. "A hospital called me. Dawson's been in a car accident."

My heart thumps once in my chest. Then his words register, and the organ divebombs into my stomach. The sounds of the warehouse fade to the background. The floor disappears beneath my feet.

"How bad?" I force out.

His hesitation tells me all I need to know. "He's in the ICU, Gray. Medically-induced coma. They said—" a loaded breath comes over the line. "They said there's a good chance he'll pull through and be fine, but that's not a guarantee."

Worry and panic hit like a wall of ice-water, flushing my body cold. I want this to be a lie. Some fake news story. A random guy with the same name as my brother. But I know Anson's already vetted it.

He speaks over my silence. "There's a flight to Ohio leaving in two hours. I already made arrangements with people to watch Lala. I'm booking us both tickets now—unless you need to wait until morning?"

Like hell I'm waiting. Dawson could...he could—

No. I shove the worst-case scenario from my head. Our family's lost enough. Dawson's not fucking following our parents right now.

"I'm not waiting. I'll head home right now to pack and meet you at your place."

Anson gives an affirmative, and I woodenly hang up.

"What's wrong?" The two softly spoken words bring the warehouse back into focus. Eliza stands before me, hazel eyes wide with concern.

"Dawson." My voice cracks. Amanda's chair scrapes against the floor as she stands. Two other team members glance over in concern.

Get your shit together. Taking a breath, I shove out,

"Dawson's been in a car accident. He's in the ICU, in Ohio. I need to go."

I'm expecting hysterics. Some mirror of the volatile emotions tumbling in my gut. But Eliza merely grasps my arm, her thumb stroking my skin.

It feels like a fucking life raft.

"What do you need?" she asks calmly.

Her question pulls me from the storm. Helps me focus.

It also slaps me with the reality of the next few days. Of all the times to have an emergency, this is one of the worst. All that panic spirals up again.

"*Fuck*," I mutter, yanking off my hat and tugging my hair. "I can't...I can't go—"

Eliza's grip firms around my arm. "You're going."

She doesn't understand. "Steve's out. We have a full schedule, and that fucking festival..."

Fuck.

I *can't* leave, but I need to. Dawson's fighting for his life. Nothing is more important than him right now. "I guess— we'll have to skip the festival, cancel some tours. Amanda, can you—"

"We're not skipping or cancelling anything," Eliza states. "You're leaving, and Amanda and your very capable team and I are going to cover everything." She steps closer, using her free hand to pull mine away from my head. "I will take care of Dave. I will get a ride back to your place. All you need to do is go home, get your things, and go see your brother."

The steady confidence of her voice is like a heaven-scent balm, breaking through my panic.

But it's not just her voice. It's the fact that I *know* she'll follow through on her word. If anyone can make hard things work, it's this incredible woman, with her stubbornness and drive and sheer capability.

And she has a damn good team with her—though she'd do it on her own, no doubt.

Eliza isn't some flimsy fucking life raft. She's a full-fledged rescue boat.

Not caring that everyone can see, I yank her to me and lock her in a hug. She comes easily, wrapping her arms around me, like us embracing is the most natural thing in the world.

It feels like it—the way she fits into my chest, her salt-tinged, flowery scent wrapping around me like a comforting blanket.

"Thank you," I say into her soft hair.

Then, because I can't help myself, I kiss her right there in front of everyone.

When I'm in the airport with Anson two hours later, slugging through security, the thought of what lies ahead twisting my stomach with dread, it's the memory of that kiss that loosens the knot enough for me to breathe.

30

ELIZA

"WE GOT off to a rocky start, and I'm willing to take the blame for that. I made some false assumptions about you when we first met, and I realize that my hostility toward you hasn't been...productive."

My words are met with a blank stare.

Taking a nervous inhale, I reach behind my back, grab the gift, and set it on the floor. "Consider this a peace offering."

Dave looks down at the plate of dried mealworms. The man at the pet store assured me they're the crème de la crème of duck treats. And while I promptly lost *my* appetite when I arranged them on the plate, pet-store-man seems to know his stuff, because Dave's little feathered tail is beginning to wag.

He takes two cautious steps forward. Glances at me, then the worms, like he thinks this is some kind of trick. When I remain still, he steps right up to the plate. His wings flutter. His tail wags harder.

Then, with a delighted chirp, he descends on the meal, absolutely demolishing it.

I watch in morbid fascination until he's done two minutes later. Then the real test begins. I grab my keys and swing the door open wide. "Come on. We've got to go to work."

He stares at me from behind the empty plate, and for a moment, I think my plan's an utter failure. But then he slowly starts waddling toward me, making his way out the door and to my car in the driveway.

God bless you, pet-store-man.

Grayson's only been gone eighteen hours, but Dave has already made it incredibly clear how unhappy he is to be stuck with me—refusing to get in Amanda's car to come home last night, then refusing to enter the house, then refusing to shut up while I tried to eat. So after dinner, I drove two towns over to acquire my bribe.

The ridiculousness isn't lost on me. I'm aware this is a wild bird, who can surely survive on its own in Grayson's absence. I could leave him outside, or let him hang at the house while I'm at the farm. But I told Grayson I'd take care of Dave, which means keeping the duck happy, fed, and in his normal routine so he doesn't throw a tantrum and destroy everything within sight. Or me.

I double-check that I have more worms in the trunk for later, then let Dave hop in the passenger seat before buckling myself in. The drive to the farm is sleepy and quiet, dawn just blooming in the sky.

It's the only moment of peace I have the entire day.

From the second I arrive, work is certifiably insane. With Grayson out, Steve away, and only one Amanda in existence, I'm covering tours with Kenny and helping with the table at tomorrow's festival, which is an hour-drive away. While I might not be a farmer, I've been on enough tours to have the script memorized, and I know how to speak well and smile at people. The team agreed to the plan when Amanda asked them last night, and even grumpy old Mark gave us a *whatever-the-fuck-you-want-to-do* grunt—though that probably had less to do with his belief in me and more with his hatred for small talk with the public.

Between my regular marketing work, three tours, and festival prep, I'm dragging my feet to the car when the day ends, Dave waddling behind me as he digests more worms.

I'm effectively beat, but not in a way I know. My eyes aren't fried from computer screens, my back isn't sore from sitting, and my head doesn't hurt from fielding asinine feedback or overdramatic "emergencies."

This is an exhaustion born from sun, sea, and conversations. It's *satisfied*. A tiredness that has me content rather than stressed as I drive to Grayson's, where a call with Suzanne is waiting—which will undoubtedly invoke all that stress I'm missing out on.

Monday's interview is only three days away, and she wants to rehearse my responses. I should be eager to practice, but right now, it feels as appealing as rush-hour traffic in Boston.

I've just pulled into the driveway when my phone rings. It's five minutes to six—our scheduled call time. Suzanne must be eager to tear my responses apart.

But when I look at the screen, it isn't her.

It's Grayson.

My chest jolts.

Not an hour has gone by where I haven't thought about him. I've been fighting the urge to contact him all day—to ask how Dawson's doing, how *he's* doing. But I haven't sent a message or tried calling, because he's with his brothers and I don't know if...if he *wants* to hear from me right now.

I'm not his girlfriend. I don't think *friend* is the right

word, either. We're *more* than casual, and I'm worried sick, but...I just don't know if I'm the person he wants to talk to in the midst of an emergency.

Though as I stare down at the screen, I wonder if his call means I *am*.

Or maybe he's just calling to check on work.

"Hi," I answer softly.

"Hey, Boston." His voice is tired and drawn, enough for me to wonder if Dawson took a turn for the worse. I steel myself for bad news.

But a thread of good-natured humor seeps into his tone as he asks, "Have you tried selling my duck to a restaurant yet?"

I glance over at said duck, who's very politely sitting in his assigned seat. "No takers, unfortunately."

A soft chuckle comes over the line. "Really, is he giving you a hard time?"

"It took a little adjusting, but we've...reached an agreement."

"Are you bribing him?"

How does he know? "You think I need to resort to bribery to get your duck to like me?"

"Yes."

"I'll have you know I'm very likeable all on my own."

"I'm well aware." His instant, easy reply makes my belly flutter. "But Dave's a little slow on the uptake."

"Don't insult my new friend like that."

He blows out a sigh. "Something tells me you'll be teamed up against me by the time I come home."

The way he says *home* turns the flutter into a flock. "You'll always be his favorite. I can't replace you."

"You calling me special, Boston?"

My eyes skate over the wood shingles of his house—the home he welcomed me into without hesitation, where we finally kicked down the flimsy wall between us, regardless of how self-sabotaging it might be.

"Yes," I answer.

There's a pause, and I bite my lip, wondering if that was too honest. If the distance has made me too bold. But he says, "I'm afraid that adjective is reserved for you. You'll have to find another one."

My smile is so big, my cheeks hurt. "Arrogant. Difficult. Bullheaded."

"You know, bulls are famous for their virility." I can practically *see* the cocky smirk on his face. "I'll happily take that compliment."

"You are..."

"Perfect?"

"I was going to say incorrigible."

"See, that's what my day was missing. A nice, multi-syllable insult. Thank you."

I roll my eyes. "Don't tell me that's why you called."

"Do you want my honest answer?" he asks, his amusement fading.

"Yes," I say, my heart kicking into gear.

A breath, then, "I wanted to hear your voice."

It's like I just drank a gallon of hot chocolate, the sweetness and warmth of his words infusing my chest. Before I can admit that I wanted the same, he clears his throat and asks, "How's work? Amanda told me you were partnering with Kenny for some tours, and you're helping man the table tomorrow."

"It's good. The tours were easy. Kenny did the driving and oyster holding, and I did all the talking. I figure tomorrow will be even easier. Amanda printed out an oyster cheat-sheet for me just in case, but I've got it down."

"Sounds like if I'm not careful, you might take my job."

"I would, but no one wears stained orange waders as well as you, Grayson."

"You just say that because you haven't seen yourself in them," he replies. Then he bumbles right along, like doling out *another* compliment is no big deal. "Thank you, again, for covering. You're going above and beyond for me. Hell, 'thank you' isn't even a good enough word for it."

"You don't need to thank me, *or* find a better word." He inhales to argue, but I cut him off. "I feel lucky to be in a position where I can help you. And it feels like a privilege that you trust me enough to help take care of things."

He snorts. "Eliza, anyone with half a brain knows that having you in their corner is like having a fucking superpower."

My dorky smile, the one he's held on my face for the last five minutes, suddenly slips. Not because he's upset me, but because I think that's one of the most wonderful things anyone has ever said to me.

I've gotten praise from professors, bosses, occasionally my parents. Kyle would say nice things about me, back when we were in love. Kitty hypes me up all the time. But to hear *these* words from *this* man—who's seen me at my worst, who's no bullshitter, whom I *respect*—it reaches right into the places where I store my doubts, the parts of me that have tirelessly strived to achieve, but quietly wondered if I'd actually get there.

And, dammit, it clogs my throat right up.

Fighting back tears—because, of the two of us, I'm *definitely* not the one who should be crying right now—I ask, "How's Dawson?"

"He's hanging in," Grayson says. "His head took a good hit. There was some swelling, and the doctors found a small bleed when he first came in, so they put him in a medically induced coma just in case. So far, nothing's gotten worse, which they say is a positive sign, but we won't know what kind of damage he has until he wakes up. There's a good chance he's fine. But there's also a chance it's catastrophic. Otherwise, he's just got some busted ribs and a strained shoulder."

I don't know Dawson, but Grayson's pain guts me. I want to take it away, bear it for him, but that's impossible. Nothing I say can make this better, but I try, anyway.

"If your brother's anywhere close to as stubborn as you, he'll be just fine."

"He's *more* stubborn than me. Might even be more stubborn than Anson." He laughs weakly before an unintelligible voice cuts him off. "Hey, I've got to go. Anson has news."

I slump back in my seat. "Okay. I, um—"

I miss you. I'm glad I got to hear your voice today. I want you to call me again soon.

Each confession is a compulsive urge, desperate to reach him. But even with his compliments, it feels like too much right now, at the end of a phone call, when he's about to be updated on the condition of his seriously injured brother. I haven't decided yet if I'm staying in Garnet Shores. Saying things like this would just make it *that* much worse—for both of us—if I leave.

So I lamely settle on, "I hope he keeps getting better."

But I'm the only one who seems to be heeding caution, because Grayson disregards my lame platitude and boldly states, as if it's a fact, "Talk to you tomorrow, gorgeous," before hanging up.

For a moment, I sit in the silence of the car. Then a giggle escapes my chest. Just a *little* burst. Enough for Dave to quirk his head at me.

And when I see Suzanne's text on my phone, informing me I'm ten minutes late to our call, I just giggle again.

ELIZA

"SHE'S BEAUTIFUL. Like a fucking goddess. And her *smile*...it just does something to me, you know?"

I nod absentmindedly as I record last week's marketing analytics on my phone. Kenny's on minute eight of musing about the love of his life, whom he hasn't spoken to yet.

"She smiles a lot, too. At everyone. She's kind like that. A total sweetheart."

My head bobs as my fingers fly over the screen.

"I heard from my buddy that she volunteers at an animal shelter in free time. Kind *and* generous. That's rare in this world, isn't it—hey, are you even listening?"

I glance up at Kenny, whose dreamy-eyed expression is beginning to clear. Feet resting on a cooler, he reclines further into his plastic folding chair, crosses his arms, and waits.

"Beautiful. Goddess. Animal shelter," I list. "I'm listening."

His eyes narrow on my phone. "Don't tell me you're working right now."

"Just doing a few things," I say, shrugging.

"Eliza, we just manned this table for eight hours straight with no breaks. It's five o'clock. We're done for the day."

Well, almost. We still have to break down the tent and clean up.

"Besides, it's Saturday. I thought you didn't do marketing stuff on weekends."

"Some last-minute things came up. But they're quick," I say, glancing at the half-broken-down tents around us so he won't see the guilt in my eyes.

There's a lot of it, too, because I'm lying.

The truth is, I'm trying to get ahead for Monday to make time for my interview. Between driving time and the inevitable traffic, I'll be gone the entire day. Technically, there's nothing *wrong* with my absence. I'll have all my marketing work done between tonight and tomorrow, and I'm not *required* to be on-site from nine to five.

But I also won't be around to help out. Amanda has the day's tours covered, but if she's sick, or wakes up to a flat tire, or some other emergency pops up at the farm...

What am I supposed to do, though? *Cancel* an interview I'm lucky to even have? I've hardly had time to consider Anson's offer, but it's so different from what I pictured for myself, whereas this interview is a literal manifestation of my goals. I've been working toward an opportunity like this all summer. I can't just...*not* go.

Grayson's team is *very* capable, I remind myself. If I wasn't here the past two days, they would have figured everything out just fine. Their world doesn't revolve around me.

It's probably the eighth time I've replayed those reassurances in my head, and they've done nothing to lift the heavy weight in my stomach.

"*Fuck* yeah," Kenny suddenly exclaims, leaping from

his seat. I blink away my thoughts to see a middle-aged man approaching with two full paper plates. "Jay, man, I've been looking forward to these all day!"

Smiling as he hands the plates to Kenny, he says, "A few fried oysters, plus some fish I caught yesterday."

These very plates are the reason Kenny wanted to hang around when most of the vendors already left. As I take in the steaming, golden morsels, I start to understand.

"By the way, this is Eliza. She's been with us this summer," Kenny introduces, placing a plate on the cooler beside me before immediately digging in.

Jay extends a hand. "I own a farm up in the bay," he says, his handshake easy. This must be the Jay who helped Grayson with his new intertidal system. "Marketing, right? Gray mentioned something last time we chatted. Are you liking it?"

"It's been wonderful," I say, though that doesn't quite capture it. The last two months feel like some kind of fever dream. One accented with salty air, big breaths, a few tears, and *Grayson*. I don't even know if there *is* a word that encompasses it all. Or him, for starters.

"The Gold boys sure got something special going, huh." It isn't a question. More like some well-known local fact. "Is it just a summer gig for you?"

"Right now, yes."

"Right now," he repeats. His gray eyes twinkle as he glances around. "Garnet Shores, this whole little stretch of coast—it's got a funny way of hooking you in, doesn't it?" His gaze settles back on me, a dimple cutting into his wrinkled cheek as he leans in. "Best part is, no one really knows it until they live here. Keeps the place quiet for us."

He pulls back with a wink and raises a hand to Kenny. "Got to break down the tent, but it was good to see you guys here." He smiles at me. "And it was nice to meet you. Maybe I'll see you around next time I swing by the farm."

Maybe.

"Thanks for the food," Kenny says as Jay walks away. Then he sets his sights on me, a grin on his greasy mouth. "Now, I'm not the best with words, but I'm pretty sure you said 'right now.'"

I really didn't think he was paying attention. Heck, he spent half the day today humming some Green Day tune while I fielded customers and he shucked oysters in the back.

"I did," I say, unperturbed, taking a bite of fried fish.

"That mean you might stay?"

There was no harm in being honest with Jay, an uninvolved stranger, but I'm not about to confess my current situation to Kenny. I don't know if farm gossip is a thing, but I don't want to start it.

When I take too long to answer, Kenny says, through a giant bite of fried oyster, "Is it 'cause you moved in with Boss?"

The fish lodges in my throat. I cough, my eyes watering. "I didn't 'move in' with him."

"But your boat's getting repaired, and you drove to work together the other day."

Turns out farm gossip *is* a thing, because I never even told Kenny I was living on a boat.

"Grayson is helping me out," I say carefully. "And it's also none of your business."

"Um, wrong," he declares. "Boss obviously likes you, as in—*like* likes you—which means his mood is tied to you. If you leave or break up or something, he's gonna be fuckin' miserable, and the whole team's gonna suffer."

If Kenny's been thinking about us this much—*shit,* is the whole *farm* thinking about us, too?

He pops another oyster in his mouth while my mind frantically searches for some way out of this trap. "You aren't responsible for your boss's moods," I say, "so you shouldn't be digging this deeply into his personal life."

"I'm not responsible for him, but I like him." Kenny shrugs. "He's a good guy. Cool boss. I want to see him happy."

Some of my annoyance ebbs, if only a little. Unsure where to go from here, I find solace in a fried oyster, hoping Kenny lets this conversation go.

Of course, he doesn't. Popping his feet up on the cooler, he asks, "So what's so much better up there than here?"

I shake my head tiredly. "It's...different."

"Good different?"

"*Different,* different." Apparently I've told some kind of joke, because Kenny starts laughing mid-chew. My hackles raise. "What's funny?"

"You make *nooo* sense." His laughter ebbs when he notices my flat expression. "If it isn't a *good* different, why the hell would you rush back there when your contract here is done?"

"It's not that simple—"

"Yeah, 'cause you're *making* it not simple. *Women.*" He blows out a breath, shaking his head. "Which place do you like more?"

It's not about *liking.* It's about my future. Besides, "I've only been here for two months—"

"Exactly," Kenny says, cutting me off *again.* Fried oyster bits flick off his fingers as he points at me. "You've only been here for two months. You gotta give it more time before you know how you feel." His tangled hair swoops across his forehead as he inclines his head. "I mean, really, why are you rushing? You can probably get a job up there any time of year. It's not like August's the only time people hire, right?"

I drop the oyster I was planning to eat, irritation eliminating my appetite.

Kenny proves he's not *entirely* socially inept when he raises his hands. "You look mad."

"I'm not mad," I ground out.

I'm tired. Overwhelmed with decisions. Stressed about my interview and skipping out on the farm. Thinking about Anson's offer. Excited to talk to Grayson tonight.

And, *yeah*, feeling the increasingly strong urge to throw a fried oyster at Kenny, who thinks he has all the answers to the world's questions, but just *doesn't get it*.

"Look," he starts softly, like he's speaking to a rabid coyote, "I'm just saying you could stick around for a little. You end up not liking it, you go back to what you were doing. You only would've missed out on, like, six months of your life up there, and you've got—" he looks me up and down— "at *least* fifty years left, unless you die in a car crash or something, but that probably won't happen because I've seen you pull into the parking lot and you drive *painfully* slow. So six months is nothing." He resumes eating, giving me an eyeful of mushed food when he adds, "If you do end up leaving, though, just give me a heads up so I can take time off and avoid Boss. I'm *not* dealing with that."

"Sure thing," I mumble. Do I really drive *that* slowly?

"Thank you."

I shake my head, fighting an oncoming headache as Kenny continues to munch away, like he didn't just try to separate me from my sanity. As he mumbles, "*Fuck*, this is so good," I reluctantly try to cool my annoyance.

He's not trying to rile me. Kenny just doesn't have a reliable filter—or *any* filter?—and he's punching a sore spot.

Taking pity, I sigh and say, "Hey, Kenny?"

"Yeah?"

"That smiling goddess, the one you see at Dyl's?"

He nods, eyes taking on that dreamy quality again.

"Swallow your food before you talk to her, and maybe she'll smile at you, too."

———

IT'S late by the time I get back to Grayson's.

I should be crawling to the couch, but I'm buzzing with energy. Not the good, productive kind, but the kind that makes your armpits sweat and brain ping-pong like an arcade machine. Even Dave seems to sense it, giving me a wide berth after delivering his standard-greeting *quack*.

Grayson texted to say he'd call me at nine—a good thirty minutes from now. Which means I currently have nothing to distract me from the guilt and anxiety and indecision that have only grown stronger since I left the festival.

I'm spiraling.

For no good reason.

My feelings are blowing themselves out of proportion, because I'm tired and hungry and haven't had a good *the-world-is-crashing-down-on-me* moment in two months. That's all it is.

I have an *exciting* interview coming up. Suzanne says I'm well-prepared. Grayson is calling me again tonight. The festival was a success. Dave hasn't tried to sabotage me since I got him the mealworms.

Everything's *good*.

But even after mentally chanting this for ten minutes as

I tidy the house, my stomach still feels like it wants to simultaneously implode and explode. It isn't just anxiety. It's heavier than that.

It's *dread.*

Like driving to Boston in two days is stepping off the edge of a plank into shark-infested waters. And it's getting harder and harder to ignore, to compartmentalize into a *they're-just-feelings* box and override with reality.

It's like my body doesn't know the difference between being chased by a bear and taking a goddamn step forward.

"You're not being chased by a bear," I state aloud. Then, hoping a cool drink can settle me, I yank the fridge open and pull out the first bottle my hand lands on.

It's one of the beers I bought for Grayson.

Grayson, who I'll talk to in—I check my watch—fifteen minutes. Who'll inevitably make me smile. Who I won't tell about my interview because...

Because I don't want to hurt him. Disappoint him. Acknowledge the possibility of me leaving out loud, because that makes it *real*, and that's...god, that's *terrifying.*

You're not being chased by a bear.

The reminder runs across my mind as the bottle's chill seeps into my hand. Except this time, the sentence keeps going.

I'm not being chased by a bear...up to my interview. No one's *forcing* me to go. No one's *forcing* me to look at options outside of Anson's offer. No one's *forcing* me to do what I've always done—to stay the course, to do something that makes me feel *this* shitty.

The simple, obvious revelation seems to loosen some of that dread. With it comes another one.

"I don't want to leave," I whisper.

Expectations, pros and cons, college-grad-Eliza's plans all shoved aside—I really, *really* don't want to leave.

Dave waddles into the kitchen, beady eyes on me like he's studying the misery plastered all over my face. Or he just sees a human-shaped blob. Whatever it is he sees, it makes him toddle all the way over to stand at my feet.

"*Quack.*"

For a moment, I stare down at him. This little emotionally abusive beast who I'm still half-afraid of, but have come so far with.

Then I shove off the refrigerator, drop the beer on the counter—because Grayson will enjoy it more than me—and beeline it to the couch. Thirty seconds later, I have Anson's proposal pulled up on my laptop screen. I've already read the PDF twice. I go ahead and read it a third time, my gut slowly unraveling.

It's *different* from what I've been working towards.

But it might be a *good* different—just like *I* am, down here.

And maybe I should start caring about that more. Folding it into my definition of success. Or, at the very least, give it a shot and see what life could feel like.

Because if there's one thing I know for sure, it's that life *before* Garnet Shores didn't feel as good as it does now. A fact deeply intertwined with the man who—no matter how much logic or therapy or willpower I throw at it—I will *never* be able to forget.

I thought I owed it to myself to stick to my goals and plans, and inevitably let Grayson go.

Maybe I owe myself the opposite.

32

GRAYSON

"I'VE SET you up for failure."

It's the first thing Eliza says when she picks up. The sound of her voice alone is enough to ease some of the heavy pressure constricting my ribs. Then her words, spoken with conspiratorial glee, effectively distract me from the afternoon's events.

I didn't even know that was possible.

"Did something happen at the festival?" I ask. Amanda reported that everything from the day went well.

"Yes. Me, smiling at everyone who came by, marketing the crap out of Gold's, and getting you a good number of new customers."

I lean against the brick wall of the hospital, sweat drawing a line down my back in the oppressive nighttime air. Fuck, I miss the sea breeze. And the woman who comes with it. "I don't understand how this equates to failure."

"Well, they're all going to be expecting my friendly face when they pick up orders or come for a tour, which means they'll be awfully disappointed when they get stuck with yours."

I shouldn't be capable of smiling, but she pulls one out of me. "How long did you spend brainstorming that whole thing?"

"The entire drive back to the farm. It was either that, or pay attention to Kenny's rendition of a Red Hot Chili Peppers album."

"Guess that means you were thinking about me today."

"I've been thinking about you a lot, Grayson."

There's no hesitation.

No tinge of amusement.

No follow-up joke.

No resignation or reluctance either, from what I can tell. Unless this Ohio phone service is warping her voice, it sounds an awful lot like she's...happy.

I was honest and raw with her on our call yesterday, not even trying to restrain myself. Because, yeah, I'm all-fuck-ing-in. I was already sliding down the slope when I took her into my home. I picked up a shit-ton of speed when she said there's a chance she'll stay in Garnet Shores. And sometime in the last three days, I've fallen completely, incapable of climbing back up.

And I don't *want* to climb back up.

I want *her*.

Even if she goes back to Boston, I'll try to make things work. Start my days earlier so I can drive up and take her to dinner. Hire another hand so I have more wiggle room on the weekends. Work around her, give her what she needs, and help keep her going.

It's obvious she feels something for me, too. But still, save for her calling me *special* yesterday, she's been holding back.

Until now.

She might as well have injected dopamine right into my

bloodstream. Crazy how one of my worst fucking days in recent memories can have a moment as good as this.

"I've been thinking about you, too," I say right back.

There's a dainty little exhale. The kind that comes with a shy smile.

"Dave's eying me. I think he feels left out."

"Well, we can't have that. Give him a kiss for me, will you?"

"I'd like to keep my face in one piece."

"Don't worry. Dave knows how much I like your face."

"Do you tell him all your secrets?"

"Baby, if I wanted it to be a secret, I wouldn't be sharing it with you," I drawl.

She's quiet for a second, and I indulge myself, imagining her blush. She's hard to fluster, which makes it that much more satisfying when I manage it.

And I *know* I've flustered her, because when she finally talks, it's a complete topic change. "How's your brother?"

My smile fades as a lead ball settles back in my gut. Not her fault, though.

"He's awake," I report. "Lucid and talking." But talking isn't the right word for it. Yelling? Arguing? Being an unrecognizable asshole? "He's got a decent concussion, but he knows who he is and remembers what happened. He'll need a few days of observation, but it seems like he's lucky."

Extremely lucky, for a guy who got into a car with someone as high as a kite, with a propensity for racing, who smashed their car into a tree. Somehow, the driver was even luckier, only spending a few hours in the hospital before walking away.

"That's great news," Eliza says softly. When I'm silent, she asks, "Right?"

"It is," I force out. "It's great news."

"But not everything is great," she cautiously concludes. "Do you want to talk about it?"

I'd rather swallow shells.

But this isn't going away. I'm going to walk right into round two the second our call's done.

I breathe deep and give her the short version. How the first thing he said when he was fully conscious was, *What the fuck are you doing here?* How the second thing was that we shouldn't have come. That he's clearly *fine,* that it was just a little accident and wasn't worth the trouble of us dropping everything.

How Anson then asked him why he got into a car with an incapacitated driver, and everything just...exploded.

"Ah, now I get it—why you came all the way out here." Even hoarse from all the tubes, Dawson's voice was unmistakably bitter. *"To rub my nose in my shit, tell me how badly I messed up, like I don't fuckin' know."*

"Yeah, Dawson, that's why I dropped everything the fucking second I got the call, pulled strings to open two seats on a full flight, and spent all of yesterday staring at your heart monitor just in case it decided to level off," Anson had shot right back. *"You got me, little brother."*

"Go the fuck home."

That one had been aimed at both of us. I'd ignored it, but Anson hadn't, and they regressed into angry little kids trading blows in the backyard until Dawson got worked up enough to lurch forward, like he might actually throw a fist. He'd immediately flopped back in pain and called a nurse for more meds, who informed us the doctor was ready to run some more tests.

That'd been about an hour ago.

When I finish, Eliza firmly states, "Whatever's going on isn't on you."

I know we did nothing wrong by coming here. It was the right choice. But this whole thing started long before he landed in that hospital bed. "Dawson always was the wild child, growing up. It never left him when he got his first contract, but he was twenty, still had time to grow out of it. But he didn't. And he's gotten more and more distant over the years."

Clearly, some kind of bullshit has been going on inside that head of his. Something that turned little Daw—who was pretty reckless but always *good* in the end—into *this*.

"I didn't do enough to stop it from happening." The confession scrapes my throat. "With Lala and the farm, I just...thought he'd figure it out."

Fuck.

"Grayson, you aren't responsible for your adult brother," she says calmly. "You're doing an incredible job helping to raise Lala. You've worked your ass off to grow what your father started. And you, just like Dawson, had to work through losing your parents, and came out the other side a *good person*. You've done so much."

Her conviction cuts loud and clear through the line, her words striking me to my core. But still, "I could've done more."

"Not without one of those other things suffering," she argues. "You can handle a lot of moving parts. But there's a limit. For anyone."

I nod, gripping onto her reminder like an anchor.

"I know there's probably nothing that can make you feel better right now. But please, just...give yourself a little credit. Don't beat yourself up."

My chest feels too full as I breathe.

It eases a fraction when she adds, "I'm the only one allowed to be a little mean to you."

An incredulous exhale shoots out of me. Shaking my head, I mutter, "I've let you get away with too much."

"Hmm. Maybe," she replies innocently.

The day's surprises keep on coming, because—like magic—my thoughts shift from self-loathing and despair to Eliza and her addictive perfume, her soft skin and cute little freckles, how sweetly she responded to me in bed.

Some might consider it fucked up that I'm able to go there right now. But I'll take the temporary reprieve. I'll take anything she gives me.

My pitch dropping, I muse, "Maybe I'll have to do something about that when I get back."

"*May*-be." She sings the word, like a dare. One that heats my blood.

"Maybe I'll think about it every night I'm here. Brainstorm a little. Practice on my own." Picture her sweet little moans and tight pussy while I do it. "I know how much you appreciate planning."

"Maybe I'll do some planning of my own."

I'm grinning again. Grinning and fighting a sudden hard-on that really doesn't fit with this day.

Up ahead, three nurses on an evening stroll turn onto the walkway I'm next to. "For such a rule follower, you have me thinking very inappropriate thoughts in a very inappropriate setting."

"Can't handle me, Grayson?" she playfully challenges.

"I can handle you just fine, Boston."

And I'll be counting down the days until I can *handle her* again. A light at the end of this dark tunnel.

The nurses approach, giggling at something one of them said.

"I should go," I say, though it pains me. Dawson's definitely done with the doctors by now, and I only told Anson

I'd been gone a few minutes. Any longer out here and I'd be overindulging.

"Yeah. Of course." She's quiet for a breath, like she's searching for words. "Grayson, he's lucky to have you as a brother. Remember that."

And I'm lucky you stepped foot on my farm all those weeks ago.

"Talk to you tomorrow, gorgeous."

The hospital's fluorescent lights hurt my eyes as I make my way back inside, weaving through sterile hallways until I find Anson leaning against the wall outside Dawson's room.

He lifts a brow. "You said you were just stepping outside. You go on a walk to Michigan?"

"Had a call to make."

He makes a point of reading his watch. "Eight p.m., so it wasn't work-related. And I just gave JJ an update."

I stare at him. "You waiting for me to fill in the blank?"

He shrugs. "Blank's already filled. How is she?"

There's no point denying his assumption.

Aside from the night he offered her the job, I haven't spoken to Anson about Eliza. He's not the guy you go to for relationship advice—and I've already made up my mind about what I'm doing. But Anson's always been good at reading people, and the fact I'm not moping around like some pathetic, heartbroken sap tells him all he needs to know.

"She's..." *Perfect. Hot as hell.* Honestly, the list of adjectives is endless, but I go with, "a lifesaver. She stepped in with tours and the festival. Didn't even ask her to."

"And I still got her marketing report in my inbox last night," he says, a pleased tilt to his mouth.

Then it flattens.

"I got a call this week from some tech startup. The lady was a fucking robot." If Anson thinks that, she must be as warm and welcoming as a brick. "She was calling for a reference for Eliza's upcoming interview."

His implication hits me like a blow to the sternum.

I remind myself the reaction isn't fair. I know she's still figuring things out. She hasn't taken Anson's offer. I've been careful to tell myself every day that she could leave and things could get harder.

But still, it sucks to hear. And it feels even shittier that she didn't tell me about her interview—not because I'm offended or angry, but because I'm sure it's a big deal to her, and I want her to share her *big deals* with me.

I haven't asked about her job situation because I don't want to pressure her, but *fuck,* I want to be there for her. At the very least, I don't know, wish her *good luck.*

Not that Eliza needs luck.

"What'd you tell them?" I ask.

"The truth. That she's fucking excellent. So much that I want her to continue working for me."

I look away from Anson's evaluative gaze. White tiles, metal carts, lifeless cream walls. Why does everything in a hospital have to be so damn depressing?

"What are you going to do if she leaves?" he asks.

I drag my gaze back to his. "Date her. If she wants that."

"How's that going to work?"

"I'll make it work."

"She's worth it?" He isn't mocking me, like I'd expect.

No, Anson's curious. He's truly wondering how, after last year's mess, Eliza got me to fall down the rabbit hole again.

Well, *he* sees it as a rabbit hole. A fruitless endeavor. A waste of time and energy that I could easily and logically keep myself out of. But with the right woman, it's *none* of those things.

God, I can't fucking wait for someone to blast into his life, surprise him with that revelation, and toss his neatly organized world upside-down.

Grinning at that thought, I answer, "Yes."

He nods to himself, considering this. Probably thinking I'm a fool, too. Then he slaps me with more bad news. "The doctor said Dawson should be discharged in three days. He also said he's asked to prohibit visitors."

I'd thought Anson was waiting outside the room because he wanted to face Dawson together, use me as some kind of buffer—not because we'd been banned. "Since when do you let someone tell you what you can and cannot do?"

His flat expression fissures, and his chest heaves a breath. "I don't know what the fuck happened to our brother, but *that*—" he jerks his chin toward Dawson's door — "I don't know what to do with that."

A muscle thrums in his jaw, a telltale sign that he's pissed. But that's not all. Because his voice sounds alarmingly thin—fragile, from someone who's as unbreakable as stone—as he grits out, "If I go in there, I'm just going to make things worse. I don't even have to open my fucking mouth."

His pain piles on my own.

Anson's a jackhammer, and Dawson's a strip of concrete that's currently crumbling to pieces. But Anson's not deliberately being an asshole. He's just being *Anson*, handling Dawson the only way he knows how, when our little brother needs kid gloves. Space.

Or maybe he *does* need tough love, for Anson to break him down until he gets his ass into gear. Fuck, how am I supposed to know?

"Are you going home?" I ask quietly.

Anson shakes his head. "I'll leave when he's discharged. I don't want to be hours away if his condition nosedives. There's a family room on the first floor I'll work out of."

I rest my hand on his shoulder. "I'm going in. I'll say bye for the night, then meet you in the car." I'm not letting some doctor tell me to stay away from my brother, and regardless of what Dawson said, we've always gotten along.

It's worth a shot.

Anson nods his agreement, and I head in, steeling myself to be a punching bag. Dawson looks up when I enter. He still looks like shit, dark circles bright against his unusually pale skin, sandy hair disheveled across his forehead. Not a good look for a star athlete.

"Told the doc I don't want visitors," he says.

"I'm not a visitor. I'm your brother."

His green eyes track me as I approach the bed. "You're literally wearing a visitor's badge."

"Well, yeah. It's part of my cover. If they knew I was Dawson Gold's brother, the tabloids would be after me."

He doesn't smile. "You shouldn't be here, Gray. It's peak season at the farm."

"And I've been working nonstop. I needed a getaway."

"This is *my* fucking mess. I'm the one to deal with it. Don't make it your problem." His anger from before is gone, replaced by resignation.

Maybe it's a new dose of drugs.

I don't think that's it, though.

"This *is* your fucking mess," I confirm straight-up. Then I grab his wrist and slowly articulate, "But you're my fucking brother, and I love you. So I'll see you tomorrow."

I let go and walk out.

And he doesn't argue.

33

———

ELIZA

MY FINGERS TAP restlessly on the hardwood table.

The gentle pop of a candle breaks the monotony of the crickets outside. Shadows seep in through the windows and dance in the corners of the room. Nervous energy makes my knee bounce beneath the table.

Any minute now.

Again, I glance at the offering set before me—and my hope crumbles.

This isn't working.

With a sigh, I shove to my feet and head to the wall, flicking on the lights. At the sudden change, Dave lifts his head, opens his eyes, and stares at me blankly. *Really? Again?* his expression asks.

"Yes, again," I mutter.

He tucks his bill back into his feathers and resumes sleeping. I return to the table, examining the tray of cinnamon rolls, utterly hopeless. In the dark, they were indistinguishable blobs. In the light, they're sad, fluff-less dough spirals smothered in too much icing.

I should've asked Joy for her recipe.

The sound of tires over gravel cut through the night, and I swing around to see headlights slice through the blinds. My heartrate clicks into its next gear. I hurry to sit back down, facing the doorway across the living room.

It feels wrong.

Probably because when Grayson walks in, exhausted from a delayed late-night flight, the first thing he'll see is me, sitting straight-backed at the head of the table like some over-eager exorcist awaiting her prey.

I shuffle around to a side seat. Clasp my hands. Stare at the wall, then the door, then the sad cinnamon buns.

Nope, this is still weird.

Outside, his truck door slams.

Maybe I should just pretend to be sleeping and greet him in the morning. It's midnight, after all. No matter where I sit, the simple fact that I've waited up for him like some loyal medieval wife awaiting her husband's return from war could be too eccentric.

Keys jiggle in the door. In a burst of panic, I dart from the table, jump over the back of the couch, land haphazardly on a cushion and pop open my laptop.

There. I'm just working late.

And randomly put cinnamon rolls out for him.

Oh my gosh, you're hopeless.

The door swings open, and I peer over the edge of the couch to where Grayson fills the entranceway. His eyes track across his home before finding me.

Instantly, they light up. He gives his space another scan as he shuffles in with his bags.

"You made yourself at home," he observes.

Even tired and stale, hair askew from a flight, he's ruggedly handsome. Those golden irises settle on me again, and his words register.

My blush is immediate.

"It's just a few things I had on the boat. Some candles, a few plants, a throw blanket for the couch. It's, um, not much. Just wanted to...I mean, I know this isn't my home. I'm not, like, actually *living* here..." His eyes dance with amusement as I sputter, cheeks burning, kicking myself for overstepping.

At the time, I hadn't thought I was pushing boundaries. Just giving him a nice setting to come home to. Finding use for my décor that was collecting dust on the grounded boat. Not, like, *nesting* here, or laying claim, or assuming I'll be spending time here in the future—

Ok, yeah. I was totally doing all of those things.

"It's nice," Grayson says, pulling me from my thoughts with a knowing smile. "Almost as nice as that smell coming from the kitchen."

I clear my throat, shutting my laptop and popping to my feet. "Yeah. Um, I don't know if you're hungry, but there are cinnamon rolls," I say casually as I lead the way to the dining area.

Oh, who am I kidding? I might as well shout: *there are cinnamon rolls here, because I spent yesterday interrogating your employees about your favorite dessert, took the afternoon off to make them from scratch, then set it out next to some flowers and a candle like it's Valentine's Day.*

So freaking *casual.*

I lean against the table, trying not to fidget as I study him for a reaction. We aren't officially in a relationship. Just because I've made my decisions doesn't mean he's made his. Sweet words and flirting over daily phone calls doesn't confirm anything. This—*kill me now*—could be so *weird* of me.

His silence eats at me as he takes in the cinnamon

buns, so I babble. "They're definitely not as good as Joy's. It's, um...I've never worked with yeast before, so they're not—"

Grayson's gaze finds me, and his expression stops my words in their tracks. He's looking at me with this soft tilt to his lips, honeyed eyes perusing my face with a gentle kind of wonder.

He drops his bags on the floor and launches into motion, removing the space between us with purposeful strides. My breath hitches. Without hesitation, he clasps my cheeks, tilts my head up, and kisses me.

It's *sweet*. Tender and slow, like he's drinking me in, and I melt right into him, hands resting on his chest. He draws back, one of his thumbs smoothing over my cheek as I slowly open my eyes.

"Hi," he says, his stubble shifting as his cheek hitches. "I missed you."

He kisses me again, one hand burrowing into my hair, lightly massaging my scalp. It's a lethal combination, that gentle touch and leisurely kiss, mixed with his heat and strong presence that wrap around me like a hug.

When he draws back again, I'm so light, I could levitate. My fingers curl into the soft cotton of his shirt. "If this is for the cinnamon rolls, you should reevaluate. I'm pretty sure they're inedible."

"It's not about the cinnamon rolls." His smile widens, and his hand slides down my neck to linger at my waist as he inspects the dish. "Besides, they're smothered in icing. How can they not be good?"

"I'm pretty sure they're sugary bricks."

"You had me at sugary." He reaches over to snag one, his other hand keeping a firm grip on me.

My phone vibrates on the table just before he makes

contact. I don't even need to look to know who it is. Grayson's hand pauses as he glimpses the screen.

"Your mom's calling," he murmurs with a frown.

"I know."

"It's midnight." His brows come together, and he straightens, his dessert-less hand finding the other side of my waist. "Could it be an emergency?"

"In her eyes, it is." My hips warm from his fingertips, and I return his touch, grasping his forearms. They're thick and sturdy, rippled with veins beneath my palms. "Based on the string of text messages she sent before making her first phone call, she just found out I bailed on the interview I had on Monday."

His worry gives way to shock. "The tech startup?"

I expected his surprise, not his insight. I hadn't told *anyone* about the interview. "How do you know?"

"Anson received a call from their HR, checking on your references." He must see my next question in my eyes, because he explains, "He told me in Ohio. I didn't mention it because I figured if you wanted to talk about it with me, *you* would bring it up. I mean," the knob of his throat rolls, "I *wanted* to mention it. Give you support. But with Anson's offer...you know what I want. I was afraid I'd end up pressuring you."

"And what *do* you want?" I'm pretty sure I know, but I'm greedy enough to want to hear it from him.

He doesn't mince words. "I want *you*." His thumbs sweep across my skin. "And for you to stay here, where I think you'll be happy—though I can work around that if it doesn't pan out."

The statements come out of him so easily, as if we've already addressed this topic. As if it's common knowledge. Our daily calls over the last week, our little lines of honesty...we've implied the *heck* out of it, but we have yet to lay it out so directly.

It snaps a final puzzle piece into place.

A dorky smile spreads across my lips. "You were concerned about pressuring me. But the thing is, you can't pressure me when I've already made my decision."

"Did you? Make a decision?" Unlike me, Grayson isn't smiling. His face isn't drawn in worry, but the tension along his jaw gives him away. I don't even know if he realizes he's being so expressive.

"Mm-hmm." I reach up and smooth my thumb over his jaw, his scruff scratching my skin. "And I just sealed that decision with an email to your brother. All I need to do now is sign the formal contract when he sends it over."

Watching realization dawn on his face is better than seeing Garnet Shores' sunrise from the boat. I commit it to memory, the way his eyes subtly widen, the happy creases that appear beside them, how his mouth softens. The liquid warmth that washes in behind it.

His fingers tighten on my waist as he murmurs, "You really *were* making yourself at home."

My chest brushes his as I lean into his heat. "I'm going to find my own place, Grayson."

"Yeah." One of his hands slides lower, sweeping across my hip bone. "But you'll be spending a lot of time here, too."

I bite my lip. "You sound so confident."

Through a chuckle, he says, "Yeah, Boston. 'Cause I am." Then he lifts me and smashes his mouth into mine.

His hands secure my legs around his waist, and he carries me to the bedroom for the *second* time in a week—which I gleefully confirm is just as hot as the first time.

I didn't know I was into Neanderthal behavior, but

wrapped up in a rough-hewn, Grayson-shaped package, it's as arousing as it is addictive.

Boston sure as heck never gave me this.

He shuts us inside his bedroom and tosses me onto the bed, stripping his shirt away to reveal his perfectly carved body and that dark trail of hair leading to *another* perfect part of his anatomy.

I nervously lick my lips and shove to the edge of the bed. I made my plan a few days ago—did some research to brush up on skills that have never been very good in the first place—and I intend to follow through.

Until Grayson stops me with a hand on my shoulder, planting me firmly on the bed, his other hand pausing on his pant button. "Nope. Scoot that sweet little ass back for me."

"But I wanted to—"

"I know."

"What, are you a mind-reader now?"

"Baby, you just zeroed in on my cock like a homing beacon and licked your lips." Even threaded with humor, his low timbre rumbles through me, flipping any remaining switches that have yet to go haywire.

"Your intent was pretty clear. And while I really fucking want that, you're gonna have to save it for later, 'cause this one's all about you."

Ignoring him, I reach for his pants, only for him to catch my hand and place it back on the bed. The ridges of his abs are inches from my nose, and I'm hit with the absurd urge to open my mouth and *lick*. Maybe it's a good thing, then, that I have an argument to make.

"I'm not the one who had a tough week. I want to do this for you. It was part of the planning I did."

He lightly laughs as he shakes his head. "Too bad, Boston."

Too bad?

His hands snake to my waist, lifting the hem of my tank top and resting on my skin. "*You* just accepted a hard-earned job offer, and I want to celebrate that." He secures his grip as he smirks. "And even before you shared that news, I'd already made some plans of my own."

With that, he propels me back on the mattress, momentum carrying him with me. I gasp, a disbelieving laugh dancing from my lungs as he shucks off my top. My cotton shorts and underwear go next, and he shoves me up the bed a little more, making room for his bulk as he swings my legs over his shoulders and locks them in with his hands.

So this *is what he meant by celebrate.*

Instinct has me tensing against him. His smoldering gaze meets mine, an eyebrow lifting. "What do you think you're doing?" His breath skims my inner thighs, and my core clenches, despite my apprehension.

"Um...lying here?" I answer weakly. What am I going to say? That I'm bracing for my least favorite position? I've only done this with Kyle and one other guy, and both were lackluster enough to turn me off forever.

Grayson taps one of my thighs. "Relax this." When I do, he pats my other leg, tensed beside his head. "Now this one."

Slowly, I comply, his soft authority making my body thrum with need.

"Just like that, gorgeous. Now rest your head back."

I study his face between my thighs, his easy confidence and calm intent. The look of a man who knows what he wants—and knows he's capable of getting it.

I sink back into the mattress.

"So good at following instructions," he murmurs, his hot breath drawing closer to the juncture of my thighs. His praise unlocks a new wave of tingles, a rush of wetness behind it.

I jolt when his lips press against my inner thigh, his whiskers scraping my skin. "You work your perfect ass off, Eliza." His low pitch reaches me as another kiss lands, this one inches from where I'm suddenly throbbing. "But right now? You don't need to do a thing." Another kiss, with a gentle scrape of teeth. "All you're gonna do is relax, baby."

That *baby* alone, in that self-assured baritone, sets off another sparkler in my core.

I expel a breath. He hums his approval, then dips his head.

He teases me, softly kissing and licking everywhere but the place I need it most. Building anticipation with a patience that has my hands curling into the comforter in frustration, my nerves tightening with need. I lift my hips to encourage him toward my clit, but he just pushes me back down into the mattress with a chuckle that vibrates through my thighs.

When he finally moves where I need him, *minutes* later, I'm strung as tight as a crossbow, my body quaking beneath him. With all his preparations, it doesn't take much. He flicks his tongue over my clit, and my hips surge up against his hand, which refuses to let me move. The little show of strength sends me to the edge, then he slips his other hand off my leg and fills me with his fingers, thrusting sternly as he *sucks*—

His name spills out of my mouth as the orgasm rolls through me.

Sensation still rocking me, I'm vaguely aware of him placing my legs back on the bed and crawling up my body. When he kisses me, I taste myself on his mouth and more need bolts through me. I've never been so turned on, so in *need* of another person, in my life.

Without a word, he draws back to reach for his nightstand. Recovering, I catch his arm. His eyes collide with mine.

"It's up to you," I breathe, "but I don't need it."

I don't *want* it—any other flimsy barriers between us.

He inhales sharply. "I'm clean. Birth control?"

I nod.

Grayson returns, and I lower back down as his body cages mine. Gaze on mine, he whispers, "I'll never get enough of you."

Then he captures my mouth in a searing kiss, and enters me with a shudder.

He keeps kissing me, our moans caught in each other's throats, even as his hips pulse faster, deeper. Even when he shifts my legs to one side and slides a hand down to touch me. Even as his skin grows damp beneath my palms, and his breathing uneven.

Everyday Grayson is hot as hell, but *this* Grayson is *intoxicating*, branding me with his body and mouth and hands that can't seem to get enough of me. With every strong sweep of his tongue, every unsteady breath, every intentional roll of his hips, he's both savoring and devouring me.

I've never felt so cherished in my life.

I've never cherished someone *else* so much in my life.

Only when I tip over the edge does he draw back, jerking out of me to come across my stomach in thick, hot ropes.

His head hangs above me as he catches his breath, and I trail my fingers through his sweat-slicked waves. My throat thickens with emotion as I breathe him in, relishing in his closeness.

He takes his time leaning back, muscled chest still expanding on big breaths. His palms trail up and down my sides, his thumbs brushing across my breasts before he pulls back and takes in the state of my torso.

"Let me get you cleaned up." He winks. "I want to get to those cinnamon buns before Dave does."

"Cinnamon bricks," I correct with a wince.

This doesn't deter him in the slightest. If anything, it makes his whole damn night, because a devilish grin lifts his lips and he says, "I actually hope they're as bad as you say. 'Cause if they're really inedible, I'll just have to have you again. For dessert."

34

ELIZA

I TAKE another sip from my tumbler as I drive down the vibrant, tree-lined street to Grayson's house, the sugary concoction lighting up my taste buds.

"*Coffee milk,*" Grayson called it, when he'd mixed it up for me this morning before I left for my swim. According to him, it's a Rhode Island staple, and thus a required part of my "living-in-Rhode-Island initiation"—a process which he's deemed "essential" and put himself in charge of.

It tastes like coffee ice cream, and I'm hoping it comes with the same sugar rush. After last night's homecoming and a thirty-minute sunrise swim, my body needs all the energy it can get.

Not my brain, though. I've never had a Red Bull, but I imagine the happy buzz lighting up all four lobes is equivalent to at least three cans. I thought I was *happy* when I treated myself to a latte, a new season of my favorite show, or a Friday night date with Kyle. But that feeling was a whisper compared to this.

My phone rings again, and I sigh. My mom texted me again while I was out swimming, but I was waiting to unpack that giant can of worms until I got back home. At this point, though, what difference does three minutes make?

Fortifying myself with another sugary gulp, I hit the green button, and her voice blares through the car's speakers.

"Eliza Bethany Attleburn. You've been deliberately ignoring me." Her greeting is steady and controlled, but the middle-name-drop shows her hand.

She's a volcano, about to erupt.

"I wasn't ignoring you," I say calmly. "I was busy last night and this morning."

"Busy with what?" There's a snap in her tone now. "Daydreaming? Throwing your life away?" I'd tell her she's being overdramatic, but that would only rile her further, and I don't want to ruin how good I feel with a Category Five argument.

Not that she cares.

"Suzanne told me about your apparent decision to just *skip* an interview Monday."

"I notified the hiring team the day before—"

"And *then*, you proceeded to ignore every single one of Suzanne's emails and calls." She says it like she's accusing me of a felony.

"Mom, I—"

"*No*," she states, interrupting me again. "There is no excuse for this level of negligence, and I will *not* allow you to continue this asinine self-destruction today."

I'm twenty-six and independent. She no longer *allows* me to do anything. But I'm too caught up on deciphering her meaning to address that verb usage. "What's today?" I ask.

"Your interview with the consulting agency."

Everything within me freezes. *Consulting agency? Interview?* I'd submitted cover letters and my resume to several firms and agencies, but I haven't accepted any other interviews. Had Suzanne agreed to it for me? Can she even *do* that?

"Wow, Eliza." Mom's bitter disappointment fills the silence. "You really *haven't* listened to a single one of Suzanne's voicemails."

No, I haven't. And I've been too busy all week to inform her I was done with her services. "Mom, I have a new job. I've already accepted the offer," I blurt.

"What job is this?"

"Marketing Director for Gold's. The vineyard, the oyster farm—everything."

On a dime, her tone shifts. "Why would you do something like that?"

Before, she was angry. Now she sounds ready to give me a hug and discuss my sanity.

"Like what?" I ask, just to hear her say it.

"Limit yourself like that," she replies, stunned. "You're better than that. Capable of *more* than that."

"I'm also capable of slowing down. Lowering my cortisol. Making life a little more enjoyable." My car bumbles into Grayson's driveway. "Besides, it's *Director* of Marketing, Mom. I report directly to the CEO. It's an incredible opportunity."

"In a small town, in the middle of nowhere."

My blood heats at how flippantly she disregards Gold's. Grayson's operation alone is more impressive than half the high-rise occupants in the city—never mind Anson's growing business.

"Have you signed a contract?" she asks.

Shutting the car off, I answer, "It's coming today."

"So, no."

I already know where she's going with this. "It's already *in writing* that I'm accepting this offer."

"Doesn't matter. You don't have that job, Eliza. It could fall through." There's a point-zero-one percent chance of that happening. Anson isn't the type to go back on his word. "And this interview could be the one. You're going."

I shake my head, chewing my lip. "No."

"Your career and life aside, do you *know* how much we pay Suzanne and how hard she works to find opportunities as good as this?"

"I never asked you to hire Suzanne."

"Eliza, we've invested so much in you," she emphasizes, and for the first time in this conversation, her words get to me, planting a little seed of guilt. "And you just want to—to —*throw* it all away because you're on a nice little vacation and you want it to last? I don't want to see you make a mistake you'll regret."

You're asking too much, I want to say. But that kernel of guilt is beginning to create fissures in my obstinance. My parents *have* invested a lot in me—building bridges, finding opportunities, guiding me through achievements since I was a child. No matter how tough or stubborn they are, how selfish their motivations were, or how painfully misguided this phone call is, I can't overlook the good they've done for me.

She must sense my weakening resolve, because she says, "The interview is virtual, five hours from now. There's no reason you can't make it. Just go. Give it a chance."

My head tilts onto the backrest, and I stare at the gray ceiling of my car. She isn't asking me to drop everything and drive to Boston. A virtual meeting will only eat thirty minutes of my day, and because I don't actually want this job, I won't have to spend any time preparing or stressing out.

If anything, going to this interview and then telling her it isn't the right fit *might* bring her a little closer to acceptance.

"Fine," I say.

Then I chug the rest of the coffee milk and try to shake the feeling that I've just placed myself back on a trail in bear-infested woods.

35

GRAYSON

SUMMER on the water in New England is unpredictable. Some days, you're baking in a water-logged desert. Others, it's cloudy and damp, or ripping with fast-moving squalls that make you question your choice to work on small boats.

But sprinkled between the extremes are some Goldilocks days—sunny and perfectly warm, with a gentle sea breeze that dries the sweat from your forehead and feels like bliss.

Today's one of those days, and I can't think of a better welcome home.

Well, except for last night.

I started early this morning, antsy to get back into the rhythm of things and catch up on any paperwork Amanda wasn't able to do. Had Eliza wanted to laze in bed and go for a repeat of last night, I would've been down in a heartbeat. But she was happy to get out for a morning swim—though part of me suspects her readiness to get up and go was for my benefit as much as hers.

Women I've dated, Mackenzie included, always wrestled with the farm for attention. They liked the *idea* of dating a farm owner, the fantasy of a man who works outdoors with his hands, until they realized they had to share me with the work schedule.

With Eliza, though, something tells me my challenge will be telling *her* to slow down.

It's perfect for me. *She's* perfect for me.

"You want to talk about him?" Mark asks as we putz toward the sorting float.

Mark's not much of a talker. It's one of the reasons I teamed up with him this morning. I'm not shoving Dawson's situation out of my mind, but I sure as shit don't want to spend all morning getting unsolicited advice and sympathy about it.

"No," I say. But Mark's met him before, so I add, "He's recovering at home now. Got a PT doing daily visits. Should be back in playing shape for next season."

Mark nods once, and leaves it at that.

But then, to my surprise, he speaks again. "She's living with you, huh?"

I eye his weathered face, regarding me from the bow. The team must've been talking a lot for Mark to catch wind of the gossip.

Need to give them more work if they're that fucking bored.

"She was renting a boat that's getting repaired right now. I'm housing her."

And I'll *keep* housing her, whenever she wants to stay the night—which'll be *most* nights. Cocky, maybe, but I'm not above playing dirty. Bribing her with coffee milk and orgasms. But I don't think bribery's even needed, considering she waited up for me last night.

I liked coming home to her before I left for Ohio, but last night?

I full-on *loved* it. Just as much as I loved seeing her cute trinkets scattered everywhere, making their claim on my place, and her adorable blush when she tried to deny it. Then I took in the cinnamon rolls and her news about staying in Garnet Shores, and my heart hammered my ribs so aggressively, the shittiest week this year turned into the greatest of the last decade.

Two-point-five months of knowing her, and she's already got all the power over me. And I'm pretty sure I've got as much over her, too, even if she won't admit it yet.

My chest is full of fucking rainbows thinking about it here, in the middle of the salt pond, hands grimy from scrubbing cages and harvesting. It only gets fuller when Mark says, "She did some things here, when you were out. As far as I heard, she didn't fuck anything up too bad."

"Glad to hear it."

From anyone else, it'd be a backhanded compliment. From Mark, who's done nothing but scowl about her, it's a glowing, sparkly five-star review.

Yeah, my girl's got a way of slithering in and making a salty bastard love her.

Love.

The last time I felt that for a woman was my early college girlfriend. Since then, it's been a lot of pining, lust, *liking.* When all those feelings appear in your chest, it can be hard to tell the difference between them. People usually turn to timeframes to differentiate. Six months of knowing someone, and you're still a sap? You've probably crossed into love territory.

But process of elimination is also a good way of narrowing things down. It's not "pining" for a woman when you've got her. It isn't just "lust" if you're addicted to them with their clothes on. And it sure as shit is more than "liking" if they occupy this much of your chest and head.

We're two minutes from the cages when my pocket vibrates with a call. I grab my phone to see an unknown number. Normally, I'd ignore it, but with Dawson...it could be a nurse, his agent, god forbid another hospital call.

"Grayson," I answer.

"Hi, I'm calling from a marketing agency regarding Eliza Attleburn, who just interviewed for a position with us. We have your company here as reference. Would you be able to answer some questions about her?"

The chipper female voice echoes in my head, drowning out the engine's rumble. The pond's gentle breeze turns rigid. The sunlight pierces my eyes. And all the stupid fucking rainbows in my chest collapse into a cloud of acrid dust.

"What do you mean, interviewed?" The question scalds my throat coming out.

"We just spoke with her about a Senior Marketing Management position. Just an hour ago, actually," the woman adds with pleased disbelief. "She's excellent. We're reaching out to several of her references before we make our offer."

An hour ago?

An *offer*?

But she's...she's staying in Garnet Shores. She took Anson's job offer. She told me this fourteen hours ago.

My thoughts wade through sludge as I try to understand. Eliza wouldn't do this. Her heart's honest. She's too fucking *good*. The woman must have her dates mixed up, because there's *no* way Eliza interviewed with them today.

But she's been working from home all day.

And how could you mistake an interview that happened just an hour ago?

There's—there's some kind of good explanation. There's *got* to be.

Like what? the devil on my shoulder taunts. *Like a shiny, new opportunity popped up, and no matter how hard she tries, part of her will always think she belongs in the city?*

"I'm sorry, do you know her?"

A *no* pounds against my throat. I want to be done with this conversation, pretend it isn't happening. But—my fingers tighten on the wheel—it is.

Eliza...*damn*...Eliza just took an interview, and the reference call mistakenly came to me instead of Anson. Good fucking thing for her, because if it *had* gone to him after she'd accepted the position, Anson might be pissed enough to rescind her offer.

If she even wants it?

Jesus.

"Hello?" the woman prompts.

"Yes, I know her," I say, forcing my voice to work.

Then I proceed to tell her about the most incredible woman I know, the one I've irrevocably fallen for, who owns my goddamn heart—who couldn't possibly feel the same way about me, because if she did, she wouldn't have said one thing to my face last night, then gone behind my back and done another over her fucking *lunch hour*.

36

ELIZA

I HAVEN'T FELT the urge to skip since I was a child, but I'm practically hopscotching around the farm when I arrive to shoot some late-day content, the afternoon sun reflecting a vivid gold on the water. My smile is overly bright, my voice too high-pitched as I make small talk with the team, but I don't care.

I just gave a masterclass-level performance in my interview.

I know this because the Marketing VP called me three hours after our video call to offer me the position. A thirty-percent increase from my last job's salary, decent paid time off, a lunch stipend, a gym stipend, an expanded cubicle next to windows, and a clearly structured promotion plan, plus a signing bonus that would cover four months' rent, and maybe a tropical vacation, too.

They wanted me so badly, they put together the prettiest list of perks that's ever been written in Times New Roman—as if a list of perks, written beneath a strict list of heavy responsibilities, makes this an impassably *good* opportunity for me. A big, exciting step in the right direction, with all the privileges that indicate forward progress.

Two months ago, it would have been. But now, my definition of *good for me* isn't as narrow. I'm still figuring out what that definition is, still questioning if changing it will even be the right choice in the end.

But my fresh signature on Anson Gold's contract should help me figure that out.

And the fact that I'm prancing around the farm with a goofy grin is a promising sign that this *is* a step in the right direction.

I'm leaning against the warehouse wall, throwing together a basic post, when Grayson's skiff finally pulls into the dock. As Mark ambles off the boat with orange baskets in his hand, I head down to say hello, the pep in my step getting peppier at the sight of Grayson's sturdy form.

It's only been a few hours, but I miss Grayson like some lovesick schoolgirl. Maybe it's silly, but there's no need to stifle the impulse. There's no *desire* to.

Not when Grayson's so obviously intent on embracing me, and I'm just as wrapped up in him.

He's turned away from me, stacking two crates of oysters when I step on the dock. "Hey, farmer," I drawl.

I'm prepared to be struck by his good-natured grin, the one his rugged face wears so well, or maybe some kind of quip.

So I'm caught off-guard when Grayson's back stiffens and his arms freeze. After a momentary pause, he resumes his work.

My enthusiasm stutters. "Bad day?"

Had he gotten a call about Dawson? Maybe there was an issue out on the farm?

"Not as good as yours," comes his flat reply.

My brows crash together. "I mean, I *did* have a good day, but..."

He jerks the crates into the air and plops them on the deck with a thud. Only then does he plant his hands on his hips and look at me.

Instantly, my bubble of happiness pops, anxiety filling the space. Because Grayson's face is impassive, devoid of all the warmth I've become addicted to.

The last time I saw this look was when he wanted me gone. Back when I was the *worst* part of his day.

I know why he's wearing that expression the instant he says, "I'm sure you did. Probably the best day ever. An interview and an instant job offer. Your dream."

I blink.

My lips part.

The cascade of implications hit me all at once, and the picture they paint is unforgiveable. Grayson thinks I pursued a job in the city today. That I told him one thing last night, and turned around and did another behind his back. I *know* how much staying in Garnet Shores means to him, and I lifted all his hopes, just to toss them aside.

He misreads my silence for confusion. "They called me for a reference, instead of Anson."

References. I hadn't even thought of that, because I wasn't taking this job opportunity seriously. I *never* was, at any point in the process. That's why I didn't tell him. But he doesn't know that, and it looks so, so bad.

"I—"

"I told them you'd be an amazing hire," he states.

My explanation halts in my throat. Why would he do that? Does he...does he want me gone? Does a simple phone call, a screwed up misunderstanding, just negate *everything?*

A buzzing fills the air, and he drags his gaze away to glance at his phone. "*Fuck*," he murmurs, then answers.

I don't know what he says, worry and hurt flying around my head in disorganized chaos. His call is short, and thirty seconds later, he jerks his phone back into his pocket, starts up the engine, and loosens the lines.

His intent sends another wave of disbelief through me.

He's...leaving.

"Engine problem by the float. Kenny's stranded. I've got to go," he mutters, his eyes everywhere but me.

I should jump onto his boat. Force him to listen and understand, talk this out. But I feel like I've been punched in the face, so I watch, numb, as his skiff drifts away instead.

I can't think, can't process. I'm mentally drowning as I rigidly retreat from the dock, barely aware of where I'm going.

Which is why I nearly crash into Amanda as she exits the warehouse.

"Shit! Sorry." My head jerks up, and there's no time to hide my feelings.

Amanda freezes. "You okay?"

Tears, delayed in their reaction, spring from my eyes.

"Alright, you're definitely not okay," she rushes out, eyes flaring in panic. "Do you, um, want to talk about it?"

I rapidly shake my head as the first tear makes landfall on my cheek.

"Okay," she breathes. "Do you want to be alone?"

I don't know what I want. I don't know what to think.

The only thing I *can* think to do right now is call Kitty, but she's unreachable.

When I don't answer, she nods, grabs my arm, and drags me toward the warehouse.

"What are you doing?" I whisper, fighting to control the wobble in my voice.

"I'm not leaving you alone like this," she states. "Workday's over, and the warehouse is empty, so we're going to go sit in the corner and stuff our faces with the cookies Steve's wife made. And if you don't want to eat, and you don't feel like talking, you can throw darts to distract yourself. We can even print out someone's face and stick it to the board."

"What if..." My mouth doesn't feel fully attached to my body. "What if I should just leave?"

"Then you leave." Amanda's lips press together. "But you should wait until you *know* leaving's the best choice."

I nod and follow her.

———

THE HALF-EATEN platter mocks me as Amanda swipes her third—no, fifth—cookie from the tray. They're chocolate chip, slightly underbaked, just how I like them. They smell delicious.

But the chips are arranged in a smiley face.

The same smiles I was doling out forty-five minutes ago, before Grayson pulled into the dock. The thought of him would make me nauseous, if I wasn't already on the verge of throwing up.

He'll be back any minute, and I still don't know if I should be here when he arrives. If he *wants* me here. My dead phone sits on the folding table, taunting me with the possibility that he's texted, saying he never wants to see my face again.

True to her word, Amanda hasn't forced anything out of me—just kicked her feet up on an empty chair, loaded a livestream baseball game on her phone, and started chowing down on cookies. A dart board I never noticed before hangs expectantly on the wall, but I don't feel like printing a photo of Grayson's face and piercing it with projectiles.

If anything, it should be a photo of me.

Because this is entirely my fault.

I didn't hide the interview from Grayson on purpose. If I'd run into him between my mother's call and the video meeting, I would have mentioned it. But I didn't go out of my way to text him about it because it wasn't a big deal. Nothing was going to change. It was a favor to my parents. Knowing he was probably buried in work, I didn't want to cause him pointless stress.

Maybe, if he hadn't received that reference call, it would have been the right choice.

Maybe it still would have been wrong.

Doesn't matter now though, because, *fuck,* I think I might've just ruined everything.

All my achievements, all the *effort* I put into doing everything well, and I carelessly ignored how one choice could impact the best thing I've ever had.

And I *know* it's the best thing—that he's the best choice I've ever made, the best gift to ever come into my life—because it wouldn't feel like my lungs and heart, my entire world, are on the verge of collapse if he wasn't.

I was heartbroken when I was fired, angry and disappointed when Kyle cheated on me. But this? It's mounting into a fucking sledgehammer, and I don't know if I can stop it. If Grayson will even give me a chance to explain.

He owes me that chance. If he really cares about me, he owes me enough credit to hear me out.

But Dawson broke his heart this week.

Just last year, that girl tore him up.

And I saw the pure joy on his face last night when I told him I was staying.

A heart that's been jerked around like his might be done giving chances.

Fuck.

Something clangs outside the warehouse. Bile shoots up my throat. A fine tremor overtakes my hands as Amanda angles her head, squinting toward the open door.

She didn't witness our exchange at the dock, but she reveals she has some idea of what's going on when she quietly says, "It isn't him," and turns back to the baseball game.

It isn't him, but it *should* be. A simple tow shouldn't take this long. Maybe he's avoiding me.

I stare at my fingers, still shaking uncontrollably against the table top.

You should go. You're reacting this way because instinct is telling you he doesn't want you here. If you leave now, you'll have enough time to grab your things from his house, and...and...

A sigh cuts through my spiral.

"I don't know the situation—" I glance up at Amanda, who's no longer watching her phone. "But if it involves him, I've got to say something. Because it can't be as world-ending as you clearly think it is."

Slowly, I shake my head. "It's bad."

She finishes the last of her cookie, then dusts her hands off. "Two years ago, when I was still pretty new, I crashed one of our boats. I'd just started driving them, and a storm was coming in as I pulled up to the dock. The wind messed me up, the bow started heading for one of the pilings, and I panicked. Hit the throttle too hard and went right into another one of our boats." She laughs to herself. "Damage was so bad, we were out of two skiffs for a week."

I can't imagine a world where Amanda got that flustered. She's always so...unbothered.

Her feet drop from the chair, and she swings to face me, leaning on the table. "I thought Gray was going to fire my ass and sue me for damages. The thing was entirely my fault. But he didn't." She shrugs. "He was upset, at first. Didn't say a word, and I thought I was done for. Then he found me about ten minutes later and told me not to worry. Said they have insurance for a reason, and that it was his fault for sending me out there alone in unfamiliar conditions."

I understand the point she's trying to make, but if anything, her story only shreds me more. *This* is the person I just inadvertently hurt. The person I might've just *lost*.

But Amanda isn't done. "I was just another employee that he'd only known for six months, and he had my back, no questions asked." She studies me. "He's got yours."

She doesn't know what I did. "How can you be so sure?"

Smiling to herself, she shakes her head, like it's the world's dumbest question. "Back when you started, when you two were going at it like little squirrels fighting over a tree branch, he'd steal looks at you all day long. Then he started correcting the team with your title when they called you the video or phone girl. Then he started bringing you up in conversations you really didn't need to be part of."

"Insults, I'm sure."

"No," she corrects, leaning back in her chair. "Neutral things. Nice things. The stuff you say about a person you can't stop thinking about, but don't hate."

Oh.

"At some point, he fell ass over head for you, giving you these longing, doe-eyed looks I don't think were even conscious. Smiling when people mentioned you, going out of his way to do things for you."

My breathing turns shallow, like inhaling too deeply might drown out her words.

"He told us to leave a parking space open for you by the office. He'd have us put the nicest pick-up bags on the lowest shelf in the fridge. Keep an eye out for you on your morning swims if we had an early shift. Tidy up one of the skiffs every day so you wouldn't have to move stuff if you wanted to film it. That day he asked Kenny and I to make that sorting tutorial for you, we were already drowning in work.

"And every single day he was in Ohio and I sent him reports about the farm, he'd ask about you—if you were working too hard, taking on too much. If it seemed like you had a good day. Every. Single. Time."

Tears burn my eyes again, but not for the reason they did before.

"You ask how I can be so sure he's got your back," she says, waving a hand in the air. "Well, duh. He's in fucking love with you."

37

ELIZA

AMANDA'S DECLARATION rings in my ears, punching through my despair.

I glance at my trembling hands.

Maybe I'm reacting this way because instinct is telling me to *get up and fix this* before it's too late.

The revelation zaps me like a lightning bolt.

"I need to go," I breathe.

The chair scrapes against cement as I jump to my feet and beeline it for the dock, Amanda on my heels.

"Okay. Let's take a sec," she coaxes, trying to keep up with me.

But I don't have a second. I never should have let him leave the dock without me.

Marching past the last slip, I scan the water. There's no sign of him on the horizon.

"I need to find him," I blurt, backtracking toward the only remaining skiff—which isn't in its slip, because it was hauled yesterday for maintenance.

The touring boat, then.

"Gray has the keys," Amanda says, reading my mind.

"But I have a friend down the road with a dinghy. He might let us use it." She pulls her phone from her pocket. "Let me call—"

"*There's no time.*" It comes out in a burst of panic, my eyes wild as I search the yard for another option.

Swim. I'll just swim to him—

Orange flashes in my periphery—a stained kayak, upside down behind the warehouse by the shore. My feet carry me toward it.

"Eliza, there's some headwind," Amanda warns, rushing after me. "It's going to take at *least* thirty minutes, even if you paddle like crazy."

"Then I'll paddle even harder." The kayak is old, edges buried in the dirt like it hasn't been moved in months, a stained orange life vest half-lodged under its front. "Whose kayak is this?" I ask, soil lodging beneath my nails as I try to unearth it.

Amanda kneels beside me, and we flip it, a cloud of dust poofing into our faces. I wave it away, revealing a paddle stuffed inside the main compartment, glowing like it's heaven-sent.

Except it isn't.

"It's Mark's."

"Well," I grab one end, giving it a mighty yank toward the water, "Mark's just going to have to deal."

She positions herself at the other end, shoving as I pull. "I won't tell him if you don't," she grits out. Two more heaves, and I jump out of the way as the kayak slides down the bank, splashing into shallow water.

I hop in after it, water soaking my shorts, and pull the paddle free before clumsily climbing in.

"Life jacket! In case you're stopped," Amanda shouts, and something soft glances off my head. I snag the vest midair and stuff it by my legs. "If you're not back in an hour, I'm getting my friend's dinghy and searching for you."

I spare a precious second to face Amanda, who's peering down at me with concern. I think this means we're officially friends, and I have a feeling she's a damn good one.

"Thank you," I say earnestly.

She jerks her chin.

All my urgency surges back like a storm tide as I shove away from the shore. My paddles are strong, but the kayak is a damn slug in the water. I pick up some momentum, only for a stiff breeze to buffet me the moment I get past the docks. Bending over in an attempt to streamline, I strain against the water, little waves splashing up over the sides and soaking my clothes.

Paddle. Harder.

My arms burn. Salt stings my eyes. It's like the entire pond is trying to push me back to shore. I pant through bared teeth, back cramping as I force the heavy kayak against wind and waves that all seem to be aimed at me. I'm a sopping mess of pain and panicked purpose when the sorting float appears in my periphery. The back of a skiff peeks out the side. Fear threatens to choke out my urgency, but I barge through it, pushing, pushing, *pushing*—

I careen around the side of the float, drop the paddle, and frantically grab the back of the skiff, gliding to a stop. Gasping for air, I cautiously glance up.

Kenny stares at me wide-eyed from a second boat, a wrench in his greasy hand. "That looks a *lot* like Mark's kayak," he says, sucking in a breath, "and he's not gonna be cool with you using it."

From where he's crouched over the engine beside Kenny, Grayson unfurls. He turns toward me in slow motion.

The burn in my lungs, the soaked fabric sticking to my body, Kenny—they all cease to exist.

Just like at the dock, his expression startles me. But not because it's impassive or withdrawn like I expect.

No—it's...*wild*. Eyes fevered, forehead creased, mouth parted, cheeks red like he's rubbed them raw with anxious hands.

"What are you—" he shakes his head a little. "You're *here?*"

His voice is as taut as his body, but I can't read the mess of emotions emanating from him. There are no signs of the steadiness I know. This man is all but cracking at the seams.

Because of me. Because of how badly I'd hurt him.

"I...I came to talk," I pant out.

His hand scrubs down his cheek, smearing grease, agitating his skin further. "Jesus, Eliza. Your phone—you've been fucking *unreachable*. I called you *eight times*." With every sentence, the pitch of his voice raises. "I ran out of gas, and we've been rushing to fix this fucking engine so I can track you down and say what I need to say."

I made this worse. Somehow, without even trying, I made this *worse*.

"I-I'm—sorry," I stutter.

His face twists in pained confusion. "Why the fuck are you apologizing?"

Where do I even begin?

But Grayson wasn't expecting a response, because he says, "You need to go."

My lungs compress. *Please, let me—*

"I can't leave," Kenny says, face furrowed. "Your boat's out of gas. You need mine to tow it."

Oxygen slides back into my chest. Grayson wasn't talking to me.

"The kayak, Ken," he bites out, stepping onto the skiff I'm gripping for dear life. Without a word, he takes my paddle, then grabs under my arms and hauls me out of the vessel.

It's pathetic, how quickly I find comfort in his grip. I'm that desperate for a dribble of reassurance. But the moment I'm steady on the boat, his hands drop away to hold the kayak steady for Kenny.

"The wind will be at your back," he tells him. "You'll hardly need to paddle."

Kenny settles inside, extending a hand for the paddle. "No offense, Boss, but I'd paddle into a tornado to get away from this."

Then he's gone, leaving us in a dense quiet. Grayson doesn't return to the other skiff, but he stays on the opposite side of this one.

It feels like there's an ocean stretched between us.

Words. Find words. Say them before it's too late.

"I'm apologizing, because—"

"Stop." It's half-command, half-plea.

My mouth closes. I watch, terrified, as his entire body shakes on an exhale.

"When you didn't answer, I thought you were ignoring me. I thought I *ran you off,* and I was fucking stranded out here, unable to do a damn thing about it until I got this engine fixed. I—" He rakes his hand angrily through his hair, taking a small, stiff step forward. "I thought when I finally got back to the dock, you'd be gone. That you were packing up your stuff from my house to leave."

"Isn't that what you want? For me to be gone?"

My words are quiet, the warm evening breeze wrapping around me, ready to whisk me away at his request. Waves lap against the skiff, a murmuring audience to the inevitable answer that'll send that sledgehammer down and break me.

"*Fuck*, no," he breathes.

Wha—

No?

He tents his fingers in front of his lips before saying, "I fucking hate that I made you think that."

For the first time since he left the dock, hope sparks in the void of my chest. But—

"You told them I'd be an amazing hire," I whisper.

"Yeah," he says loudly, sweeping a hand out. "Because you *are*." His hand drops as realization dawns. "Jesus, *that's* what made you think I wanted you gone?"

I'm too busy trying to protect myself from mounting hope to speak. My silence spurs him into action, his long legs eating up the deck between us before stopping just out of reach. He smells like salt and sweat, his shirt stained with grime and grease, hair more unruly than it was this morning, but he's the most handsome man I've ever laid eyes on.

"I was upset. I've *been* upset, from the moment I got that reference call. Then you showed up, and hearing your voice—the one I look forward to hearing every fucking day— just jammed in the knife. Reminded me how un-fucking-likely it is that you'd ever want to stay here, with me. Kenny called before I could get a handle on it."

His chest moves on a burdened breath, voice slowly returning to normal. "But I want to see you happy, Eliza. That's all I fucking want. It might suck, but people are allowed to change their minds. I think you'll be happy here, but if...if you changed your mind, and going back to Boston is what'll make you happy, then that's all I want for you. Doesn't matter if it eats me up."

And it *is* eating him up—the thought of me leaving.

It's clear as day, now.

"You're a fucking star. You'll shine wherever you go. And if you don't think Garnet Shores is big enough for all that shine, then who am I to fault you?"

All the hope I've been trying to tamp down erupts, filling me up, rocking me with relief and ecstasy and something else that injects straight into my heart.

It only grows more intense when he says, "I've already thought about how to make things work. Taking early shifts to meet you for dinner. Working the schedule to get more Saturdays off." He hesitantly reaches for my hands, like he's afraid I might jerk away and dive into the water.

When he makes contact, my hands tremble beneath his calloused fingers.

"If you don't want that because of today, because I've upset you, it'll *fucking* kill me, but I get it. I was an ass. Hell, I've been an ass half the time I've known you. But if you don't want that because you don't think it'll work, I'm dead-set on convincing you it will."

"Grayson." His name is like a revelation coming off my tongue. Hope and worry battle behind his blazing eyes. "I'm not going."

He blinks.

A smile splits my lips. Maybe it isn't appropriate to smile when wisps of distress still cling to him. But in the wake of everything he's just poured from his heart, I can't stop myself. How could I, when I'm standing before the man who barged into my life, scattered all my well-laid plans, stripped away the cage and opened the goddamn door? The man who sees me, knows me, makes me feel like I'm already flying?

"That interview—I was never going to take the job. I didn't even know it was scheduled until this morning, after you were already gone. I only went to get my mother off my back. It didn't *matter*."

His lips part, and I twist my hands, wrapping them tightly around his wrists. "You were busy at work, and it was just a chore in my day. I was going to tell you at dinner. I didn't want to worry you unnecessarily."

He stares at me, wide-eyed. His lips waver, until finally lifting on a disbelieving smile.

"*Fuck*, Eliza." He pulls a hand away to rub his hair, his laugh hoarse, incredulous. "You did a hell of a lot worse than worry me. *Jesus,* woman."

Without warning, he grabs my biceps, snaps me to him, and bear-hugs me. He's in desperate need of a shower, but his arms, his solidness, his all-encompassing presence feel like home. The skiff bobs as a wake rolls in, and he easily adjusts his stance, keeping me steady and secure in his embrace.

"*Fuck,*" he swears again, squeezing me harder, even as the boat stabilizes. "You're staying?" He asks like he doesn't trust his ears.

"I start with your brother in September. It's contract-official." My voice is muffled by his chest.

"I..." he pulls back, cupping my face. Some of his worry returns. "I tried to understand. I didn't think you'd flip things like that, but, the facts—I mean—"

I lift to my tip-toes and press my lips to his, stopping his explanation. His thumbs stroke my cheeks as he gently kisses me back.

I don't want to pull away, but it's important he understands. Still, his roughened fingers linger, feather-soft on my skin like they can't bear to let me go.

"Grayson, I know how it looked. This is on me." He opens his mouth to argue, but I don't give him the space. "I was never going to take that job. I shouldn't have even *enter-tained* the idea. But I felt like I owed my parents, and in the process, I forgot what I owe *you*. Sorry isn't a good enough word. I almost—" my lungs spasm with emotion— "I almost lost you in the stupidest, most idiotic way."

He shakes his head. "Impossible," he snorts. "Can't lose me when I'm in love with you."

My pulse stutters.

The way he says it, like it was obvious, just an offhand comment—

He's in love with me.

It will replay in my head forever. That...he just...*oh my gosh.*

"I wasn't going to say it so soon, but talking out of my ass earlier didn't scare you away, so I figured this probably won't, either."

All at once, my pulse recovers, then goes into overdrive. My heart thunders in my chest, screaming its truth.

I listen.

"I love you, too."

Just like that, the tears I've been fighting all evening flood my eyes, a few unruly traitors spilling over. I tilt my head away, but Crayson tightens his hands, bringing my face right back to his.

"Got salt water in my retinas again," I sputter.

He laughs and kisses me, my tears salty against his lips. I breathe through it, and by the time he pulls away, I've reclaimed a sliver of composure.

Eyes shining, his palms coast down my shoulders to my hands. He glances at my soaked clothes. "You arrived in a kayak, but it looks like you swam," he says with amusement.

A giggle bursts out. "It probably would've been faster if I did. That thing is a tank." I roll my aching shoulders, then peer around his body at the other boat's open engine. "Please tell me you fixed that engine before Kenny left. My arms are noodles. I might be able to hold a wrench for you, but otherwise, I'm useless."

"Don't worry. Just need to screw something in place, and we're good." He winks. "Though I wouldn't mind being stranded out here all night with you." His gaze lifts above me. "Or at least until sunset."

I tilt my head to see the orange cast bleeding over the sky as the sun tracks toward the horizon. There isn't a cloud in sight.

This sunset's going to be *pristine.*

Unmissable.

I don't have to say a word. Grayson breaks away to pull two towels from a deck compartment, laying them down like picnic blankets. Then he takes my hand and tugs me down with him, situating me between his legs, my back to his front.

"I'm soaking wet and smell like seawater," I warn, even as I tuck myself into him.

"Baby, I'm sweaty and smell like a workday."

Neither of us cares. His arms fold around me, cocooning me in his heat, and my chest glows as warm as the sky.

This is what bliss feels like.

Wet fabric itches my skin, my arms ache, and I only have a few weeks to learn everything about the wine industry, but I've never felt more at peace. My brain—the engine that never quits—is *quiet.* All of my headspace has been filled by this man and his presence and the fact that he's *mine.*

Well, there is *one* niggling thought.

"Can you text Amanda that I'm alive? I don't want her

to worry." Or race out here on a boat thinking I've drowned, just to see us all cozied up.

"Of course." One of his hands leaves to send the message, before wrapping around me again, even tighter than before. Sealing us together.

His torso vibrates against me as he says, "You know, I'm surprised you're waiting until September to start with Anson. Your contract at the farm is done mid-August."

Of *all* the revelations, that's what's sticking in his head?

Planting a cheeky grin on my face, I lean to the side and catch his gaze. "I'm not sure if you heard, but I'm a pro at giving tours now. I figured I should donate you two extra weeks of my time to show you how it's done."

His grin is stunning. "Alright, Boston. We'll see what you got."

Unable to help myself, I reach for his scruffy jaw, and urge his mouth toward mine. Just before I close the distance, I wink and add, "And I heard the grumpy, hot oyster farmer doesn't want a social media girl, but I'm having far too much fun being a pain in his ass to leave him so soon."

EPILOGUE
GRAYSON

October

THERE'S a crispness to the autumn air, warning of shorter days and frigid temperatures ahead. But it does nothing to wick the sweat from my forehead as I haul ass down the basketball court.

With fall in full swing, we're preparing the farm for winter, which on top of our normal operations has made this week especially grueling. At this point, my engine's running in the red. Doesn't help that it's been months since we last played, and all the sprinting and jumping doesn't come as easily as it did in my teens.

Not that Eliza or JJ give a damn.

Steadying his breaths beside me, Anson's in the same rickety, tired boat as me. Lala just got over a nasty week-long sickness, and he pulled a few sleepless nights to help her through it.

"C'mon, Uncle JJ!" her little voice shouts from the sideline, where she's curled up beside Anson's dog, arms slung around the German Shepherd's torso.

"Took care of her all damn week, and this is what I get," Anson grumbles under his breath.

JJ observes his scowl as he dribbles down the court. "Don't you worry, Miss Lala. We're kicking their butts."

"I wouldn't go *that* far," Anson argues.

JJ pauses at the half-court line, a shit-eating grin on his face. "Hey Lala, remind me of the score?"

She peers at the little notepad splayed on the pavement beside her. "Sixteen to...nine!"

Anson's jaw hardens, and JJ's smile only widens. "That's right. Thanks, honey."

Eliza arrives, a wash of flower-scented air coming with her as she sets her legs wide, back to me. "You boys need a break?" she goads over her shoulder.

She's breathing as hard as I am, but she's bouncing on her feet like a caffeinated bunny. Not that I'm surprised. Nothing—and I mean, *nothing*—gets her revved up like a good challenge.

And I don't mind that one bit. Whether I win or lose, I always come out on top, because she's hotter than the summer sun like this, her chin all stubborn and eyes fiery.

Hell, she's hot *all* the time—when she leaves another trinket of hers at my place, or pads around my kitchen wearing nothing but my shirt, or gushes about some new genius marketing strategy she's developed for Anson. The only wines I know are reds and whites, but when fancy, multisyllabic words like *Zinfandel* and *Cabernet* come out of her sweet mouth, I'm ready to replace that big vocabulary with moans.

A muffled *wump* yanks me back to the court. Eliza's got the ball in her hands, already dribbling toward the basket. *Fuck.*

Before I can take two steps, she pulls back, shoots, and drains it.

"Gray, what the hell are you *doing?*" Anson yells, eyes bulging as he chases after the ball.

Just obsessing over my girl.

There's no need to say it. Everyone knows I'm completely, irreversibly gone for Eliza Attleburn. When she's in the room, I can't keep my hands off her. When people ask how I'm doing, I somehow turn the conversation to how brilliant she is. I stop by Anson's office at least three times a week now, when I used to avoid it like the plague.

I'm walking around with big cartoon hearts in my eyes— and I'm happy as goddamn clam about it.

Except right now.

Because I'm objectively sucking ass, and Boston's starting to get *real* cocky about it.

Proving my point, she shoots me a cheeky wink and says, "I think he's just traumatized from last time. Knows he can't win, so why bother?"

Fuck, I love that mouth of hers.

She runs to the sidelines to give Lala a high five, and Anson comes up next to me, dribbling the ball. "In case you forgot, you're not on a fucking date. You can do the whole love-blind bullshit later. I need to win fucking *something* this week."

"That new neighbor of yours not running away as quickly as you'd hoped?"

"No, but she will. That thing's not up to code, no matter how hard she tries," he mutters.

I first heard about her in September—the new owner of the broken-down house on his vineyard. Turns out the elderly owner passed away a few months ago and left it to her granddaughter in the will, hence why Anson's lawyer's letters have gone unanswered.

He figured he could buy the new owner out, no bullying necessary. She's young, and the place needs a shit-ton of work to be livable. But she's actually *staying* there, trying to fix it up, despite Anson's increasing pressure. And it's driving big brother up a wall.

Doesn't help that he thinks she's pretty.

"She made us fucking soup last week," he mutters.

I cock a brow. "Was it good?"

A tendon snaps in his jaw. "It's always fucking good."

"It's okay to be scared, you know," JJ taunts up ahead, observing our quiet exchange.

Beside him, Eliza nods, a solemn expression on her face. "I'm proud of you for just showing up today. Facing your fears."

Alright, that's it. Time to eat your words, gorgeous.

I glance at Anson. "Blitz," I tell him.

Then we explode down the court.

JJ comes up to defend Anson, but he whips the basketball to me, and I'm barreling to the basket before Eliza can catch me. In it goes.

"Two points!" I shout at Lala, who scribbles on her notepad.

On JJ and Eliza's next drive, Anson steals the ball and sinks a three-point shot. Suddenly, they aren't smiling anymore. But I am.

JJ passes the ball to Eliza, and I crowd her right side, forcing her to dribble with her weak left hand. She tries to skirt around me, but she runs straight into my body with an *oof*. A little growl escapes her throat as I force her to retreat.

The ball fumbles in her hand.

"Sorry, baby," I apologize. Then, like a shameless bastard, I swoop in, steal the ball, and sink another basket.

16 to 18.

Lala groans in despair on the sideline, while Eliza shoots daggers with her eyes. I wink right back, then watch as she and JJ conspire at the end of the court. He argues against something she says, but she persists. She isn't taking no for an answer.

"Get ready," Anson murmurs.

JJ dribbles up to him, deceptively slow, then starts to move. Eliza darts past him, forcing Anson and I to switch defense. I see their next play form before it sets in motion. Remember it well from our game in June, when I'd run Eliza over.

She's about to set a pick.

Considering how badly I'd laid her out last time, it's no wonder JJ resisted her plan. *Stubborn woman.*

Feigning ignorance, I chase JJ as he moves. In my periphery, Eliza stops in my path, bracing for impact.

And I give it to her.

Ducking low, I scoop her up and over my shoulder without breaking stride.

"*Grayson!*" she yells, hands scrambling for purchase on my back. I lunge as JJ shoots, going for the block with my free hand.

An epic play—if I actually made it. But the ball brushes just past my hands, swooshing into the basket. JJ throws his hands up in victory, hollering like he's won the NBA finals as Lala cheers and storms the court.

"*Grayson, put me down!*" Eliza shouts, legs jerking against me. Instead, I secure my grip on her thighs. "JJ, help!"

But her teammate's occupied down the court, hefting

Lala up on his shoulders. A second later, they're running victory laps around the court, her wild giggles filling the air as she holds onto JJ's head.

Anson watches them, shaking his head in annoyed disappointment—but I catch the quirk to his lips. It broadens into a smile when JJ speeds up, sending Lala into a fit of squeals.

Eliza must be appreciating the scene too, because she stops struggling against me.

I jostle her once, then start for the parking lot.

"Hey!" she says, wiggling again. "The game's done."

"Sure is."

"So let me down!"

"No can do, Boston. You need a lesson about self-preservation."

She snorts, falling limp again. "What are you going to do? Just cart me around? That's fine. My legs are tired from whooping your ass."

I don't bother replying to her sass.

Instead, I step up to my truck, turn around, and gently press her torso between my back and the metal, effectively trapping her.

Realizing her predicament, she tenses. "Grayson?"

A giant grin on my face, I tighten my grip on her so she doesn't fall.

Then I start tickling the backs of her legs.

Immediately, she's a fish out of water, flopping against me as she squeals. "*No no no!*" Trapped as she is, her efforts don't do much, and I pick up the pace, gleeful as Dave when he catches a worm.

Discovering that she's ticklish might be one of my favorite revelations from the last two months.

"This isn't fair!" she pants out, trying to shove us away from the truck. But I'm too heavy to budge.

"With all that chirping you did on the court? This is *definitely* fair play, baby."

She tries tickling me back, but my nerve endings don't work that way. "This—this is—" she squeals as I tickle her inner thighs— "*bullying!*"

I snort. "Bullying implies I've got power over you, but everyone knows it's the other way around."

"*Grayson!* Please!"

My fingers stop, drifting up to her ass as I hum to myself. "That's a nice word, Boston."

"You're insufferable."

My fingers return to her legs in warning. "Now, that's *not* a nice word."

Her body shakes against me, a laugh bubbling out of her. "Put me down."

"Ask nicely."

She huffs, and it's an effort to stem my chuckle. "*Please* put me down."

"There. That wasn't so hard." I step away from the truck, open the back door, and swing her down, careful her head doesn't hit the doorway as I place her gently on the seat.

Her face is flushed red from being upside down, hair all over her cheeks, lips twisted in a scowl, but her eyes are bright and lively.

Happy.

It's a familiar sight, but it still hits me in the sternum every time—seeing her glow, watching her thrive. Knowing I contribute to it.

I reach out, tucking her hair behind her ear. "You might

not care about getting yourself run over for a casual basket-ball game. But I do."

She half-heartedly rolls her eyes. "You wouldn't have run me over."

"Did you forget what happened last time?"

She leans her cheek against my hand, nestling in. "No. But back then, you didn't know what I was capable of. You also hated my guts."

"You're half-right."

"Which half?"

I sweep my thumb over her cheekbone. "That I didn't know what you were capable of. I didn't know you'd steal my heart." I slide my hand to the back of her head, tangling it in her soft hair. "But I didn't hate you, then. Couldn't have, because you were already wiggling your way into my heart, even if I didn't know it yet."

A smile spreads over her lips, warm as honey.

Ducking into the cab, I say, "Now you're there to stay."

Then I kiss the hell out of the woman I love.

Thank you for visiting Garnet Shores. I hope you enjoyed your stay!

Really, though—*thank you* for opening the pages to this story. With all the books that exist in the world, it means so much that you spent your time in this one.

While this book might be fiction, New England summers *are* pretty magical, and I hope you get to experience one some day.

One last note: reviews play an important role in helping readers discover an author's work, so if you have a minute to spare, please consider leaving one.

-Megan

ACKNOWLEDGMENTS

I started writing this book for pure fun. No plans to publish. No commitment to even finishing it. I was completely drained dry from my full-time job, was worn down from marketing my fantasy trilogy, and felt like I'd wasted another beautiful Rhode Island summer. So, in an effort to feel those summer vibes and find my creative spark again, I decided to chase this story idea.

Turns out, it was one of the best experiences of my life.

I love this story. I love the world of Garnet Shores. And I'm so thankful to everyone who's helped me put it into the world.

To Jared, my husband/rock/barista/baker/therapist/best friend—you are the ultimate life partner, and I'm grateful for you every hour of every day.

Mom, Olivia, and Brigitte—it's a blessing to have people I can trust with my ugly early drafts. Thank you for being in my corner.

Christine Drummond, it feels...unfair to have you as my editor. Like, *what do you mean*, I get all your talent and skills and brainpower poured into this book? Thank you for helping me make this story better, and I can't wait for you to blow up as an author. (Trust me: you want to read her books.)

Megan Jayne Designs, you were a joy to work with on this beautiful book cover!

I also want to shout out my small but mighty street

team. It takes a village to get a book going, and I'm so, so appreciative of your support.

And, finally, a *massive* thank you to all my readers, cheerleaders, quiet supporters, family, and friends who keep me going. Every page read, message, post, review, and happy thought helps me get closer and closer to my dreams. This wouldn't be possible without you.

ABOUT THE AUTHOR

Megan Monte's first stories were born on the sidelines of her brother's soccer games as an elementary schooler. What began as a way to entertain herself became an infinite obsession with getting lost in fictional worlds, either through reading or writing them. As much as she loves getting lost in characters' adventures, she also likes to create her own in real life. When she isn't writing or reading, you'll find her surfing, hiking, skiing, cooking, traveling, or spoiling her pup in New England, where she lives with her husband. (P.S. If anyone has any recommendations for long, cruisy left-hand surf breaks, please email her.)

<u>Stay Up to Date</u>

Website: AuthorMeganMonte.com
Instagram: @authormeganmonte